"About eighteen months ago, we laid our hands on several satellites built by Martin Marietta and placed in cold storage by the government. In ten months of operation, we've discovered six major mineral fields in unknown but accessible zones. But in the fall of 2014, the scientists handling the system discovered something they weren't looking for: a single point in the old Congo that registered a magnetic emission twelve thousand times stronger than anything detected before."

Paul felt his curiosity rise.

"At first we thought the emission might point at mineral deposits, so IMC didn't inform the Congolese government or Gécamines, the country's mining supervisory board."

"Let me see if I understand." Paul poured another drink without taking his eyes off Milford. "You say at *first* you assumed the presence of minerals in large quantities, but it's obvious that wasn't so. Otherwise you wouldn't be here. What's the depth?"

"Over four miles."

Paul whistled, his geologist's instincts alert. "What have you found down there?"

Milford stared at him for what seemed like a long time; Paul suspected the old miner was weighing how much to tell him.

"No idea, but whatever it is, it's hollow."

Paul straightened. "What do you mean, hollow? A cavern?"

"I don't know. *Nobody* knows. There's a hollow space; call it a cavern or whatever you like. But it's big. Enough to house a fifteen-story city block . . ."

carlos j. cortes

perfect circle

bantam spectra

PERFECT CIRCLE
A Bantam Spectra Book / December 2008

Published by Bantam Dell
A Division of Random House, Inc.
New York, New York

This is a work of fiction. Names, characters, places, and incidents either are the product of the author's imagination or are used fictitiously. Any resemblance to actual persons, living or dead, events, or locales is entirely coincidental.

Bantam Books, the rooster colophon, Spectra, and the portrayal of a boxed "s" are trademarks of Random House, Inc.

ISBN 978-0-553-59162-0

Printed in the United States of America
Published simultaneously in Canada

www.bantamdell.com

OPM   10 9 8 7 6 5 4 3 2 1

For Shawna,
friend, lover, champion,
editor, and critic

acknowledgments

I want to thank my wife and fellow writer, S. J. Thomas, my editors Anne Lesley Groell—*bruja* extraordinaire—and Joshua Pasternak, and my agent Kristin Lindstrom for their hard work, faith, and generous assistance in the completion of this book.

The following people also read parts of the manuscript and offered helpful criticism: Deb Cawley, Michael Goodwin, Nemecio (Chito) Chavez, Susan Curnow, Jim Jiammatteo, Treize Armistedian (a *nom de plume*), Donna F. Johnson, Ian Morrison, Andre Oosterman, Jeffrey Kuczynski-Brown, Brian Otridge, and Leonid Korogodski. I thank you all.

perfect circle

part one

discovery

The beginning of
knowledge is the
discovery of something
we do not understand.

frank herbert

This can't be happening. Ken Avery stuck his fists deep into the oilskin's pockets and stared at the yellow-clad figures swarming around the drill head. Streams of water dripped from the brim of his sou'wester, blurring his vision.

The men glared at the spinning rod. Someone had painted a depth marker on the tube as a reference, but the white blur didn't show more than negligible progress: a paltry four inches in forty-eight hours. Ken could have sworn they were willing it to advance, but the steel pipe revolved doggedly without sinking any deeper.

A large man separated from the group and approached Ken with a sour expression fixed on his puffy face.

"Now what, boss? Another bit?" Mark asked with the lilt of an Irish accent.

"I've run out of ideas."

The eyes of the crew pivoted in his direction. After all, he was the geologist, the corporation's wonder boy with all the answers. Now he had none. One of the roustabouts swore, kicking at the revolving tube.

Mark tilted his head toward the tents. "Any news from the brass?"

"Nope, same as before. Keep drilling."

Ken's orders were to extract a core sample from the soil at a precise point, less than three feet across. It was a simple procedure: A hollow tube fronted by a drill bit pierces the earth with the help of lubricant slurry. The tube fills with sludge and debris. The product is a mud column, an extruded rod of pliable earth with information from the subterranean layers. The depth? That was the clincher: 18,000 feet was the previous world record. They had passed that mark over a week ago.

The head office never gave Ken many details. He didn't know what they were looking for, but whatever it was they hadn't found it. Yet. Every day at 16:00 local time, 08:00 in Texas, IMC mandarins could read his report on the contents of the core bit—or, so far, the lack of it—as they sipped hot cups of java in cool, plush offices while the damn hole ate $20,000 diamond cutters like they were cotton candy.

Ken moved closer to the derrick, sinking into the red clay. Slimy mud oozed up the sides of his boots. The heat–humidity–sweat combination was unbearable. Every pocket and pore were packed full of Congo mud.

He looked up as a bolt of lightning ripped the sky, followed almost at once by a clap of thunder that vibrated through his chest.

The whole project had been a bitch from the beginning, and the odd tightness in his gut told him it was far from over. Ken drew back his upper lip and blew off the drop of rain dangling from the tip of his nose. He didn't know what he had done to deserve this cursed assignment; he was no friend of God but neither His declared enemy.

Ken peered past the sheets of rain and the powerful arc lights. The jungle seemed almost solid, a jumble of lianas and shrubs beneath stands of umbrella trees and hardwoods.

He reached under his hat. His scalp still felt strange without hair. After the headshakes and smiles at his ponytail when he arrived, he had presumed the drillers' crew cuts were a macho thing, a clannish livery. Now he knew better. After the first week, Ken's hair had matted into an uncomfortable tangle of red clay and drilling slurry, a mess no amount of soap and rainwater could clear. There had been only one solution. Ken joined the clan and shaved his head.

"We've two bits left," Mark added. "When those two are gone, we'll have to drill with our dicks."

Ken didn't know what to say. The cutting head's sophisticated microturbines, powered by the slurry's awesome pressure, had secured the record depth, but each bit had been worn down, smooth and shiny, burnished like a new coin.

"You must have *some* idea about what's down there," Mark insisted. "What am I supposed to tell the men?"

"Keep drilling."

After the first drilling-head failure, someone suggested a tenacious basalt layer lay beneath. However, that wouldn't account for the condition of the bit. Ken ruled out diorite and nephrite jade, both prevalent in the area. Each bit was of a special alloy encrusted with a new generation of industrial-grade diamond, much harder than either of the other minerals. They should have gone through *anything* underground like a hot knife through butter. But they didn't.

Now Ken worried because the roughnecks, men familiar with harrowing working conditions, were spooked by the cutter's inexplicable behavior. In normal circumstances, the men stayed under cover after their grueling shifts—sleeping, having a beer, playing cards, watching a DVD. But not now. Now they huddled around the spinning tube and stared at the depth gauge.

○

In the solid jungle, the roughly circular clearing produced a well of soaring green walls blazing under the harsh light of mercury projectors. But the glossy walls of exuberant greenery changed to impenetrable darkness scant inches beyond the light, where, on the forked branch of a towering bubinga tree, a naked pygmy huddled. The tiny man, clutching a drab satchel to his chest, squatted immobile but for his bright eyes, which darted between the roughnecks and the drilling rig. His skin, gleaming like burnished ebony, blended into the wet bark so well that even in plain view an untrained eye would have missed him.

When he took to the trees after the men cleared the jungle to set up their machine, his four-foot-six frame had been better padded and clothed: a simple loincloth tied with a supple thong around his waist. But rain and a meager diet had taken their toll. His once-thick lips had shrunk on a gaunt face, and his loincloth was long gone;

prolonged exposure to the persistent rain had rotted it away. Not that it worried him; his attention was riveted on the drama slowly simmering twenty feet below. He pursed his lips, tried to blow a bubble, and repressed an urge to laugh about his predicament. His pack was depleted and he hadn't napped in forty-eight long hours, but he wouldn't dream of closing his eyes now that the fun was about to start.

Jereh stirred and gripped the stout branch tighter with his toes. He checked the white smudge on the pipe, then glanced past the engineer. Jereh eyed the group of roughnecks and the rig's cabin, where the operator controlled torsion and drilling speed.

It was a monstrous undertaking. Dead in the center of the clearing, an orange structure soared fifty feet into the air next to a cradle holding countless tubes, flanked on one side by metal shacks and on the other by a squat canvas tent. On the ground, a group of figures decked in bright yellow crowded a tube rapidly rotating into a flat platform.

Jereh had been in the trees for weeks, moving between spots to mark and record the different phases of the core-drilling. The skin on his shoulders, legs, and back was peeling. He would resemble a molting hyena when he returned to his village at Mongwange and gave his report to Leon Kibassa.

At the beginning of his vigil, thirty-five long days ago, Jereh had fashioned a cone-shaped cape with long bracken that he tied around his head. Twice, when he had ventured to the ground, Jereh had passed for foliage when the roughnecks were within a couple of yards—an advantage of being small, although he towered over most of his tribesmen. But the constant wetness at the dome of his head had softened his skin and exfoliated his scalp, exposing the bone despite frequent applications of okapi grease. A cap from an elephant's ear leaf helped for a while, but it amplified every droplet, and Jereh needed his hearing unimpaired.

He dug into his shoulder bag for a piece of duiker jerky and froze when he detected movement. Without altering his position, he picked up a slug and popped it in his mouth. No sense in wasting protein, he reasoned. At least water was no problem. He could drown by sticking out his tongue.

On the other side of the clearing, a narrow tunnel entrance opened between stands of *Albizia* and *Celtis*. Jereh stared into the blackness, straining his eyes to see the contour of a gray mass. "*Hunwa.*" He rolled his tongue around the Masaba word. "*Hunwa*, my friend, the greed of men stands in the way of your final rest." The old elephant had arrived four days ago. The drilling crew hadn't noticed.

The path to the elephants' graveyard bisected the clearing, smack through the middle of the rig. Jereh could sense the animal's bewilderment. The elephant was old and had sunk in the mud. He would die there.

He fingered a *panga*'s handle. "I'll help you, my friend. I'll end your suffering soon." Jereh tensed. A subtle vibration. A minute change of pitch in the whine of the turbines. He dropped six feet to another branch and leaped sideways to a nearby tree, an observation point closer to the tent with the assay table.

He gazed at the white line. The shaft had dropped a

quarter inch. The crew hadn't noticed. Too subtle for them. He appraised the fastest route to a branch over the samples tent and the spot where he'd cut a tiny slit in the waxed canvas.

From a pouch around his neck, Jereh picked the last of the khat, made a small wad, and pushed it into his mouth. Feeling the rush, Jereh pressed with his tongue and placed the mush inside his lower lip. Then he reached back in the bag, retrieved a high-speed camera, and snapped off several frames.

○

Ken mopped his face with a soggy rag. He blinked. The white mark had disappeared. Alarm bells blared as the pipe plummeted and the brakes slammed into the gear-head.

With feverish urgency, the men attacked the tube with tongs and oversize power wrenches, unscrewing sections as the steel tube returned from the depths. When the end surfaced at last, Ken heaved the yard-long front coring section and sprinted toward the samples tent, the crew right behind.

Under the glare of the inspection lights, the men stared in silence at the mud-streaked cylinder, as pirates before a chest. The rain stopped and the sudden quiet sounded exaggerated.

"Your shift, Pedro," Ken said, handing a blunted chisel to the man. "You open it."

Pedro inserted the blade in the side groove of the can-ister, twisting and levering it as he worked along the seam. With a wet slurping sound, the container split in two, displaying the contents of the core.

The chisel dropped from Pedro's hand. *"Santa Madre de Dios!"* He stepped back and made the sign of the cross.

chapter 2

The room's darkness was broken at intervals by six small table lamps, one in front of each leather chair. Along one wall, heavy drapes smothered the windows that once let in light. The atmosphere in the room was stuffy with the echoes of ancient corporate battles. Four mute witnesses guarded the council chamber: four large oil portraits, four serious men with cold eyes.

Hugh Reece, president of the International Mining Corporation, would chair the forthcoming meeting. Though mining was the main line of business, the corporation was active in other fields—biotechnology, genetics, and microelectronics—but shy of the limelight; IMC was a private company.

The causes for Hugh's previous thirty-six sleepless hours were in front of him: a report with perforation details and the laboratory analysis, a diagram with multicolored lines, and scores of names identifying the contents of the core drill. It was all there: the electromagnetic signature with staggeringly high-energy output, low proton surge, incredible neutron exchange, and quark decay.

Trying to relax, he closed his eyes and conjured an image of Alaska—the lands of his Kutchin forebears and birthplace of four generations of miners who had forged the largest private corporation in the world.

Hugh felt a pang of loneliness, an overwhelming nostalgia, as his mind reeled from the awesome discovery in the Congo. He wanted to share with his kin the magic of this moment. *I am homesick after mine own kind.* Ezra Pound's words, but fitting, and a paradox. Hugh had no kind or kin left, just Paul and the four ghosts in the paintings. He made a brief, wry movement with his mouth, stretched his neck from side to side, and rubbed his temples.

For the next couple of minutes, Hugh remained in a slumberlike trance, his large, manicured hands resting on the papers. He felt the slight movement of his fingers, a nervous trembling and a harbinger of the descent to his private hell: the dark hole of memories.

Paul, my boy, where are you?

His grandson was gone. *Paul, you should be in the Congo, opening that shaft, leading the greatest exploration in history. Where are you now?*

When had the estrangement begun? When had the dynasty ended? *His* dynasty. *Paul, what have I done? What have we done?*

From a side door, the directors filed in and took their seats.

Hugh opened his eyes and savored a deep breath. Like a general inspecting the troops, he let his gaze wander along the oval table. *Machiavelli was right. Better to be feared than loved*, he thought, as he nodded, acknowledging Owen DeHolt, Stewart Goss, and Milford Crandall to his left and Eula Kauffmann and Justin Timmons to his right. His gaze touched on the empty seat of the late Walter Reece, his son. Hugh pushed back his chair. Straightening his legs, he removed his moccasins and swept them aside with one foot.

"On April twenty-sixth, a test team in the Congo completed a preliminary exploration. The core-drill contents have been with us for over forty-eight hours. We now have a definite analysis." Hugh paused, glancing toward the end of the table. Milford was rubbing his eyelids. *You couldn't sleep either, old miner?* "As usual, Milford, Owen, and I are aware of the technical data. We've upped the project's status from potential to definite. The previous low-priority station is now critical."

He eyed, in turn, Eula, Justin, and Stewart. "The rest of you have been involved in compartmentalized aspects of the project. Now it's time to evaluate the full picture." Then he closed his eyes. "What do we name this operation?" Hugh asked, to no one in particular.

Silence.

"Suggestions?"

"Sphere? Ituri?" Stewart offered.

Owen frowned.

Hugh glanced at Justin, just in time to catch a faint twitch at the corner of his mouth. "Justin?"

"Isis."

The goddess of magic. An insightful choice, but Hugh could bet the cause of Justin's merriment rested with the goddess's relatives. Perhaps Osiris, her brother and husband, god of the underworld, or the other brother, the dark one: Seth, god of chaos.

Hugh nodded. "Project Isis it is." After a pause, Hugh turned to the red-haired man on his left. "Owen, how do we get Project Isis on the road?"

The dim lights picked out Owen's liver spots, barely cloaked beneath his receding and unnatural russet hair. Hugh, Owen, and Milford were technicians with mining experience; the other three were just professional bureaucrats.

"The challenge is colossal," Owen began, his whitened teeth gleaming. "We've discovered something magical. Why magical?" he asked rhetorically. "*Magical, divine,* or *supernatural* were the tags man appended to anything that escaped his understanding, until science came to his rescue. But science can't help us in Ituri; science can't even accept what we've cored: an object that shouldn't be there, can't be there, and yet it is." He paused to square his papers. "But the depth..." He shook his head. "Frightening. Our scheme will need virtuoso engineering and vast resources. To do it in secret is madness but essential."

Magical and madness. Hugh liked the choice of words.

"Under Ituri, there's a buried structure," Owen continued. "An ancient and sophisticated buried structure. Again, I'm at a loss for words. *Ancient* is inadequate; *prehistoric* would fit the find more accurately. The preliminary findings are extraordinary. We *must* go down there. The problem is *how.*"

Hugh peered at Eula, the legal adviser. Her posture was straight—not arrogant, just strong. She stopped doodling and met his gaze. Hugh noticed that her forehead was lined but the skin around her eyes was smooth, as if all her life she'd only frowned.

"What's the problem?" asked Stewart Goss, the chief financial officer. "You dig a hole, go down, and fetch whatever it is to the surface. That's the way to do it, isn't it?"

Hugh straightened and shook his head with dismay. Stewart was good at his job, with an old-fashioned accountant's zeal, but he was no miner.

Owen gripped the table's edge with both hands, adopting the tone of a professor harassed by bored, lackluster students. He had taught geology at a private college before joining the company twenty years ago.

"It's not a question of just drilling a shaft," he explained patiently. "In fact, it's a hell of a lot more complicated. The drill hit pay dirt at over twenty-two thousand feet."

Stewart dragged a finger along his collar. Hugh cringed. Stewart had a habit of hooking a finger between his neck and too-tight shirt collar. After a short time, the fabric was grimy, as if he hadn't washed it in a month.

"Okay," Stewart said, "but a shaft is a shaft. We need to go deeper perhaps, but the damn South Africans have been digging deep for years. I fail to see the problem or why we'll need 'vast resources.' "

"Let me tell you the facts with figures, the only language you'll understand," Owen continued, staring at Stewart. "The depth of the find is 22,497 feet. That's almost as deep as Everest is tall. Are you with me so far?"

"That's an exaggeration," Stewart said.

"Is it? Everest is a trifle over twenty-nine thousand feet, not a hell of a difference if you consider we have to dig instead of climb. Nobody has ever sunk a shaft to such depth. The South Africans you mention gave up when they reached the seventeen-thousand-foot mark. I tell you what." Owen reached for his legal pad and scribbled a few numbers. "If you fell off the Empire State Building, you'd hit the pavement in about eight seconds. If I hurled you down that shaft, it would take two very long minutes for your body to hit the bottom."

Hugh, his hands joined under his chin as if in prayer, turned with bored annoyance to Owen. "We're not getting anywhere. Get to the point. Tell us how we run the operation. That's what we need to know."

The ex-professor collected the documents into a pile, adjusting the edges with care. "Officially, the caper with the test drill was to survey the land for uranium."

Everyone at the table knew it, but Hugh mused that saying it eased the way for a lecture.

"That's the purpose of the exploration licenses we have. I've studied the figures from the number crunchers. If we follow this line, we need to drill twin fifteen-foot shafts with forty-ton crowns. To extract uranium from such a depth, the ventilation problems will be huge. Without parallel shafts, the radon gas would fry the men's lungs."

At the foot of the table, Milford, the chief technical officer and a mining engineer of exceptional talent, nodded from his seat next to Stewart. Out of habit, he rubbed a dime-size bright-red birthmark in the center of his forehead.

Owen peered at Milford and continued with the monologue, counting on his fingers.

"Hot rocks at that depth. We'll need refrigeration."

Owen glanced at the finance man, who sweated profusely despite the air-conditioning.

"In addition, *we* will need to line the shafts—"

"Are we sure about the lining?" Hugh interrupted, running his finger over the chart with strata details.

"No way to avoid it, Hugh. We have zones of compact calcite that may crumble," Owen answered before resuming the outline. "We'll need to build a town, perhaps an airport, stores, and"—he finished the fingers of one hand and started with the other—"a damn expensive and complex infrastructure. On the conservative side, once we factor in Murphy's Law, we can expect anything between two and three billion. To be honest, four billion wouldn't surprise me if we integrate the huge amounts of baksheesh, or good old bribes if you prefer, that we may have to fork out." Owen paused, perhaps to let the numbers sink in. "That's a summary of the engineering. Of course, there are other considerations besides nuts and bolts."

Stewart shifted forward on the chair as he slammed his open hand on the tabletop. "What are you talking about? Hell, we know there isn't uranium, or any other mineral, in that part of the country. Why should we build a full mine? Isn't a hole enough?"

Owen darted a glance at Hugh and started to rise, his face flushed with anger, when Eula raised a placating hand.

"Take it easy, guys," she said. "Owen's right. After the satellite detected the anomaly, we asked the Congo government for exploration licenses. It wasn't easy, because Ituri is a national park. It was also *expensive*. Right then we made a quick assessment of the zone. The folks at the geology department gazed at their crystal ball, and the uranium proposal popped out of the hat. Although there are no traces of it for miles around, our exploration permits are for uranium."

Justin Timmons cleared his throat. "Why uranium? To throw everybody off track? It seems flimsy. Why not pick something that is present in known quantities? Something that would lead to fewer questions?"

"The guys at geology aren't geniuses, but they're not stupid either," Owen answered. "In fact, because of the surrounding substrata formations and the geological age, the zone *could* be uranium rich."

"Therefore," Eula continued, "the only reason we have to stay here is to develop a uranium mine, although I fear that, as Owen pointed out, the problems are not just technical. We know the Congo government issues licenses to any hillbilly who asks for one. After all, if you don't find anything, they know where *not* to look in the future. But when it comes to mining permits, they'll expect to have a full-fledged project request with good-looking figures, proven reserves, and other juicy things." Eula paused and adjusted her cuffs, pulling them over her wrists. "I imagine Owen will have no problem producing a core-drill report out of thin air to justify the improbable." She stared at Owen, a sly smile on her lips. "If memory serves, it wouldn't be the first time."

Owen was about to argue when Hugh silenced him with a curt wave of the hand.

"The Congo Mining Administration is really Gécamines, staffed by French-trained scientists and engineers and a throwback to colonial times. Let there be no doubt around this table," Eula pressed on. "Inspectors from Gécamines will have their noses up our asses, sniffing at everything, not to mention the local boys—pygmies, Bantus, Nilotes, and whoever happens to be passing by. Gentlemen, what will we tell them when no traces of anything associated with uranium appear anywhere?"

"You want to sink billions in a godforsaken country for remnants of some geological structure we haven't even seen? That we might not be able to sell?" Justin, the chief of security, demanded, incredulous. His tone was so refined that he could have freelanced as a speaking clock. With hair plastered with gel and thick bifocals, Justin looked like a hotel night porter ready to produce Alka-Seltzer to nurture a guest's hangover.

Hugh knew that behind the inoffensive facade was a computer genius who controlled a legion of specialists entrusted with feeding the corporation's gargantuan nervous system.

Justin stood and wandered to one of the windows. After a heartbeat, he shook his head. "You're beating around the bush. Details and money aren't the core problems," he said without turning to face them. "The Congo's been at war for decades." His voice lowered as he turned. "*Everybody's* at war with one another—state, rebels, tribes, warlords, neighbors, every Tom, Dick, and Harry. War is a way of life there; the country has been bleeding for generations. You're plotting to sink the deepest mine in the known universe, dead center in the thickest and most impenetrable jungle, in a national park in the middle of a war zone. Hugh, are you serious about this?"

The patriarch stared at the documents on the table before answering. "You've read the Project Isis reports.

Have no fear about coming up empty-handed. We know there's something four miles down. We don't know what it is, but we can't leave it there." With a grimace, Hugh bent over the table and stared at everyone in turn. He noticed that Milford, still sober-faced, had remained in the background. *You're far too quiet, my friend. I know that look.*

"We must go down, regardless of the cost," Hugh concluded.

"There may be another way," Milford said, drumming his fingers on the chair's arm. "A capsule—a special vehicle."

Hugh suppressed a smile as he noticed the four pairs of eyes converging on Milford's birthmark. *Now we'll get this show on the road.* The meeting had been a necessary farce from the start. Hugh was waiting for the moment when Milford would bring his awesome intellect to bear on the matter.

"We could drill a thirty- or forty-inch exploration shaft with a solid lining using a rotary crown from a derrick." He drew a circle with his hands. "Of course, under the auspices of sending a drone to measure temperature gradients, radon concentration, or whatever. Call it an oversize core drill."

Hugh saw Justin's eyes go wide.

"Afterward we could design a drone with lateral laser-drilling capability and thin automated probes, ostensibly to analyze the shaft and gather data. We can invent some state-of-the-art engineering procedure to justify the odd drilling."

"You said lasers?" Owen asked. "What about the electronics? The electromagnetic pulses would fry them."

Milford nodded. "I never said anything about building such a drone. Just designing it, for Gécamines' benefit. In fact, we would build a very different drone." Milford paused and inserted his thumbs into the pockets of his bright-yellow waistcoat. "If we find any large elements, and if it's worthwhile, we can always think about extraction and sinking a larger parallel shaft or shafts. Of course, this is an oversimplification, and *drone* is the wrong word. I'm thinking of a cylindrical vehicle, maybe self-propelled . . . and *manned*."

Stewart jerked upright, opening his mouth like a startled lamprey.

Hugh felt a half-forgotten warmth spread through his loins. *You magnificent bastard! A manned vehicle, no less.*

"Perhaps an all-mechanical contraption," Milford continued. "The electromagnetic emission of the site prevents the use of electronics, but a man could go explore whatever's down there."

Milford followed Justin's progress as he returned to his seat.

"No doubt the exercise would be expensive and complicated but nothing compared to sinking twin full-size shafts," Milford continued. "Later, if we have to, we can always claim we've made a mistake or that the exploration data doesn't warrant a full-size job. We pack our gear, blow the shaft, and get the hell out of the country." He paused. Hugh held his breath as he sensed the argument's conclusion nearing. "Now all we have to do is find a guy with the balls to get into a coffin-shaped elevator and drop one and a half thousand floors below ground."

For the next few seconds nobody spoke. Meshing mental cogs—appraising, analyzing, and weighing the pros and cons—was almost a physical sensation in the background.

"Who, Owen?" Hugh asked, laying his hand on Owen's forearm.

As if talking to himself, Owen murmured, "All we need is a man with the *cojones* to ride a casket down a tight hole. Someone who knows how to assimilate and analyze whatever he happens to find down there and knows how to be discreet. He must care about his job and this company. *And* be a brilliant geologist."

Hugh jerked his hand from Owen's arm, as if the flesh were poisoned. Like a boomerang, hurled years before and returned out of thin air, Owen's words hit him with full force. He had described Hugh's errant grandson. *Paul, where are you?* He glanced at the empty place on his right. Walter, his son, could never return to his chair, but would Paul?

Hugh gazed at the portraits on the wall. Messing with the gods and destiny was a risky business. He breathed deeply as he pictured dog-eared pages with the meticulous inquiry of his son's death, buried at the bottom of his safe with the flight-recorder analysis and folder containing the last minutes of Walter's life. Two years ago, but it seemed like yesterday.

To be truthful, the idea had buzzed inside his head for a long time; he'd thought of it as a devious puzzle, a mental exercise like the *Times* crossword, until one day he decided to play God and the idea metamorphosed into a plan. A plan that ultimately ended his son's life and turned his grandson into an enemy. *Was it the dream of an old man bent on testing fate? No, a gauntlet thrown to the gods would be a more accurate description.* Everything has a beginning, often difficult to pin down, but Hugh couldn't let it go. He wanted to find the exact moment— the wistful breath of air in a clenched fist, the slight gesture of a wrist, the movement that set the dice in motion.

Hugh leaned back and closed his eyes. "I need to think. Let's adjourn for an hour. Have lunch."

After hearing the door close, Hugh stood on his bare feet and padded to a credenza. He eyed the apples in a Lalique bowl and selected a large one with a small blemish, a dark spot the size of a sequin. *We're all flawed, aren't we?*

When did the dice start to roll? Maybe when wasn't as important as why. *Why did it have to happen?* The rhetorical question took him by surprise. He'd only wanted to ensure his lineage. *Was that so wrong?*

He ambled to the far window and parted the curtain a fraction. Far below, herds of little people jostled and rushed to their little offices and their little lives. He polished the apple on his shirt, over his belly, and took a big bite, avoiding the flaw. His only grandson was sterile. Susan, Paul's departed little bitch of a wife, had given Hugh the proof—a vial with Paul's sperm. Still fresh. Handed to a trusted courier at their doorstep. *How had she managed it?*

Hugh eyed a band of errant sparrows outside the window. Susan had consented to be implanted with a thoroughbred Reece embryo. An eagle. So what if he had to blackmail her? It had been easy. The cow liked threesomes with Mrs. Yu's teenagers—little girls plucked from the rice fields. Walter agreed to supply his seed. How was Hugh to know that Susan would fall for her father-in-law? She was giving him a blow job when they crashed in the canyon.

Terminal blow job. Hugh took another bite from the apple. The coroner had to dig Walter's dick from Susan's mouth with a crowbar. Before Hugh could react, Paul got his hands on a copy of Susan's autopsy and the biopsies, which confirmed the paternity of the fetus she was carrying. Paul's father. Hugh eyed the apple. A drop of juice clung to the skin. With the tip of his tongue he lapped the runaway fluid. Paul had found recourses and friends, like the biologist who carried out the DNA tests. *I hope you like your new posting in Alaska, Dr. Schroeder. May you rot in hell.*

Milford must have helped Paul. Hugh felt a pang of jealousy; Paul and Milford had always been close. He rotated the apple and took another bite. Paul had zeroed in on him and screwed IMC good. *Almost bankrupted us. Made us foot the bill for the accident in Bangladesh. What a waste of money!* All because of a few hundred dead peasants who had been starving anyway. *Is the score settled? Did you get redress for the disenfranchised? Such an idealist. You could have had me killed, or done it yourself, but you didn't. Instead, you tore apart the company—my company, my life.*

Hugh splayed his toes and tried to grip the carpet's luscious pile. *Bet you won't screw up the company when it's yours. There are no dying hillbillies in the Congo. No moral considerations; just business.*

The corporation had scores of expert engineers, geologists, people of proven loyalty. But would they stay loyal with the stakes so high? What about the directors? Would they think him mad to entrust this mission to his treacherous grandson? But Hugh knew better. Paul's past actions were personal, nothing to do with the corporation, just aimed at his grandfather's pocket and his beloved IMC, where Paul knew it would hurt the most.

The greatest coup in history. I'll make you an indecent proposal and you'll grab it 'cause you're a sucker for challenges. Yes, you'll do it, 'cause I can't. We're the only miners left of our kin. I can't take that elevator down to magic. But you will. Of course you will, my boy. You'll lead Project Isis for the company, for me, and because you're a Reece.

He dropped the curtain and peered at what was left of the apple: the core and a piece with the blemish. He took the last bite with relish, then tossed the core in the garbage.

One arm folded across his belly and the other outstretched, Hugh Reece waltzed back to the table, pirouetting on bare tiptoes. He sat on his chair, his chest heaving with rumbling laughter. He leaned back and closed his eyes. A couple of minutes later his breathing settled into a deep and rhythmic pattern.

○

Hugh snapped awake from his impromptu siesta, instantly alert, as the directors settled in their chairs. "You were saying, Owen?" The phrase was rhetorical, because he already knew the follow-up.

The others stared at Owen DeHolt with understandable foreboding, holding their breath.

"This is far too important," Owen said. "It should be a Reece. It should be Paul."

Humanity's greatest discovery in modern history. Hugh

pictured the headlines, musing that he didn't give a damn about humanity. What the find would do for the IMC was another matter.

"Preposterous," Hugh spat to no one in particular. It sounded as effective as it was calculated. "Am I hearing the counsel of my board? The men and woman who came close to killing my grandson? Now you're nominating him?"

"Just a minute!" Justin stood, his face contorted in rage. "Don't try to pass that carcass off on us!"

Hugh Reece laughed inwardly, still looking at no one. "You've got a poor memory, or at least a damn selective one." He lifted his head and stared at Justin and then at Eula, the smile dissolving from his face. "I remember a board meeting in this same damn room. How long ago was that, Owen? A couple of years?"

Owen stared ahead in silence.

Hugh stood and leaned over the table. "Perhaps your eminences have amnesia? Have all of you fuckers forgotten?"

Eula was the first to react. "Please, Hugh, it was an accident; we've all paid our dues." She stood, her palms upturned in a soothing gesture. "Let bygones be bygones."

"She's right," Owen agreed.

Hugh relaxed his fists and glared at the executives in turn. Milford returned an angry stare. Hugh straightened to his full height.

"Paul, then," Hugh repeated with sneering undertones, his attention on Owen's eyes, waiting for the tiniest of sparks, the slightest body-language giveaway to betray his knowledge of Paul's whereabouts. Nothing. *So, it's not you.* Hugh had lost hope of discovering Paul's hiding place despite a cartload of money spent on detectives and other less-orthodox investigators. But his gut told him someone close knew. Time to raise the ante. "And who on this board will bring the black sheep back into the fold?" Hugh enunciated the question with care, academic, as though eliciting no answer.

"Paul has never been a black sheep."

Everyone turned again to Milford.

"IMC and all of us in this room betrayed him," Milford reminded them. "He's been manipulated, used, and insulted. I'm in this hideous den of iniquity with you, but I'll have to live with that." Milford rubbed his forehead and seemed to reach a decision. "I'll speak to Paul."

All the faces angled in Hugh's direction. So, Milford *did* know where Paul had been all this time. *Gotcha!*

chapter 3

The mule labored along the path between Colquizate and Dulce Nombre de Culmí—little more than a dirt track of pits, uneven ground, and loose rubble. In the dry season, a few neighbors, the doctor, or the parson would come and go. The alternative was an eighty-mile detour along a road clinging to its last sheets of paving.

But bad weather sobers men. In May, when the rainy season starts in Honduras, they use the path only for matters of life or death. But the centuries-old *Vereda del Diablo*, the Devil's Path, persists like a wretched dream on the slopes of the Agalta cordillera, halfway up between the rugged peaks and the Olancho Valley.

The man, covered with a tarpaulin knotted with a rope at the waist, sang off-key *rancheras*—old hands' tales of sorrow and broken hearts—amid the din of the deluge and the splashing hooves.

A few yards ahead was a large rock with a smaller one balanced on top—a curious arrangement, its profile resembling the Moai of Easter Island when they still had their hats. The rider stopped at the formation and slapped the mule's neck, coaxing the animal to the right between the trees. The man leaned on the mule to take the new track and swore in Spanish, questioning the animal's ancestry and damning the water that trickled along the hood's rim and drenched his shirt.

The sheer incline, like the rest of the trail to Dulce Nombre de Culmí, was covered in dense groves of pine and oak, with a scattering of other trees—splendid mahoganies, Spanish cedars, balsa ceibas, *guayacos*, rosewoods, and *chicozapotes*. The forest formed a tunnel, usually soft-lit through the leafy canopy but now darkened by the torrential rain. On the floor and between the stones, water trickled in muddy streams toward the valley over a mile below.

After half an hour of arduous climbing, Manuel Negroponte reached a small clearing at the foot of a rocky wall—an imposing vertical escarpment one hundred feet high. A crevice split the rock.

Manuel dismounted, lost his footing, and almost fell when the mule reared and kicked. He swore again, grabbed the reins, and half-dragged the animal through the crack, trawling the tarred canvas behind.

A narrow path led through the fissure and turned right after a few steps. The bend widened at a cave's entrance. A curtain of dense foliage and thorny bushes camouflaged the opening. Manuel pushed the undergrowth aside with a hand and pulled on the reins. "*Entra de una vez, mala puta!*"

He stopped and held the animal by the halter, senses alert, waiting for his eyes to adjust until he could see the familiar contours and the signs of habitation.

The space was almost circular, about thirty feet in

diameter, sloping to one side where a pair of mules were tied to a post. On the other side, a pile of planks, a few wooden props, and an old barrel—with picks, shovels, and other tools—sat on a stone shelf. Further up in a niche, a rumpled sleeping bag lay over slats, a pair of knapsacks off to the side. Manuel breathed deeply. The tang of hot ashes, smoked timbers, and dung was a welcome change from the scent of rain and wet earth.

On the floor and next to a demijohn of water were the remains of a fire. The embers glowed under an aluminum pot, blackened by use, hanging from a tripod made of branches.

Across from the entrance, a tunnel opened, its curious geometry following an inclined seam in the rock. The walls, although parallel, leaned to the right. The floor, made of compacted excavation rubble, forced the visitor to walk with his feet touching the right wall and his head a couple of inches from the left. The shoring system was ingenious; a solid wooden beam parallel with the floor inserted into a housing cut into the rock and held in place by a stout vertical post.

It looked tilted and botched. Manuel smiled at the strange optical illusion, but he knew the shoring was sound. He'd helped dig the tunnel but, until now, he hadn't seen it finished.

He tied the mule with the others, undid the rope from his waist, and stretched the tarpaulin over posts. He scratched his cleft chin before entering the unlit tunnel.

The gallery, cut between two volcanic plates, extended for about a hundred yards toward the mountain core at a slight slope. Humming a tuneless melody, Manuel walked with an arm extended as he followed the alluvial strata. The air was damp and a hint of a draft told of another opening somewhere.

The corridor ended in a cave where the darkness was not complete and wispy tendrils of vapor danced in lazy swirls against the shadowy background. He stopped and looked upward, his eyes adjusting to the scant light. High up, between an inverted forest of stalactites, a bright spot shone like Sirius. Manuel smiled in the gloom, remembering when he had descended through the hole, high above, a year before.

The business had been dicey—a real act of faith, to say the least. When they reached the top of the mountain, Paul had picked up a small stone and dropped it through the hole. A few seconds later he pronounced, "One hundred yards," as if reading from a mountain guide. Manuel doubled the dynamic cord, making it one hundred twenty-five yards long, secured it to a nearby tree, and threw it down the hole.

He had rappelled six hundred feet in six seconds from a moving helicopter once, but that was in the army, when he was twenty and crazy. Thirteen years later and out of shape, the descent was slow, especially when the rope played out.

"Straighten your legs," Paul had called from above. He did, and landed in water up to his knees.

Manuel stifled a laugh and, with a movement of his hand, swatted away the memories as if they were flies.

In contrast to the now-dry corridor, the sides, ceiling, and floor oozed water. Large drops fell from the calcium-salt formations into bowls hollowed out in the limestone floor through the millennia, a pleasant staccato noise amplified by the cave walls.

Manuel wandered to the center of the cave and a small, calm lake, its surface rippled by falling water. Eyes closed, he lifted his head, letting drops run down his face. With the tip of his tongue, he tasted the liquid with satisfaction. It was warm, slightly sulfurous, with the same spicy smell that filled the cave.

Where are you hiding? He followed the sound of muted thumps, sliding through a narrow crevice with difficulty. Moving sideways, he scraped his back against the rock, his nose inches from the opposite wall. He continued in darkness until the gash widened enough to accommodate his bulk. Suddenly, the passage opened into a chamber where a hurricane lamp shone brightly.

Manuel watched the familiar lank six-footer, in jeans and a sleeveless T-shirt, working on the opposite wall. He looked good. When Paul moved, the light caught the long white scar to one side of his forehead, partly hidden by waves of dark, unruly hair.

Bracing himself against the wall, Manuel remained in shadow and observed. Perched atop an assembly of planks roped to posts, Paul was inserting wooden wedges along a cleft in the rock. A three-foot-wide black seam snaked from the ceiling and traversed the whole wall. Manuel stared in fascination at the curious procedure, following the long fingers.

When it appeared Paul was satisfied with the number and distribution of the wood slivers, he poured water on them, following a precise order from the outside in to the center. After repeating the maneuver several times, he waited, his eyes glued to the crack, fingers absently rubbing a green doughnut-shaped disk dangling from a thick gold chain around his neck.

In subdued tones at first, then with increasing intensity, cracks sounded within the rock. When the noise ended, Paul put his nose close to the stone, sniffing. From a distance, he looked like a rutting male detecting a female. In slow motion, Paul drew back from the formation, following the seam's interstices with his gaze.

He reached for three larger tapered pieces of wood and inserted them in the center and sides of the cleft. A splinter may have pierced his finger, because he drew a thumb to his mouth and sucked, but he never took his eyes from the crack. Taking the water can in the other hand, he moistened the wood again.

Manuel bent down, picked up a small stone, aimed at an empty drum, and hurled the rock with force. The stone's impact was deafening, made louder by the rock walls. Paul jumped backward as if propelled by a hidden spring and tripped over the water can, which clanged against the rocks, adding to the noise. He tried to stand upright but lost his footing and fell on the seat of his pants, his eyes still glued to the crack, which had widened.

Paul searched the rock face but couldn't zero in on the cause of the noise. He detected movement on the periphery of his vision and tensed. His eyes found the convulsing ebony giant and he let his breath escape, composing his face into a frown of mock anger. Slipping between the planks, he pounced on the laughing man and shook him.

"Son of a bitch! You scared me to death, chin-ass! My, but I'm happy to see your ugly face, you bastard."

Manuel slapped Paul's back and grinned. "Let me see

you, honky." He paused to inspect Paul's face. "Yes, you do look good—a little pale from hiding in this hole, but fine."

Paul rolled his eyes and snatched Manuel's forearms, then dragged him toward the platform. "It's been over a month. Come, let me show you something."

The men climbed over the wooden structure to reach the rock face where the wedges had loosened a slab of mineral.

"Give me a hand with this beauty."

Inserting their fingers in the crack from both sides, they dislodged the chunk and, with some effort, laid it on the floor. Wood-grainlike patterns traced across the bluish-black surface. In places, fiery red bursts flashed, reflecting the light from the lamp as if small windows permitted a glance into its internal fire.

"Isn't it awesome?"

Manuel tilted the chunk a fraction sideways, as if to catch the light from another angle. "It is, but I don't know what the hell I'm looking at."

"This is seam opal, you idiot. It's worth a small fortune."

"*How* small?"

"If the seam is as deep as I think, perhaps thirty to fifty million."

Manuel took a deep breath and crossed himself. He looked again at the black block. "Lempiras?"

Paul shook his head. "Yankee dollars. This beauty alone is worth more than half a million."

Manuel whistled as he looked at the piece on the floor and then at the huge vein on the wall.

"Stop calculating." Paul followed his gaze and understood the confusion at once. "That's not all opal, not by a long shot."

Paul went to the spot where he'd been using the wedges. After rummaging between some rags, he picked up a small flask and took a swig from the container before passing it over.

"Opal forms when water filters into cavities left by rotten wood. The water carries mollusks and other microscopic organisms. These collect until the cavity is full. This is the result."

Manuel knelt to slide his fingers over the surface irregularities. "Do you mean that this is made of bugs?"

"In part. Somehow the wood got trapped in the rock, and when it decayed it left a hollow, a mold if you will. Over the millennia, the cavity filled not just with bugs, grasses, and silica-rich things but also with other material, creating the oxides that give opal its different colors and character."

"That's not *all* opal?"

"Of course not. That's a seam of organic carbon and manganese oxide with lots of opal in sight. And the good bits, the gem-quality stones, are these spots here and here." He pointed to the iridescent pieces. "We'll see what's inside the seam. It's rare to find opals of such quality. Black-seam opal may sell for three thousand dollars a carat, as expensive as low-grade diamonds." He lit a cigarette and tossed the pack to Manuel. "But don't worry. There's enough here for both of us."

Manuel lifted his head and looked at Paul. "You discovered the seam and you're working it. What do I have to do with it?"

Paul smiled at his friend. Manuel was younger, thirty-something, and a couple of inches shorter. His muscles bulged through his short-sleeved checkered shirt, which was open to the waist. The locals said that Manuel's deep-clefted chin was a sign of beauty because it looked like miniature buttocks. *Chin-ass* had stuck as a nickname. It was great teasing fodder for Paul.

"You showed me the way in here through the mountaintop and lent me a hand with most of the tunnel. Now you can help me dig it out and move the opals to the village." He stood and offered his hand, palm up. "I need you, buddy. We're partners in this little caper, okay?"

"I have to work the farm," Manuel stuttered, rising to his feet, though a broad smile lit his face.

"Do me a favor, man! Hire the whole damn village. We've a problem *here*, not on your damn farm. If word gets out, we'll have a rush. We have to work the seam between us, with a couple of men from the village at most. Besides, you're plantation labor. You know how to dig!"

"I'll give you plantation labor...white bread." He wrapped his arms around Paul's waist and lifted him two feet off the ground. "Damn Yankee! You'll turn me into a bourgeois, but you have a deal, partner." He laughed and rocked Paul up and down. Suddenly he dropped him on the planks. "Shit! I forgot. They're waiting for you in the village."

"Who?"

Manuel shrugged. "Don't know. Last night, Joaquin came to see me. He asked if I knew where you were, because two Americans—friends of yours, apparently—were looking for you. The two guys came yesterday on the bus from Tegucigalpa and put up at the hotel. Joaquin insisted that it was urgent. You know how these things are. We had a couple of drinks. I promised to have a look around."

"Did he say what they look like, the two Americans?"

"He said they seemed like important people."

Paul took a swig from the flask and tried to imagine who they might be. He sighed, giving up. "Well, it's about time I surfaced. I miss the village."

"The village?" Manuel raised an eyebrow and smiled. "That's all?"

Paul caught the leer on his friend's face and threw a punch to his arm. "Get lost."

"Sure thing."

Paul laughed and batted his eyelids. "I've been underground for so long that I'm even finding you...attractive."

Manuel raised his hands and backed off a pace. "Hey, man, that's not in the contract."

Paul bent down at one end of the slab. "Give me a hand with this. We can take it down to the village and start figuring out how to sell the opals on the quiet."

Unexpected visitors were a bad omen. Paul rubbed the smooth line crossing his forehead and tried not to think.

○

In a little over an hour, they had the animals loaded for the return to Colquizate. They wrapped the opal in a hemp bag and loaded it onto the spare mule with other samples, the small field laboratory in a wooden box, a rifle, and their backpacks. Manuel led the mules while Paul followed, carefully stepping over mule droppings.

The men re-covered the opening after they exited the crevice. Unless someone was looking for the cave, they would never see it behind the vegetation.

The return trip took the rest of the day. The din of the storm made conversation difficult. Manuel led the way, covered with his oversize tarpaulin. Paul followed, wrapped in an army cape, the hood held to his face with a piece of elastic. One last mule brought up the rear, tethered to Paul's with a rope.

Lulled by the rhythm of the animal and the rain's cacophony, Paul drifted. *Has Grandfather died? No*, he decided, answering his own question. Milford could have used his sat-phone. Paul hated the idea of inheriting a desk job in Dallas. He tried it once and almost went insane.

The image of his grandfather woke Paul's own inner demons. He shivered under his cape. In a weird way, he understood the reasons behind the old man's demented plans: the dynasty's perpetuation. Paul knew he would always love the old man. But, at the time, he had wanted to see Hugh Reece dead; more than that, Paul had wanted him to suffer. The task had been easy: find what a man most loves and you will know his greatest weakness. Strike at it and you will break him. His grandfather's heart had been the International Mining Corporation.

Paul straightened his back and adjusted his sore buttocks to the saddle as he considered that he had spent the best part of the last two years bumming around—what he called jolly follies. The feeling in his gut told him that things were about to change.

But the thought of taking over IMC filled him with dread. He could never do it.

And there was Carmen.

Time seemed to have stopped in Colquizate. The place
had the air of poverty, sadness, and neglect that sometimes clings to Central American villages. Groups of
houses huddled along the hillside below in no recogniza-
ble pattern—drab adobe walls topped with curved red
tiles that blended with the rocky terrain.

As they rode into the village under a heavy downpour,
Paul noticed Don Eduardo looking out a window of his
house. Paul waved.

With fewer than three thousand inhabitants, the village was small. Hidden from sight, however, lurked a
prosperous community. Coffee growing and a fiery
liqueur, flavored with the burned sugar from the coffee-
roasting process, formed the backbone of the families' in-
comes, further bolstered by products like cloth, leather
goods, fruit preserves, dried sausages, natural cosmetics,
and—in a discreet fashion—a rare sinsemilla marijuana
of singular quality.

Colquizate's seemingly paradoxical success arose from

two unique reasons: geographical isolation and the fact that none of the town's industries was lucrative enough to attract hustlers. Its remote location was due in part to the extraordinary talents and vision of Eduardo Fontcuberta Gonzalez, the mayor of Colquizate. During his third term, the region's politicians tried to bestow on the town an asphalt road to Catacamas. It was a poisoned gift. Easy access formed part of a plan to co-opt the village's wealth. Quick means of approach would promote traffic in both directions, and with the newcomers would come the predators.

At an epic meeting, much laughed about in cantinas, the wily Don Eduardo cajoled the government representatives into funding a sewage plant instead of the road. In fact, they said, the mayor maneuvered the politicians into "leaving the coins and taking the shit."

Paul blessed the mayor's foresight. He'd been able to retain his anonymity here.

When they reached the fence of Paul's house, Manuel jumped off the mule and approached, his oversize poncho dragging in the mud. "You're sure about not wanting me to come along? You know . . . to meet those people."

Paul shook his head as he dismounted.

Manuel opened his mouth as if to say something, held Paul's gaze, and shrugged. He jumped on the mule's back, clicked his tongue, and slapped the animal's rump.

Paul opened the gate, pulling the mules toward the stable behind the house. He lit a kerosene lamp, unloaded the beasts, and hung saddlebags and rucksacks from hooks on a beam. He undid the harness, drying the mules with old blankets before emptying half a sack of grain mixed with straw into the manger.

"Today there's no full treatment," he said, excusing himself, "but tomorrow I'll give you a good brushing down."

One of the animals turned its head, as if in understanding. Paul laughed, slapping the damp neck, then split some yams with a machete and added them to the fodder.

"This is compensation," Paul muttered, rubbing the other mule's flank. "Dessert instead of a beauty treatment."

He dimmed the lamp, sat on a stool, and lit a cigarette. At times like this, he questioned his self-imposed exile. There was a price to pay for choosing the less-traveled road. He tried to put faces on the two men, no doubt the bearers of bad news. Just a handful of people knew where to look for him, people from faraway places.

Paul shook his head in frustration. It had only been a question of time. He felt angry, cross at his own ingenuity. To be left alone was too much to ask, perhaps even unreasonable. He couldn't run forever. *Run.* It all boiled down to that—withdrawal, escape, obscurity. He flew from ghosts, from the nightmares, from his name and his past, but he knew that starting again would be impossible. There was no second chance, just new performances with old actors. Other than his grandfather, he was the sole survivor of the Reece dynasty, heir to the family fortune and IMC. To expect that the long arm of Hugh Reece, alive or dead, would never reach out and pluck him back to reality was naive.

Another wave of agony washed over him as he thought of Carmen. Could she ever adjust to life in a crowded city? He shuddered. It would be like clipping the wings of an eagle. Susan, his departed wife, had been the love of his youth—light, without the depth and the meaning afforded by maturity. He hadn't been emotionally prepared to share himself fully. Carmen was different. He loved her with his being and his soul. He couldn't imagine any sort of life without her.

The smell of coffee and food met him at the door. A whirlwind dressed in white detached itself from the stove and rushed to him, throwing tanned arms around his neck. Paul dropped the backpack and kissed her without haste, from the heart.

Her lips were cool, moist as the air. She tasted like mangoes.

Once again, he marveled at the intoxicating aroma of clean, bare skin, empty of perfumes or artifice. His eyes unfocused as he breathed in her fragrance.

"I've missed you," Carmen purred.

"I've missed you too." An understatement. At the mine, he had yearned for her with a need that went beyond the physical—a longing not even the endless hours of grueling physical labor could assuage. He belonged by her side; it was a deep-seated feeling of completeness, unlike the despair he once felt for Susan. How strange to think of Susan now, while he held another woman in his arms, but it lasted just for an instant, like a dull pain in his side. Paul broke the embrace, stepping back and staring into her dilating irises. "Are you trying to seduce me?"

She stood with arms akimbo and frowned at him. She was young, mid-twenties, with raven hair reaching to her waist. Her oval face held the aristocratic cheekbones of the Sambo–Mosquito Indians, and her large, slanted eyes were so dark there was little visible separation between pupils and irises. Now they blazed with anger, at odds with her smile.

"Of course I'm trying to seduce you." She hugged him again, looking up, wrinkling her nose. "You're soaked."

"Mmmm . . . I never complain."

Carmen's smiled deepened. "But I don't smell like a mule, dopey."

"No, you don't."

She grabbed his hand, dragging him to a door on the other side of the kitchen. "Come, I've a hot bath ready for you." She opened the door to a small room, and steam wafted from a huge tin vat filled to the brim. Paul never used the artifact, preferring to shower with the roof tank's tepid water instead. He glanced into a corner where a metal bucket bubbled over a wood-burning stove.

"I've heated the water at least five times. You've taken a long time to get here," Carmen complained. "It's about time you install a water heater."

"How did you know I was coming back today?" he asked, but he knew the answer.

"I saw Manuel taking to the hills. I heard some guys were waiting for you, so I came. Satisfied?"

"Not yet." Paul delighted in Carmen's smile as she pushed him into a chair, undid his shoelaces, took off his clothes, and guided him into the bath.

"Be careful!" Paul shouted when she dumped the first bucket. "It's scalding!"

She rubbed his arms and legs with rough hemp and green soap, humming as she pretended to ignore the obvious signs of his arousal.

"I feel wicked making you suffer," she said, laughing.

"I have a remedy for wicked girls."

"Let me guess..."
He reached for her.
She took the remedy.

○

Paul entered the hotel, freshly bathed. The bar was busy despite the rain. With the mayor were three other men who made up the town's police, plus the sergeant, Joaquin. To one side stood Manuel and Raul Diaz, a huge farmer reputed to pull a plow faster than oxen.

Paul was used to seeing all the men at one time or another, but not all together or intent on staring down a lone stranger. He stopped by the door, followed their line of sight, and rolled his eyes as he recognized their focus of interest, a man who looked like a punch-drunk boxer: Mark O'Reilly. Paul darted a glance at the men crowding the bar, as the intent behind the bizarre scene made sense. After learning of the stranger's interest in Paul's whereabouts, the mayor must have rallied the town's muscle to look after him.

Mark sat on a couch with his shiny lizard boots on a small table, the only guest in the lounge that also doubled as the hotel lobby. He wore a dark suit, the tie loosened and white shirt unbuttoned at the neck. He seemed out of place under the reading lamp in the tiny Honduran town. From the plastered hair to the scars on his face and the broken nose, he reminded Paul of a third-rate actor in a low-budget gangster film. His hands were enormous, disproportionate, strong, causing the book he was reading to shrink out of scale.

Paul smiled tentatively, noticing with apprehension

that the men at the bar had left their glasses and started to move in unison.

Mark must have spotted the peripheral movement, because he stopped reading and looked in their direction. He dropped the book and stood clumsily, knocking over the table and dumping newspapers on the floor as he leaped toward the door with a speed and agility at odds with his bulk. Paul remained glued to the spot, watching the action unfold.

Manuel, standing nearest the charging man, reacted first. He stuck out his leg. Mark tripped and fell, bellowing in annoyance. He tried to stand up by placing both hands on the floor. Paul heard metallic snaps. Mark flexed his knees, pivoted his head, and stared toward the black orifices of four automatic pistols—held in the Weaver stance by four men with cold eyes. He lurched in horror, only to find Paul by the door.

Paul shook with laughter, approached Mark, grabbed him by the arm, and helped him up. He slapped his back and offered his hand. Mark took the hand and shook it with both of his, the palms covered with the telltale matte areas of calluses. Hands used to hard work.

"Goddamn, Paul, these guys mean business. For a minute there, I felt like Dillinger."

Manuel, the mayor, and the police officers shared confused glances as they holstered their guns. Paul eyed them in turn. "Guys, next time you can bring the cannon and the cavalry."

The mayor scratched his chin and grinned. Paul threw his arms around the shoulders of Manuel and Joaquin. "Let me make the introductions. This brute," he nodded at the American rubbing his side, "is Mark O'Reilly, a half-Irish bastard, but the best mine supervisor you'll ever know. These," he turned to the other men, "are my friends: Don Eduardo, the mayor of Colquizate; Joaquin, the police sergeant; Benito; Manuel; Pedro, the hotel owner; Julian; Santos; and the little guy is Raul." *Little, my ass.*

The men all shook Mark's hand.

"Holy shit, what a show. You look like a Special Forces unit."

Laughter soon replaced the first tentative smiles, for Mark's words were delivered in thickly accented Spanglish. Paul signaled Pedro to pass around the liquor. Everyone waited for Mark to drink first. Mark emptied his glass with a gulp, reddening as he swallowed the fiery liquid.

"Je-e-esus!" he stuttered, choking and coughing at the same time. "You're going to kill me one way or another today." He peered at the empty glass. "What the fuck is this?"

"*Quitapenas.* Local moonshine," Paul answered.

The mayor bent in two with a rich baritone laughter. Benito, one of the police officers, mopped tears with the back of his hand.

Pedro came from behind the bar, tucking a rag under his belt, and refilled Mark's glass. "*Si que son flojos los Irlandeses. No saben hacer aguardiente en su tierra?*"

"Aye, laddie," Mark replied, "we do make fine spirits in Ireland. I thought t'were the best in the world—'til now, that is."

Mark was prepared this time. He downed the *quitapenas* and smacked his lips. "Have to take some back." He winked at Pedro and slapped his back, making the short man wince. He offered his glass for a fresh refill and then put his arm around Paul's shoulder. "What was that all about?" Mark asked before downing the third shot.

"Friends."

"You can't go wrong with friends like that," Mark said. He eyed Raul, who boldly stared back at him. "I guess the tiny guy at the rear was to finish me up, in case the firing squad failed, right?"

The banter continued for another hour, until the mayor hinted at an early-morning call. He nodded to the others. In a few minutes, only Manuel remained at the bar. He offered Mark his hand. "I'll leave you to it, guys. Call if you need something."

At the door, where Mark had fallen, Manuel stopped, extended his arms with a rigid finger pointing at the floor, and pretend-fired several times. Then he left, laughing.

Paul remained silent for a while. Mark grabbed the bottle and pointed to Paul's empty glass. "One for the road?"

"Are we leaving?"

Mark glanced toward the stairs at the lobby's rear. "*I* am."

Paul nodded and took a seat at a table. Mark filled the glasses and sat in the chair opposite.

"Who's with you?" Paul asked, niceties over.

Mark shifted, eyeing the dark liquid in his glass before answering. "Milford."

Paul stole a glance toward the stairs and frowned.

"We didn't know how long it would take for you to turn up. It could have been days," Mark explained. "And we agreed to take turns waiting down here. He's probably napping or watching a game."

An awkward pause followed and Paul nodded. "The bastards chose well. They knew I wouldn't talk to anyone else. What's this all about, anyway?"

Mark shook his head. "I don't know. We hit something in the Congo, something big. The guys who were on site have been sent on vacation, isolated, and replaced with security people. I swear I don't know what's happening."

"Where in the Congo?"

"Ituri."

"Were you there?"

Mark hesitated for an instant, then nodded.

"What were you doing?"

"Deep coring."

Paul was surprised and relieved at the unexpected turn. *Hugh is alive and well. We're talking business.*

"You were there but don't know what's going on?" Paul persisted.

"We drilled *into* something, but they didn't tell us what." Mark shifted, obviously uncomfortable. "Please don't ask me about details."

IMC had isolated the drilling team—all but Mark. Paul nodded. Mark had been with the company for twenty years and was a senior field engineer, a master tool-pusher; trusted.

"Do you think there's any reason at all why I should talk shop to a representative of IMC?" Paul asked. As he spoke, he realized Mark's role as a chaperon for Milford. To grill the man was unfair.

"I don't know. I could give you a dozen reasons, but I think a couple would do: curiosity, or the simple pleasure of saying no."

"Perhaps you're right," Paul said, pouring the remaining liquor into their glasses. "Besides, I've missed Milford. Tell him I'm waiting."

Mark stood, assented with a nod, and turned on his heel toward the stairs.

Paul closed his eyes. He saw the disaster schemed by IMC in Bangladesh projected against his eyelids. He hadn't been able to accept the inconsistency that Susan had died in a plane crash while flying inside the Grand Canyon with his father when she'd told Paul on the phone only the night before she would be playing a minor bridge championship downtown. Naturally he had to find out the truth, and he did; it almost cost him his sanity. He'd tracked down Lucy Fielding, the Las Vegas resident examiner, only to find out that the almighty Hugh Reece had descended on her morgue with a judge, the chief of police, and Governor Swan in tow. Within minutes, they bulldozed Dr. Fielding and spirited both corpses away. But not all the evidence. Paul returned from Las Vegas with the tiny tissue samples the pathologist had kept and thus opened a lively can of worms. The tests were conclusive. Susan was two months pregnant; he'd been gone for three. After more tests and DNA-typing results of the Las Vegas samples and his own, another two stunning discoveries were made: He was sterile—probably a genetic disorder, but there was no doubt about it—and Susan was carrying Walter's child. An heir conceived by the decree of a scheming patriarch. Betrayed by every member of his family, Paul had retaliated, aiming for Hugh Reece's dark soul. He crippled IMC. The outcome? A deep wound between the last two Reeces, the only survivors of the mining dynasty who'd awed the Wall Street boys and had them salivating for the day when the corporation would go public.

Paul opened his eyes and saw Milford approaching alone.

"Hello, miner." Milford opened his arms.

Paul rose and hugged the old engineer, then gripped his arms. "You look well, you old pirate. I'm happy to see you."

A few minutes to eleven, Pedro, already closing the hotel for the night, brought two pots of coffee and a raffia-covered bottle. He arranged everything on the table and left, switching off all the lights except the floor lamp.

"I can see you're well settled in this town," Milford said. "They seem like good people and they cover for you. Holy cow, how they cover you! Nobody had ever heard of or ever seen any Paul. I explained to the mayor that I was an old friend from IMC on a family errand. I bet he had my ID checked before sending for you. But they've been watching us like vultures since we got here." He nodded toward the bottle. "I suppose the rope is to keep the glass together. What's inside, battery acid?"

Paul smiled, poured some *quitapenas*, and offered a glass to Milford.

The engineer sipped, smacked his lips, and nodded. "I can see why you look so good. This is better than embalming fluid." He sipped again. "Anything in these mountains?"

"Not much. Just a couple of tons of the finest and biggest seam opals you've ever seen," Paul answered with a malicious smile.

Milford slapped his knee. "I knew it! I knew there'd be a mine somewhere nearby. Tell me all about it."

Paul peered at the displaced miner with a hint of sadness. Milford was not old by modern standards, perhaps a trifle over sixty. But as a miner, Milford was indeed misplaced; his time had passed. At some point in his life he took a wrong turn, chose the wrong gallery, the one leading to the corporate labyrinth instead of the pit with the vein of gold. He got lost in tunnels with spiders and snakes and other hideous creatures of darkness, like in a real mine, except the snakes wore Armani and were the most venomous in the world.

Paul knew the engineer felt cheated by his own decision. But no one had forced him to go one way or the other. With no one else to blame, you can't hate, condemn, and despise those who caused the miscarriage, only your own face in the mirror.

"A few months ago, a friend showed me a hole on top of a hill, just two feet across but three hundred deep," said Paul.

"You calculated with the stone?"

Paul nodded with affection. Milford had taught him the shortcut to kinematic equations when he was fifteen. It consisted of dropping a stone and counting in half-second dashes. Multiply that number by a variable and you had a good estimation of depth. Over the years, Paul learned to adjust the factor with uncanny precision.

"We lowered ourselves with ropes to a natural cavern. Then I followed some lines until I hit a broad carbon seam."

"We?"

"Yeah, me and Manuel Negroponte."

"Local?"

"His mother is. His father's American, an ex-Green

Beret sergeant. After he mothballed the uniform, he set up an ostrich farm here and rooted. He also grows the best bud south of Texas."

"Ostriches and pot? Sounds like a good place to retire. But you were telling me about how you found the opals."

"The rest is boring. I found a weak draft and opened an entrance on the side of the hill. I used the rock faults and the slope to make an asymmetric portico. Now instead of using ropes I can walk straight in."

Milford finished his drink and poured another. "Damn, I envy you."

"That's your fault, old man. Nothing's stopping us from packing a couple of mules and looking."

Milford shook his head, melancholy in his gaze. "I'm too old and soft after all these years shuffling papers. I couldn't lift a pickax off the floor. Now I pimp around delivering messages."

"I wondered when you'd get down to it."

Milford nodded. "First a few details you don't know. About eighteen months ago, we laid our hands on several satellites built by Martin Marietta and placed in cold storage by the government. Damn defense cuts. Nice units with metastable-helium magnetometers, magnetic anomaly detectors, and superconducting quantum interferometric devices."

"That's a mouthful," Paul quipped.

"No, *this* is a mouthful." Milford emptied his glass in one gulp and grimaced. "If you lit a match now, you would have to come and fetch me in Hong Kong harbor."

"You'll never change," Paul chortled, and refilled the glasses.

"We realized these tools could give us an edge, so we

struck a deal with the government. The pact couldn't be simpler: We pay for the balance of the project—thirty percent of the total value—and foot the bill for the launch. In a crisis, the government can take control of the system, but it's a good agreement, flexible for both parties. On one hand, the administration has the setup ready in case they need it. On the other, IMC controls an extraordinary tool, a space bloodhound capable of scouring vast tracts of land for minerals."

"How precise is the detection?"

"Very. In ten months of operation, we've discovered six major mineral fields in unknown but accessible zones. The system has paid for itself several times over."

Paul followed Milford's words, impressed.

"In the fall of 2014, the scientists handling the system discovered something they weren't looking for: a single point in the old Congo that registered a magnetic emission twelve thousand times stronger than anything detected before."

Paul felt his curiosity rise. Twelve thousandfold was a huge level of magnetism on the tesla range.

"At first they thought it might be a calibration error or a natural phenomenon."

"There's no natural phenomenon with such a signature."

"A sheared solar flare—"

"Okay, I'm sorry." Paul raised a hand, interrupting the explanation. "I forgot we're talking about space-mounted sensors. You thought the sensors could be giving the wrong origin of the anomaly: solar instead of earthly, right?"

"Right. That evening nobody went home. We waited

for a pass of the nearest satellite and obtained the same result. We repositioned another two satellites to triangulate the location and corroborate the source of the extraordinary emission. It's located in the middle of almost uninhabited terrain. Initially, we thought the emission might point at mineral deposits, so IMC didn't inform the Congolese government or Gécamines, the country's mining supervisory board."

"Let me see if I understand." Paul poured another drink without taking his eyes off Milford. "You say *initially* you assumed the presence of minerals in large quantities, but it's obvious that wasn't so. Otherwise you wouldn't be here. What's the depth?"

"Over four miles."

Paul whistled, his geologist's instincts alert. "What have you found down there?"

Milford stared at him for what seemed like a long time.

Paul suspected the old miner was weighing how much to tell him.

"No idea, but whatever it is, it's hollow."

Paul straightened. "What do you mean hollow? A cavern?"

"I don't know. *Nobody* knows."

"IMC is plotting a four-mile shaft to explore a cavern? Wait a minute. If you know the formation is hollow, you've cored it."

Milford gave a deadpan expression, then smiled, offering no verbal response.

"You can drop a camera, have a look. Most expensive minerals are nonmagnetic."

"I never said anything about minerals."

Only something of enormous importance would force his grandfather to search for him, Paul thought.

"What the hell's down there?" Paul pressed.

"I told you, we have no idea." Milford wasn't smiling now. "There's a hollow space; call it a cavern or whatever you like. But it's big. Enough to house a city block."

"Holy shit!"

"That's not all. There's an electromagnetic pulse vibrating in erratic bursts, so powerful that any electronics fail. We can't use telemetry."

"What about electrical gear?"

"Dicey. Are you familiar with electromagnetic pulses?"

"Only in regards to nuclear weapons."

"That's good enough. EMPs induce high voltages in coils," Milford explained. "With sophisticated shielding, we can bypass the effect, but most of the gear will have to be mechanical. There are two alternatives."

Paul's eyes narrowed as he listened with increased attention.

"We can drill a twelve-inch shaft and drop a robot. If we manage to get around the problem of shielding, the technical problems are colossal. There could be water, excrescences, and countless other obstacles in the way, not to mention the challenge of trying to gather samples. A twelve-inch hole and remote control is madness.

"The second proposal is a thirty-inch hole to drop a manned all-mechanical probe. It's logical. The cost of going from twelve to thirty inches is nominal, and the possibilities are enormous: mechanical instrumentation, flexibility of movement, and the irreplaceable analytical ability of a man."

"A four-mile dumbwaiter," Paul muttered. Suddenly he understood the reason for Milford's errand. *You can't be serious!*

"We're talking about a vehicle capable of transporting all the equipment and instruments necessary to carry out a thorough exploration, with an expert to collect samples and images. We could even make multiple descents. The craft would be the key. Maybe we could deploy a base camp down there, use the vehicle as an elevator."

Paul steepled his hands and mentally replayed Milford's words.

"Ituri is a national park; the Democratic Republic of Congo is a war zone," Paul said, shaking his head in disbelief. "You'll never get away with opening a mining operation there. Even if you bribe the government and buy half the warlords, you'll have to deal with the international community—the French, the Russians, and anyone with a satellite aloft. News will hit the papers; the environmental lobby will have a field day—"

"No, they won't."

"Why?"

"We'll be watched, I know, but they'll leave us alone until we announce the success of our exploration and our designs to undertake a full-fledged mining enterprise."

You don't intend full exploitation, Paul realized. *You're hoping that whatever is under Ituri can be accessed, and recovered, through a thirty-inch tube.* He wondered how many more details Milford was prepared to put forward.

"First, I can't believe IMC is crazy enough to sink billions in a shaft to peek inside a cavern. Second, Gécamines won't stay on the sidelines while IMC carries out a mysterious exploration in their country. Third,

IMC has dozens of capable engineers and geologists. Why are you telling *me* about it?"

"I can't tell you any more, Paul. My instructions are final. If you agree to join, all the data will be waiting for you. If not, you don't need to know, simple as that. If you accept, you'll have to see it with your own eyes to evaluate the find.

"We've told Gécamines we're developing a state-of-the-art project: a thirty-foot shaft for production and six thirty-inch shafts for a new system of forced ventilation with high-performance turbines at different levels in the mine. They don't know about the EMP. They think we're after uranium. Evacuating radon gas would be a prime concern, and the small shafts are a dazzling solution. The project is viable, innovative, and sound from an engineering angle. We propose to start with a single thirty-inch shaft for testing and sampling with a sophisticated drone capable of drilling holes sideways to insert probes. Of course, we don't intend to carry out the project as submitted. But you've probably already guessed that much."

In a corner of the darkened lobby, a battered grandfather clock struck a single dissonant note; eleven thirty.

"You're the ideal person," Milford continued. "A brilliant geologist, young and in good shape, a major IMC shareholder and future owner. Paul, in the guts of the Congo there's something that will affect humanity. I would give my right hand to be the first one down, but I'm too old. It's there. Hillary didn't need any other incentive to climb Everest."

"Who suggested including me?"

"Owen."

An alarm went off in Paul's head. IMC's operations

vice president was the archetypical loud and coarse Texan, and a phony. He dyed his hair and wore shoes with inserts. Paul didn't trust him.

"Before you decide, consider who you are. Forget your grandfather. Everybody makes mistakes in the name of egotism, pride, greed, or simple stupidity. You can hate and despise him, but you're a Reece. IMC was built with the blood of your forebears. It's the magnum opus of a dynasty. Your great-great-grandfather John risked everything to chase his son Tobias's dream. Father followed son. So there's no gold in this one; but there is magic. . . ."

Paul stared into Milford's eyes and realized he was right. He was a Reece, and curiosity had the best of him. His heart skipped a beat.

"What substrata did the drill go through?" Paul asked.

"Sediment at the higher levels, basalt farther down."

It was exposed once, covered by an eruption, and filled with alluvial deposits. It could be anything.

Paul shuffled his options. He had fallen into the trap. Milford had inoculated him with the most powerful venom known to man: miner's fever. Gold, diamonds, emeralds—it didn't matter. As soon as he had heard the words *vehicle, tube,* and *four miles,* Paul knew he had to pilot it. But Milford didn't know it yet.

"How far does your authority go?" Paul asked.

Milford let out his breath and smiled. "No limits."

"I want full jurisdiction running the show. I'll bring my own security."

"I don't think they'll accept that."

"I thought you had total authority," Paul snapped. "It's

not negotiable. *I* am the only one who can toy with my life. Take it or leave it."

Milford remained silent for a couple of seconds. "To hell with the board. We've got a deal, miner!"

Paul wondered if this was how pacts with the devil were made.

"Will you come back to Dallas with me?" Milford asked. "I have a jet at Tegucigalpa."

Paul nodded. "I need to sort out several things tomorrow morning. I'll be ready at noon."

"Fine." He raised his glass. "Let's toast to miners, absent and present."

Paul clinked his glass with the engineer's. "To absent and present miners."

They talked for two more hours. When they parted with a bear hug, Paul had clinched a deal for Colquizate's opals, and all that was left of the *quitapenas* was the bottle and the rope.

chapter 5

Paul heard Carmen's light, quick footsteps approaching the door. He rose from the kitchen table, his heart heavy.

After the conversation with Milford, he called Don Eduardo and explained that he would be away for several months. Later, he had a bite to eat with Manuel and discussed his plans, in particular the procedure to extract and prepare the opal. He left a sat-phone with him—a plain device the size of a fat credit card—with precise instructions for its use. Afterward, he went home, grabbed a few hours of restless sleep, and awoke early. He knew Carmen would be around at first light. News traveled fast in small communities and the police sergeant, Carmen's father, would be one of the first to know.

She appeared at the door, her slight figure outlined against the reddish dawn. Without a word, she moved to him and buried her head in his chest.

Paul held her close, tilting her face to him, a finger under her chin. He kissed her on the eyes, the nose, and the mouth. He could taste the saltiness of her tears. He would have lingered longer, but she pushed him away.

"When are you leaving?"

"In a few hours." He drew her next to the table and poured two mugs of coffee. In clipped sentences, he summarized his conversation with Milford.

"I'm frightened, Paul." Her eyes brimmed with tears. "You have enemies. Your grandfather has enemies. *He* is your enemy."

He held a finger to her lips, silencing her.

"I'll be careful, honey. I'll get things done in Africa and come back to you."

It was but yesterday we met in a dream. The words from a Lebanese poet echoed in his mind as he hugged Carmen. *And I of your longings have built a tower in the sky.*

She kissed the tips of his fingers. Carmen sniffed and turned around, offering the tiny buttons that fastened her dress. "I need you now; I'll cry for you afterward."

Much later, Paul gathered his meager belongings with the graceless lack of precision men embrace when they are casting aside one life for another.

chapter 6

Paul knocked on the glass that separated the driver from the passengers. The partition slid down. "Yes, sir?" the chauffeur asked, looking into the mirror.

"I'll walk from here," Paul said, before turning to Milford. "I need to clear my head."

Milford nodded, understanding.

For a while Paul pondered the contrast between a humble village of adobe houses, in the middle of nature's ordered chaos, and the Dallas residential area in a modern city. To his eyes, full of the wilderness and the arcane symmetry of rock outcroppings, the city looked artificial, an abomination of pagan forms. The lines were too clear-cut and the differences too sharply defined.

A riot of oleanders divided the thoroughfare. He found a suitable place and sauntered across. Paul sniffed the air, smelled the rich garden earth, and surveyed the familiar outlines, glad to see the house, the neighborhood, and the street. He stopped across from his home. After setting down his worn leather rucksack, Paul sat on the curb, under an arbor of bougainvillea, and lit a cigarette.

Memories assailed him with a strange third-person aftertaste. He felt like a soldier returning home from the trenches. The past he'd buried for so long could no longer remain contained. He had changed, and the building across the street was not home anymore: an empty house but for Lupe, his housekeeper.

Paul felt the heat of the cigarette's cherry in his fingers and lit another. His eyes followed a cat walking daintily along the edge of a fence. Paul eyed the trimmed lawn and the garden—hydrangea, iris, a clump of geraniums and black-eyed-Susans. *Susan, I failed you.* He could defend his incompetence as a husband, but he had failed her as a friend and could find no excuses for that.

His eyes misted over as he viewed the geraniums. He'd been blind to the lesson a geranium had taught him several years before. Back from checking some unusual strata at an open cast mine in Bolivia, he missed his flight and was stranded for a full day in La Paz. With nothing to do, Paul strolled through the city and discovered a vast open-air market, where he spent the next couple of hours. Dazzled by an orgy of colors and smells, he ambled past countless stalls, eyeing piles of fruit, noisy poultry in wooden cages, and knitted garments. After Paul bought, without haggling, a few trinkets from an old Indian woman in a homburg hat, she had pressed a small cotton bundle into his hand. Inside, Paul found a gnarled stick with a lump of matted roots at one end. "It will bring you luck and return your love tenfold," she had said. He didn't think again about the gift until he returned to his hotel the same evening. When he emptied his pockets, he found the wrapped stick and dumped it in the waste-basket.

The next morning, one hand on the doorknob to go check out, his eye caught the cotton fold. He hesitated, backed into the room, and rescued it. Risking a fine and a dressing-down by U.S. customs' inspectors, he smuggled it into the country, bought a small pot, and planted the stick. A few weeks later, velvety leaves with a pungent citrus smell sprouted from the misshapen wood. The pink geranium thrived on a corner of his desk at IMC, lovingly tended by regular watering and treats of fertilizer pellets. When Paul resumed his hectic traveling, he entrusted a janitor to water the plant during his absences, and the old man did for a while, until someone younger replaced him. Paul must have noticed a sadness creeping over the plant, the browning of its leaves' edges and dwindling petals, but the novelty had worn off and he chose to ignore it. He would pour a glass of water into the plant's container if he remembered, assuming the janitor would do the rest. One day, after a horrible month reopening the deep-lying Recsk copper-ore body in Hungary's Matra Mountains, Paul returned to find a pot of cracked dry earth and a dead stump on his desk.

His marriage had shared the geranium's fate.

As the top geologist at IMC, Paul globe-trotted to solve major issues requiring his hands-on involvement. When forced to stay at home, he would fidget in his office, yearning for the mineral tang of deep galleries and the dash to faraway places. Susan wilted, and he was too busy trying to emulate a corporate Indiana Jones to notice. Their daily phone conversations, which had once lasted for hours, now dwindled to infrequent pastiches of pleasantries. Sometimes, they communicated only through hurried messages on each other's cell phones or e-mails with single-line paragraphs. And, at other times, there were no calls at all.

Paul had seen the writing on the wall and had done nothing about it. Instead, he sought refuge in statistics. One in two marriages went sour. He deceived himself further with excuses to hold on to his mining obsession. Susan might have been the mirage of a summer romance from his student days—a chimera of permanence with a stranger—and their marriage might be on the rocks, but they would always be friends.

When his world caved in, his analytic brain screamed at his attempt to shrug off blame and flashed pictures of wasted geraniums into his dreams and waking thoughts. Later, when he painfully reconstructed his grandfather's harebrained scheme, he realized that Susan hadn't stood a chance against his grandfather. Together they could have thwarted Hugh Reece's demented plans, but on her own, Susan had been a lamb before a cunning wolf. And now she was dead. Paul felt an overwhelming feeling of guilt, of having failed her.

With a last glance at the geraniums, he grabbed his bag and crossed the street.

Standing alone in the predawn light, comparing his memories of Central America to his reminiscences of home and his marriage, Paul realized he had spent two years collecting vindications for past failures. Understanding that, the ache he'd carried around the hills of Central America lifted with the dew evaporating from the lawn.

His hand rose to the ragged scar on his forehead, a

reminder of his brush with death on another continent. Paul shook his head to exorcise his demons as he walked across the granite paving stones. He stepped onto the mat.

"Hello, I'm home."

No key was necessary. The house would recognize him by appearance, eye, and voice scan. The lock clicked and a tiny LED changed from red to blue.

Melancholy returned when he opened the door. The lights came on, subdued, as if prolonging the welcome. The furniture, the Navajo rug, the accessories, everything was in place, clean and gleaming, the same as the day he left. Even the Bernard Buffet canvas with the slight pitch, a tilt he corrected mechanically every time he entered the house, was there. Paul ran his fingers over the wood and straightened the frame. After a short delay, the picture settled back to its natural position: crooked. He went to his study without turning on any more lights.

After heaving the knapsack onto the desk, Paul wandered toward the kitchen, looking for coffee and something to eat. The lights came on and Lupe appeared, wearing a white cotton nightgown and a thin woolen shawl over her shoulders.

She stopped, a hand darting to her mouth in surprise. Gathering her nightgown, Lupe drew toward Paul, standing on tiptoes to hug him.

"Sweet Jesus! You look so handsome!" She stood back from Paul, inspected him, and hugged him again.

He looked down at her and ran a hand over her thick gray hair as she sobbed in silence. She had been with the family for many years. In a way, she'd been the closest to a mother he could remember.

"I've missed you, Lupe." He bent down to pick up the knitted shawl that had fallen to the ground and followed her as she scurried to the kitchen.

"I have nothing in the house. I could have prepared breakfast. How was I to know?"

Paul smiled and sat at the table.

"You'll never change, Lupe. I'm sure you have enough food stored somewhere to feed an army."

Lupe fixed ham salad sandwiches and put water in a pot to boil. Paul wolfed down the sandwiches and looked on as Lupe fussed about the kitchen. From a cupboard, she took down a hand-cranked coffee mill darkened by age. She emptied beans into the funnel and turned the handle with energy, filling the kitchen with the sharp aroma of coffee. When the water boiled, she emptied the ground coffee into the pan and stirred a couple of times with a wooden spoon, then poured the mush through a cloth strainer into a thermos jug.

Paul watched the precise liturgy he knew by heart from the countless times he'd seen Lupe make coffee for him in the past.

She brought the coffee and two mugs to the table.

"You've been away a long time."

"I know."

"We still have the same telephone number," she admonished. "You could call more often."

He hadn't called her since Christmas. "I know, Lupe."

"You had me worried."

He got his cigarettes and lit two, something he used to do whenever he chatted with her. Afterward, Paul leaned forward and smacked a kiss on her weathered cheek. "Are you mad at me?"

She lowered her head with a coy smile. "Of course not. I can't wait to hear about what you've been up to all this time."

Over the next hour, Paul narrated sketches of the last two years for the small Mexican woman who probably knew him better than anybody else.

chapter 7

Paul checked his mirrors, pulled to the curb before the security building, and waited for the uniformed armed guard to approach the car. From a distance, it was difficult to discern a rent-a-cop from a trained expert. Studying him, Paul thought the guy could be the latter; it was something in the eyes. Paul fished in the glove compartment for a card and passed it to the guard, who looked at it, read the name, cocked an eyebrow, and asked him to wait. In seconds, the steel doors started to slide and the guard returned to the car with a grin—the face a professional uses in the rare instances when he wants to be remembered.

"Welcome, Mr. Reece. They're waiting for you at the labs." He raised a finger to his cap as a salute.

Paul maneuvered between the buildings and through a large square. Sprinklers worked overtime on an island of crape myrtles and the usual manicured lawn. Behind, a white brick building with large tinted-glass windows caught the glare of the strong sun. He looked for a space between the vehicles and parked the car. A brief rainfall had left a smell of fresh greenery and damp asphalt in the air. As he got out of the car, the door to the building opened. Milford and Owen came out to meet him, with a woman he'd never seen before trailing behind.

Owen came forward, grabbed Paul's elbow, and pumped his hand.

"Paul, you look *great*." He stared at Paul's face. "I expected a deep tan after so long in sunny places."

"Hello, Owen."

Owen widened his smirk. "Where have you been hiding? Mexico, perhaps?"

Paul glanced at Milford, wondering how discreet the old miner had been. Milford must have sensed the conflict, because he stepped between them, the bright red birthmark on his forehead prominent, like an Indian *bindi*.

"You look well rested after your beauty sleep. Though it hasn't helped jack shit," Milford said, smiling. "This is Dr. Lynne Kennedy, the director of geological services."

Paul eyed the DGS. She wore a dark-blue pinstripe business suit with an unbuttoned lab coat thrown over it and black pumps. In her early thirties, he guessed. She had cognac-colored intelligent eyes and cheeky laughing dimples. He liked her at first sight.

Paul glanced sidelong at Owen with a half smile, relieved by Milford's intervention. As he shook Lynne's hand, he remembered her predecessor. "Will Dr. Weiss join us?"

"Not unless you've got a Ouija board," Milford answered. "Dr. Weiss paid a hell of a price for his Viagra; he passed away on the job, like Attila or Alexander."

"A shame, but there are worse ways to die."

"Yup." Milford grabbed his arm and propelled him toward the building. "Come, miner. I'm dying to see your face when you see it." He lowered his voice to a whisper. "Easy, pal, they don't know. I cooked the plane's log, greased the local traffic control, and the crew owes me one. For all they know, I picked you up in Mexico."

They entered the building and descended two flights of broad stairs in tandem.

Paul glanced around. "This has changed."

"We've enlarged the underground labs," Owen explained.

The steps ended on a semicircular landing with several stainless-steel elevator doors at the far end.

"Here we submit to the gestapo's tender mercies," Lynne whispered.

Paul was aware of the guards' stares. He noticed the Tasers on their hip holsters and the stun billy clubs. *I'll be damned. We've gone all-electrical around here.*

He cringed as he watched mechanical arms, peppered with scanners, extending from a desk.

After clearing security much tighter than he remembered, he entered the elevator with the others, absently rubbing his eyes reddened by the retinal scan, an oblong tag dangling from a thin chain around his neck.

"Say, Paul, where have you been hiding all this time?" Owen gripped his forearm and pressed. Paul glanced at Milford, who remained stone-faced.

"Here and there, bumming around."

Owen increased his grip and leaned nearer.

"Bumming around, perhaps, but Milford knew where to find you, no?"

Paul stared at Owen, taking in his strong aftershave mixed with a hint of stale breath. A warning bell rang deep within his head.

"Let's see what you've got," Paul said when the elevator stopped.

They paused at a wall recess and grabbed lab whites hanging from a line of coat hooks.

On ten rows of tables rested cylinders of a dark material with different tones and textures. More than four miles of earth, marked with thousands of familiar small disks, flags, and yellow cards bearing notes, codes, and numbers.

The core-drill contents. The sample, extracted from the tubes, had been transported in boxes from Africa and restored to its original sequence with painstaking precision. He took in the codes on the nearest table, and once he learned the drilling's direction, he strode to the end of the core, the last piece recovered from the deepest point.

Toward the center of one table, the cylinders went from six to four, and then two, up to the 22,400-feet mark. From that point onward, a single piece continued toward the end of the table and ended abruptly. Paul walked up to a point with several markers and checked the data. "Up to this point we have basalt," he noted, "and here the structure changes to a compact calcite."

At the end, where the cards and markers played out, Paul stopped dead and felt the hair on his neck and arms stand on end.

He stared at the straight line where a jet-black material started without transition, opaque and matte. Paul lowered his head and pressed a nail over the surface. He moved his hand away, surprised to see the stuff recover its shape. The black band, four inches thick, ended in a sharp, straight line. Another blue-gray speckled material followed, with lighter inclusions and shiny dots, round and spaced with artificial symmetry. His legs started to tremble, forcing him to grip the table. From the lab coats came a small burst of nervous laughter.

"This shit is reinforced concrete!"

"And the black band?" Owen asked.

"Some elastic material. Neoprene maybe."

"Not bad at all," Owen said, approaching the sample. "This beauty is the closest you can get to reinforced concrete and neoprene, but there are some extraordinary differences."

Milford came and patted Paul's shoulder, his expression that of a teacher who has broken through to a slow but earnest student. "And the magic of this whole affair is in those differences."

"Neoprene is a good guess," Lynne explained. "It is indeed an elastomer. Nevertheless, the likenesses stop there. This material has properties like nothing we know. How they managed to put it together escapes us, and we've done over a week of intensive analysis."

"They?" Paul asked.

"Take it easy, boy," Milford said. "One thing at a time."

Lynne pointed to the seam where the materials joined but didn't touch it. "The sample was a fraction under twelve inches thick, equally split between the two materials. Now it isn't complete. We've taken two inches from the juncture of the materials for analysis. The elastomer, the black material, has two principal characteristics: It's inert—not affected by organic solvents or hydrocarbon compounds—and almost fireproof. When it reaches a temperature over a thousand degrees Fahrenheit, it hardens and becomes rigid, changing to a shiny gray color, like polished steel. In that state, it can withstand high temperatures without deformation. Don't ask me how high. We tried carbon subnitride, the hottest flames we could get."

"There are hotter flames, no?"

"Not that we know of. Anyway, at just over nine thousand Fahrenheit, the sample didn't feel a thing. Then there's the matter of what you call concrete, for lack of a better name. These inclusions"—she pointed at the clear elements—"are strange metals, and the stuff in the darker areas, where normal cement would be, is a synthetic resin similar to epoxy but much harder and denser. The reinforcements"—she pointed at the shiny dots—"are placed in a radial spread, crisscrossing to form cells. The armature is ferric but with high nickel, chromium, and molybdenum content."

"Stainless steel?"

"Hardly. It contains osmium, tungsten, and several rare earths. This is a material that preserves its magnetic characteristics." Lynne paused as if gathering breath and darted a nervous glance toward the sample. "The result is a metal ten times stronger than titanium, with a quarter of its weight."

"Stronger than titanium with a quarter of its weight? That's impossible."

"This material is made of tiny bubbles. In fact, most of it is air, like a sponge made of nanoparticles."

Suddenly he understood, his uneasiness deepening. If the lab data was accurate, just the sample could be worth billions.

"How hard is it?"

"Local penetration, scratching, machining, abrasion, or yielding?" Owen asked.

The man couldn't forget his academic roots. "Mohs' scale will do."

"Nine, but damn close to ten."

Harder than corundum and only a step softer than diamond. "How did you drill into it?"

"Wearing down a fortune in crown heads. It took two full days to drill through the last couple of feet."

Milford cleared his throat. "Next time it won't take so long."

Paul waited, but Milford didn't offer anything else. "So, all this is amazing," he said. *And frightening.* "Does anybody know what it is?"

"The closest guess we have," Owen replied, "is a magnetic condenser—a contraption to gather energy from the earth's magnetic field and concentrate it."

"Because of my conversation with Milford the other night, I can see how you could reach that conclusion," Paul agreed. "This can't be a naturally occurring geological phenomenon. I was referring to the reason for building it."

"We've surmised the builders wanted to draw attention to its location."

"Draw attention? To something buried more than four miles beneath the surface?"

"I suggest we adjourn somewhere else. I've had it with standing up," Milford said, massaging his knee.

"Fine with me," Owen said, gesturing for the others to exit first.

A minute later, they were riding an elevator much

larger than the first. "What do you think about it, miner?" Milford asked.

"Fascinating, puzzling, and . . . frightening."

Lynne chuckled. "Those were almost my exact words after the early analysis."

"Almost?"

"Yes, I believe I used *terrifying* instead."

They exited on the ground floor.

"You know what they say about great minds," Paul said, smiling.

"You flatter me, Mr. Reece."

"Just Paul."

"Don't waste your breath," Owen whispered to Paul when they reached a door. "She's married with two kids."

Paul flinched at Owen's coarseness and was about to reply when he caught Lynne's sharp look and the slight shake of her head.

Paul beamed. *You have this moron measured up.*

Lynne's office was large and split into two areas. The first held a conference table with chairs and auxiliary furniture. To one side was a low sideboard with twin plasma screens and videochip slots. A wide arch opened into the next room, occupied by Lynne's desk, a samples display cabinet, computers, and videochips stacked in shelves.

"Excuse the mess." Lynne punched her intercom and ordered coffee, then joined the others at the table.

When everybody was seated, Paul turned to Milford and caught a glint in his eye. The old buzzard was waiting for the obvious question he'd been mulling all the way from the lab. "Why will it take us less time to drill into it next time?"

Milford smiled, darted a glance in Lynne's direction, and nodded.

"We've found other"—she seemed to grapple for the right words—"fascinating properties in these materials. Although Owen correctly pointed out that the 'concrete' has a Mohs' nine hardness, it's very brittle and shears off like flint before a sharp blow. Then there are the armatures. Inside the sample we found a joint, not welded, just butted."

Paul waited for the punch line.

"The rubberlike material is weird, to say the least. Abrasion with a fast tool, such as a rotating crown, produces heat and the material hardens, but with something cold and slow, like a knife, you can cut through it like putty."

"That's what I meant," Milford said. "Next time, all we have to do as soon as we detect extraordinary hardness in the substrata is to bring the crown speed almost to a stop. The teeth will sink into the rubber and push it aside."

"And the 'concrete'?"

"No chance of using a hammer. We'll have to drill through by brute force, wearing down several tools, but since the rubber makes up half the structure's thickness, it will take half the effort."

Paul nodded, questions piling in his head.

"By the way," Milford said. "We've christened the operation 'Project Isis.'"

"Whose idea was it?"

"Justin's, but Hugh approved it."

Paul nodded. Isis. Magic. Just like Hugh to go for such a name.

○

"The data we have up to now confirm the construction is between fifty and sixty thousand years old," Milford began. "It's impossible to come up with a closer estimate and difficult to appraise the materials with conventional methods. We've tried carbon-dating the samples. Both the resin and the rubber contain organic compounds, but the results are inconclusive. In fact, we've had to extrapolate the data from the formations around the sphere."

Paul raised his eyebrows.

"That's right, a sphere. There's a slight three-dimensional curve in the sample. As for the source, we can only venture that its origin is earthly, perhaps the work of a civilization before ours. A civilization that no longer exists."

Paul bit his lip and shook his head as he tried to put his thoughts in order. Everyone was making efforts to sound nonchalant, but under the hard data lurked a whiff of uneasiness, even fear. "How did you reach that conclusion?"

"We'll get to that in a minute—"

"I need to clarify something here," Lynne interrupted. "The origin's hypothesis is conjectural. It could be a previous civilization. Of course, that would go contrary to history and established scientific theories. On the other hand, there's always the possibility of a nonearthly civilization."

There. She had voiced the thought he'd purged twice

from his mind. Paul shifted on his seat. *I'm a scientist. Aliens don't exist.* It was beginning to sound like a mantra.

"The word is *alien* or *extraterrestrial*," Milford clarified, reaching to loosen his tie.

"That's far-fetched," Owen piped in. "It supposes erecting a complex industry for material production. Transport of raw materials from space is illogical if we consider the scope of the project and, besides, all elements in the sample we've cored are abundant in our planet."

"I don't follow your logic," Paul said.

"What can't you follow?"

"Like you, I don't believe in aliens or interstellar travel, but your reasons for dismissing the possibility don't make any sense. If the materials are all over earth, aliens could process them in their ships."

"You've got to be joking."

"I'm not. You assume producing these materials needs a complex industry, and the opposite might be true. Alchemists produced complex chemicals with next to nothing."

"Fine," Owen conceded, "but consider the sophisticated bars. Their geometry is almost perfect, calibrated to a ten-thousandth of an inch. That needs an industrial process."

"If we are dealing with compounds we don't understand, isn't it also possible it was created by a process we cannot conceive? Isn't it also possible that aliens lived on earth before humans evolved or spread and did manufacture such an object, leaving only when we rose on our hind legs?" Paul caught the gleam in Lynne's eyes.

Owen frowned. "Anything is possible. The only thing

we can be certain about is the awesome technology behind the materials."

"The sophistication is in the mix? The alloys?" Paul asked.

"Right. Had we unearthed a thousand-year-old steel artifact, say a weapon or agricultural tool with no signs of rust, we would be baffled."

"Because all steel eventually rusts, stainless or not."

"Right. In all fairness, we should refer to SS as 'rust resistant.' Ordinary stainless steel—an iron–carbon alloy with added chromium—is fine for some uses but poor in saline and other aggressive atmospheres. For these applications you need to add nickel, molybdenum, nitrogen, and other bits and pieces in the right amounts. An ancient forger, using impure ores, could have possibly stumbled on a batch with enough of these materials and crafted something. Modern metallurgical assay would expose the fluke; the sample would be spiked with other useless elements."

"I follow. If the artifact showed the exact levels of nickel, molybdenum, and nitrogen, we could be certain the steel was formulated by someone who knew his stuff."

"Yes, but don't forget all the elements you've mentioned are common. Anybody could have crafted rust-resistant suits of armor many centuries ago, had they known the formula."

Milford chuckled. "And the folks at Allegheny Ludlum would have had a fit."

Paul frowned.

"You've just described their Superaustenitic Steel."

"I see." Milford's uncanny repository of mineral and alloys data never ceased to amaze Paul.

"Anyway. The technology is sophisticated, but the elements are not. For the sake of argument, let's assume the sphere was built by people from earth." Owen lowered his gaze, drummed his fingers on the table, then reached for his pencil, only to put it down after a heartbeat, as if he didn't know what to do with it.

Paul nodded, a surreal sensation settling on his shoulders like a mantle.

A young Asian man, stocky but curiously light on his feet, entered and deposited a tray of mugs and a thermos on the table. He darted a quick glance around and locked eyes with Paul for the briefest of moments before leaving quietly. Paul eyed the departing figure in jeans with an *I love bottlenoses* sweatshirt, imprinted with a pair of cavorting dolphins, and frowned.

Milford poured the coffee and Lynne continued where Owen had left off.

"After much discussion, someone suggested an artifact similar to the monolith in that film ... *2001*, wasn't it?"

Paul flinched. "You can't be serious!"

"Let me finish," Lynne insisted. "That gave us the idea that it could be an artifact designed to be detected by a future civilization when it reached a certain technological level."

Milford leaned in Paul's direction. "Imagine we want to leave something for our posterity far into the future or we're faced with a catastrophe, something that threatens the survival of the species. We would be in deep shit. How could we leave our message? How could we design a structure sufficiently robust to withstand millennia and to ensure discovery at the right time?"

Paul nodded. The argument was sound, although it raised more questions than it answered.

"Imagine the following scenario," Milford continued, reaching once more to his tie. "According to history as we know it, ten thousand years ago we lived in caves. One of our ancestors finds a container, a book, or a chip. First, he would check to see if he could eat it. Then he would throw it away or burn it. Anyway, it would be lost."

"All that sounds fine," Paul said. "But if a total catastrophe occurred, there would be no one left to profit from any data."

Milford shook his head. "That's unlikely. It's difficult to wipe out a whole species—in particular one as adapted and numerous as ours. Even if a reasonable-size meteor struck the planet, some would survive."

"Same after a global nuclear calamity," Lynne agreed.

"That's what I can't understand," said Paul. "An advanced civilization wiped out without a trace sounds like fantasy to me. I mean, how can you make China's Great Wall disappear, or Stonehenge for that matter?"

Owen, who had begun doodling on his pad, stopped and nodded at Lynne before answering in her place. "We have racked our brains about these contradictory issues; it's a question of perspective and time. The Great Wall isn't a good example; most of the sections we know are fewer than eight hundred years old, built by the Ming Dynasty. Other sections are a thousand to fifteen hundred years old, but the whole construction would have long disappeared without maintenance. Years ago, I read an article about Chinese scientists who found, using space-imaging radar, parts of the wall buried under sand. Other stretches built parallel to the present one had crumbled into dust."

"Stonehenge is à better example," Lynne added, pausing to square her pad. "But also young—a mere four thousand years old. Of course, we don't know if the people who built the present structure did it from scratch or repositioned the stones."

Paul looked at Owen. Either his questions were too obvious or the IMC had done its homework. Either way, there were too many unknowns. And then there was the fidgeting. Perhaps he was hypersensitive after his first brush with something his mind couldn't grasp, let alone explain, but he could have sworn fidgeting fingers, busy pencils, creaking shoes, and recalcitrant tie knots pointed more to fear of the unknown than excitement.

"Fine," Paul conceded. "Let's accept for a moment that buildings erected by men can erode away and disappear, but you said before that it was unlikely to wipe out the whole human race from earth. I agree."

Owen opened his palms as if pleading for understanding. "Paul, after a generalized catastrophe, say a pole meltdown, whoever remained alive would return to the Stone Age."

"What about mitochondrial DNA evidence? It suggests a short span since the human species emerged."

"That's a good point," Lynne said, "but others subscribe to the bottleneck theory that we were more diverse until a disaster squashed us back."

Owen shook his head. "We can't answer all the questions; we're only guessing. DNA evidence covers millions of years. Here we're talking of tens of thousands, a moment in evolutionary terms."

Paul realized that nothing would be gained with added speculation, although everybody had failed to mention the obvious: The structure existed. Therefore, however dubious its origin, someone had built it.

"Sorry about the long interruption, Milford," Owen said. "Carry on with the details about the ... thing."

Milford placed his mug on a coaster and dabbed a tissue to his lips.

"The construction concentrates a disturbance in a small field. On the ground, you would have to walk over it with a magnetometer to detect it; an implausible scenario. We could argue it was designed for detection from a great height, even from orbit."

"I was thinking about that," Paul said. "If it contains a message, why not leave an orbital body, something circling earth that could be detected when we had space-flight capacity? Sooner or later, we would have found it."

"We discussed that, too, but experts agreed it would be far-fetched. Orbits decay with time, and small objects fall back into the atmosphere and burn up because of earth's gravity. Besides, if something caused large disturbances in earth's structure, satellites would be lost."

Paul was beginning to fathom the implications of the find. From an economic viewpoint, the materials alone were priceless. The black elastomer could replace high-performance refractory cladding in ovens, satellites, aircraft, and spacecraft. The light metal and the hardened concrete would revolutionize construction. *And that's just the shell!* He glanced around the table. Milford was again adjusting his tie and Lynne stared at his restless hand. *Shit*. Paul clumped his fingers into a fist and bunched his toes.

"Other considerations are even stranger," Owen said. "The object's construction suggests that it would be difficult, I would say impossible, to explore it in depth by remote control. It looks as if it was designed to force some*body* to go down instead of some*thing*."

"Just a minute," Paul interrupted. "When I spoke with Milford, I didn't know all the details, but I had the idea we were talking about a hollow space or a cavern or something like that. I asked why you didn't use a camera. I thought he said it was impossible."

Milford shook his head. "No, Paul, I said we had to go down, but I never said we hadn't done a visual inspection."

"You *have* dropped a camera?"

"Correct," Owen answered again. "After the drillers pierced the sphere, we replaced them with a scientific team. The scientists collected gas samples, tested the bore and the sphere for biological contaminants, and decided to risk dropping a camera."

"Risk?" Paul didn't like the choice of word.

"To film, we needed light...."

"I see." Paul caught Owen's drift at once. "You feared light would trigger something."

"You could say that. Anyway, we rigged a camera, with all the limitations of a three-inch tube, and mechanically fired a magnesium flare. The shuttering mechanism was also mechanical. You see, when we tried to use a video camera and a flash, we couldn't get it to work because of the magnetic pulse. We ended up using old eight-millimeter film technology. The results were poor. And . . . yes, we triggered something."

A flurry of half smiles and nervous glances rippled along the table.

Owen signaled to Lynne, who stood, loaded a videochip, and waved her hand before the screen to switch it on. One of the plasma monitors came alive.

"We've enhanced the images," Milford said. "After the film was processed, we could only see snow."

The images were of still pictures that showed a bizarre display of hundreds of cylindrical bars sticking out of a sphere in the center of the structure, like a round pincushion inside a hollow ball. Milford moved an unsteady laser pointer over the image. Whatever it was, the symmetry in the blurred image removed whatever rationale Paul was clinging to. It reeked of advanced technology.

"From studying the samples' inner curve and extrapolating measurements from the film, the outer sphere is about a hundred fifty feet across, and the smaller one about thirty feet. Thus, the distance from the shell to the inner core is about sixty feet."

"A hell of a drop," Paul said.

"You bet. As you can see, a probe on wheels, or even tracks, couldn't maneuver between the bars, and we couldn't drop it on top of the inner sphere. There's no room. We couldn't avoid fouling the cables, and radio control is impossible. That construction is like a Faraday cage. Anyway, even if such a vehicle could be made, it would fall off when it tried to reach the underside of the construction."

"It's like steps," Paul muttered, leaning closer to the screen.

"Yup," Milford agreed. "I'd bet there's an opening somewhere on the inner ball."

"Why do you say that?"

"Have a look at this area here." He pointed to an almost imperceptible lighter square beyond the inner sphere. "The guys who enhanced the film pointed it out. The angle and size is right for inner light from the core sphere escaping through a rectangular opening."

Paul squinted, but even with a flight of imagination it was difficult to determine if the shape was real. Milford was observing his reaction with attention and a slightly cocked eyebrow. There had to be something more. "Go on, what's up your sleeve?"

Milford fingered the remote and the screen went dark. "We lowered the camera again without a light, and the inside of the main sphere remained pitch black. Now watch carefully." He pressed another button and the original scene of grainy bars filled the screen. After few seconds the image started to dim, while the phantom square in the background became more apparent until it eventually disappeared also.

Paul suppressed a shudder. "That's what you meant by triggering something...."

"Right. We lowered the camera several times. For this sequence we adjusted the timer so the flare would die off while the camera was still in the sphere."

"And you think there's light in the inner sphere, reacting to any light outside it."

"It's a possibility."

Although the coffee was stone cold, Paul reached for his mug. His mouth was unpleasantly dry. On the screen, the bars formed once more.

"We believe the internal framework is for support. It has no reason to be there, otherwise—at least, none that we can think of. It seems as if the engineering of the double construction, the outer shell and the inner sphere, would force someone to go down. A vehicle would have to be like a chimpanzee to move between the bars."

"We considered a monkey...." Owen said.

Paul sniggered.

"Seriously," Owen assured him. "But we didn't know one with the right credentials."

"Well, you knew *one*," Paul muttered.

Everybody laughed without taking their eyes from the screen.

"Of course, we may be suffering from the Moon syndrome," Paul said.

"Pardon?" Owen frowned.

"The camera filmed from a static point. We can only see the inner sphere's top face. Who's to say the inner sphere is not connected by a pillar, or any other solid structure, to the outer shell? Then, there wouldn't be an opening anywhere but through my imaginary support structure on the side we cannot see. Access to the inner sphere would then be outside the outer shell."

"Then why the bars?" Owen asked. "If there were a pillar underneath the inner sphere the bars would be redundant."

"I suppose you're right," Paul conceded. "It's sensible to assume the bars are all around the inner sphere and for support. But the theory about the bars being there to force someone to explore comes crashing down if you drill straight through the shell, through the bars, and into the—" Before he finished the sentence, Paul bit his lip.

Lynne smiled as Paul digested the flaw in his argument. "We discarded such a possibility. First theory, we suspect the inner sphere's construction would make drilling impossible." She stopped the film and waved the lights back on.

"Theory number two," Milford announced. "Distant neighbors with a nasty sense of humor, afraid that one day we may compete with them in the universe, install a *gift*, something we'll discover when we have space flight. Like horses after a carrot, we drill ahead, and *boom!* One planet fewer to worry about. There could be all kinds of beauties inside—germs, prions..."

Paul shook his head, unconvinced. "That's not a logical assumption. They could have done it a long time ago when we were still tree-hopping. They didn't need to make things so complicated. Still, when we breach the inner sphere we must guarantee the integrity of the shaft. A containment system is a must."

Milford nodded. "When you browse through the preliminary designs, you'll see that we've considered how to effectively seal the shaft."

"If you want something weird," Lynne said, "Chodak, my assistant—the guy who brought the coffee—thought it could be a signal to our advanced neighbors, something to tell them that we were ready as meat or cheap labor."

When the forced laughter ebbed, Milford intervened with an uneasy look at Lynne. "That's illogical. An advanced species would have all the genetic tools they needed to clone slaves, although I must say the thought of a flock fattening on a planet makes me nervous."

Paul felt a tightening in his gut and looked askance at

Milford. He turned toward Lynne. "The young man who brought the coffee knows about this?"

"He has a grade-four security clearance," Lynne said in a defensive tone.

Owen intervened to explain about the dynamics genius he had shanghaied from MIT—a Chinese scientist of Tibetan extraction.

He's one of yours. "Who else knows?" Paul asked.

"Clearance four and over," answered Milford with a clipped tone that Paul found unnerving. "Directors and twelve other people, including three senior geologists at the labs. Eighteen people all told."

"Let me finish," Owen broke in. "I think the only sustainable theory, considering the evidence we have, points to some information or data. A time capsule. It may be a warning or perhaps contain the knowledge of ancient earth inhabitants—or generous space travelers."

"To sum up," Paul intervened, "we don't know its origin, who built it, or what it's for."

"That's a fair assessment," Milford chuckled.

"Right," Owen said. "But there's no doubt that any materials or artifacts recovered from the capsule's exploration would shake the foundations of science and civilization and would catapult IMC to the top of the corporate pyramid. Even with no additional material gains to be had, we must go down. It's there. That's reason enough."

"I wonder if we have the right to keep the project secret," Paul said.

Milford reached for his arm with a warning look. "I think your ethical doubts will dissolve when you've had time to think about it. Consider this: If we made Project

Isis public, it's possible we would have a new world war on our hands."

Paul wondered about Milford's look. What was the old engineer trying to warn him about?

"Think about it, miner," Milford continued. "Churches, clergy, governments, media, all the crazies of this world, visionaries and apocalyptic prophets, all converging on the Congo for their own particular reasons—businesses, mafias, adventurers, organizations, the dregs of the world. It would be a disaster."

"In addition, the sphere may be empty; it could be just an object," Owen pointed out, and raised a hand to forestall Milford's rebuke. "I mean, empty of artifacts. We know the materials are priceless."

"I agree the matter is more complicated than it seemed at first," Paul admitted. "Perhaps it wouldn't be a good idea to publicize the project. I imagine it will all depend on the contents of the structure, if there are any."

"That was the board's decision," Owen informed him. "For once, we have been able to agree on something important."

Lynne stood and walked to her desk, returning with a slim folder. "I've prepared a report for you. Here are the project's outstanding points and some of the sketches of the Autonomous Manned Probe—AMP for short. It's been cleared with Owen."

Paul realized that he was being maneuvered into a confrontation. Milford had not warned Owen of his status, and Lynne hadn't needed to add the last sentence. "I don't need the digest, just the raw. I prefer to do my own analysis."

"I'm sorry, Paul," Owen said. "I feel raw data would be useless to you. Too sensitive."

Paul turned toward him. "I've been meaning to talk security and other issues with you."

"The security measures are excellent," Owen said, patting his oversprayed comb-over. "This morning I met with Justin Timmons to organize the procedures for the drilling site in the Congo and—"

"Just a minute." Paul eyed him squarely. "As of this morning, I have full authority over Project Isis, and that includes security both here and in Congo."

"I don't think that now is the—"

Paul silenced Milford with a wave of his hand. "On the contrary, I think that this is the exact time and place to clarify authority and responsibilities on this project."

"If you'll excuse me." Lynne started to get up.

"Lynne, remain where you are—please."

He turned again to Owen, who had blanched.

"From now on, I'll have the final say in all details of this operation—who does what, how, when, and where. Let me clue you in on something, Owen. I don't deal in innocence. I've spent too much time in the real world."

"There's a chain of command here," Owen's voice was raised a fraction.

"There's a new one now," Milford intervened in a conciliatory tone. "I spoke with Hugh this morning and he's agreed. Paul's in total charge of this project." He pushed the comm-pad in Owen's direction. "You may check with Hugh."

Owen swallowed, his eyes blazing with ill-contained fury. "That won't be necessary."

"Fine. That's settled," Paul said in an even tone. "Ask

Justin to send his head of security to see me. By the way, I'll need a place to work."

"You can use my office," Lynne offered. "I spend most of the time at the labs. I'll have all the raw takes and the AMP's design data brought over."

Milford checked his watch. "It's almost noon, and I scheduled a meeting with Donald Watson, the head of R and D, and his guys at thirteen-thirty. You remember Donald?"

Paul rolled his eyes. "How could I forget? He's quite a character."

"Right. I suggest we grab something to eat."

Paul rubbed his stomach. "Good idea. I thought you were trying to put me on a diet."

"On the contrary, miner. You need to keep in shape. God knows you're going to need it."

"I have a couple of calls to make," Owen announced as he stood. "I'll catch up with you at the cafeteria." He turned on his heels and hurried out of the office.

"Phew! That was unpleasant," Lynne said, smiling nervously. "Beginnings are complicated times, but he'll get over it. Isn't that so, Milford?"

It was Paul's turn to smile.

"Yup."

"I'll tell you what," Lynne said. "After lunch, I'll organize a workstation for you here on the large table, with access to the raw-data files."

"Great idea. Thanks."

They left the room and strolled along an atrium on the side of the building toward the cafeteria. Walking under the warm sun filtered by dark glazing, Paul was amazed at the changes that had taken place in the Dallas research center since he was there last, two and a half years before. The single strangest aspect was the youth of the staff that walked the corridors. Acne and an air of informality contrasted with the IMC's stark conservative policy of a few years earlier.

I must be getting old.

"Mr. Reece?"

Paul stopped and turned to face a pint-size young woman, her bright eyes sparkling on a flushed, freckled face.

Milford continued with Lynne to stop a few yards away, as if eager to prove he didn't want to eavesdrop.

Attempting a smile, Paul hesitated before reaching for the flat cellular phone on the young woman's outstretched hand. "Paul Reece."

The soft breath at the other end of the line, hollowed by the electronic signal's void, flashed a striking image in his mind—an image Paul had often attempted to exorcise from his consciousness. "How are you, Grandpa?"

"Older and wearier, but fine."

Paul narrowed his eyes and took a deep breath. "I thought the saying went, 'older and wiser.'"

"I'm weary of seeking wisdom. I listened to your exchange with Owen. You handled him well. I'm proud."

"Thank you, Grandpa, but it would have been simpler to draft a memo informing everybody of the rules."

"Sometimes choosing a simple path can be a mistake."

Paul shook his head, trying to keep his mounting anger in check. "At school, they taught us the shortest distance between two points is a straight line."

The young woman had backed off toward the mezzanine.

A dry chuckle. "Indeed, but in the real world, it is not a question of simple or complicated but expected or unpredictable. If your opponent knows beforehand the road you're likely to choose, you're giving him advantage if his heart craves ambush."

"I thought everybody at IMC was on the same side."

"An idealistic mirage, my boy. Soldiers of fortune, that's what they are, mercenaries with no allegiance other than their own. *Beware, no enterprise is more likely to succeed than one concealed from the enemy until it is ripe for execution.*"

"Enemy? You've borrowed from Machiavelli."

"You look good."

Next to Milford, Lynne looked in Paul's direction and waved before turning on her heel toward the cafeteria. Paul darted glances at the bulbous domes of 360-degree cameras on walls and ceiling. He spotted three, but there could be many more. Something snapped inside and a jolt of adrenaline flashed through his system. "All-seeing, all-knowing, and pulling at people's strings. Still playing at being God?"

" 'Next time I see your face, I'll kill you with my own hands.' Those were your last words to me, and you have me at a physical disadvantage. Is the hatchet buried?"

Paul swallowed. Since his arrival, he'd dreaded his instinctive reaction to a first contact with Hugh after so much bad blood between them. Now he felt a mixture of elation, relief, and a weird sensation of embarrassment at the depth of his longing for his only kin. "IMC was in the wrong in Bangladesh; it was only fair we made amends."

"It was an accident, later compounded by incompetence. Nobody wanted it to happen."

"But it did, Grandpa, and the company ruined the lives of good people. They clamored for justice and I ensured they had it."

"It's always easy to fire with the king's powder."

Hugh had a weakness for colorful metaphors. "Our powder, Grandpa. The money was also mine, or would have been."

"Is the hat—"

"Yes, Grandpa. I wish it hadn't turned up the way it did, but it's over." It had been over for a long time. "You are my only family." He was about to add "and I love you," but the words died before leaving his throat.

"I'm glad. Anyway, you know where our home is. Drop by for dinner sometime."

Paul's anger waned. Hugh's voice had a fringe of something soft and vulnerable. "Grandpa?"

Silence.

"It's nice hearing your voice."

"Take care, my boy."

Paul stood immobile, looking through blurred eyes at the droning cell phone, replaying Hugh Reece's words, sifting through his conflicting feelings, relieved at the recurring discovery that no matter how much he tried he would never be able to stop loving the old buccaneer.

"Are you finished?" The young woman said in a low, husky voice that would have been sensual had it not been tainted by a whiff of stale breath.

"Thank you." Paul handed her the phone back, followed the overplayed swing of her retreating hips, and sighed.

Milford neared, running a hand through his hair and stealing a glance toward the ceiling cameras. "I spoke with Hugh," Milford said, "but I didn't have the time to straighten things out with Owen."

Paul blinked to clear his eyes and made a conscious effort to marshal his thoughts—"change the chip," as Carmen used to say when depression loomed near. He linked his arm with Milford's and propelled him toward the end of the corridor. "You're an awful liar. You wanted me to have a showdown with him."

Milford grinned. "Let's say I wanted to see if you had left your balls in the mountains."

"What's Owen doing now? Calling Grandfather?"

Milford's expression became tense. "I think you and I need to chat about the power struggles and internecine wars around here. Lorna will rig us some of her meat loaf this evening. You *do* remember Lorna, don't you?"

Paul pictured the striking Southern belle in a dark dress next to Milford at Susan's funeral. "I look forward to it."

"That's settled. We can talk about the whale of a time we'll have in Africa."

Paul stopped and turned around to face Milford. He peered into his friend's eyes, taking in the sparkle of excitement, then he shook his head slowly.

"Sorry, miner, but you're not coming."

"W-what do you mean by that?" Milford stammered. "Who's going with you?"

"Owen."

The look of confusion deepened. "Are you out of your mind?"

Paul planted both hands on Milford's shoulders, ignoring the curious looks of employees circulating through the gallery.

"I want him close by, where I can see him." Sun Tzu's advice flashed in his mind: *Keep your friends close and your enemies closer.* "Call it a hunch. You, my friend, *must* stay here to watch my back."

○

After lunch, they strolled unhurriedly through an atrium along the side of the building to a meeting hall in the research center. The air seemed electric, with a striking atmosphere of contained, contagious excitement.

Paul turned to Milford. "I'm worried about this project's security."

The old engineer turned and took Paul's arm. "Don't be deceived, miner. All the people working in the labs and development departments—I mean the Indians, not the chiefs—are on IMC scholarships. They have all graduated thanks to corporate endowments. In any case, they have security clearances that would have made the Manhattan Project proud."

"That's fine, but we're not dealing with mineral deposits."

"Right. Besides the eighteen people I mentioned before, everybody else believes we're testing for uranium in the Congo."

"And the vehicle?"

"We've circulated a red herring. The coring team drilled into a vast cavern, probably a tiny section of a vast network. Within such a subterranean formation, there could be minerals—perhaps gold or diamonds—susceptible to mining by conventional means, if we can explore it."

Paul mulled over the new information and nodded. "Yes, that could work and at the same time would give us an excuse to tighten security. You've mentioned the bosses at the labs and a few key personnel. What about the rest?"

"The executive and management personnel involved are old IMC hands who have been with us for a long time; trustworthy. We try to limit the spread of data as we get it to the groups working on specific issues, keeping to the uranium and the cavern, but you're right. Something like what we're about to pull off is hard to keep secret in an environment like this. Still, I doubt you'll find a higher security level anywhere."

Owen joined them at the entrance of the meeting hall and listened to the closing sentences of Milford's explanation. "The problem is that there are lots of people with the need to know in order to produce effective work. I imagine you've noticed that the logistics of this project are awesome. We have very little time for a number of reasons, and the quantity of plant and equipment to be moved is simply colossal."

"I only hope that with all this rush we don't bungle the whole thing," Paul said.

"Amen," Milford murmured.

The hall was a small amphitheater with armchairs in circles, like a lecture room. Each seat had its own flexible-necked fiber-optic lamp and a folding table on the arm for taking notes. Already there was a group of men and women standing close to the front. Paul recognized Lynne, Chodak, and Donald Watson, the chief scientist among them.

As they entered the hall, a jovial middle-aged man in

an oversize lab coat peeled away from a group and strode toward the newcomers. "Paul, my boy! My, I think you've grown since the last time I saw you." The man hugged him and slapped his back several times.

"You always exaggerate, Donald." Paul returned the hug. Donald was a tall man, with wavy hair, slightly bulging eyes, and a certain disheveled air, like the archetypal mad professor in the movies.

The three men and Lynne sat in the front row as the others scattered behind them, and Donald climbed to a podium. "We have with us the vice presidents of operations and development, the director of geological services, and Mr. Paul Reece in charge of the project. The purpose of this meeting is to brief Mr. Reece on the new shaft architecture, the operation systems, and the transport vehicle."

"Just a second," Paul said. "Do we need such a large room?"

Donald nodded. "This is the only place with a large projection screen."

Paul looked at the people scattered about the auditorium. "Come closer, and we won't need to shout."

"Thanks for springing me out of this hole," Owen said in a low voice. "Milford just told me."

"I thought a little honest work would get rid of your potbelly."

Owen straightened with an offended look and a faint smile. "You're just jealous, you bum."

Paul turned to the rostrum. "We're ready, Donald. Let's see what kind of a crazy caper you've concocted."

Donald breathed deeply and nodded toward a freckled, red-haired youth. He did not wear a lab coat but faded denims and a cotton Caltech T-shirt. The young man climbed to the stage and stood by a workstation, then he reached to a panel and dimmed the lights.

The opening title, *Project Isis*, on a field of blue faded to a Katia CAD drawing depicting a tube section and showing the union thread on an overhead screen. Donald took a laser pointer from his top pocket and directed the red dot to the drawing.

"As we can see in this section, we will use a perforation parallel to the existing sample bore, with a rotating thirty-inch crown, exactly three feet from the core bore. Since the target is less than one hundred and fifty feet in diameter, we can use sensors in the sample bore to control the verticality of the shaft by standard telemetries at first and low-frequency pulses later, if we manage to find a way around the EMP. Otherwise we'll have to fall back to old technology."

"You mean drilling by ear," Paul chuckled, "like our forefathers."

"More or less, but we have excellent specialists to ensure correct deployment with a small margin of error. The instrument laboratory is preparing drones, sensors, and guide equipment for delivery in two weeks."

"What about the tubes?" Owen asked, pecking at a palm-held.

"We've ordered half-inch tubes from Guillam-Dennis here in Dallas, with a standard forty-foot length and a weight of slightly over two tons each. The bore's jacketing column will have a total mass in excess of one thousand-two hundred tons, nothing to worry about. I can't tell you anything about drilling that you don't know already. It's a standard operation, except for the depth."

Paul offered no comment.

The screen changed to a drawing of a long cylinder with both ends rounded and shaped like a torpedo.

"The vehicle we are designing is twenty-two feet long—about seven meters—with two compartments of about seven feet each. The instrument controls are over the top compartment, and the entrance is through the lower section. Initially we think a single person will make the descent, with the top zone for removal and storage of," he paused, "samples. In future descents, however, we may want to take down two people. In that case, we'll remove some of the instruments. This won't be a problem, since the initial design already contemplates that possibility."

Paul followed the bright laser dot as it moved along the cylinder's different sections.

"The technical modules are above and beneath the manned compartments. The top module houses three forty-eight-volt motors, each a little over one horsepower. Through planetary gears, the motors drive three striated cylinders in hard metal, shaped like the interior of the tube. In the center and lower part of the vehicle are six smaller cylinders in high-density neoprene for centering, braking, and stabilizing during the descent. In both the upper and lower modules, there are oxygen and water tanks and two sets of lithium–carbon monofluoride batteries with a two-thousand amp-hour capacity."

He paused while a number of line drawings showing different internal views and cross sections traveled slowly across the screen.

"As you can see, there is a battery of connectors for the life-support systems during the exploration in the lower module, together with elements to facilitate exit and entry and fastening lines, a winch, and other accessories.

"The speed of descent will be quite fast, six feet per second with the vehicle coasting. Gyroscopes attached to the drive wheels will provide braking, so that the vehicle can make the trip down in about one hour. The ascent will be slower, two feet per second, about three hours to reach the surface.

"The analysis laboratory is preparing tables with the temperature gradients and the capsule's gas contents, which will help us considerably to determine the precise final design performance criteria." He paused, pocketing the pointer. "We've split the design team into two groups: mechanics and instrumentation. The engineers here are from the mechanics team, and they're also designing the suits and hand tools."

Paul nodded. "Right now, the mechanical aspects of the vehicle are the important issues. Tomorrow I'll get up to date on the instrumentation. For the mechanics, the only important aspect is size, power consumption, and weight. Right?"

Donald nodded and sat down next to Paul.

"Are you personally supervising the whole design, Donald?"

"For over two weeks now I have delegated everything else and concentrated exclusively on this."

Paul nodded and turned to the engineers. "Fine. If that's the case, we won't detain these people any longer, and we can adjourn somewhere to discuss matters and procedures."

Lynne glanced at her watch. "I'm afraid I have a video-conference scheduled. I'll catch up with you later."

As everyone stood and filed toward the exit, Donald pointed to his office at the other end of the corridor.

The room was similar to Lynne Kennedy's office, although with better furniture. On one wall was a huge map with hundreds of colored pins deployed. The four men sat around an oval table.

"Let's order some coffee and get down to defining strategy," Milford said.

Donald went to his desk and lifted the phone. Milford took off his jacket and loosened his tie.

"That's the best idea you've had all day," Owen said, following Milford's example.

Donald came to the table with a pack of yellow legal pads and a cup full of pencils. "By the way, when does perforation start?"

"We're ready to go right now," Owen said. "People are waiting for marching orders. We have heavy machinery in South Africa and Nigeria. We can get stuff airlifted to Kisangani and from there to the site on cargo helicopters."

"Another thing," Milford added. "We have an agreement in principle with the Congolese government and Gécamines, the state company. We can start work at once."

"How long will you need to clear the ground and build quarters, storage, and personnel transport?" Paul asked.

"I can have cabins and the infrastructure to start clearing inside a week. In about two weeks I can be ready to plot the ground and pour the slabs for generators, the fuel tanks, administrative quarters, service cabins, and dormitories." Owen consulted his palm-held. "We can start in four weeks, just when the first sleeving tubes and the drilling gear arrive."

"All right," Paul agreed. He turned to Owen. "I think you should leave in two weeks to establish the communications base and the infrastructure for logistics before they start the clearing. Meanwhile, you and Milford can organize the logistics agenda and your own coordination. I'll stay here with Milford for two to three weeks to supervise planning and building of the equipment and the vehicle. In about four weeks, five at the most, I'll see you at the site."

"Sounds good to me." Owen continued to peck at his palm-held.

"Well, gentlemen." Paul eyed the three men in turn. "We've got a hell of a job to do. Now, where's that fucking coffee?"

chapter 8

Deputy Director of Operations Dario Hindman gathered several document folders as his driver pulled into the usual slot under a marine corporal's watchful eye. He locked them in his briefcase and waited for his bodyguard to open the door. The corporal raised a hand.

The train of events they had triggered flashed through Hindman's mind. The sensor buried under the tarmac queried a microprocessor in the car, sending a signal to the central computer. Once authenticated, the soldier received confirmation on his handheld. The system had been a bitch to install, but after six months there hadn't been a single glitch.

A few seconds later, the corporal checked his PDA and waved them through.

The trio, with the driver marching point and the minder in the rear, strode at a brisk clip toward the Central Intelligence Agency's main building.

Hindman entered the building flanked by both men, walked across the terrazzo-crafted logotype, and paced to the left admittance zone, where his escorts released him with a curt nod. He patted his jacket's pocket, drew out a small ID pad with a thin chain, and slipped it over his head. The pad was a prop to reassure visitors. What mattered, in the restricted areas of the building, were the implants.

After security, he mounted a flight of stairs. A uniformed marine nodded.

"Good morning, Mr. Hindman."

"Hey, Josh."

Hindman stopped as the sensors locked on the ID implant behind his right ear. The light blinked green and he transited the security gate. Deep in the bowels of the building, the computer would follow his implant's unique signature and the whereabouts of its wearer.

He pressed his thumb to a small mirrorlike rectangle on the side panel and the door glided sideways. Hindman entered the narrow elevator and waited for the sensor to lock. The door closed and the elevator rose automatically.

A few seconds later the door opened, revealing a large marine sergeant in combat fatigues with an H&K MP-5 crossed over his chest. He waited as the soldier eyed a side panel, where Hindman's authentication code would be displayed, before standing aside.

At the end of the corridor, he submitted to a retinal scan. The door opened with a metallic snap. It led into a large boardroom. A woman and three men sat at the table. The room smelled of leather and lemon oil.

Hindman placed his briefcase to one side of a chair and scanned the familiar faces: to one side, Aaron Greenberg, deputy director of intelligence, and Rhea

Paige, chief analyst; to the other, Anthony Bouchard, the Africa controller, and Luther Cox, another veteran running one of the least publicized departments in the organization, one that did not exist in any official form. His department, external operations, was omnipresent, handling tasks of dubious legality. The agency shied away from being associated with its deeds.

"The cream of the crop," Hindman muttered. He sauntered to a sideboard, where he poured Perrier with a slice of fresh lime into a cut-glass tumbler. As he sipped his water, Hindman eyed the foil stickers on the holographic facsimile machine and the sat-phones, government labels marking secure channels with hard encryption. On the far wall, flanked by American flags, a portrait of President Edwina Locke added a splash of color to the sober wood paneling.

Luther Cox leaned back, balancing his chair precariously on two legs. Of average height, lean, with a quiet bearing and a small nose, he looked like a sales representative or an accountant. Hindman reflected that Cox's bland appearance had been a godsend in his dubious line of work. Underestimating his inoffensive looks had cost both civil and military personnel a great deal on every continent.

"I'd say we're scraping the bottom of the barrel," Cox rejoined, looking at Bouchard—a tall, distinguished black man whose knowledge of the African continent was as legendary as his hostility toward Cox.

"Nah! Had we dredged that deep, we would have found your anonymous father there," Bouchard countered.

Cox glared at Bouchard. "One of these days I'll close your stinking mouth."

"With yours, sweetie pie?" Bouchard pouted, batting his eyelids.

"Jesus. Shut up, will you?" Hindman said as he sat next to Greenberg.

He eyed Rhea Paige, taking in the undone buttons on her blouse. It was obvious she didn't give a damn about professional decorum. She had a nice ass, though. Whenever he had walked behind her, he'd always felt an itch on the palm of his hand. He wasn't sure if he wanted to caress her derriere or smack it. He studied her ponytail and her arms, downy with light hair. *Much too intelligent for a natural blonde. Frightening.*

They all turned and stood when Scott Foust, CIA director, appeared at the door. He motioned for everybody to sit down.

Hindman glanced at Director Foust, as always impressed by his aristocratic bearing. Foust was crowding sixty, tall, and imperially thin. He walked with the distinctive gait of the career soldier. His full head of bluish-white hair set off his tanned face with striking contrast.

"Please, sit down." A quick smile. "This is not a documented meeting. No recordings or babysitters." Foust nodded toward the wall's two-way mirrors and the fiber-optic ceiling pin cameras. "No need for subtlety." He balanced tiny eyeglasses on the tip of his classic nose, over which he gazed at the others like an eagle pinning its prey.

Everybody sat and opened their briefcases, spreading file folders and tablets on the table. Hindman's fingers brushed the attaché by his side but left it closed. He didn't need any papers. He had pored over the documents for several days.

"You've been meeting over the past few days to evaluate the lay of the land," began Foust. "I've read your input, Hindman. That's why I called Cox and Bouchard, to bring them up to date on the, shall we say, most noteworthy background points."

Hindman raised his eyebrow as he digested the precise wording of Foust's comment. *The old buzzard hasn't mentioned the full contents of the file. We'll have to tread gingerly.*

"Where are we?" The director glanced at Hindman.

"IMC is under full battle orders. They know the depth, size, and probable age of the structure. They will explore the find regardless of the cost. As anticipated. They've even given a name to their operation: Project Isis."

"Egyptian mythology?"

"Yes, sir. The goddess of magic."

"I see. Do we know what's down there?"

"We know as much as they do. It's a manufactured spherical hollow with a smaller sphere inside."

"Could they be mistaken about the data?"

"I don't follow you."

"I mean, is this for real?" Foust tapped a file by his side.

"IMC has some of the finest minds in the country, and our source is good. To make sure, we ran their raw take here. It checks."

"Age?"

The director had read the report, that much was obvious, but he wanted reassurances.

"Fifty thousand years—give or take a few hundred."

"No mistake?"

"No, sir."

Foust looked at him but said nothing.

"IMC engineers have a workable project to drill a narrow shaft. They plan to drop a manned vehicle. Instead of years, they can be at the sphere in months."

"A *manned* vehicle? How large?"

"Very small. In fact, short of thirty inches in diameter."

"That's clever," said Aaron Greenberg. "Small and manageable. But the thought of being locked up inside is the stuff of nightmares."

"Timetable?" Foust pressed.

"Four to six months. Our main concern until now has been the time frame. If the operation took years, it would have been a bitch to keep it under wraps," Hindman replied.

Foust nodded, pecking at his tablet. "Do we know who'll be in charge of . . . er, Project Isis?"

"Paul Reece, the prodigal grandson."

Hindman knew Paul Reece's file by heart.

"Fine," Foust breathed. "Now he can keep it in the family. I take it that our source at IMC is trustworthy and not compromised in any way?"

The mole's identity was omitted from the briefing the others had received, Hindman realized. "Our source's product is first class, as usual," he assured Foust.

Foust nodded. "What are your thoughts about Hugh's choice to head the exploration?"

"Poor devil. Paul Reece is a rich kid who's been pushed around by his family. A bit communist but without affiliation to any major group or political party. He had a problem with the Cubans, but we covered it up when he reached Honduras."

"Why?" Foust asked.

Hindman blinked.

"Why the cover-up?"

"Um . . ." Hindman coughed on his fisted hand. "He was a passenger in a drifting cargo ship, one of ours, towed into the Island of Pines by the Cubans. A group of dissidents helped him flee the island. When he reached Honduras, Paul Reece forced us into a trade-off: his silence for our help in covering up the wretched affair."

"Forced us?"

"Well, it was our operation—a shipload of military spare parts, choppers, and other goodies."

"So he had us by the balls."

Hindman nodded. "We lost track of him for a couple of years, until he surfaced for this job. He'd been bumming around Central America."

"For a poor devil he did a good job of taking a powder for a long time," Cox commented.

"He did *not* take a powder. As I said, there was a problem with a Cuban operation," Hindman explained, staring at Cox. "The wrong person in the wrong place at the wrong time. Then there was a fight at Aserita in Honduras; clowns from your department, courtesy of your predecessor. Two men—a local and one of ours— were wounded in a dirty scene involving Paul and a young woman. After the debacle, we had no reason to keep tabs on him."

He caught a hint of a smile from Rhea Paige.

Much too intelligent.

"When we got a whiff of this operation," Hindman

continued, "his name popped up. Four weeks ago, we sent someone to Aserita impersonating a Honduran immigration officer. The village principals, who remembered the brawl well, said that Paul had left soon after the incident, on his way to Nicaragua."

Foust raised a hand while scribbling on his pad. "He left Honduras two years ago, correct?"

Hindman nodded.

"How did we follow up from there?"

"I was getting to that, sir. To tie up loose ends, the agent traveled by mule to Colquizate, the village of the citizen wounded in the affair. The injured guy, Manuel Negroponte, insisted he hadn't seen Paul since the incident. Nobody in the village had ever heard of an American or anybody called Paul Reece."

"Did we check in Nicaragua?" Greenberg asked.

"It would have been complicated. This agency doesn't boast many fans in that particular spot; no operatives."

"How did IMC know where to look?" Cox intervened.

"According to our information, he kept in touch with his lawyers and one of IMC's directors, Milford Crandall."

"Can we lean on them?" Cox asked.

Hindman caught a sparkle in Paige's eyes. She was enjoying the exchange. He turned abruptly toward Cox. "Are you suggesting we strong-arm one of the most reputable law firms in the land and the officers of IMC?"

Cox bit his lip. "Of course not. It was just an idea."

"An unfortunate and reckless one, I'd say," Bouchard pointed out with a smile.

Foust slid his eyeglasses nearer the tip of his nose.

"Why choose a man like that for such a delicate enterprise?"

"Three reasons," Hindman replied, "all sound. As a professional, Paul is brilliant. He's an authority in geology with the experience and capacity to interpret anything in mining or industrial geology. He's been in mines since he was a kid. The second is that IMC can count on his discretion. Let's face it; this is a potentially profitable adventure. If it succeeds, it may keep the corporation at the forefront of industry for decades. The materials of the sphere's shell alone have the potential for scores of patents, let alone any contents."

"Do we know the nature of the materials?"

"Yes, sir, from IMC's lab data. I'll have the file sent over." He locked eyes with Foust.

The director raised an eyebrow, jotted down a line, and nodded. Hindman didn't want to discuss the colossal implications of the materials until they were alone.

Before returning to the previous issue, Hindman paused to down the rest of his water. "The man is a Reece. Even if he didn't overlook the Bangladesh affair, he's turned a blind eye to other shenanigans, like the Biotec adventure. I think Paul got mad at the old man because of his wife's involvement and hit him where it hurt the most: in the pocket.

"The third reason: Hugh doesn't have long to live. Paul's the last of the dynasty. When the old hawk dies, the whole kit and caboodle will be his. It's logical to presume he wants to profit from the raid they're planning."

"If that's your opinion," Foust replied, "then we've followed through this operation more as an exercise than anything else. IMC is a legitimate and loyal American corporation. Why should we be involved?" Foust paused and checked his notes. "Is there any other data, anything else?"

All eyes converged on Greenberg as he took off his glasses and polished the lenses with a square of chamois.

Greenberg's Intelligence was the CIA's most important division. Thousands of people collected statistics from the media, the Internet, and other sources. Departments scoured the waves, listened to cell-phone exchanges, taped land phone lines, and eavesdropped on conversations in theaters, restaurants, and civilian aircraft. They coded the data and fed it to supercomputers looking for coincidences and matches with scores of different criteria. Specialists further digested the collated intelligence, assigning it to one of hundreds of different areas. The division had many more or less autonomous branches, each looking after a segment of industry or some part of the planet. They fed the agency's directors—departments like Bouchard's—which coordinated practical matters somewhere on the globe. After the Cold War, Greenberg's department was state-of-the-art in marketing and counterterrorist intelligence. Hindman glanced toward Paige, Greenberg's chief analyst.

"If you could bear with me for a few minutes..." Greenberg peered at Hindman and then the director. After a slight pause, he rolled his eyes a fraction toward the other three. "Perhaps we should examine the nature of the materials IMC has recovered from the Congo and a few data snippets, say, *less* publicized and *more* confidential."

Aaron Greenberg was in his late forties, pale and fair-haired with china-blue eyes. He wore an unbuttoned vest and a drab tie. As the CIA's ops director, Hindman had endured his share of arguments with Greenberg, but there was no doubting the man's genius.

"It may be best to limit these details to those with a need to know," Foust said.

Cox, Bouchard, and Paige exchanged quick glances and then filed from the room.

Foust rang his secretary, asking for some coffee to be sent in.

"I'll leave the materials to you, Dario," Greenberg began when they were alone. "My concern is Paul Reece. Several muddy issues are bothering me, paradoxical details, voids in Paul's character we ought to review."

Hindman nodded.

"I've followed the chain of events leading to the break between Paul and IMC," Greenberg continued. "To tell you the truth, it's been a sobering exercise. This has been a typical case study of what happens when you have a small, localized infection and, instead of treating it, you compound the problem by messing about with it. The infection spreads and soon, instead of a minor inconvenience, you have a major crisis."

A slender smile, soft as candlelight, rose to Foust's lips.

"The whole thing started when the senior Reece brewed a harebrained idea. The dynasty was in danger because his son, Walter, didn't give a damn about IMC. Walter had sired a son, and to his mind had done his bit. So Hugh Reece focused on his grandson. Paul had been married to Susan Schaefer for several years without producing a child. The old man grew restless.

"Hugh decided to play his hand at divine intervention," Greenberg continued. "When he found out

Susan's father was in a tight spot with the mob, he pounced on the opportunity. The poor jerk—more through negligence than intent—had caused Domenici Giammatteo and his bunch to lose fifteen million on the purchase of a plot of land. The godfather was madder than hell."

Hindman nodded encouragement at Greenberg.

"Hugh Reece sent for Susan and explained the ways of the world to her. He offered to lean on Giammatteo and get her father out of the mess. Please don't miss this point: Hugh Reece can twist Giammatteo's arm and those of hundreds of the most powerful people in this country, but more about that later."

Foust raised an eyebrow and scribbled something on his pad.

"The patriarch secured Susan's cooperation with a little added enticement. He offered to destroy some juicy videochips of her cavorting with underage girls at a local brothel. The bitch was hooked."

"Did Paul know about Susan's pastimes?" Foust asked.

"I doubt it. The husband is usually the last to find out."

"Carry on."

"When they found out about Paul's sterility, the old man had Susan implanted with an embryo fertilized with Walter's sperm in exchange for twenty million dollars. Walter stepped in and offered to do it for free. I think he loved his father more than his own son, but this is a personal opinion.

"Hugh Reece sent Paul flying all over the world on routine jobs and, in the end, to the Bangladesh mines. There the plan started to come apart at the seams because of a stupid and unforeseeable set of coincidences.

"IMC had problems in Bangladesh. Blast water from one of the galleries filtered through into the town's underground water supply, contaminating it with organic mercury—"

"Blast water?" Foust interrupted.

"The technique for dislodging coal seams. They make holes in the mineral and insert high-pressure water lances to free the coal."

"The mercury was in the coal and contaminated the water used in the extraction process?"

"Right. Then the contaminated water mixed with the town's drinking water, resulting in countless victims of mercury poisoning. It's called Minamata disease. It made headlines some years ago. IMC's solution? Blow the gallery to smithereens, sealing whatever proof there was of the whole fuckup."

Foust penciled another note. "*Could* they have kept the lid on it by destroying the problem's source?" he asked.

"No doubt. Several inspectors from the Bangladeshi ministry were on their payroll."

Foust darted a quick glance over his specs. "No inquest? No investigation?"

"It seems as if IMC had a contingency plan. They intended to lay the blame on the mercury coating of grain seeds supplied by a relief agency.

"Paul knew nothing about the cover-ups," Greenberg clarified. "He showed up at the mine. The guys IMC sent over to take care of things mistook him for a snoop. They bashed him over the head and blew the gallery to hell. First problem."

"They blew the mine up with Paul Reece inside?" Foust asked, raising his eyebrows.

"Yes. IMC operatives didn't know his identity at the time. Meanwhile, Walter and Susan were flying from Dallas to Winslow, back and forth to the Biotec Foundation with the implant business in full swing, when Paul's papa decided to show off for Susan. He flew his aircraft into the Grand Canyon, managing to smash the plane with both of them inside. This was the second problem."

Greenberg paused for a moment and sipped coffee from his cup.

"The remains were carted off to Las Vegas. There the chief butcher, Lucy Fielding, conducted the post-mortems, finding out that Susan was pregnant. She also noticed the telltale marks of curious manipulations. Out of the blue, IMC cavalry landed at the mortuary, with Hugh Reece leading the posse. Along with the local judge, they bulldozed the pathologist and retrieved the remains with what they thought were all the samples. They dashed back to Dallas, leaving behind a pissed-off woman with—unknown to them—the biopsies of the fetus in her fridge. This was a hell of a third problem."

"With families like that you don't need soap operas," Foust commented.

"The old man found himself alone," Greenberg continued. "In one fell swoop, he'd lost his whole family— but not quite. Before blowing the gallery, some workers snuck Paul out through a side shaft. The miners were from the Chittagong Hill clans, the people IMC had been poisoning and killing for years. A whale of a fourth problem."

"Why would they do that?" Foust asked.

"Do what?"

"I mean, Paul was IMC, the guilty party."

"Probably the locals thought of kidnapping Paul to lean on the IMC."

"Why didn't they?"

"My take is they discovered an ally."

"I see. Carry on."

"Now the plot thickens. The Bangladeshis told Paul about the cover-up. As he recovered from his wounds, Paul learned about the death of his father and wife. He returned to Dallas an angry man, only to find out, through Milford Crandall, that his grandfather had ordered the termination of the three guys in charge of blowing the gallery. The boy added two and two together and brewed a devious plan. The first thing he did was to spirit the three operatives out of Asia: Michael Didier, Gordon Turner, and Rolf Bender—three ex-marines on whom we have thick files. Friends of Paul. This was a towering fifth problem. Paul Reece had bought muscle."

"*That* was Hugh's great mistake," Hindman added, "allowing Paul the opportunity to get his own private army."

"With the help of his new pals, who owed him their lives, and that of an able hacker—who we've since got on our books—Paul got hold of Susan's full dossier. The pathologist was the decisive factor. Paul tracked her down. She handed him some deep-frozen tissue bits. Sometimes a guy puts a quarter in the slot, pulls the handle, and *does* get the jackpot. This was not just the sixth problem but also the straw that broke the camel's back."

Greenberg went to the sideboard and returned with a

fresh mug of coffee—deep-blue china with the agency's logotype in gold. Hindman and Foust remained silent, waiting.

"This rosary of botched jobs and coincidence led Paul to the Biotec Foundation—a complex of laboratories and installations that has done many jobs for the Pentagon and this agency.

"Paul's hired hacker, in classic American fashion, emptied the databases. For good measure, he released an awesome worm in their server farm and crashed the whole thing for days. Paul's life insurance. With his back well covered, he pulled the rug out from under his grandfather's feet. He leaked information to the press. The papers had a field day. The company was found guilty of the Bangladesh fiasco and had to shell out the biggest compensation in history. Now you have, in a much-abbreviated form, the life and miracles of the IMC's Autonomous Manned Probe pilot, Mr. Paul Reece."

Hindman marveled at Greenberg's feat of memory. He had checked no papers during his recital. The intelligence community had many drones, and a few smart people, but Aaron Greenberg was a superstar.

Foust remained silent for several seconds, eyes narrowed, his head cocked to the left, as if listening to a distant sound. "You mentioned the Biotec Foundation. Is there more to Hugh Reece's power?"

Hindman cleared his throat. "Biotec has an impressive menu—radical plastic surgery for witness protection and identity changes, illegal operations and transplants. You name it."

"Explain."

Hindman ran a finger over the side of his mug.

"Transplants require donors, a commodity in short supply. If anyone able to pay a fortune needs a transplant, they will scour the globe for a suitable donor. Russia, South America, and China have provided thousands over the years."

"I still—" Foust clamped his mouth.

"Yes, sir. Tramps, illegal immigrants, inmates, and any unlucky bastard Biotec has managed to bag."

Greenberg pressed his lips, his eyes fixed on a point of the opposite wall, as if debating an intractable conundrum. "Scores of senators, several presidents, and hundreds of others have paid up to ten million for the service. It's the hammer Hugh Reece has over Domenici Giammatteo and hundreds of powerful people."

"I see," Foust said, "but what has this to do with Paul Reece?"

"Among the Biotec files were thousands marked *client* and *donor*. Paul had the means to bury IMC *and* the whole damn country. Nevertheless, he just slapped his grandfather's wrist. A couple of billion is nothing to IMC. But here's the amazing bit: He copied the files, depositing them in triplicate in secure places as life insurance. At least one of them is in Chittagong, where Paul Reece is as holy as Buddha.

"Then," Greenberg continued, "there's the matter of Paul's conscience. He never demanded his grandfather shut down Biotech. He managed to disappear and reappear at will and is now in charge of an operation that may change humanity. And we're going to be left out in the cold."

"You think so?" Hindman asked.

"I don't *think* it. I damn well *know* it!" Greenberg shot back. "Paul Reece is hiding something."

Hindman shifted on his chair. The scenario Greenberg had painted was frightening, and he didn't have the full picture of the Congo discovery. Up until this moment, he had considered keeping the full extent of what was underneath Ituri outside the discussion. But after Greenberg's caveats, he couldn't justify holding back the information.

"Greenberg's analysis opens a radically different perspective to this inquiry."

Silence.

"And I fear there are other issues to consider about IMC's discovery."

Foust didn't say anything, just leaned back, cradled his fingers on his lap, and stared over his reading glasses.

"Our source at IMC is at the very top."

"Who is he?" Foust asked.

Hindman was about to take refuge behind a need-to-know declaration when he realized it wouldn't wash with the director. But that didn't mean he had to lay down all his cards.

"Owen DeHolt, a vice president and member of the board. He'll be Paul's second in the Congo."

"Carry on."

"The sample brought back to the surface contains two sophisticated materials: a type of rubber and a metal. The rubber is precious: It hardens with heat. As a refractory material it's miles ahead of our best ceramics. IMC will make a mint out of the patents and licenses. The metal falls under a different category. According to our source's report, it's not so much the alloy that's unusual but the way it's made."

"What's so strange about it?"

"It's like a foam: almost weightless, but with the strength of titanium."

Greenberg nodded. "I've read the specs. If IMC manages to reproduce it, and we must assume they will, such a material will revolutionize many industries. We would be able to build aircraft at a fraction of their current weight, which would use less fuel and be much cheaper to operate. Providing we keep the formula secret, Boeing would monopolize the industry and the European Airbus would go to the dogs."

"Nice," Foust muttered.

"But when IMC briefed Paul Reece about these materials, they kept quiet about the best," Hindman continued.

"How could they?" Foust asked. "I thought he was in charge."

"He is, but Hugh wanted to have an ace up his sleeve. Let's face it, after the Bangladesh fiasco, he has every right to tread carefully with Paul. Call it need to know. I don't doubt Hugh will fill Paul in with all the details after he pulls off the Congo stunt. Besides, none of these materials has an immediate use."

"How so?"

"Having a sample of a material is useless unless you have the know-how and technology to replicate it. It may take years of research and laboratory work to fathom the processes."

"Carry on," Foust said.

"They showed Paul a core of concrete lined with the

rubber and reinforced with the metal, but they didn't disclose everything they found in the concrete's inner layer. Most of it is made from a synthetic resin with superb properties and worth a fortune to someone like 3M, but mixed with it there are several kinds of flecks and thin strands.

"One of the flecks is a transparent metal with similar mechanical properties to aluminum. It could replace all of our existing glass. The other type of fleck—or buckyball, to use the same terminology they used—is a sophisticated semiconductor that produces visible light."

Greenberg frowned. "What's so strange about that? LEDs do the same thing."

"Yes, but light-emitting diodes use electricity and transform a sizable portion of energy into heat. The material IMC found inside the cement doesn't need any apparent source of energy. The thing produces broad-spectrum white light with practically no heat. This means efficiency. Such material could replace all the light sources in the world."

"And the strands?" Foust asked.

"That's the best of the lot. They call them buckytubes and there are two types. One is a superconductor at room temperature."

"Meaning?" Foust insisted.

"To name a few uses: supercomputers on a pinhead, electric motors with a fraction of their present weight with unheard-of power running on a few volts, as well as electricity generation and distribution with a tenth of the cost. In a nutshell: our energy problems solved."

"And that of our allies—at a price, of course," Greenberg muttered.

"Of course."

"And the other?"

"They still don't know. The structures are like odd-shaped tubes and seem to accelerate molecules."

"What's the use of that?"

"As I've said, the IMC scientists have drawn a blank so far."

"Why didn't you include these details in your report?"

Foust was polishing his glasses again, and he hadn't altered the pitch of his voice. Translation: He knew the answer.

"You said it before, sir. If IMC—a loyal American company—lands a windfall, our nation would benefit, and we have the means to profit, if not control it."

"We could classify these materials as strategic and meter their distribution," Foust mused.

"Precisely."

Greenberg straightened. "In this scenario, to do nothing would be reckless. God only knows what our idealistic friend Paul Reece is plotting."

"Sharing the goodies with the world's disenfranchised?" Hindman asked.

"Or worse," Greenberg said. "I listened to a transcript of Paul's briefing when he took over the project. His exact words were: *I wonder if we have* the right *to keep the project secret.* The emphasis is mine, but his thoughts are there."

Foust studied both men. "What do you suggest?"

"We must act. The President will back us all the way," Greenberg said, and darted Hindman a glance.

Hindman realized that Greenberg was asking for his sanction to overstep his charter. He nodded.

"The Congo is about to implode again, as it's been doing intermittently for the last seventy years or more. If a rebel army attacked the IMC base before the vehicle returned to the surface, we could send our people to salvage whatever American interests remained in the zone. We would have every right in the face of public opinion. It's worked before."

"Pull the rug from under their feet?" Foust asked.

"Why the hell not?"

"Torching the woods to get a fox. Sounds familiar." Foust made another note on his pad.

"After we bring out the black bags, we would give Mr. Reece a hero's burial. People would mourn him. I don't believe the Bangladesh guys holding a copy of the Biotec data would do anything about it. He would be the regrettable victim of a war in an unstable country—the great American hero. The material from the operation would come home with us. End of the matter. IMC would continue in business, under control, depending on the nature of the finds."

"What's your opinion?" Foust asked, turning to Hindman.

"I agree with Greenberg. Paul Reece has never taken a step back in his life."

Foust appeared to mull over the matter for several seconds, but Hindman guessed that he'd already made up his mind. Foust was conservative about department operations, but this was explosive, too important to risk.

The craziest part of the intelligence business was that you couldn't trust *anybody*, but you had to trust *somebody*. Hindman had trusted his best source—one that neither of those present knew anything about. According to this informant, when Paul Reece got hold of the stolen files, he discovered that they were encrypted with a hard key. A key he didn't have. It would have taken a long time, grinding the code in number-crunching main-frames, and a team of experts to unravel it. Since he didn't have a pressing need to use his evidence, he just made the copies and stowed them in safe places. Paul had never opened the stolen files. He didn't know a thing about Biotec's crimes.

chapter 9

The roar in the helicopter cabin was deafening. The pilot's eyes roved the instruments: radar, speed, altimeter, torque, pitch, collective, and back to the radar screen. Rain fell like a thick liquid curtain; wipers pushed it from left to right. The flying machine swam, as though immersed in a shapeless clear mass devoid of beginning or end.

Paul had landed with the corporate jet at Kisangani, the capital of the Upper Congo, after a fourteen-hour flight from Dallas and a refueling stop at Tenerife.

At Kisangani, a helicopter pilot had been waiting at the jet's steps with two polite immigration officers and a military jeep. The one driving the jeep—a neat young man with dimply cheeks—quickly metamorphosed into a howling banshee. After reversing his cap back to front, he'd thrown himself screaming into a suicidal, zigzagging drive. They had barreled between airplanes moving on the taxi lanes toward a waiting helicopter. Somehow, despite the jerks, skids, and jolts, his partner produced a rubber stamp from a shirt pocket, ink pad and all, and endorsed Paul's passport. Within a few seconds he had returned the travel papers, though not before performing a technically perfect sleight of hand with the two hundred dollars folded on the last page. On arrival, the driver had reversed his cap and smiled.

The pilot was a sullen man. After introducing himself as Peter, he had climbed at once into the helicopter and started the turbine, all the time looking at the sky and cursing as the engine warmed.

Kisangani, Paul thought—like most large cities in central Africa—appeared almost idyllic from the air: thousands of tiny houses spread over a vast surface, contrasting with the commercial centers, the large buildings, the concrete blocks common to every city. Between Kisangani and Kinshasa flowed one of the navigable sections of the Congo River, a fluid road linking both cities. Out of his right window, Paul watched the river port, where a seething throng of small boats scudded amid their bigger cousins.

There was no mistake; the continent was Africa. Once in the air, Paul stared down on a thick sea of dark green surrounding the city. The equatorial jungle, blackish under the gray light of storm, appeared eager to recover open space lost to tall buildings, to claim dull gray concrete ribbons of road. Dense masses of rosewoods and ebony mingled with irokos, sapeles, wenges, limbas, agbas: colossal trees one hundred feet tall or more, their branches reaching to the sky like green limbs in a wild explosion of life. Paul cringed, imagining he could feel the jungle's hankering to devour the small houses of men.

Once they were airborne, the water started to fall, without warning or progression. His eyelids, heavy after the long trip from Texas, closed as he adjusted the safety harness. He knew the data. Rains were constant through the year in equatorial zones, in particular during July and August in the Upper Congo. Flights to the site were madness in such conditions but necessary; otherwise they would have had to postpone drilling for a full two months.

The helicopter struggled through the turbulent air, rising and falling like a mad roller coaster. Paul blessed the inventors of the automatic rotor and rudder controls; flight would have been impossible without them. A thousand and one things could go wrong on a zero-visibility flight without open landing ground below. Ignoring the hollow sensation in his stomach, Paul tried to doze and stop thinking about the dangerous flight and the daring pilot.

Unbeknownst to anybody, he'd spent a long night with his grandfather, reminiscing about times gone by and discovering that Hugh was still capable of drinking him under the table.

Hugh had given a day off to the staff and commandeered the kitchen to produce a memorable goulash they later washed down with Bikavér Bull's Blood. The old Hungarian recipe recommended noisy belches to help digestion, and they followed its advice to the letter.

"There are two sides in this corporation: the blood— you and I—and the mercenaries, those who would fall on the corporation carcass like famished vultures if given half a chance." As Hugh opened their second bottle of wine, he'd grown somber. "Out there, you'll be on your own, boy. Regardless of what you do, communications will leak like a sieve; we might as well broadcast any private conversation. You see, this corporation is too large—too many steps, too many filters, and too many mercenaries with their ears to the ground. If I ever have to warn you, I'll find a way outside the normal channels."

"Why do you think you'll need to warn me?"

Hugh hadn't answered straightaway. He sniffed at the cork and nodded absently, as if the smell confirmed a dearly held belief. "Project Isis is as great as it comes, straight out of a science-fiction tale, only it's real. But time is our enemy. With the passage of every hour, we run the risk governments or competitors will get a whiff of what we're seeking in Ituri. If they do, the rules of the game will change."

"In what way?" Paul knew the answer but posed the question anyway.

"No rules."

"Sounds like fun."

"Attaboy." Then Hugh had refilled their glasses and raised his own, steady, as if nailed in midair. "And when you're done in Africa, go fetch your woman, adopt the next Reece, and come back home."

The previous weeks had been a maelstrom of activity. After the initial slow, shaky beginning, IMC's formidable machine had meshed into gear, accelerating like a huge, well-oiled mechanism.

In Dallas, Milford had seized the reins of the operation. He had closed off the logistics center with an impressive security deployment, organizing the departments with a small army of administrative personnel commandeered or stolen from almost all the corporate divisions.

In the Congo, Owen had managed to obtain Gécamines' collaboration through Mafia tactics. He hastened permits and licenses with the world's best grease — millions of dollars in bribes. Rolf Bender, savvy ex-marine that he was, had designed the project's security logistics from Dallas. Gordon Turner and Michael Didier, the other confederates in the Bangladesh affair, were in the Congo as well: Gordon in charge of security, and Michael running the satellite links with real-time audio and video.

Startled by a sudden change in the noise, Paul opened his eyes. Blinded by a blazing sun, he fumbled for sunglasses in his shirt pocket. Below, a landscape of savanna — low hills, high grasses, and patches of bamboo with splashes of green vegetation — rolled by. Masses of trees stretched to the horizon. He glanced at the pilot, who seemed more relaxed, now chewing a stick of licorice.

Paul followed the pilot's finger and unhooked a headset dangling overhead. The cans muffled the engine noise to a whisper.

"I hope you had a good sleep," the pilot drawled.

"Just resting my eyes."

"That's one way of putting it. At first I thought the gearbox was grinding, then I realized it was you snoring."

Paul smiled. He eyed the landscape under the helicopter. "How long?"

"An hour, more or less." He checked the instruments once more. "We've taken a detour to skip the storm, to the confluence of the Lukwaye River and due north. The town on the right is Banalia. Now we'll follow the Lokoma River below through Malili and Mondjale." The pilot pointed to a map in a plastic folder dangling from the center column. "If we could have flown a straight line, we would be there already, but with the damn Banyamulenge on the rampage, it's wiser to go around."

"Understood."

"You know the region?"

"I'm familiar with the geography. We've been studying the area for a month, but this is my first time in the Congo. A few years back we did some coring at Al Sharkïyah in Sudan. We used the airport of Juba, about twelve hundred miles to the north." Paul shifted in his seat to stretch his legs. "Everything went fine until we clashed with the locals. For a while we had to use a landing field in Bangassou in the republic of Central Africa, no fewer than three hundred miles from our camp."

The pilot nodded. "I've never been to Bangassou, but I know Juba. It's a pimple on the ass of Africa."

Paul smiled. He let the pilot ramble and watched the forest fly by under them. As they cleared a hill covered by dense vegetation, the landscape changed. A large tract of deforested land gaped like an enormous scar in a depression. Tracks of heavy machinery scoured the red earth. The clearing's size surprised Paul. After studying the satellite photos, he expected something more compact. The site centered a square almost half a mile to a side, surrounded by a perimeter fence, posts, and wires shining under the blazing sun.

Hundreds of multicolored containers were piled on concrete strips, marked with the logotypes of corporations and shipping lines. Paul recalled the layout diagrams in Dallas. *What's that?* he thought as he noticed a corner missing from the square layout. To the right, long rows of cabins, painted blinding white and sitting on concrete slabs, were the personnel quarters. The tallest building, the three-story administrative complex, consisted of two blocks assembled from large containers with stairs on the outside.

Scores of telecommunication antennas and satellite dishes reached into the African sky, like the dorsal plates of a stegosaurus, and thick bunches of cable snaked along the metal roofs, disappearing into the buildings.

"They've chopped down half of Ituri to drill a damn hole."

The pilot glanced sidelong at Paul but offered no comment. He steered the helicopter into a wide arc, toward a concrete slab adorned with a white cross. After banking to slow the craft in midair, the pilot leveled off, touched down, and began the shutdown sequence. Paul opened the door. The blast of sauna-hot air made him gasp. He collected his knapsack from the back before jumping to the ground. Though he knew it was three feet higher, Paul bent his head in the unconscious reaction to the rotor overhead.

Michael Didier waited in a jeep beside the slab. "My son, what a blessing for my impious eyes, to see you still in one fucking piece, albeit frayed at the edges. Didn't we get our beauty sleep?"

Paul shook his hand, comforted by the sight of a familiar face. "I've told you a million times, Michael: Your vocation is the cloth, if possible at a remote monastery with a nunnery nearby."

Michael joined his hands and bowed his head in a

saintly gesture. He was as tall as Paul, on the sunny side of forty with short dark hair. A scar to the side of his mouth gave the impression of a permanent leer. He wore a sleeveless black T-shirt, '60s style. Tanned skin covered a set of flat muscles, compact, smooth like a swimmer, giving him a predatory look.

"The tender mercies of a woman—balm for my tormented soul, my brother. You know? If they taxed dicks around here, it wouldn't affect me, due to longtime unemployment."

"Have you never heard of self-employment, Father?"

The pilot handed Michael two large canvas bags. He threw them one after the other onto the jeep's rear seat. "Coming with us or staying?" Michael asked.

"I'll stay. Need to get back to Kisangani."

Paul climbed into the jeep and waved at the pilot. Michael had already started the engine and was busy grinding gears. Paul opened his rucksack, pulled out a padded envelope, and passed it over to Michael. "Here's something you lost."

Michael took the envelope, emptying the contents into his hand. The midday sun blazed off a Submariner with a thick gold wristband.

"I didn't have time to get it gift-wrapped, and the box was too bulky," Paul said.

Michael caressed the Rolex. "Thank you, boss, but you shouldn't have."

"No shit. First, 'my son,' now 'boss.' Here, give me back the watch."

Michael laughed and pulled his hand away, sliding the timepiece onto his wrist. "Forget it. I was being polite.

I didn't mean it." Then he fixed Paul with a serious expression. "Thanks."

Paul recalled the odyssey two years ago when he, with the help of the Bangladesh clans, arranged to have Michael, Gordon, and Rolf spirited out of the country to escape Hugh Reece's henchmen.

They had left Bangladesh from Chittagong to cross the Gulf of Bengal in a leaking wooden craft in choppy seas: two days of bailing water overboard with buckets. The crew—two Chakma tribesmen who could speak only Bengali—laughed their heads off at the three Americans with green-tinged faces and red-rimmed eyes.

The Chakma put them ashore at Haldia, in the Ganges Delta, where a man called Patel picked them up. Patel spoke only Hindi and drove a truck of chickens, with whom they shared the two hundred fifty miles to Cuttack. There, another Indian—small, chubby, and very black, but with a perfect Oxford accent—gave them false passports with visas and a large wad of rupees, similar to the Bangladesh taka but larger. The wad disappeared with the purchase of train tickets to Bombay, a trip of more than twelve hundred miles. On the train, Michael managed to sell his gold Rolex timepiece to a merchant for one thousand dollars, a twentieth of its value, although he'd won it at poker. With the loot, they moved to the other end of the train and spent the four-day trip in relative comfort. At Bombay, another Indian gave them fresh clothes and four tickets to Jeddah in Saudi Arabia with a party of pilgrims. They had to wait three days. With the money from the watch gone, Michael had removed Gordon's gold tooth with a screwdriver and sold it to buy *chapattis* and curried rice. From Jeddah they flew to Barcelona, Amsterdam, Mexico City, and Chihuahua. They drove to Ciudad Juarez and entered the U.S. through El Paso with another set of passports. Altogether, it was a two week odyssey. When they finally reached the continental U.S., they had no money or anything left to sell.

After the jeep stopped, Paul and Michael sat in the vehicle and lit cigarettes. Paul surveyed the frantic activity around the central zone. Two bright-yellow Liebherr cranes maneuvered materials and tubes above a swarm of men in orange overalls and hard hats. He gazed from a distance at the colossal drilling platform, the labyrinth of tubes pumping refrigeration slurries to cool the crown bit and return it to the surface from the bottom of the hole. To one side of the tower was an open pit to recycle the slurry and separate the solids. A backhoe dredged the slush pit, loading trucks that had oversize pneumatic wheels. The trucks transported the mud to the edge of the site, piling it into sloppy mounds.

On the other side of the tower, one derrick positioned long lengths of drill pipe on a cradle; another moved a blue container with the IMC logotype in large white letters. From a cabin covered with vibrating corrugated sheet metal, a battery of diesel generators on steel mounts contributed to the general din. Roaring motors and the metallic clang of steel against steel echoed against the encroaching greenery.

From the control cabin next to the rig, a man in a white hard hat waved in the general direction of the jeep. Paul shielded his eyes with a hand to see better against the bright sunlight. Mark O'Reilly. Paul waved back, threw down the cigarette butt, then jumped into the thick red mud. "Anybody looking us up would think we're drilling or something."

Michael made a farewell gesture. "I'll drop your things in your cabin. If you need something, I'll be around."

"Fine. What about Gordon?"

"At the office, preparing tonight's roster."

"I'd better head in." Paul gestured toward the administrative building.

"Later, boss," Michael said, saluting before barreling out.

As Paul approached the stairs, he ran into a dark-skinned woman. He pulled back. The standard orange overalls and rolled-up sleeves didn't hide her shapely body. She carried an armful of rolled drawings.

The woman eyed him and then tapped her white hard hat. "Put one on."

Paul backed up another step, eyeing her—an ebony beauty with high, aristocratic cheekbones and pouting lips. Long black curly hair gathered at the nape of her neck with a bright yellow scarf. For an instant he considered introducing himself, but thought better of it. He shouldered his bag, took a hat from a hook, and decided to follow the woman toward the drilling tower.

From ten yards away, Paul observed the drilling platform. A custom-built flywheel for opening a large diameter hole rotated around a wide sleeve with a four-inch cylinder inside. The shaft descended in slow motion at the cutting rhythm of the bit. The sleeve—the tube down which Paul would travel—sank at the same rate. He leaned on a pile of empty wooden cable spools, staring at the smaller cylinder with white marks spaced every three feet. Paul clicked the chronometer on his wrist as he followed the cylinder's slow descent. He measured the speed of perforation, although the exercise was pointless; he couldn't calculate for the hardness of the strata through which the bit was moving.

After a few minutes, the drilling slowed to a standstill.

A loud horn blew, sounding like a submarine on a crash dive. A dozen men sprang from nowhere and dashed toward the motionless platform. With the precision of mechanics replacing tires on an Indy car, the men set friction collars on the shaft and pulled it until they reached a threaded joint, then disconnected the pipe with a large motorized clamp. One after another, the men pulled out thirty-six-foot lengths of pipe, fastening, blocking, twisting, and unclamping between cascades of viscous brown slurry.

Paul counted the pipes until the crown reached the surface—a formidable mass of dented cogs on tungsten blocks, over three feet high, weighing several tons. A man knelt next to the crown, inspecting the cutting teeth with care, then signaled the crane operator to lift the bit.

One of the men jumped over the crown assembly and fastened his sling to a hook. He directed the procedure, riding the cogs like a cowboy. The cranes swung their massive arms toward the tower, one with a new deep-blue crown dripping thick oil, the other with a steel sling. The man fastened the webbing support to the worn bit with spanners dangling from his belt.

When the first cutter set was loose, the new one moved into position as the man unhooked his harness. He then jumped from one crown to the other, rearranging all the connections. With the new cutter installed, the rest of the men converged on the platform and assembled the pipe in its original order. They moved aside as it started to rotate once more, gathering speed.

Paul checked his watch. Sixteen minutes to replace eighty-four thirty-six-foot lengths of pipe and a crown. These were the best IMC had, specialists better paid than many executives, with bonuses per foot drilled. The roughnecks were the frontliners of any prospecting company.

He noticed Mark O'Reilly in front of the control cabin talking to the woman and pointing to something on the sleeve pipe. They looked toward him. Mark's head bent toward the woman's. She covered her mouth with her hand, and Mark's laughter rang out over the infernal din of the machinery. Paul smiled, turning on his heel and walking toward the logistics and administrative block.

Before reaching for the doorknob, he hung the hard hat back on a hook and tried to get rid of the mud on his boots. Scrapers were located on either side of the stairs, but the mud was tenacious; Paul did the best he could. On the steps leading to the upper levels, he glanced at a painted sign: *IMC/Gécamines 0, Security 1, Logistics 2,* and an arrow pointing up. He stood aside as a young man with a sheaf of papers in his hand barreled down. After another look around, Paul climbed the steps up to the third level.

From his vantage point, he could see the whole camp. The strange layout of the clearing was obvious. *Why did they cut a corner?* he wondered. The drilling rig was in the upper left quadrant of the square, but the fence had been angled, excising the corner. As a result, the rig was close to the wires, a security headache. After watching the frantic activity for a few minutes more, he opened a door, entering a small office containing a table and a couple of chairs. The air in the cabin was cool and dry, in contrast to the clammy atmosphere outside. The racket dropped when the door closed behind him. There was no one in the room. Following a sound of voices, he ambled down a narrow passage, past several doors, until he reached the end of the walkway and the last door.

Owen DeHolt, looking tanned and healthy, stood screaming into a phone, his face contorted with rage. He lifted his head and smiled when he saw Paul.

"I don't give a rat's ass about your orders. I want those containers cleared this afternoon and moved during the night!" Owen listened for an instant. "Now, you listen, bozo! I want the parts here before the morning shift. I'm not going to stop drilling because of your stupid pap— You don't have any papers? Then make some! But get my crates on the chopper."

After slamming down the receiver, Owen politely asked, "Have a good trip?"

"Long, boring, like all trips," Paul answered, amazed at Owen's ability to morph as needed. "How'd you manage air-conditioning? Man, you're set up like a Turkish pasha!"

Owen gestured Paul toward an easy chair and sank into another one. "Rank hath its privilege. I'm telling you, this project has brought me back to life. I'd forgotten about opening a field—the smell of sweat and diesel. I've missed it."

"Everything okay?"

"The planning's been faultless, at least up to now." He tapped his head, smiling. "Knock on wood."

"Why so much clearing?" Paul asked. "We would have had more than enough space with a fraction of it."

"Ah, the clearing." Owen leaned back in the chair. "That's Julius Mbembe, the regional administrator's payoff. When he saw our proposal, he insisted on drawing the limits more than double what we'd done. We had to do some fairly stiff negotiating to get even reasonable concessions."

Paul smiled as the ruse became obvious. He had worked with many corrupt officers in Third World countries.

"We're talking big dough here," Owen continued. "The motherfucker has taken out an enormous bunch of timber; we even had to move it down to the river to keep him happy. If you saw the ebony, mahogany, and bubinga we've hauled out of here, you'd fall flat on your ass. Massive logs, first-class. I bet he's netted a million bucks out of them, and he wanted more. If we hadn't stopped, we would still be doing the lumberjack routine for the son of a bitch. We used two tons of dynamite blowing out the stumps." He opened his arms wide. "We made craters as big as Vesuvius."

"Stumps?"

"This is a sharp bastard we've got here. After we cut down the trees, he forced us to dynamite the stumps so the Gécamines inspectors couldn't count them. Then he brought over a swarm of men to pick up the leftovers. We had to load the wood onto trucks—*our* trucks, by the way—after each blast, night and day. You should've seen it. He took hundreds of tons of firewood to sell."

"The man's an entrepreneur."

"An entrepreneur? A conniving bastard, if you ask me. He charged us for removing the wood."

Paul laughed.

Owen got up, went to the fridge, and broke out a six-pack of beer.

"What are your plans?" he asked, throwing one to Paul.

Paul detected a subtle change in Owen's voice. The sparring was over. Now it was down to business. "To get this job done as soon as possible."

"And afterward?"

Like any two-bit poker player, Owen would give an arm to know how the other would play his cards.

"I'll get on with my life."

"Where?"

"Look, Owen, my life has nothing to do with you or anybody else. I take it as it comes."

"Won't do, Paul. IMC's a private corporation with an arcane chapter: The property passes along the bloodline. You're next after Hugh. He can't last forever."

"You're worried about your job? Worried I'll take the company public when my grandfather dies?"

Owen took a swig of his beer, staring at Paul. "Many people have given their lives to IMC."

"Let me put it this way. I want to know what's down there. When this is over, nothing will have changed," he lied.

"And when Hugh dies?"

"Then I'll have to make a decision. But until then, stop pushing me."

Owen nodded. "Remember, Paul, this corporation is home to more people than the Reeces."

Paul stared into Owen's eyes and nodded once. "I won't forget," he assured him before changing tack. "By the way, who's the arrogant pretty thing I've seen around?"

The vice president of IMC took a long pull on his beer and cleaned the froth from his lips with the back of his hand. "Nice going, Hawkeye. Dr. Shermaine Mosengwo is the Gécamines inspector detailed on-site. Don't be deceived by appearances. She's a competent mining engineer, intelligent and experienced. Besides, I don't think she swallowed the uranium-mine tale."

Paul narrowed his eyes. "Why do you say that?"

"Call it a hunch. But don't underestimate her. A couple of days after we got here, some of the native hands—two guys who looked like overfed gorillas and were plastered to boot—tried to have a go at her between the goods containers. I believe they're still in the hospital—broken arms, ribs, and sundry other damage. Since then, the men get out of her way as if she had the pox. Exquisite manners, you know—ladies first, let me hold the door for you, madam, and all that bullshit."

Paul mulled over the information. "Interesting. What about our ties with the government?"

"Great. We had the normal rush of backhanders at first, the old baksheesh routine, but as soon as Gécamines got into the picture, there were no problems. Everything works like clockwork, perhaps even too smoothly."

"That's the second time you've hinted at something

fishy. What's Milford's impression? Have you spoken to him?"

Owen nodded, setting the empty can on the table. "He pooh-poohed the whole thing. His take is that the Gécamines people are biding their time to see where the operation leads. They know our side of the project: a central large-diameter shaft from which galleries will spread radially to work the mineral seams, and several smaller shafts perforating its perimeter for ventilation. The samples we've given them can pass examination, provided it's not too thorough. This first shaft can be justified as one of the ventilation perforations we are doing to test the ground and get more-accurate data."

"Justified?"

"We have to start somewhere, and a test bore is reasonable, providing they believe we'll follow it through with the rest of the project as submitted. But I tell you, I have the heebie-jeebies. Too easy."

"Have you got something tangible? A detail, incidents?"

"That's the problem; I can't put my finger on anything substantial. Call it foreboding, but it's eerie. No parts have gotten lost. We've only suffered delays of hours, never of days or of anything critical. Take today. We have forty cutting tools in Kinshasa, the second delivery from Norsk Hydro. The consignment was held up yesterday, but I bet you before the day is over they'll release it. Nevertheless, they're not essential parts; we have crowns to last us a week, maybe two."

"May be coincidence," Paul muttered, uneasy. "How many Gécamines inspectors are here?"

"That's another thing. Only Shermaine."

"Just that woman?"

Owen nodded. "When I'd been here two or three days, before we started drilling, a Congolese air-force chopper appeared out of nowhere to drop her off. Of course, she had faultless credentials."

"I imagine you checked her out."

"Yup. Besides the documents, we snapped some photographs, ostensibly for security passes. I took the photos to Kinshasa. They not only certified her credentials, they also vouched for her. She has unlimited authority straight from the president. Her father, Étienne Mosengwo, is the sidekick of the Kabila dynasty: first for the father, Laurent, now for the son, Joseph. They are Bantus from the Kasai tribe. She's a princess. Impressive, no?"

"A job for daddy's girl? I can't believe it," Paul mused. "Doctor?"

"Yes. In geology. The Sorbonne, 2006, when she was twenty-four, and later postdoctoral studies at MIT and Caltech."

"Impressive."

"She questioned the final few feet of the bore."

"I thought Gécamines would. What did you tell her?"

"Exactly as agreed. Our target is to drill down to 22,500 feet, a world record. A few feet short of that depth, we've cored through a vein of nephrite jade. That will entail using some advanced crown heads we've designed, but after we clear the vein we will have reached our objective."

"We will indeed. What did she say to that?"

"She asked why go through the jade. Stopping a few feet shorter would save us money and hassle."

Paul waited.

"I told her that 22,500 was a nice round figure and be-sides, when we dropped our probe, we wanted to inspect the jade to ascertain if it would be worth extracting."

"Did she buy it?"

Owen shrugged. "She hasn't commented further. Strange, no?"

"You bet."

"Anyway, the reports and files on all this and a lot more are in your office next door. Come."

Paul followed him into a large space composed of two rooms, the first with a long table, the other with a desk like Owen's: institutional gray steel and linoleum. On one side was a file cabinet, a videochip reader, holo-printer, and a router. On the table was a PC with a dock-ing station for Paul's tablet computer.

"I hope you'll like it here," Owen said with a sweeping gesture. "It's sunny in winter, breezy in summer."

Paul smiled. "I'll be fine. How long before we finish the perforation?"

"We're doing fine, but soon we'll hit basalt. Now we're pumping slurry a couple hours a day. As soon as we clear three thousand, we'll go to four, then six. When we hit 20,000 feet, we'll be pumping more than a whole shift. Then the final hurdle: the damn con-crete. By the way, have you seen the AMP? How does it look?"

Paul recalled the frantic activity he left behind in Dallas. "It's . . . awesome. Scary, but they're doing a super job. Let's hope it works. One serious error will be the last for me."

The engineer's face turned serious. "There won't *be* any errors, I can assure you."

"Amen to that." How Owen thought he could assure anyone of anything baffled Paul. "Where's security? I want to say hi to Gordon and get up to date."

"Below us. I have a few calls to make now, but I'll join you later. Here, let me walk you to the entrance and introduce you to Matthew. He looks after the comms, the agenda, and darts about like a rabbit."

At the entrance, which doubled as reception, the young man Paul had seen running was separating holocards into piles.

"This is Mr. Reece. He'll move into the corridor offices. You'll be aiding both of us now."

The young man, not older than twenty, stood and shook Paul's hand with an awed expression, perhaps intimidated by the name.

"Welcome, Mr. Reece."

"Thank you, Matthew. Can you transfer calls from here to other departments?"

Matthew shook his head. "No, sir. I can communicate with you at any point of the project by landline. I can also transfer outside calls to your office or to Mr. DeHolt's, but only through the central switchboard."

Paul nodded. "I'll need an internal phone to be in contact with Mr. DeHolt's office, an Internet connection with hard encryption, a pager, and a sat-phone."

"I'm sorry, Mr. Reece, but security controls all communications. You'll have to ask them."

Paul turned to Owen, searching his face for any sign of displeasure at having to route all his calls, even personal ones, through the site security, but Owen remained deadpan. Paul cringed because he was left with the same unanswered dilemma. Could he trust Owen? Either Owen had not made any unofficial calls or he had a way to evade security.

Owen pushed open the door. "Everything clear?"

"Yes," Paul said. No, he thought.

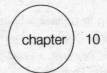

chapter 10

Twenty-two, twenty-three, twenty-four...

Jereh slid to a lower branch, stretched his arms like a tightrope walker, and trod along the bough for a few yards before leaping to the ground. *At least this time it wasn't raining.* He ran a hand over the multicolored dome of his head and thought back to his stint when the drillers cored under a constant deluge. His scalp was healing but still felt strange under his fingers. Forty feet ahead, through a tangle of creepers and lianas, he caught the glint of razor wire.

He trudged back, around a clump of thorny acacias, to a raised mahogany root. Jereh barely missed running into a hissing white colobus. "Ayayay! No need to get angry, Bemba. Here, have some nuts."

As the monkey flopped down to shell its treat, Jereh leaned over the animal to rescue from the harness on its back a beer-can-size box containing a repeater capable of bouncing a particular signal to a satellite transponder. With deft movements, Jereh unlatched the tamper-proof top to replace a battery with a fresh one from his knap-sack.

"Now, be a good boy, Bemba. Climb back with your pals. Tsch, tsch."

The colobus tilted his head, as if considering the re-quest, and scratched his belly, seemingly satisfied. After making a face, the animal grabbed the remaining nuts, swung around on his rump, and bolted up the mahogany to a safe height.

Jereh edged a few steps and darted to a hackberry, climbing the lower branches with ease, fingers and toes seeking purchase on the warty bark. Over the recent months, he'd spent more time in an area one hundred yards around the derrick than at his pygmy village, a good three days away.

After reporting to Leon Kibassa with details and pho-tographs of the coring, he'd hoped to relax a few days, perhaps visit Makemba a few hours upriver and discuss the dowry with the family. It was about time they settled down. But Leon's plans didn't encompass rest or ro-mance. *To avoid detection, change positions every thirty seconds.* Leon Kibassa's words had sounded innocuous. Now, after hours of darting from one tree to another, the old man's warning took on a different meaning.

From a forked branch fifty feet from the ground, Jereh could view the camp unimpeded. In the foreground, the drilling rig, painted bright yellow, contrasted against the dark forest background. *Like a wasp on a bongo hide,* Jereh thought.

Five, six, seven...

He eyed a tall man standing to one side of the ma-chine.

Ten, eleven...

Jereh had seen him check his watch.

What are you counting? The time until you hurl your-self down that tube? Fifteen, sixteen, you'll drop like a leka na-ma. Jereh chortled. He found the image of a banana snake sliding down a hollow vine funny. *Nineteen, twenty. You look too big to fit in that tube.*

A powerful horn blasted, hushing the forest sounds.

Twenty-three, twenty-four...

Another rising of the pipes, another bit replacement.

My friend, at this rate you'll be there very soon.

chapter 11

Several khaki-uniformed men sat at workstations, staffing traffic desks and satellite links. A man in a blue cap bent over a counter, stabbing at a tablet PC with his stylus. He looked up when Paul closed the door.

Paul smiled, seeing the badge attached to the security guard's shirt pocket: *SA*. Security Associates, the company he owned with Rolf, Michael, and Gordon. Paul choked a laugh: He'd reformed three inveterate bums. A *fine gravestone epitaph*. To cap it all, according to his accountants, the company showed a handsome profit.

"Something I can do for you?" the man asked.

"I'm Paul Reece. I'd like to see Mr. Turner, please."

The man straightened, an alert shadow scurrying across his eyes. "May I see your ID?"

Paul dug up a wallet from his back pocket and pushed his driver's license across the counter. The guard eyed it. His hands moved below the counter and a dimple on the desk microphone lit up. At the mention of his name, there was a muffled thump and a door on the rear wall opened. Gordon Turner emerged, smiling from ear to ear, wagging his arms like an oversize fowl as he marched to the counter.

"I'll be damned! It really *is* Paul!"

He wore khaki shorts and thick knee-length socks— like an outdated WWII vintage desert rat in tropical gear. Only his black skin and shiny dome spoiled the illusion. A compact man, Gordon gave an immediate impression of great strength.

"I'm still alive," Paul chuckled.

"What are you standing there for? Come in, man. Make yourself at home."

"I see you keep polishing that head of yours." Paul shielded his eyes and squinted. "The shine is blinding."

"Envious of my glow, that's what you are." Gordon stared at Paul's face. "Man, you look like shit."

Paul followed Gordon to his office, the only private area in the security complex. As he went in, Gordon dragged a chair to the desk.

"I heard you had a good trip. Rolf called from Dallas. I'm up to date on their side of the operation. Where do you want to start?"

Paul loved Gordon's professionalism: down to business, pleasantries for later. He felt a sudden ringing in his ears and swallowed hard. Gordon smiled.

"You won't clear your ears by compensating." He pointed to a grapefruit-size bulbous dome on the ceiling. "High-frequency chaff. We don't want recordings or any joker with a laser taping our conversations from the jungle."

"I see." Paul's eyes roamed the office, taking in the frugal all-steel furniture, a few books, telephones, and a couple of computers. No papers. Large-scale maps of the region occupied the far wall. Next to the desk, a gun-metal credenza supported three flat screens displaying diagrams and colored dots.

Paul told him about security in Dallas, the AMP's design, and the surface's isolation module to prevent possible contamination. He didn't skip his reasons for accepting the challenge; Paul wanted Gordon to have a clear picture of his motives. When he finished, Gordon's face relaxed, his eyes softer.

"Thanks, man."

"Now what about letting me in on what *you've* been up to?"

Gordon glided one hand over his head. "Shoot."

"The setup. The perimeter fence. Reasons?"

"We're in Africa." The answer came as a papal pronouncement.

"No kidding. I hadn't noticed. What has that got to do with it?"

"Bear with me. We've all kinds around here: buffalo, monkeys, leopards, mongooses, bongos, elephants—"

"You're joking! Elephants in these hills?"

"There's a species of elephant, not too big but dangerous. Anyway, the animals partly justify the fence. So do tribes."

"Same ethnic group?" Paul asked.

"Hell, no. Nilotes and Sudanese from the north. Azande, Mangbetu, Banda, and Barambo in the forest. Not to mention the Mai-Mai, the Interahamwe, and God knows who else."

Gordon swiveled his chair toward the far wall and

pointed to a detailed map of the region with a large white dot and several colored pins peppered over its surface.

"We're the white dot on the map," Paul guessed.

"Right. The pins represent villages or settlements. The locals endure a hard life. Screw the idyllic view of contact with nature. These people do little besides starve."

Gordon pointed at the screen nearest to Paul. "That's the boundary system. A standard electrified fence. We cleared the ground three feet around the perimeter and sprayed it with a conducting varnish to improve operation."

Electrified fences? "Aren't we overdoing it?"

Gordon shook his head. "This country's at war. We switch it off during the day and power it at night."

"Okay, go on."

"The fence has two settings. In the nonlethal mode, the energizer's output is a pulsating DC voltage of ten kilovolts between fence loops: minus five on one loop, plus five on the other. In lethal mode, the phase is reversed and nonpulsing."

"A ten-kilovolt whack?"

"Correct."

"And the razor wire?"

"That's more for show than anything, to mark the boundary. In addition, there are resonating wires running through the fence. They detect attempts to breach it."

No mention of guerrillas or warlords, Paul thought. On the windowpane, a large fly with an iridescent-blue abdomen rubbed its head between its front legs. "Incidents?" Paul asked.

"About fifty every twenty-four hours."

An alarming number, but the security chief's voice sounded dispassionate.

"So far we've not had any problems with the army or armed groups," Gordon said as if reading Paul's mind. "Nothing."

Just as Owen had voiced misgivings about Gécamines' behavior, Gordon sounded edgy about the *absence* of trouble.

"How many security workers?"

"One hundred thirty-seven, counting Michael and me."

Split into eight-hour shifts, it meant over forty security workers on duty at any one time.

"This middle screen tracks site personnel. The dots are color-coded. The number next to the dot identifies the subject."

"How does it work?"

From his desk drawer Gordon produced a small tin. He twisted the lid and eased a bright-red bracelet onto the blotter. "Yours."

The object looked like a solid strip of soft plastic with a Velcro fastener. "Am I supposed to wear it?"

"We're supposed to." Gordon tapped an identical bracelet on his wrist. "White are security personnel." He pointed in quick succession to three sectors on the screen with tightly packed dots. "Security center, sleeping quarters, cafeteria. Pink dots are IMC administrative staff; blue, field workers; green, technical and scientific; and red, executive staff."

"I see." Paul leaned over the table for a closer look. "Who's red-three?"

"Yours truly."

Paul studied twin dots in the same point on the screen. "So," he tapped his bracelet, "this is number one?"

"We wouldn't have it any other way; pecking order."

"Are you after a raise?" Paul asked, grinning.

"Well, now that you mention it..."

"Get lost." Paul stood, picked up a paper cup, and poured himself some coffee from a carafe. He offered the cup to Gordon, who declined. "This circle is the derrick?"

Gordon nodded.

"I imagine red-two is Owen. Who's red-seven?"

After reaching for a remote-control pad, Gordon clicked several buttons. The center screen scrolled, stopping at a live feed from the derrick area. More button-punching zoomed the camera to a close-up shot of Owen and Mark in animated conversation. No sound. Paul made a mental note.

"Mark O'Reilly. And before you ask, red-four is Dr. Mosengwo, red-five is Michael, red-six is—"

"Wow, stop, stop." Paul raised a hand. "You better give me a list."

"I'll do better." Gordon swiveled his chair to face a workstation and stabbed a finger at several points on the screen. "There, you have it on the secure intranet. As soon as you log in, it'll be there."

"What about Internet access?" The question was academic. He'd already guessed the answer.

"No way. If you need to send any mail, use the intranet to send text files and a list of recipients to the security office. We reverse procedure with incoming mail. Plain English, no encryption, no attachments."

"I like it," said Paul, impressed.

"I thought you would."

"And the other screen?"

"Our perimeter scan; we call it our jungle eyes. Heat sensors with mass discrimination. It detects any warm object within a twenty-yard band outside the fence, but only if it has a mass over one hundred ten pounds."

"What happens if it weighs less?"

"The system ignores anything lighter, unless the thing remains static or within a narrow zone for more than thirty seconds. See here? Those four dots have large masses, over five hundred fifty pounds. They're bongos. Two men are already there."

Gordon had mentioned bongos twice already.

Five hundred fifty pounds? A picture of a large pig formed in Paul's mind. "Bongos?"

"A mother of an antelope. Big horns and white stripes."

"What will the men do to them?"

"We don't wage war on bongos. We use a spray that smells of leopard's piss."

"I see."

"Now, here there's a group of small objects, between twenty and forty pounds. Monkeys. Damn pests. They leap over the fence and onto the derrick."

"Why the thirty-second delay?"

"A buffer to avoid overloading the system. There's a lot of rodents. Without the mass discrimination we'd be swamped with alarms."

"What about humans who weigh less than a hundred or so pounds? There are pygmies in Ituri, small-framed."

"Here's where the discrimination helps. Once inside

the detection perimeter, they would have to move all the time to avoid detection."

"Ah. To ambush or use weapons, you need to be still."

"You've got it."

Paul stood and neared the window. "I remember hearing in Dallas that the drill head had to be moved and compensated for by a slightly angled drilling. Is that the reason for the truncated corner? It places the derrick damn close to the fence."

"Couldn't be avoided. Can you see that opening in the jungle? There." Gordon pointed to a clearing and a narrow track.

Paul narrowed his eyes and nodded. Thirty yards away from the fence and over a bare patch of land, a sparse multicolored cloud glinted at intervals under the strong sun.

"What on earth is that?"

"Mocker swallowtail butterflies. We tried everything, but the damn insects wouldn't move. Other than constantly spraying insecticide, nothing would have worked, and a biologist sent by the Congo government would hear nothing of it."

"You tried ultrasounds?"

Gordon nodded. "No joy."

"But that area is bare of vegetation. Who keeps it clear? And the trail?"

"The users have unshakeable rights in these parts."

"Users?"

"Elephants. It's *their* trail."

"You must be joking."

"I'm not. Every time we built the fence, they pulled it down. Eventually, we gave up and moved it back."

Gordon's last words were drowned in a mighty commotion. The cabin vibrated. Through the window, Paul gaped up at an enormous dark-green mass with several blue containers with the IMC logotype dangling from its belly.

"Where'd you get the Skycrane?" Paul asked.

"Ask Owen. He struck a deal with the guys at the Russian embassy and bought two. It makes you sick. We buy American choppers back from the Russians. Sikorsky will turn in his grave."

They followed the machine as it landed on the heliport, dwarfing the men on the ground.

"What about Dr. Shermaine Mosengwo?" Paul asked.

Gordon smiled. "I can tell you Michael's hot for her."

"Michael? You're kidding."

"Nope. And you know what's hilarious about it? She hasn't given him a second glance."

"Serves him right after his never-ending cavorting; still, he must be having a hard time."

"Probably. She's an enigmatic woman, full of surprises and with a perfect background."

"It seems perfection worries you." Paul returned to the table.

"That's Rolf's opinion. I agree. Don't pay any attention to what I say. When you plug into the intranet, read the report. Somebody sanitized her résumé. She studied in Europe and the States; nothing else. Clean as a whistle."

"What about here, in her own country?"

"Shermaine Mosengwo is a high executive at Gécamines with political connections. Untouchable. On a personal level, she's attractive, polite, sometimes arrogant. Doesn't mix with anybody here. She works and locks herself up in her cabin. The most interesting issue about her is her phone. She uses an odd cell phone."

"You said we didn't allow private phones. You mean she has a sat-phone?"

"Nope. Cell phone it is."

Paul stared at Gordon, waiting.

"Her phone works and it shouldn't. It doesn't use any known transponder."

Paul shook his head, not catching Gordon's drift.

"All cell phones work on a given frequency. Everything in the system uses them—repeaters, amplifiers, satellites, and the rest of the cellular network." Gordon nodded toward the window. "There are no repeaters out there."

"All traffic uploads to a satellite transponder. What's curious about that?"

Gordon smiled. "We tagged her phone's frequency, an odd one, much higher than the range blanketed by our suppression setup. She doesn't upload to any communications satellite. Her signals bounce from an odd repeater in the jungle."

"You just said there aren't any repeaters out there."

"Yeah, I know. But this one moves."

"What?"

"We triangulated it a few times in different locations, always in thick jungle. When we made it to the site, we only found trees. No marks, no tracks, no repeater."

Paul leaned back as he pondered the implications of an uncontrolled communications line. "Can't we intercept her calls?"

"Nope. Her cell phone works on a band ten times

higher than the standard. It's a squirt transmitter. Sound familiar?"

Paul thought for a moment. He'd heard Manuel speak about squirt transmitters but didn't know anything about them. He shook his head.

"The device records sound in thirty-second blocks, compresses it, and sends it in a single burst lasting a few microseconds."

"She doesn't communicate in real time?"

"No. First, she talks as long as she wants. Then the contraption goes on, sending pulses. Afterward, when the gizmo receives a pulse, she listens. It took us two weeks to figure that out."

"You can listen to her conversations?"

"We can listen to the pulses, but decompressing and decoding them is impossible. The doctor cares about her privacy."

"That's not what I meant. She must be calling from somewhere—her office, the head..."

"We've bugged her suite to the hilt, pal. She hisses and spits."

"Yes, I've noticed."

"I don't think you have. I mean she doesn't use words. She hisses, spits, clicks, and whistles."

"A code?"

"No idea. Two linguists from Kisangani University ran the tapes and drew a blank. Not an African language or dialect. Same result from home. We tried at half a dozen universities. No dice."

"Interesting," Paul muttered. An untouchable government inspector with secure communications under his own nose. "Gordon, starting tomorrow I'd like a perimeter-incident report and tapes of our mystical doctor's conversations."

Gordon nodded. "Today's reports are already on the mail server. I'll send them to you daily."

"Another issue. How do we communicate with IMC?"

"Coded, hard crypto direct with some boards supplied by the corporation. The setup uses boards in pairs: one in the transmitter and another in the receiver. Can't be hacked."

"What about your communications? Are they secure?"

"As secure as theirs. Our equipment is more sophisticated because we use a hired sat-transponder. IMC runs their satellites with added security. All our communications go through SA headquarters in Dallas. If you want to talk to Paris, for example, the message goes encrypted to Dallas. From there it's routed in the clear to its destination, almost in real time."

"Almost?"

"There's a two-second delay: one on the uplink and another on the downlink."

The coffee was stone-cold. Paul downed the last of it and leaned back. Too many details to absorb. Tight security and drilling according to schedule. The rest could wait. "How are you doing?"

"Couldn't be better. I love it here. I wish we were closer to Kinshasa, but one can't have everything."

Paul caught Gordon's drift but played along. "What's in Kinshasa?"

Gordon grinned. "Ass."

"Jesus, first Michael and now you. Must be the heat." Paul endured the routine of having his hand mauled by Gordon once more. "I need to be accessible. Let me have a pager. Also, install a fiber line from security to my office and between Owen's office and mine. Any problem if I use my own sat-phone?"

"Yeah, it won't work. We have a permanent multifrequency scan. As soon as your phone tries an uplink, our equipment will detect it and screw up the signal. In the first week we sent eight workers home for transgressions."

"And Dr. Mosengwo?"

"Come on, Paul. There's nothing we can do about it. She's government, for God's sake. We're in *their* country with a dicey license. She represents Gécamines. We can't touch her." Gordon propped his feet on the edge of the table. "Let's face it. In this game, there're two sides. We're one and she's the other. Our rules don't apply. She's the heat."

Paul nodded. It had been a stupid thing to say. Their stay hinged on Gécamines' sanction.

"We use radio with encryption codes," Gordon continued, "even if we're buying toilet paper, and short-range talkies on the site. The roof antenna covers two miles. If you need to make private calls, lift your phone and tell the number to the operator. Archaic, but it works."

"Other than Dr. Mosengwo's, there are no phones besides the secure lines here?"

"Right."

"Nobody can call without going through the switchboard?"

"Nope."

An alarm bell sounded in his head. Owen could be clean or could be using plain-language code. "Do you check Owen's traffic thoroughly?"

Gordon's eyes narrowed. "Any reason I *should*?"

Paul bit his lip, considering alternatives. "Let's say I want to check if our reports coincide."

Gordon's frown deepened.

"Let me have his transcripts also."

"Business or personal?"

"Both."

"Anything I should know?"

"Play along, Gordon. It's a hunch."

"You're the boss," Gordon said. He picked up a tablet and pecked at it.

"What am I supposed to do with my phone?"

"Keep it switched off," Gordon answered without interrupting his jotting. "Leave it in your safe."

"Looks like you've got everything covered. Where's the cafeteria? I'm starving."

"Follow the cabins on the left. It's a block between this group and the dormitories."

"Fine. I'll see you later." At the door, Paul turned. "By the way, I'm happy you're here with me."

"Sure, Paul. The feeling's mutual."

As Paul closed Gordon's door, the officer staffing the counter approached with Paul's knapsack. He'd left it in Owen's office. "They brought your bag. Here's your pass, Mr. Reece. Until your face is familiar to everybody, security personnel may ask to see it."

Paul accepted the plastic card and inspected the holograph. In the blurred background he could make out the chopper he flew in from Kisangani.

He checked his watch. *Midday*. Paul eyed the liquid-crystal upper window on the hybrid timepiece: 82. He had worked out that the job would take four months from start to finish. Two-thirds left. In eighty-two days, he would enjoy Carmen again. For an instant, Paul recalled their early-morning and late-night chats. Those would have to end now. He hated crowds.

chapter 12

Paul headed for the cafeteria, then thought better of it and stopped to inspect the office building's layout. There were doors on both sides of open metallic stairs. The one on the left bore no markings. On the right and half hidden by a steel frame was a small plate: *Field Offices IMC*.

Paul stepped around the staircase and opened the unmarked door into a small vestibule with a table and two chairs. Beyond, through an open internal door, Paul spotted Shermaine Mosengwo leaning over a large drawing table, studying some glossy black-and-white photographs. She glanced in his direction, smiled, and walked over.

"Welcome, Mr. Reece. I regret the earlier confusion." She spoke in a low, husky voice, as if sharing deeply emotional secrets. "How could I have been so stupid? You look like your photo, except for the scar. That threw me off." She offered her hand for a short, firm handshake. "Please sit down. May I offer you some coffee?"

She was taller than he remembered. Her eyes were expressive. He could have sworn they were laughing.

"That's the best offer I've heard all morning, Doctor. I was on my way to the cafeteria."

"Shermaine, please. I hate the *Doctor* bit between colleagues."

"No problem, as long as you call me Paul."

"Deal."

Paul laid his knapsack aside and sat in one of the chairs, stealing a glance at Shermaine's retreating figure. As she marched past the drawing table, Paul froze. He could have sworn a tiny hand had sprung from underneath the cluttered table and grabbed at her shoelaces. He chalked it up to a lack of sleep. Seconds later, Shermaine brought two earthenware mugs without handles. He accepted the drink with a nod: strong, aromatic, without sugar.

She rested her mug on the table and sat across from him. After patting her pockets, Shermaine produced a packet of Gauloises. Paul shook his head at the silent offer and dug into a pocket for his own.

"What do you think about the exercise so far?" she asked.

"Normal controlled chaos and larger than I'd imagined. But nothing out of the ordinary."

She nodded, raising the mug to her lips with both hands, like Lupe. Handsome hands with long, slim fingers and short, clear nails, contrasting with the raven skin. Paul thought the handcrafted mug, with its irregular features, matched the supple fingers.

"Will you take over directing the works from Mr. DeHolt?"

Paul did not answer at once. He took a drag on his cigarette, inhaling, mulling over her blunder. Shermaine had not asked how he liked his coffee.

"At IMC we believe in teamwork. This exercise will be run by all the officers in charge, as a group. Mr. DeHolt will continue to direct procedures, although the overall responsibility will be mine. I doubt you'll notice any change."

Shermaine set the mug on the table and stabbed the cigarette butt into an earthenware ashtray. She crossed her hands in front of her knee; her leather boot rose halfway up her leg. The lace was undone. "You know Africa, Mr. — Paul?"

He smiled. "Not really."

"But you have been in the continent several times — Sudan, Burkina Faso, Chad, Zimbabwe, Mali. Yet you don't know Africa?"

"You seem well informed."

"I told you, Gécamines provided me with a résumé of your *career*."

The stress on the last word hinted at other tidbits in the so-called résumé.

"Yes, you did."

"You've still not answered my question."

"A question with many answers. I've been on this continent several times in the past fifteen years. I've done studies, coring, and tests. I've also opened mining sites almost everywhere. I know the history, geography, geology..." He paused to peer into her eyes. "The answer to your question, however, must be no. I don't know Africa. It's hard for a Westerner to steep in the warmth of the earth and understand the currents that join and tear

Africans apart." Paul drank from his mug as he wondered what had prompted him to make such a statement.

"I think you know a lot more about Africa than you admit. I'm surprised."

"Because I'm white?"

"Because you belong to another world. We are in the Third. There are two more, higher up."

"A few years ago I visited Vienna."

"Mmmmm . . . I love Vienna," she said dreamily.

"I had to buy hydraulic props from Holtermann-Krebs. I closed the deal in a few hours instead of days. Had time to kill."

"The Schönbrunn gardens." Shermaine's voice sounded wistful. "I once enjoyed a sinful cup of coffee, topped with fresh cream and sprinkled with cocoa."

"Yeah, waiters in morning coats serving outrageously expensive coffee." He remembered the palace where Sisi and Franz Joseph necked themselves silly—now a tearoom for tourists. "The last evening, as I was having a drink, I heard the city's mayor declare on TV that he hated tourists but loved visitors. I understood what he meant." Paul stared at Shermaine. "You see, I don't know Vienna any more than I know Africa. I've never been a visitor in either place."

"But you've *worked* in Africa. You've had *contact* with men and women. . . ."

"Perhaps, but as a tourist, as a stranger. Infighting is a way of life here. Values are different. How can I understand Africa?"

"You speak in generalities. Infighting? There are men and there are children. The young display behavior at times considered criminal, sadistic, or evil if done by adults. Others are playful. They make mistakes society understands as the normal foolishness of youth. Society sanctions, even encourages it; they think it's part of growing up."

Paul took a drag of his cigarette. He hated lectures and couldn't understand the sudden shift in the conversation.

"The same happens with nations," Shermaine continued. "They all have a right to infancy and adolescence. To hold a child up to the moral standards of an adult, to measure performance according to set standards, is madness. Africa is young, regardless of its geological age."

It sounded like a well-researched speech. Even her breathing was controlled.

"Like all children, Africa is weak, frail, and defenseless. That doesn't mean inferior. On the contrary, perhaps we're the future. In a way, I think your country is jealous of the child and wants to return to childhood. But it's too late. You must start again."

Paul couldn't figure out the uncalled-for pitch of idealism. But two could play at the same game.

"Africa is not a country," he countered as he ground his cigarette into the ashtray, "and certain parts of it are far from defenseless. I don't like the analogy."

Shermaine raised an eyebrow. "You don't like it?"

"No, I don't. You compare a continent, with as much blood on its hands as Africa has, to a child. The idea alone is controversial enough. But to say we should excuse the young? To wave off murder as a folly of youth? Never. Childhood is a place where one's vision is clouded by ignorance or stupid idealism, either of which can be lethal to a nation."

He could swear she had paled.

"True clarity and candor spring from a different source," he continued. "From a personal knowledge of what it is to be a nation. This is something the nations of Africa have had stolen from them by imperial powers. Perhaps African nations are more like orphans subjected to abusive foster parents. Countries here are experiencing the growing pains other nations went through centuries ago, without any guiding hands or any real knowledge of what works and what doesn't."

People often forget North America didn't start from zero. The immigrants had been a motley lot, but many had been born and grown up in monarchies already on the path to democracy. "No country wants to be like the African nations with their never-ending revolutions." Paul smiled. "Don't misunderstand me; a little revolution, now and then, can be healthy. I think America could do with another one now that we've reached a midlife crisis."

A spark crossed Shermaine's eyes. It wasn't anger but merriment. He thought the edges of her lips twitched.

She's egged me on. She wanted to study my reaction. I'll be damned. She's pulling me by my nose ring.

"Enough of my soapbox." Paul tried to cover his tracks with the sinking feeling it was too late. "What I said was impromptu, in haste, driven a lot more by emotion than thought."

"It's unusual that you can think along those lines."

"Because I'm white?" he asked again.

Shermaine shook her head with impatience. "I was referring to your sensibility. Perhaps because you're a man."

Paul leaned back and laughed. "I wonder if you're not

being judgmental about men. Where I'm from, it's called feminism."

It was Shermaine's turn to laugh, displaying the blinding white of her teeth in contrast with the dark luster of her skin. "I live in a world ruled by men incapable of accepting an intellectually superior woman. If you compound it by being black, it can be a threat to their masculinity."

Paul smiled and lit another cigarette. "I'm sorry, Shermaine. My masculinity is still intact despite being with an attractive, intelligent black woman. Give me more time to feel castrated."

Shermaine's nose flared. Then her face broke into a broad smile. "You're pulling my leg."

Paul stood up and collected his knapsack. Despite the thick rubber soles of her boots, he was a good four inches taller when she stood. Paul stepped back to give her room and offered his hand.

"Thanks for the coffee." He enfolded her warm hand for an instant. "I've got to grab something to eat. Page me if you need me." Over her shoulder, he stole a quick glance at the photographs she had been studying on the table.

Damn! It's the probe I'll be using to ride four miles down that tube!

○

Shermaine stood rooted before the door, unsure, unbalanced from the sudden conclusion to the exchange. She replayed their conversation. The report's take was wrong. Paul was still an idealist at heart. Notes in Paul's dossier detailed why he fled IMC, a few lines about the accident and the death of his wife and father, but a bizarre silence cloaked the last two years. What had happened to the man?

She folded three fingers of her right hand, leaving thumb and pinkie outstretched. *Could it be?*

Shermaine collected the photographs, placed them in a portable safe-box with thumbprint lock, and rescued a bright-yellow envelope with Paul Reece's curriculum. She rested it on the table. There it remained unopened. She had committed its contents to memory. Shermaine knelt by the table to fasten her shoelace and caressed tiny fingers reaching through the mesh.

Shivers rushed over her arms and back. *He really did say "the warmth of the earth." I didn't imagine it.* Her skin remembered the sultry, firm touch of his fingers, sensitive and no doubt expert. Heat spread over her loins. Shermaine's eyes popped open, shocked by the response of her body. With an effort, she pushed the warmth away.

If there's a possibility, we must know. Gods, if it were possible! If Paul Reece has come to collect the colors of the rainbow, the circle would close, and it would be perfect.

Shermaine meditated until gentle tugging on her finger brought her back to reality. *"Kooko bya kekhe umu inzala im imulya,"* she whispered. The little monkey was hungry and scared, not used to the strange odor of the white man. From the galley, Shermaine had picked up a few tamarinds, and she now pushed them into the colobus cage. The monkey had learned fast that treats came only as a reward for good behavior and silence. Afterward, she bolted the outer door. Shermaine glanced at the ceiling and the spots with the pin microphones.

Do you need a beacon, Paul Reece? A hand to guide

you? Shermaine narrowed her eyes. *No, you're much too intelligent for that. Perhaps a trail of crumbs.* Sitting back down, she dug a phone from her pocket and hissed, spat, clicked, and whistled with calm concentration for over an hour.

chapter 13

The stocky young man released the backpack's heavy straps and rubbed an arm across his sweaty forehead. He glanced across the moonlight-bathed desert inside Arizona's Barringer Crater. Carefully, he laid his pack on the ground. He stood up, stretching his compact anatomy. Above bulging shoulders, his thick neck fused with the line of his head—a strange optical illusion reinforced by short-cropped hair over a square face with proud cheekbones and slanted eyes.

The ground was hard, almost empty of vegetation: a huge basin, a crater. A millennia-old footprint and mute witness of a colossal meteorite impact.

A tiny movement at the fringe of his vision and a slight sound caught his attention. Chodak stole toward a small bush and parted the low undergrowth to follow the efforts of a beetle pushing its precious ball of dung under the moonlight. *Ateuchus sacer*, the sacred insect of the Egyptians. *Fancy seeing you in Arizona*. The man released the branches, rubbed a hand over the plant, and drew it to his face. *Artemisia tridentata.* Wormwood.

For a long time, he studied the night's clarity and the magical display of a myriad of sparkling stars. Of humanity's inventions, nothing could match the lubricating properties of money, and large amounts of it in particular. A Lear had brought him from Dallas to Winslow in a little over an hour, where he'd collected one of the new tiny-engined compacts for a twenty-mile drive. Access to the Barringer Crater had been forbidden after hordes of New Age initiates attempted to descend its treacherous walls to enact their wishful ceremonies, resulting in sundry damage and broken bones. Tourists had to keep to an esplanade and admire the colossal impact site from above. Knowing he would eventually need to use the crater, Chodak had sold a dubious tale of needing aerial measurements of the crater for his doctorate to a pair of bored-looking guards with shaking heads. A thousand dollars, a vow of discretion, and the promise of a few thousand more had changed the shakes into nods and the frowns into smiles. Weeks later, passing through the closed gates had been a matter of more nods and a bulging envelope.

Chodak hadn't planned to visit the crater more than once, to announce success in Ituri, but Shermaine's call was of sufficient importance to merit the extra trip.

As if returning from a trance, he stood and checked the glowing tritium numerals of his watch. With economy of movement, he unfastened the backpack's buckles and spread its contents on the ground: several large white plastic tubes, packets of a puttylike material, batteries, and cables. He laid a tool pouch and a leather case on the empty backpack.

In a few minutes, Chodak joined the tubes, placing objects and putty packs inside with the batteries. With cable, a pair of pliers, and insulating tape, he made several rudimentary connections, threading thin wires through the assembly.

Finished, he backed up to appraise his work. Before him stood a six-foot-tall model of a Saturn V vehicle, the kind rocket hobbyists flew all over North America. He produced a GPS from the leather case and gathered some readings. Later he trimmed the model, laid the instrument back in its case, searched in his trouser pockets for two plastic boxes, each the size of a cigarette pack, and deposited one on top of the leather case. Toggling a small switch on the second one, he lit a tiny diode. Then he approached the rocket, opened a panel above his head, connected several wires to the box, set the device inside, and closed the section.

Chodak secured the GPS in its case and returned it to the backpack. After threading his arms through the straps, the young man pocketed the other box. On his way toward a rock cliff, he detoured to check the beetle's progress and have another rub at the bush.

A hundred yards from the model, he paused, pulling the box from his pocket. The box had two buttons, a small switch, and a four-digit red display. With a flick of his thumb, Chodak toggled the switch. The screen lit up: 00:00. He checked his watch and sniffed the wormwood's sharp tang on his skin, his eyes on the moving second hand. When the watch showed 01:15, he pressed the left button. The zone around the model lit with a flash. The rocket's white column rose. A few seconds later, only the nozzle's flame was visible.

Chodak stared at the altimeter screen, watching the racing numbers slow as the contraption reached the vertex of its parabolic flight. Then the numbers froze, to race in a fast countdown as the exhausted rocket fell.

As the altimeter neared four thousand feet, he pressed the second button. Seconds later, the model crashed a hundred feet away, with a blinding flare from a phosphorous capsule inside, and burned the wreck to an unrecognizable mass of molten plastic.

It was 1:17 in the morning.

Without haste, Chodak strolled toward the wreck. With a little luck, he should make it back to his apartment in Dallas by five with ample time for a long shower and breakfast before setting off for work at the usual time.

When the polymer mass that once was a model rocket cooled to the touch, he gathered the lump into his rucksack, swung toward the rock wall, and clambered a steep incline toward the security guard's cabin and the parking lot.

○

Three minutes later and thousands of miles away, a tiny man dressed in a saffron-colored tunic took the single sheet of paper a young boy offered him with both hands, his shaved head bowed in reverence. Kunchen reassured the boy, whispering soothing words before sending him back with a soft pressure on his shoulder.

Kunchen mused that huge uplinking antennae were a poor copy of what earth provided free with her old scars.

A feeble signal, broadcasting from the correct height and amplified a billion times by the crater's shape, not only had reached the monastery almost instantly but now raced to the stars. He donned small eyeglasses and stepped to a wall where two thick wax candles radiated soft yellow light into the room.

"Nestor, a signal."

Kunchen glanced toward a tall shape emerging from the shadows. He tried to read hesitation into the slow steps but failed. Nestor neared in silence, his feet encased in soft tabi. "Yet the first bringer of unwelcome news hath but a losing office, and his tongue."

"I doubt Henry the Fourth meant a young monk," Kunchen chuckled. He raised the paper to the light. After a moment's hesitation, he let his hand drop.

Kunchen's eyes roamed the circular room, taking in the Sanskrit crowding all available surfaces. He stopped at the figure by the candles. Nestor, dressed in a black silk tailored suit and turtleneck, remained motionless. Kunchen eyed the smooth features of his elongated face. The color of his skin fused with the dark garments, yet his jet-black eyes captured the monk's attention. Eyes suffused with unbearable sadness. "Yet humble papers can be harbingers of joy." Kunchen offered the document to Nestor.

Three long and tapered fingers, flanked by a pair of thumbs, reached for the message. Kunchen watched, fascinated by the graceful movement of the symmetrical hands.

After reading, Nestor sat by the small dais. He inhaled deeply several times and folded his legs. From the tray next to a small brazier, Nestor selected a small lump of incense, deposited it over incandescent coals, and studied the curlicues of the rising smoke. He sighed, hands on his knees, eyes closed.

After a moment, he opened his eyes. Pure joy sparked in his deep-black irises; his lips moved in a voiceless whisper. His delicate fingers folded into his palm, Nestor brought the thumbs of his hands together to shape a circle.

chapter 14

Towering arc projectors shone over the drilling platform. The flywheel, a massive steel slice, rotated under the machinist's watchful eye. Despite the pelting rain, the machinist's gaze never shifted from the shaft, its white depth marks at times blurred by a never-ending warm-water deluge.

When the last depth mark stood three feet over the platform's surface, he glanced at Mark O'Reilly and hit the clutch. The inertia from 20,000 feet of suspended pipe strained the steel block against its brakes. As a claxon blared, the crew sprang onto the derrick from nearby cabins.

Defying the downpour, roughnecks charged the pipe like swarming insects, bright-yellow wasps dripping water under bright lights. The capstan motor fired, belching a thick plume of smoke from its towering exhaust. A new pipe descended. In a few minutes, the crew adjusted its thread with pipe tongs, wrenches the size of a man, suspended from heavy chains dangling from steel girders overhead. The table moved, rotating sluggishly once more, straining to spin the tubes, gaining speed, while the men trudged back toward the cabins through the sticky mud.

In the control module, Mark followed the operator's hands as he tuned levers and controls, his eyes glued to speed, weight, and torsion indicators. Mark swiveled the ledger, then wrote on the first available line: 05:47, 20,000 ft.

"I'll go tell the men," he said.

The machinist nodded. Mark grabbed a yellow canvas hooded cape before darting outside. When he reached the cabins, sprinting and skidding on the reddish mud, he collided with another cloaked man, who lifted his head and stared. Mark fumed, his hair soaked, water running down his face, the hood now knocked to one side.

"Right of way to the right!" said the familiar voice. "You're not in Ireland!"

Mark scowled as Paul grabbed his arm, marching him into the cabin. "Damn!" Mark complained. "First you attack me, now you shove me around!"

"You wanted to stay holding hands?" Paul pushed his hood back, grabbed a dark-green towel, and threw it to Mark. With another, he wiped his hands and face.

The men ignored them, slumped over in exhaustion, nursing hot coffee mugs in clammy hands. Their faces looked drawn, red-eyed after seven straight hours of the same routine. On the rear wall, two bulbous electric lights flanked a large clock. The first light, orange, flashed a five-minute warning before the drill stopped. The second, red, triggered the horn and sent the men running.

"Guys, we've hit twenty thousand feet," Mark announced. He grabbed their towels and threw them into a plastic bin.

After a few tentative smiles, one of the workers lifted his metal cup without much enthusiasm.

"You Irish don't know how to announce good news," Paul teased. "Everything you say sounds like a funeral. Watch and learn."

"Guys, we've hit twenty thousand feet!"

Mark frowned.

"I've just said that."

"Not like me, you haven't."

Paul opened his raincoat and produced a bottle of whisky from Islay in each hand—exquisite fifteen-year-old Laphroaig.

A salvo of profanities broke out as men jumped over benches, their mugs miraculously empty. Laughing, Paul passed a bottle to Mark, who pulled a generous swig before filling the mugs. The whisky tasted of peat smoke and the water of Lake Nam Ban. Paul followed suit and swallowed a gulp.

"Best breakfast I've had in three months," one of the drillers grumbled before wiping his mouth with the back of his hand.

Mark edged closer to Paul. "How did you know we would reach twenty thousand?"

"I did some rough numbers. The stratum at this depth is homogeneous, but I almost missed it."

He glanced at his bottle, more than three-quarters empty. "I'll take a drink to the machinist. The bum will stop the rig and go home if we leave him out." Paul donned his hooded cape again, waving around as he opened the door.

One of the old hands raised his mug. "He may be rotten with millions, but he's no son of a bitch, that one."

"You're right there, pops." Mark stared into his empty mug. "He's a miner."

chapter 15

"Beer?"

"Make that two." Paul glanced toward the lone figure of Michael Didier hunched over a table at the far corner of the cafeteria.

The steward fished two large cans from an under-the-counter fridge and raised an eyebrow to a pile of plastic glasses. Pleased by Paul's negative, the man panned a wand over the offered bracelet to record the transaction and nodded.

"Drinking alone?"

Michael blinked a few times, like a man groping for misplaced glasses.

"Hi, Paul. I was miles away."

No, you weren't. Paul dragged a folding chair to the tiny table, slid one can across, and pulled the ring from his own.

Paul raised his beer a fraction and took a long pull. Michael was having a rough time. Others, perhaps inured by the stress of hard work in a war-torn nation, may have missed the signs, but he had watched Michael, the inveterate womanizer, suffering a hefty dose of his own medicine.

Several times, he'd spotted the way Michael watched Shermaine. At first Paul thought the lecherous Canadian was up to his old tricks, trying to add another notch to his already plentifully decorated belt, but soon he changed his mind. Michael had changed. His stream of obscene jokes had dried up and he had taken to hanging out alone when he wasn't on duty. In other circumstances, Paul would have thought nothing of it. Michael was a big boy and, in a wicked way, he deserved having his ego mauled by the ebony beauty. But there was another angle to Michael's crush on Shermaine. Paul spent most of his free time with her, and he couldn't fail to notice that Michael had started avoiding him.

"You were drinking alone."

Michael frowned, and the small scar on the left of his mouth twitched. He looked around. The only other guests were two off-duty security guards playing cribbage. The next shift wasn't due for another couple of hours, when the place would teem with workers.

"Obvious, no?"

"Years ago, I spent a few days in China, casing a company for a joint venture. One evening, Xu, my interpreter, asked me to join her family in a seasonal celebration: an autumn gathering when folks get together to dine and welcome the fall first moon."

"It sounds as good an excuse as any to celebrate."

"Right. She drove through a poor quarter of the city, unlit streets lined with high-rise tenement blocks. There were no shops underneath the buildings, just forests of concrete pillars where entrepreneurs had set up bars. They were open on all sides, with scores of plastic-covered tables lit by a few kerosene lamps and the flicker of a TV nobody watched, showing soap operas brimming with medieval bearded nobles and prim-looking courtesans. In China, most people you see sporting a beard are probably actors. As we drove past, I noticed many tables with one man nursing a beer alone. It was such a surreal sight that I asked Xu why so many single men sat by themselves.

"'Tonight is a gathering night,' she explained, 'but, as with almost everything Chinese, there's another side to it. Tonight is also a night for remembering, for missing loved ones, for sadness. These men mourn a love lost or a departed friend. Tonight they drink alone, sharing drink and silence with whomever they miss.'"

"What did you do?"

Paul locked eyes with Michael. It was a personal question.

"I asked her to take me back to my hotel. She didn't argue; turned the car around and said something like, 'I understand, you need to drink alone.'"

"And?"

"In the West we deal with our small or large miseries anytime and anywhere. The concept of setting time aside to take stock of one's life and mourn the ones with whom we've shared days or years has depth. It's cathartic. I emptied the bar in the room of anything alcoholic and cried myself to sleep."

Michael ran a finger around the edge of his beer can.

"Thanks."

"I've remembered that anecdote several times in the

past weeks. At times I am glutted with sensations. Then I get to my room to restock my emptiness, to stretch my nights and fill them fuller and fuller with dreams. I miss my woman."

Michael raised his head and a spark flitted across his dark eyes.

"You know? At times I wonder why most of us try to hide our feelings, as if sensitivity were bad teeth."

Paul's hunch had proved right. Part of Michael's problem was thinking he, the boss, might be having an affair with Shermaine.

"You bastard. . . . Is it so obvious?"

Paul shrugged. "I've been there before; call it déjà vu." He nodded toward the counter. "Your turn to buy, pal."

chapter 16

Morning had won. The rain's drumming on metallic roofs stopped without warning. Paul raised his head, surprised at the unexpected change, and concentrated again on the drilling records. At the present rate, they would reach the capsule in ten to twelve days—a record. They had set up new precision standards for the industry. From a side drawer he took a calculator and punched the keys, amazed at the results. He checked them again and scanned several sheets of paper spread over his desk. With a smile, Paul returned the calculator to the drawer. He joined his hands behind his neck.

This will shave off a couple of days from total drilling time, and the AMP will be here in a week.

He leaned on his desk and slid a finger over the silver picture frame. Each time Paul gazed at Carmen's photograph, it stole his breath. He checked his watch. The window showing the remaining drilling days read *12*. Add perhaps two days to explore the sphere and a few more to wrap things up. *Less than three weeks*, bruja. *In three weeks, I'll be with you again.* : . .

Paul swiveled his chair to reach inside the small safe built into the wall and retrieved an envelope, delivered into his hands by Owen. This envelope, rife with all the *top secret* labels and other paraphernalia reserved for confidential memos, had arrived two weeks earlier in the IMC pouch and contained a single sheet of paper.

Isis Clearance

001

Eyes only

Copy one of one

Preliminary visual report
Sample Isis 0011-SK2F1126
Third layer
Internal face

The complete sample is a core taken from a hollow spherical body and consists of an elastic layer over a rigid one of identical thickness, the latter reinforced with metallic cylindrical elements. The rigid layer is bonded on its upper face to the elastic material. Its lower face (corresponding to the inner surface of the hollow spherical body) is fronted by a third layer, until now undetected.

The material of this layer is an unidentified conglomerate of synthetic resins with a thickness of 1.6 mm and a density 1/200th of the rest of the sample. The structure of this layer is spongiform arranged like an oversize planar fullerene and incorporates other structures with buckyball and buckytube shapes.

Fullerenes:
The fullerenes' structure displays a stable 70°F regardless of the temperature of the rest of the sample without obvious energy source.
Role of this structure and nature of the phenomenon: unknown.

Buckyballs—types #BB1 and #BB2:
BB#1 displays a strong luminescence without local temperature increase or apparent energy source.
BB#2 is highly transparent but shares atomic weight, mass, and other properties with aluminum.
Role of these structures and nature of the phenomena: unknown.

Buckytubes—types #BT1 and #BT2:
BT#1 performs like a superconductor at room temperature.
BT#2, under the transmission electron microscope, displays a compound cylinder/conical shape (one end) much wider than the other. Computer simulation suggests gas molecules may be accelerated by these tubular structures.
Role of these structures and nature of the phenomena: unknown.

Role and nature of the internal third layer: unknown.

Donald Watson
Director, R&D

Underneath, Paul identified Hugh's longhand on the scribbled *Read and destroy.*

After reading the memo, Paul was furious. It was obvious Hugh had known about the third layer and kept it from him. Then he calmed down, studied the memo, and locked it up in his safe. Hugh had chosen to play his cards close to the chest, and Paul couldn't blame him. His grandfather had waited to determine if he could trust him to the full. *But why now?* Obviously, Hugh had decided it was time to show Paul the complete picture. The third layer's existence didn't alter Project Isis. If anything, the structures included in the layer made reaching the sphere even more imperative. *Unknown.* No wonder Hugh had said nothing about the third layer; the structures spelled energy sources. How many people knew besides Hugh and the lab scientists? The rest of the IMC board? Did Owen know? Milford?

The telephone pulled him from his reverie.

"I have Dr. Mosengwo on the line." Matthew's voice sounded out of breath, as usual.

"Put her on."

Almost a full week had passed since he last saw Shermaine. She'd been in Kinshasa until that morning. According to security, she had returned less than thirty minutes before.

"Have a good stay in the civilized world?" Paul greeted.

"Indeed. I've filed my reports. My colleagues are very impressed."

She paused. Paul heard her taking a drag from a cigarette.

"The data looks good. Hmm...I want to speak to you in person. Doing anything now?"

Paul's mind kicked into overdrive. How could the data look good? So far, the formations they were drilling through showed not a trace of uranium. *Would she doctor the reports?* "I was going to the cafeteria," he lied, "but if you're making coffee, I can fly right out the window."

She laughed—the deep feral peal he found so unnerving the first time they met.

"I've coffee ready; much better than the tar they serve at the cafeteria. And, Paul, you've got enough time to use the stairs."

Before her trip they had spoken often, in her office or strolling around the site at dusk. Besides her obvious intelligence, the woman had a phenomenal liberal education. Together they debated many topics and sometimes argued with gusto. They had kept, however, a prudent distance, a barrier neither felt the need to breach. They avoided personal issues, touching on studies or work but never talking about family, friends, or the past.

A few days before, Paul had met with Owen and joined in on a videoconference given by Milford and Lynne during their regular get-together. Initially, Lynne called in Chodak, the dynamics specialist tasked with running the vehicle's simulation, for a progress report. It was delivered with aplomb, listing the minor glitches they had encountered and proposing sound alterations to the probe's design. Once the technical brief was over, Lynne left with Chodak, paving the way for the real reason behind the videoconference: Gécamines. The consensus had been that the Congo government would begin to show suspicion at the lack of telltale material from the drilling. Reports flowed daily to Dallas and, of course, to Shermaine, as Gécamines' on-site representative. *The data looks good?*

Careful not to mix up his papers, Paul collected the documents and locked them in a drawer.

"I'll be at Dr. Mosengwo's office if anyone is looking for me," he told Matthew as he crossed the vestibule.

Paul couldn't hide his surprise when he entered Shermaine's office. She sported light canvas trousers and a colorful T-shirt stamped with *I love bottlenoses* and a pair of cavorting dolphins. Her feet, with squared, manicured nails, were cradled into leather sandals. Three thin gold bands shone on one toe.

"Aren't you out of uniform?" he teased as he took the mug she offered him, racking his brain to fathom why her T-shirt seemed familiar.

Shermaine laughed and sat across from Paul, crossing a leg and swinging her foot.

"I don't think it would be fitting if I went to the ministry in work clothes. They would think I was pushing publicity for IMC."

She held the mug with both hands, as usual, and brought it to her lips, then held it close to her chest. "I have some documents that I must deliver to Leon Kibassa in Shawaiti, a village about forty miles west of here," Shermaine explained, her tone intense. "Leon is a spiritual father of my people, the Kasai, and a good friend of my family. In a way, he was my mentor until I left for Europe. He's a special man, as close as you will ever get to a true spirit of Africa."

Shermaine set the mug down on the table, an enigmatic smile on her lips. "I thought you might like to escort me. If you want to know about Africa, you might find the answers to some questions."

Paul thought about Shermaine's word choice while he

lit a cigarette. *Escort?* He recalled Owen's tale about her fighting skills. "Which answers?"

Her smile widened, but Paul could have sworn her eyes grew cloudy, tumultuous. "It will depend on your questions. I sense you're seeking answers, but I'm not Leon. I can't give them to you. He can." Her voice dropped to a whisper.

Subconsciously, Paul had already accepted her offer.

"Your invitation is tempting and I'm a weak man. When do we leave?"

"If we leave in thirty minutes, we could get there before nightfall and be back tomorrow or the day after at the latest."

Ample time to pack a shirt, but not enough to analyze the implications or discuss at length with the others. Crafty. "Fine," Paul said. "I'll rearrange my work schedule and collect some things. Shall we go by chopper?"

Shermaine dismissed the idea with a shake of her head.

"Shawaiti is in thick jungle; a helicopter couldn't land there. An SUV would be better. There's an acceptable road about a mile and a half from here."

What if he had declined? Would she have gone on her own? Paul doubted it. He stood, sensing the ghostly pull of strings, feeling like a marionette. Paul nodded, his hand already on the door handle. "I'll get the SUV and pick you up in about half an hour."

○

Paul found Owen in his office and entered without knocking. The engineer lifted his head from a pile of papers, admonishing Paul with a finger. "I've been told you didn't miss the twenty-thousand mark. You could have called. By the way, where the hell did you get the Laphroaig?"

"Damn, news flies around here. I've got two bottles left for the day we drill into the outer sphere."

"Even if I have to stay on duty all night, I won't miss it. How's everything?"

Paul sat in a chair and stared at the engineer. "I'm off for a couple of days. A sightseeing tour," he explained matter-of-factly. "I need to disconnect for a while."

"What's there to see in this damn country?"

"Shawaiti, forty miles to the west. I'm going with Shermaine."

Owen leaned back with a worried frown, his eyes inspecting Paul's face. "You're a big boy now, Paul, but I think... It's a huge risk."

Paul nodded. "That was my first reaction, but there's more to it. Her colleagues at Gécamines loved the reports."

"They did?" Owen's frown deepened.

"*Very impressed.* Those were her exact words."

"There's something odd about that woman—her behavior, her damn phone, so many coincidences," mused Owen. "A couple of days in the jungle is no picnic. Gordon will blow a fuse. Security will have ample time to worry about your safety when you're off-site."

"I agree with you, but there's something more in all this. Shermaine wants me to meet someone."

Owen's eyes narrowed. "Who?"

Paul had considered the answer to that particular question on his way to Owen's office. Nothing could be gained by mentioning Leon Kibassa's name, and he might regret it later. In a flash of inspiration, he betted on Owen's scant culture and lied. "A Mr. Kurtz."

"Who's that?"

"No idea. Shermaine has to deliver documents to him. She suggested I escort her." Paul paused to rub his scar. "To tell the truth, it was more than a suggestion. I have a hunch this operation would be in danger if I refused. Personal security has nothing to do with this. She came back this morning from Kinshasa with the invitation arranged in advance."

"Precisely. It could be a trap, a setup for kidnapping. I don't know." Owen's alarm seemed genuine.

"It's got to be something simpler. It may be a courtesy invitation. Anyway, call Gordon. Ask him to join us for a minute."

Owen touched the internal direct telephone pad and spoke in terse tones with the security chief. A few minutes later Gordon sat with them, shaking his head emphatically, as Paul outlined his plans.

"I agree with Owen about the risk. It's too high. You should at least take some men with you as an escort detail."

"I don't think there's any risk involved. I can't explain it, but my gut tells me it's important."

"Your gut or your dick?"

"Gimme a break, Owen, that's got nothing to do with it." He noticed neither man was impressed. "I have a hunch, that's all. Look, if somebody wanted to stop this charade from the African side, they could kill it in a minute. Gécamines could slap a moratorium with whatever excuse and swarm the site with inspectors."

Owen nodded. "You're right there. I've been waiting for flack from the Gécamines crowd for some time now."

"It's obvious they're helping us. At least, *somebody* is."

"Why do you think somebody is giving us a leg up?" Owen asked.

"When I came from Dallas, that was the first issue you pointed out, Owen. Besides, have you guys noticed this country is at war?"

"Paul's right," Gordon commented. "I've been worried sick for ages at the prospect of a guerrilla attack. We fly the choppers daily on a fifty-mile square. It looks as if this part of the forest has inexplicably become a neutral zone."

Paul noticed the shine on Owen's forehead despite the air-conditioning.

"This is the first opportunity we've had to find out what's behind this," Paul added.

Both men remained silent. Was the meeting with Leon Kibassa a personal courtesy from Shermaine Mosengwo or something darker? Yet he loved the idea of spending time away from the site. *Was that all?* Paul smiled as he pictured Carmen. *Yes.*

"Look, Gordon, I've seen a Hummer somewhere tucked away in a shed, and I'd rather drive a tank than one of your crappy military jeeps. Fit tracers and a pulse transmitter. Have we got something like that?"

"If you've already decided, why bring me into this? Why ask what I think?"

Paul's voice took on an edge as he locked eyes with Gordon. "This is important and a risk worth taking."

"Are you pulling rank on him, Paul?" Owen asked softly.

"I don't think that's necessary; after all, I'm not a prisoner here. Am I?"

"No, but you're critical to this operation."

"We'll fit some locators in the car," Gordon said, conceding. "The pager you carry"—he produced one from his own pocket and pointed at a small red key—"has this panic button. Once you press it, it sends out a continual stream of pulses. By triangulation, we can find out where you are. If you get into trouble, use it. At least we can come and pick up the pager."

"You're always so optimistic," Paul said. "Let me have some weapons, just in case. Drop a gun in the glove compartment for show. Something fancy. Then tape one under the driver's seat and another one in a waterproof bag in the spare."

Gordon nodded, fished a small radio from his top pocket, and gave a stream of short instructions to someone named George.

"You could check in every two hours and before you turn in at night. The SUV has a GPS, a Magellan. Are you familiar with it?"

Paul nodded.

"Send your coordinates every time you call. Now, where are you going? At least we can draft an emergency plan and have it ready."

"Shawaiti, forty miles west, toward the Upper Congo."

Owen stepped to a large map and traced with a finger. Paul and Gordon joined him.

"Here it is," Gordon said. "Looks inaccessible by air. More or less six miles from the river and the savanna."

Paul peered at the spot, nose almost touching the map. "I offered to take a chopper to the river. We could have flown and then cut across the jungle, but Shermaine said it was crazy."

"I agree," Gordon said. "Even a short distance can be a nightmare in this jungle. About a mile and a half from the site's south entrance, there's a track to the river. A trail runs parallel to the water and splits in two. The right branch passes within half a mile of Shawaiti."

"I'll have to report this . . . unusual incident to the head office."

Paul froze and stared at Owen. When he spoke, his voice was cold. "You're doing your damnedest to force my hand, Owen. As director of this operation, I could tell you that you're pissing against the wind. I could order Gordon to deny you access to communications. I could order you to write your damn reports *and* place them on top of my desk to await my signature." His voice rose and he crowded into Owen's personal space. "I could bundle you into the next chopper and send you back home."

He looked at the men in turn and forced a blinding smile to his face, pleased at their bewildered expressions. "But I won't do that. Each of us must perform his duty as conscience dictates. No?" He patted Gordon on his shoulder. "Anyway, guys, I'll pick up some things and see you tomorrow or the day after."

Paul hurried to his quarters. He collected a travel kit and a change of clothes, a radio, spare batteries, his hand-held, a towel, and a few packs of cigarettes. When he had everything on top of the table, he stuffed the objects into his leather knapsack.

When he got to the site office, the Hummer was already there. Shermaine waited, holding a canvas carrier.

Paul took her bag and placed it with his own on the rear seat. He glanced toward the upper levels, where Gordon watched, a worried frown spoiling his glow. Owen was nowhere in sight. *You couldn't wait to grab the phone. Is it time to make a play for your thirty pieces of silver?*

chapter 17

The air conditioner kicked in with a slight groaning of the overhead compressor, further circulating air that smelled of mildew.

"Did you get this monster out of a sewer?" Shermaine complained, lowering the window. She had changed into tan slacks and a matching open-necked shirt.

"It's been locked up in a shed for weeks," Paul replied absently, the image of her T-shirt with dolphins hovering at the edge of his consciousness like an old ache.

He slowed down and popped his head out the window to signal the security guard. The man must have been informed; he didn't wait for the SUV to stop before opening the gates.

After clearing the camp's esplanade, they followed ruts left by trucks and heavy gear, deep gouges leading into a living tunnel, the last holdout as the jungle reclaimed the wide swath cut by machinery. The track was clear for a hundred yards, flanked by agbas and irokos, but it soon changed. Vines dangled overhead like green ropes, brushing the Hummer and sounding like lovers' feet struggling for purchase on a tin roof. Paul suppressed a smile. *Why lovers' feet? A thief would produce the same noise.*

The humidity soon became unbearable and they closed the windows again. The air conditioner started to work in earnest. Large drops of water began to fall on the Hummer from condensation and residual raindrops from the night before. The light dimmed. As they cleared a tight bend, darkness swallowed the SUV, wiping away all traces of the mid-morning light.

Paul switched on the headlights and fog lamps, lighting the wisps of water vapor. A thin, vacuous fog rose inside the leafy tunnel, steam tendrils unfolding, regrouping above like a flimsy curtain. "I hope this track will take us somewhere," he said. "Otherwise we'll have to go back in reverse."

Shermaine looked through the windshield. "I would have never believed the trail was so bad. When it opened just a few months ago, the road was wide enough in most places for two trucks to pass."

Colossal trunks, anchored to the soil by a network of raised roots, spread out like inverted pillars in a gothic cathedral. Hungry tubers, searching for the scanty nutrients in the jungle soil, formed a maze of barricades over the narrow path. Paul drove around the largest potholes and lattices of roots.

"Now I understand the source of Conrad's inspiration when he wrote, *The powers of darkness have claimed him for their own,*" he muttered, swerving to avoid a large root.

"That's a lousy quote; Marlow was referring to Kurtz," Shermaine laughed. "Now you know how Stanley must have felt when he crossed this jungle over a century ago, on foot."

"I don't know about that, but when I spoke to Owen and Gordon Turner I mentioned that you were taking me to meet a Mr. Kurtz."

"You're kidding!"

"Nope. That's the first name that came to mind. It seemed fitting at the time."

"What would you have said had either of them been familiar with Conrad?" Shermaine asked.

Paul shrugged, dropping a gear. "I would have made some excuse, I suppose. I could have claimed that I didn't get the name right."

"I knew you wouldn't mention Leon Kibassa's name."

There it was again. The unpleasant sensation of being maneuvered. "Did you?"

"Yes."

"Now I suppose I should ask why. Is that how the script goes?"

"I'm sorry, Paul." Shermaine laid her hand on his arm, exerting gentle pressure. "You're annoyed. I've demanded your trust and been unfair. The answers you seek aren't mine to give. Please, trust me a little longer."

Paul understood Shermaine's language. Trust. It all boiled down to that. He trusted her. It was like a sixth sense. *There's something in the way you hold a coffee mug.* Paul nodded, then looked with increasing apprehension at the canopy, a solid mass of foliage that blocked most of the natural light. In places, where the high cover parted, large herbaceous plants bunched in huge mounds, trying to capture the scant filtered brightness. In other places, where workers had imposed order by clearing small trees and low branches, narrow shafts of equatorial sunlight pierced the gloom. Dense masses of nettles, climbers, vines, and short-lived shrubs invaded the track, making progress grueling.

After an hour's drive in thick jungle, they reached a wider path. Little more than a natural track, it showed few signs of use by animals or vehicles.

Paul stopped the SUV and chuckled. "If we carry on at two miles an hour we may get to the village next week—if we don't get lost first," he added, after doing a 360 to view the surroundings.

Her face serious, Shermaine pointed at the track. "That's the road, there. If we follow it to the right, we'll go straight into Shawaiti. The road's fine."

Paul looked at the mud track. Half-eaten nuts and fruits, some the size of a melon, carpeted the floor.

"Fine?" he asked, raising an eyebrow. "If this is your idea of a good road, what the hell is a bad one like?" He exploded in laughter.

This time Shermaine joined him. "If you stop being dopey and get on with it, we'll be there in no time."

Paul felt a pang of longing. *Dopey*. Carmen's favorite endearment. "Yes, ma'am. In no time at all."

He put the SUV in gear and maneuvered the vehicle between potholes full of mud, tinted dark brown by the tannin of rotting leaves.

"Ituri is the largest forest in the world. You can't expect a freeway to a village with two dozen huts."

"No, ma'am, one cannot expect such a thing," Paul answered meekly.

"You don't want to argue today, do you?" She took a cigarette from her shirt pocket and another from Paul's pack on the dashboard. She lit both and put one between his lips. "A few years ago, we would have had to clear our way with a machete."

"Well, we've only just started. There's still time for that."

Over the noise of the engine and the compressor on the roof, the drone of insects was audible—in particular, the sharp clicks of cicadas. He doused the lights. The sun pierced the canopy often now and lit the road.

After covering only thirty miles in over five hours, the light changed. The day was turning gray. Glimpses of the sky, visible at times through breaks in the canopy, showed a leaden mass of clouds. Coming around a bend, Paul hit the brakes, eyeing with uneasiness a puddle stretching across the width of the track. There was no room to drive around.

"Just what we need," he mumbled. He disengaged the gear, set the hand brake, and got out.

Sweat broke out on his brow and back as he walked toward the water's edge, papyrus leaves sticking to the soles of his boots.

At the edge of the mud hole, Paul found a long branch and broke off a section at the tip. He maneuvered the improvised gauge as near as possible to the water's center, prodding to check the depth. No more than knee-deep. He tried the sides. Fighting off the insects, he returned to the SUV.

"It's not deep," he announced.

Shermaine remained deadpan.

He drove the SUV gingerly into the water, the first gear whining. As the Hummer reached the exact center of the pond, it sank into the mud. The water reached the doorsills. They were stuck.

Shermaine laughed as Paul rocked the gears, trying to get traction, but the vehicle sank deeper. If they opened a door, the Hummer would flood. Water started to seep through the floor.

He opened the window all the way and twisted himself out of the SUV, making full use of the roof grips, then jumped without letting go, noticing the mud's powerful suction on his boots. In water up to his crotch, Paul slogged to the front of the SUV and loosened the winch cable. He heard a splash.

"You don't get to have all the fun," Shermaine said, wading toward him.

Paul smiled, freed the reel, and pulled the steel cable out. "Try to get to that acacia tree over there. But look out for thorns."

Shermaine laughed. "I'm touched by your concern, but I'm a native, remember?"

Leaning forward, she trudged to the edge and climbed out of the water with the help of some vines. Paul came along behind, dragging the cable.

He heard a splatter in the water, as if a stone or a fruit had dropped from a great height. He watched concentric waves spread across the surface, followed at once by another splash and then many others in all directions. Then the invisible sluice gates opened and torrential rain began to fall forcefully with a deafening noise.

Paul slipped, disappearing under the surface. An instant later, paddling like an awkward duck, he made his way to the edge of the sinkhole, still holding the cable. Cursing and dripping mud, he crawled on all fours to where Shermaine was kneeling, shaking with laughter. He thrust the end of the cable at her with mock anger.

"You don't look any better," he shouted. Drenched and muddy, she had lost a sandal, and her bare toes squirmed for purchase in the soft mud. She stood, pulling at the cable with both hands, and wrapped it around the acacia.

Paul waded out to the Hummer. The muddy water boiled under the torrential rain. He toggle the winch and it started to turn painstakingly, the noise of its gears lost in the racket of the deluge.

"Stay clear of the line between the tree and the winch," Paul shouted over the racket.

Shermaine nodded and moved aside.

He climbed on to the hood, watching. With a crack, the cable came out of the water and grew taut. Holding on to the roof, he slid inside, slopping mud everywhere. The Hummer rocked a little as the cable grabbed. He turned the switch. The engine turned over for a few seconds and caught with a deep growl, spitting a cloud of white smoke and water vapor from the flooded tailpipe. The Hummer inched out of the sticky mud, climbing and skidding up the steep bank.

Once out of the water, Paul waited until Shermaine unhooked the cable before leaning over the seat to open the door. Water rushed out, catching Shermaine off guard. She slipped and grabbed the door with both hands, then climbed aboard with all the elegance of a hippo and collapsed on the seat, closing the door. The windows clouded with humidity. Paul reached for his knapsack, produced a towel, and handed it to her. She nodded with relief and rubbed her face.

Shermaine passed the towel back, wet and muddy. Paul grabbed it and wiped himself off, depositing as much mud as he removed. A chirp issued from within the rucksack. Paul riffled for the comm-pad and depressed a key. "Gordon? We're near Shawaiti, but we've stopped for a while, admiring the flora."

He watched Shermaine light a cigarette and apply the ember to a leech attached to her foot.

"We're also looking at the fauna, engaging and cuddlesome as it is. We'll call as soon as we reach the village."

"Checking in with Mother?" Shermaine inquired as she hiked the other trouser leg and inspected her skin for other parasites.

"I'm an important asset to my company. It's normal for them to be uneasy if I decide to take to the jungle and play Tarzan."

She wiggled her toes and put both feet on the seat's edge, circling her legs with her arms. She stared at him. "I understand your team's concern, I really do. But I guarantee that you're in no danger."

She parted her toes and searched between them. "*Niguas*. Larvae of acaridae from the high grasses. They can burrow under your nails or between your toes."

Paul fished his cigarettes from a shirt pocket, inspected the pack, lowered the window a bit, and pushed it out. He rescued a dry pack from the knapsack and lit two.

"Another man, perhaps a lesser character lacking my iron resolve, would fear that armies of bellicose natives are waiting for the rain to end to pounce on us with poisoned arrows. Not me. To tell you the truth, I wouldn't swap this picnic for a luxury cruise, though I would face a charging rhinoceros with a peashooter for a cup of coffee."

"You drink an enormous amount of coffee," she said, resting her head on her knees. "I don't see how you sleep at night."

"I used to get up tired in the morning. Low blood pressure. So this doctor prescribed something that gave me the shakes. Took it only once. When I returned to the clinic, an intern recommended I forgo the pills and drink coffee. Said that's how he survived med school. A wise young man." He winked at Shermaine. "But every cloud has a silver lining. The same doctor told me I'd live to be a hundred. Anyway, I carry some coffee candy for emergencies like this one. Not the same as the real thing, but then, you can't have everything."

Shermaine uncoiled like a cat and smiled, placing a hand on Paul's arm. "Stop, white man. Oh, ye of little faith! You don't think I'd let you die of hypotension in the middle of the Ituri?" She then turned, rummaged through her canvas bag on the rear seat, and came up with a small thermos.

Paul rubbed his palms in delight. "Has anybody told you how lovely you are?"

"Has anybody told you what a materialist pig you are? You only want me for my coffee."

"That's not true, Shermaine. I also love your flask."

Shermaine removed the cap and opened the thermos. The delicious aroma filled the SUV.

They drank, listening to the drone of pouring water. He glanced at Shermaine over the cup's rim. She rubbed her hand on the window to remove the condensation and peered outside. She had repeated the same operation three times already since the rain started.

He eyed her feet and the sharp transition between the glossy ebony of the upper skin and the light tan of her soles. He'd often wondered why the areas between the toes were much paler.

"You like my feet?"

"The different skin tones are interesting."

She wiggled her toes. "One of the gifts of being Negro; we have multicolored appendages."

"Can't you get a tan between your toes?"

Shermaine laughed again. "Probably, but I suppose there's less melanin there."

The rain stopped with the same suddenness as it started. Paul jumped out—and promptly sank ankle-deep in goo.

Shermaine also left the SUV. Suddenly she straightened and stiffened, as if listening to the jungle. She gestured for Paul to switch off the engine, then she stepped through the foliage and disappeared.

Paul thought she might be relieving herself behind a bush. He decided not to follow.

She reappeared a minute later, flashing a wide smile.

"You look like you've found paradise."

"Better than that." She opened the rear door of the Hummer. "I've found a bath."

She took a pouch and a towel from her bag and went back to the shrubs through which she had disappeared before. "Come on! We must get there before the insects."

Paul followed Shermaine into the bush. At the end of the narrow path was a small lagoon with tannin-colored water. A small torrent cascaded down from a stone outcrop, where gray sand and dark-veined rocks made a little beach.

Shermaine stopped on the sand and took off her shirt and trousers, laying them on a stone. Propping herself against a rock, she slipped off once-white panties that were now stained brown with mud. She held them by two fingers, making a face, and dropped them with the other clothes.

Paul gazed at her naked body. She had an incredibly long back, like a figure in an Ingres watercolor, and small, taut breasts. Her body shone with a film of sweat.

"What's the matter, Paul? Never seen a naked woman before?"

Paul shifted his gaze, sat down on a stone, and undid his shoelaces as Shermaine walked to the water, dove in, and swam. From the center of the lagoon, she raised a hand. "Come on in. It's warm and there are no crocodiles."

The murky water was warm and soothing to his sweaty skin. Paul went under, scrubbing his hair and face, then surfaced, blowing and wheezing. He swam a couple of easy strokes toward Shermaine. She was under the fall, the coppery water cascading over her face and shoulders.

"Superb, don't you think?"

Without waiting for an answer, she dove toward her clothes and walked across the sand, dripping water. Shermaine picked a bar of soap from her bag and returned to the waterfall.

"Turn around and I'll wash your hair. It's filthy," she said.

Paul stood somehow, testing the floor with his toes, and sat on a mostly immersed rock. Shermaine squatted behind and lathered his hair. He relaxed and closed his eyes. *Carmen.* She would make him kneel in the shower to wash his hair. A feeble excuse. He teased her about the crafty ruse. Their showers lasted as long as the warm water from the roof tank held out.

Shermaine pushed his head under the waterfall and declared the operation a success. She passed the soap to him. "Your turn. By the way, did you bring other clothes?" she asked.

"I have a T-shirt and some shorts in my bag."

"These will take a long time to dry. Too much moisture in the air. Best we change in the SUV and lay our clothes on the backseat."

As they rested under the sun, Paul eyed her. His eyes lingered at the mound of shiny tight curls between her legs. *Damn, damn, damn!* His heartbeat increased as his adrenaline pumped. Perspiration formed on his forehead. His body had reacted unconsciously, but not his mind. For a fleeting moment, he wished Shermaine could metamorphose into Carmen. His gaze traveled her length without haste, stopping at the high cheekbones and the large eyes that looked at him with a sparkle of mischief.

Shermaine stood, collected her clothes, and walked toward the Hummer. Paul grabbed his gear and followed, eyeing her buttocks as she tiptoed along. At the SUV, Shermaine opened the door and leaned inside. She got her bag and put it on the roof before passing Paul his rucksack. She studied his erection and shook her head. "It looks to me like you've got one hell of a problem today," she teased. She slipped on clean panties, adjusted a pair of shorts, and knotted the tail of a blouse over her stomach.

Paul rummaged inside his bag, hoping the damn thing would go down once he had his clothes on. He dressed with clumsy movements. Shermaine chuckled. As he bent down to adjust the laces of his boot, he froze. The reddish clay on the ground held the imprints of the SUV's tires, his soles, and one of Shermaine's feet. To a side, half hidden by the shadow of a fender, there was another imprint. Paul stared at the sharp contour of a smaller foot, broad, with splayed toes. He felt the hair on the back of his neck stand on end.

○

High in an iroko tree, Jereh eyed the Hummer, following the contour of the land it would have to cross to rejoin the track. No problem there. He glanced at Paul's erection and chuckled. Biko-batà bo, *three-legged man. I wonder how long that condition will last now. You should thank me for the careless footprint. You owe me.*

It hadn't been hard to follow the SUV; they would have made better progress on foot. At times, Jereh had waited for the SUV to negotiate bends and obstacles. He spied a movement among the acacias. Nzambe and Dibenga would be splitting their sides laughing at the sight of *biko-batà bo.*

During his foray on the ground, Jereh had checked the Hummer, substituted the Magellan's processor card, and noticed the weapons. *You don't need guns. Your life is precious.* Yesterday, as they filled the ditch with water from the falls, Nzambe hadn't believed the vehicle would stick in the clay. The young always doubted the elder's wisdom. Jereh sighed and stretched his aching limbs. He would find a suitable place to cross the track and rejoin Nzambe and Dibenga. The road to Shawaiti was clear; Nandi and his men would make sure of that.

○

"Enjoying the jungle?"

Paul snapped out of his trance. Someone, a child perhaps, had been in the Hummer while they bathed.

"I thought I saw something," he said, starting the engine.

"Mmmm?"

"A movement and strange noises." He peered at Shermaine. "There was a child's footprint in the mud."

"Perhaps monkeys. This is their habitat, you know."

Paul nodded and drove the SUV carefully toward the track. After two miles, the road leveled, and Paul risked a higher speed. They cleared a bend and a stretch of river came into view. The scene was breathtaking—an azure river-and-sky mixture. Paul stopped the Hummer and whistled.

"The Aruwimi River," Shermaine announced.

Close to the water, Paul spotted a band of huge, gangly birds.

"Kulokoko," she said.

"They look a little like pterodactyls." Paul selected a gear and revved the engine. The kulokoko screeched and took off in heavy-winged flight.

After negotiating a blind curve, Paul hit the brakes. A medium-size elephant blocked the track ahead.

"Now what?" Paul asked.

"She has priority."

"She?"

"Isn't it obvious?"

Paul searched in vain for telltale signs on the elephant's rear, feeling a little silly. "I see. Actually, no, I don't. Will she move aside?"

"I doubt it, but you can try."

The animal ignored the horn and walked at its own sedate pace until it disappeared into the jungle.

As they meandered back to the river once more, Paul connected the Magellan, noted the coordinates, and got in touch with Gordon. Shermaine checked a small map and guided them toward a road that showed signs of frequent use. They reached the village one hour later, seven hours after leaving the base camp.

chapter 18

Paul maneuvered the SUV between thatched huts toward a clearing flanked by towering irokos. *Must be the town square*, he thought before glancing up. Shermaine was right. A chopper wouldn't have been able to land.

A gaggle of children, some naked, others in tatters that were once trousers or T-shirts, crowded the Hummer. The bravest hung from the rear, climbing the fenders. Others walked to the side, looking on with curiosity. Shermaine pointed to a space between the largest huts abutting the jungle, away from the square.

A spindly man in threadbare shorts peeking out from under a shirt printed with large one-dollar bills rushed over to meet them. He hugged Shermaine and rattled away in Lingala. The kids crowded Paul, staring at his hairy legs, pointing and giggling.

"This is Malu Kilundu, the village leader," Shermaine shouted over the children's din. Malu yelled at them, waving his arms like a windmill. The kids scattered but regrouped a few yards away.

"*Ey, mondele! Bonsoir!*" Malu greeted, offering a large, calloused hand. "Was your trip good?"

Paul smiled. *Mondele*—white man—one of the few Lingala words he knew. "The rain delayed us a bit, but we had a pleasant journey," Paul managed to say in rusty French.

Mosquitoes swarmed like a fine mist around them. Shafts of reddish sunlight lit up swirling beetles and crow-size bats. Moths and cicadas spiraled at the forest's edge. Malu waved his hand to ward off the insects, a futile gesture. "Later, when we light the fire, the mosquitoes will go." He didn't mention the larger insects or the bats. Paul imagined these would keep them company.

Malu took Paul's arm and led him to a spot where tree trunks served as benches. Skillets sizzled with onions, okra, and chunks of fish in palm oil. A trio of women in rainbow robes pounded plantains into mash with carved mallets. Several women tended to a large sitatunga antelope skewered on a steel shaft. Paul figured the carcass weighed a good four hundred pounds. They turned it over the embers, adding aromatic herbs to the fire at intervals, basting the meat with dark juices dripping from the roast and gathered in a trough.

An old woman, her earlobes deformed by gaping holes, offered them large green seeds, like coconuts, the tops knocked off with a machete. Paul inspected the oversize seed. He turned it around in his hands and took a sip of the liquid. It had a sharp taste, sweet, with a hint of acidity. "Should I ask what this is?"

"This," she glanced at her seed, "is Malafu milk."

"Is this a Malafu?"

Shermaine laughed. "No, silly. That's a hollowed-out gourd. The milk is Malafu, made from the sap of several trees with a little vinegar added."

Paul nodded, then glanced toward a large basket piled with blackened monkey carcasses, their eyes and mouths wide open in terror, as if they had been smoked alive. His hunger subsided. He eyed the seed, sighed, and drank, hoping the vaccines he'd endured over the years would hold up.

"How many people live here?" Paul asked Malu, seated at his side.

"It varies, depending on the season. Now we are about a hundred fifty, but most of the men are on the river waiting for the *Ebeya*."

Paul looked at Shermaine.

"The *Colonel Ebeya* is an institution in the Congo. It's a special riverboat. You could call it a river train: six or seven two-story flat-bottomed barges that can carry more than five thousand people at a time—"

"Five thousand? That's the capacity of our largest cruise liners."

"Well, the *Ebeya* is no cruiser," Malu chuckled. "No restaurants, cabins, or bathrooms; only deck passage."

"How long does the trip take?"

"It runs between Kinshasa and Kisangani, over a thousand miles of Congo River, about once a month."

"It doesn't sound like a pleasure craft." A month afloat on the Congo River? On a rusty deck?

"Nobody rides for pleasure. It's a floating market. The people wait on the riverbank and paddle out to it in canoes. They tie on and barter with the merchants on board." Malu pulled from his gourd, a trickle of liquid dribbling down his chin. "For the river people, it's often the only way to get medicines the forest can't provide, rice, and other basic staples in exchange for jungle meat: monkeys, crocodiles, pangolins, palm worms..."

Another villager joined them, a young man with a strange beard of sparse, long hair.

"Before, there were more boats. Onatra, a government agency, ran three ships," the newcomer explained. "Now only the *Ebeya* is left. When it goes—and it will soon because it's old—we will lose our means of communication and barter." He offered his hand. "My name is Wanga-Walek."

"Wanga-Walek is a medical doctor, a rarity here," Shermaine said. "He studied in France and spent several years at a hospital in Kinshasa. He returned to his birthplace here a couple of years ago and stayed. Now he looks after a few villages."

"Practicing medicine without equipment and almost no drugs must be difficult," Paul said, regretting his words when he noticed the man's eyes narrow.

"In a way it's difficult, but in another way more liberating than in Europe or America. We don't have the government breathing down our necks or malpractice suits to worry us. There is nobody to keep us from healing."

Shermaine slapped his arm. "Wanga-Walek, you should be ashamed of yourself!"

"You're right, that was uncalled for." He made a palms-up apologetic gesture. "In a society as poor and fragmented as ours, the Western idea of medicine is senseless. Ever heard the African Lord's Prayer?"

Paul darted a look toward Shermaine, taken aback by the sudden change of subject.

"It begins, 'Our Father, who art in the ghetto—'"

"Leave him alone," Shermaine interrupted. "The way society works is not his fault."

"No, he's right," Paul cut in. "I've been living the last two years in a village in Central America, where the quality of life is superior to that of North American cities, due, among other things, to the style of medicine." Paul dragged his boot on the ground and glanced sideways at Shermaine. *Now you know where I've been the past two years.*

"That's interesting. In what way?" asked Wanga-Walek.

"There's greater emphasis on natural medicine and diet," Paul explained. "Pharmaceuticals are used only as a last resort. Let's face it, a great percentage of illnesses in my country are self-inflicted."

"If you think like that," Wanga-Walek said, "your colleagues must find you a difficult man to work with. Am I right?"

Paul stared at the doctor for an instant. It was difficult to dislike the guy. "More difficult than you could ever imagine, but no complaints or regrets. I've found friends everywhere and don't have any enemies worthy of respect."

"Must you respect your enemies?" Malu asked.

"Yes," Paul answered. "You can despise the idiot and pity the sick or ignorant but never call them enemies. An enemy is an opponent only if he's worthy of respect."

"An interesting idea. I'll mull it over. There must be a chink in it somewhere," Wanga-Walek said.

"The chink is that every day there are fewer people to respect. Potential enemies are becoming harder to come by."

"Now you're being sarcastic, Paul." Shermaine turned her head toward the cooking area.

Paul followed her gaze in time to see one of the women put an armload of something similar to thyme under the roast.

A cloud of aromatic smoke billowed from the embers to spread over the clearing. Malu coughed as he waved his arms to dispel the smoke. "The women will smoke us to death."

Paul laughed, stood, and backed off a few paces.

Several men entered the clearing, carrying armloads of branches and larger pieces of tree trunks. They set the fuel aside and built a complex pyre in the center of the esplanade.

"There'll be singing and dancing in our honor," Shermaine whispered to Paul.

Malu brought a large bucket full of water and bottles of Primus, the local beer. Paul took a pull from the warm bottle and lamented the absence of refrigeration.

Something golf-ball-size smacked into Paul's head. He glanced down and saw a large armored beetle writhing at his feet. A boy with pretzeled legs grabbed it and hobbled away with his prize catch.

As the sun dipped beyond the treetops, the forest voice took on a different tone: the cries and calls of its dwellers becoming more urgent as they jostled for branch space to spend the night. He closed his eyes to breathe the distinctive smell of Africa: pungent sweat of dark skin mixed with the forest's moist breath and the aromatic smoke of hardwoods. It was obvious the villagers had been waiting for them. The roast must have been started in the morning. Paul felt a gentle tug on his strings, the sensation of being a marionette deepening.

Twilight gathered; people started crowding around the perimeter, lying on ground rugs and coarse mats taken from the roofs. A small group of men, trailed by three kids in codpieces, crossed the square with baskets full of fish, clothes, and vegetables. The men disappeared into one of the larger huts while the three kids stopped at a distance, eyeing the group.

"It looks like the *Ebeya* has been by," Malu noted. "Now they will hang the fish to keep flies from ruining them."

Paul did a double take, suddenly realizing the kids were tiny young men. *Pygmies.*

Shermaine stood up with a delighted cry.

"Jereh!"

One of the three pygmies rushed forward, tossing a canvas shoulder bag aside to wrap his arms around Shermaine's waist.

Paul checked Jereh's pleasant face, stopping where the dome of his head was streaked with lighter swaths of skin, reminiscent of the pelt patterns of some felines.

The other two pygmies closed on Shermaine and hugged her as well. For an instant she looked like a proud mother welcoming her children.

"Come, come, you must meet our guest." She turned toward the group by the spit and shooed the pygmies ahead.

"Jereh, this is Paul Reece, and these are Nzambe and Dibenga. Old friends."

Paul awkwardly shook the small men's tiny hands, gazing at Jereh's colorful head. The streaks looked like recent scars.

"To what do we owe the pleasure of your presence in Ituri, Mr. Reece?" Jereh's voice sounded far more sonorous than Paul had expected, and he spoke in flawless French.

"Please, call me Paul. I'm...er," he darted a quick glance sideways, "prospecting with Shermaine."

Jereh smiled and his eyes shone, but he didn't speak, as if waiting for further clarification.

"We're testing a possible source of minerals."

"In Ituri?" Jereh and his pals neared the fallen trunks and sat down after dipping into the water bucket for beers.

Shermaine pulled from her beer and drew a hand to her midriff to stifle a silent burp. "Don't look so shocked, Paul. They live here; it's their home. Imagine someone drilling holes in your backyard."

Paul eyed the pygmies in turn and shrugged. "If we're successful, a uranium source will benefit your country with much-needed income."

"Our country is the forest. When you're done, our sole inheritance will be a scarred earth." Jereh raised a tiny hand to still Shermaine's protest. "I'll shut up."

Malu chuckled. "Our guest must be wondering if

coming here was such a good idea. First Wanga-Walek, and now you."

"Wanga-Walek has mistaken his calling; he should have chosen philosophy. Don't listen to him." Jereh smiled and reached over to grasp Paul's arm. "I suppose you mean well—progress and similar romances—but it doesn't do anything for us. Ah, look at that: a treat." Jereh nodded to a woman nearing with a woven platter with what appeared to be brown nuts, similar to peanuts in the shell.

Dibenga dipped into the fruits and the others followed suit.

Paul took one. Jereh watched him.

He popped it in his mouth, nodded approval, and ate another.

"Keen on palm worms?" Jereh asked. "You're a gourmet."

Damn! I'm eating larvae. "I didn't know they were worms, but they taste good."

"Worms are a luxury, sought after and expensive, in the same league as caviar," Shermaine explained. "These people are too poor to eat such delicacies. They gather palm worms and sell them on the river. Today is a special day because of our arrival."

Dibenga whispered something to Nzambe, and they started laughing in curious high-pitched voices reminiscent of a bird's warble. Jereh rattled away in Lingala, and soon everybody was in stitches.

"Am I missing something?" Paul smiled, feeling a little foolish.

Wanga-Walek popped another worm in his mouth

and gestured to Dibenga. "Our friend here has pointed out that these are supposed to be aphrodisiac."

Paul smiled, reaching for the palm worms. "If that's the case, I better benefit from this therapeutic wonder."

Shermaine choked and sprayed a thin mist of beer as she bent in two, while the pygmies rolled with laughter.

I'm definitely missing something, Paul thought.

On the square, several men sat with percussion instruments, some made from baked clay, others from skins stretched over large gourds. They started a syncopated rhythm, followed by a song much like a spiritual. More voices added complex harmonies.

Shermaine put her hand through Paul's arm and drew closer. "You listen to African music in the States?" she asked.

"I like *any* music, nothing in particular."

"Artists like Tabu Ley, Samaguana, Bella-Bella, or M'Pongo Love have influenced many composers in the West. It's music from the soul. Stirring, isn't it?"

Paul nodded and gazed into her eyes. Carmen's had the same quality—a dark and bottomless pit where a man could fall forever. He sighed.

A cacophony of shrill shouts broke the spell. Beyond the roast, several men struggled with a crocodile, its jaws roped shut. The thrashing black reptile whacked the legs from under one of the men, who fell on his rump. Bystanders roared with laughter. Another man pounded the crocodile's skull with a thick branch until it stopped struggling.

"By the way, where is Mr. Kibassa? I thought we came here to see him."

She pointed to one of the huts slightly off to one side. "Don't worry, he'll come out later. He's probably asleep or meditating. When the time comes, he'll see you."

Paul heard her voice change. A deep respect, something close to reverence, appeared when she spoke of Mr. Kibassa, something that increased his curiosity.

It was dark when the villagers started to file past the roast. They hacked off large pieces with a machete hanging from a rope and carried them away on palm fronds. Shermaine got in line and returned with two portions. In the meantime, Malu brought more beer.

They sat on the ground, their backs propped against huge trunks, and ate the aromatic meat, watching the fire and the shadows playing against the walls of the huts. The music never stopped, even while everybody ate. They sang between bites like a well-rehearsed choir, though Paul suspected most of it was ad-libbed.

As he ate, Paul could not stop thinking about all the little details that somehow failed to fit. Except for Malu, Wanga-Walek, the pygmies, and the children, the villagers showed very little interest in him. He felt an invisible barrier. They knew his name, and they were obviously expecting the visit, although he saw no means of communication. Nobody came near Shermaine, although her face was clearly familiar.

A well-padded and handsome woman stood, wrapped in a colorful tunic where orange splashes swam on a mauve background. She neared the fire. Soon the only sounds were the crackling of burning wood and the hushed jungle noises—insects whining and frogs croaking.

The woman raised her hands, staring at Paul through the flames. She threw her head back. A powerful wail rose from her throat as she closed her eyes. The bongos began a steady beat. The howl softened. The percussion gathered cadence and rhythm as the woman held what seemed a never-ending note. She spun like a dervish, undulating her hands, then slowed as her arms and torso arced toward the fire, drawn by an invisible force. One by one, other women joined the chant.

The hair on Paul's neck and arms stood. He shivered and darted a glance at Shermaine. Her eyes were closed. She breathed in ragged gasps, her face taut, a pained grimace on her face.

The chant continued unabated, each phrase bouncing back between singer and chorus in a never-ending mantra. At intervals, a word changed and the melody rose a semitone, only to drop back in the next cadence.

Paul's legs shook. The strange chant echoed inside his head. He felt disoriented and frightened—until Shermaine's hand found his.

The woman stopped. She gasped as sweat dripped from her face. With eyes shut and arms spread, she mouthed a litany. The choir echoed in a tense crescendo. The bongos stopped.

Shermaine stood without letting go of Paul's hand.

"Leon Kibassa will see you now."

Feeling like a bewildered child, he followed Shermaine to a hut, where a curtain of strings, beads, and shells chimed soft tones in the feeble breeze. Shermaine released his hand and gestured toward the entrance. "He waits."

Surprised, Paul spun around and mouthed a plea, but she shook her head. "I can't come with you." She walked away.

The villagers stood in silence, staring at him with somber faces. To a side, Jereh, flanked by his pals, gave Paul an encouraging nod. He turned, suddenly assailed by an uncanny sensation: His journey to the hut's door in a forsaken African village had started a long time ago.

Paul parted the curtain and lowered his head to enter the hut. Gradually, his eyes adjusted to the dark and he could see coconut matting on the ground. The hut looked empty, except for a brazier casting dim light and a few cushions stacked in a corner.

"Come in, Mr. Reece. Please, sit by me," a voice said in faultless, cultivated English.

Paul squinted, straining for the source of the deep, richly textured voice. He walked toward the rear and stopped, disconcerted. Among the cushions rested a tiny man, no larger than a seven-year-old child, wrinkled, his skin the texture of old bark, his hair and beard a pure white. *Another pygmy.*

Rumbling laughter—by all appearances impossible from such a tiny body—tumbled out of this figure. "Sit down, Mr. Reece." He pointed with a thin hand to the cushions by his side.

The old pygmy watched him intently. He was nude, and Paul noticed to his surprise that his pubic hair was also white. The man followed his gaze and laughed again. "When hair turns white, it does so all over. Did you not know?"

Paul smiled. "I never thought about it, but it seems logical."

"That's the problem with most ideas. They're so obvious we're often surprised by the logic. You seem taken aback, perhaps puzzled?"

"I must confess that I didn't expect a pygmy. I met three nice young men before, but I guessed they were visitors."

"I see. I understand your confusion, but I'm also a visitor here. I live with my people further inland. This village was a satisfactory place to meet you. That's all."

Before Paul could ask another question, the old man added a small piece of wood to the brazier, sending up a stream of sparkles, like ephemeral meteors. "Did you enjoy the song, Mr. Reece?"

Paul leaned back against the thatched wall. He gathered his legs and glanced toward the chirping strings of shells animated by the dancing fire outside. The drums sprang alive again, but nobody sang. He was being appraised—an examination he couldn't afford to fail.

"I didn't understand its meaning, but the performance was moving. I found it unsettling."

"Care to explain?"

"I can't describe it. I shivered, my legs trembled. The voices were...I don't know how to explain it. Special, penetrating."

"Is that all?"

"No. I was also afraid. I felt an inexplicable dread when I listened to the last part."

Leon Kibassa stared at Paul, then nodded in silence and turned to the fire.

"What do you know about the people of Africa?"

Paul didn't understand the question. *What does one ever know about people? What does the onlooker's perception have to do with the reality of others?* "Shermaine asked me the same thing. I know some facts, and I've seen images."

"Ah, facts and images." Leon chuckled. "That's a good place to start."

Paul held his breath as Leon opened his emaciated arms wide, as if priming to take flight.

"In the beginning, nomads and pygmies peopled the jungle," Leon said in a portentous voice that seemed to echo from the hut's walls. "The nomads became villagers. The women shared responsibilities and the means of subsistence. Those who settled along the rivers found that fishing and tending farms on the banks was less trying than living in the jungle. In the end, they formed communities. They trusted pygmies to supply labor and meat. We relied on farmers for salt and tools. Villagers amassed possessions, but the pygmies did not. In time, tribes developed and controlled labor and barter."

"Do you mean the beginning of Africa or the beginning of history?" Paul asked.

Leon drew a tiny hand across his forehead. "Both, Mr. Reece. The beginning is the prehistory of the world, millions of years ago, here in Africa, where everything else started. 'In the beginning was the word,' says an excellent book. We could add that the pygmies were there, right along with it."

Paul tried to remember everything he'd ever learned about anthropology and shook his head.

"You mean pygmies were the first men?"

"Pygmies peopled earth before anyone else, even before the white-skinned chimeras. Those came much later." Leon chuckled. "That song you heard tells the history of this continent and its people. We can speak later of ancient history. Interested in modern Africa and the tribes?"

"I am."

"The savanna empires once imposed their will on the pygmies. Then came the Portuguese, who made slaves of free men and women and pillaged the continent."

"Your people were slaves?"

"No, not us. Too small to be good as slaves. We became witnesses—witnesses to the passage of great civilizations, great nations, and great tyrants. Stalin, Mao, Hitler, Pol Pot...Our people smoked by the fire and tried in vain to understand human stupidity."

"I'm confused," Paul said, his brow furrowed. "Your nation is insignificant in the scheme of civilization. You've not contributed to its development and you're close to being—" Paul bit his tongue.

"Savages?" Leon smiled. His eyes sparkled as if he enjoyed Paul's discomfiture. "It's just a question of perspective, believe me. However, let me tell you about the song." He shifted and scratched his crotch without concern for Western proprieties.

"The last part of the stanza speaks of Terra, the Mother Earth, and Africa, her womb, where pygmies have observed man's collective folly. We've seen nations rip one another apart and rape the earth, fighting for copper, gold, rubber, or diamonds. During that time, we stayed in the heart of the jungle, with no hurry, schools, or banks, with no hospitals or clergy. Our unique customs

236 carlos j. cortes

and respect for life singled us out as guardians of ancient history and humanity's destiny."

"I don't follow you."

"We're not interested in riches or power, so anything entrusted to us is safe." Leon drew nearer and laid a hand on Paul's thigh. "Our language has close to two hundred words for laughing and just one for crying. The words today and tomorrow are the same. There's no word for asylum. We do not understand the concept. That was Terra's song, sung to the mother, performed for you. You are a fortunate man. Few strangers have heard that song and fewer still shared your feelings."

Paul drew up his knees and bent toward the fire. "You brought me here. Why?"

Leon seemed to ponder an instant and chuckled. "For a moment I was tempted to tell you that you came to me, but that would be dishonest. I would be playing with words. I made you come because I wished to know you. Ah!" he said in response to Paul's stare of surprise. "I know your public history and that of your family. I also know about your private life, your small and large miseries. But I wanted to meet the man. I wanted to see who looks at you from the mirror in the mornings. Who draws inside your eyelids at night."

"But why?"

The wait seemed long and the silence thick as Leon laid another piece of wood in the brazier. "Because what you are trying to reach in the entrails of Terra belongs to us. I must decide if you are worthy among your brothers or just a mercenary from your corporation."

Paul remained rigid, the unpleasant chill along his spine spreading through his body. "I don't understand."

"In a few days you will set sail on a dangerous voyage, seeking treasure for your country and your corporation. Among the marvels and astonishing riches hidden in the depths is the legacy of our kin, the birthright of Terra's children. No nation, state, or company has any right to that."

"You know what's down there? How? I don't understand," he stammered.

"Questions often have many answers. And you've posed two. Let's start with the last. How do we know? The legend we've nurtured for thousands of generations speaks of beacons for the birds. Have you noticed that migratory birds travel in straight lines to a point where they veer, as if correcting their flight plan?"

Paul shook his head, more confused than ever. *Beacons for the birds?* "I've never heard of that, but I can't imagine birds changing course over a precise point. It must be over a broad area."

"Indeed it is, but any dowser could pinpoint the exact location with a forked twig or by studying the habits of local fauna." Leon chuckled as if recalling a private joke. "You had to move your carefully triangulated drilling point to a side."

Paul recalled Gordon's security detail, the necessity of moving the drill head over to make room for ... "The butterflies?" Paul pictured the swarm of insects.

Leon nodded. "Yes, butterflies mate over the room, and the elephants keep the area clear of growth."

"What do you mean—the room?"

"The legend is complex, and words may have changed over the millennia, but we've kept one line intact: *At the bird's beacon, a room holds the colors of the rainbow.* So you see, Mr. Reece, to answer your second question, we don't know what is below the surface beyond a room with the colors of the rainbow."

A room with the colors of the rainbow?

"For your corporation, this is about money and power. We're familiar with advanced materials. Any fool can surmise that materials can be analyzed, their formulas copied and processes replicated. Is that what you hope to recover?"

"What do you want from me?"

"It's simple." Leon's eyes seemed to gather all the light from the fire. "From the room—or sphere, if you want—you must rescue our inheritance, the legacy of our forebears: the colors of the rainbow. Then you must share them with your brothers. That's all."

"But..." Not only had they known all the time about the structure but also its shape and contents. The great IMC had been led to do the work for people whose representative was a white-haired pygmy.

"What legacy? How do you know there's a sphere down there? How can I collect colors?"

"Please, Mr. Reece, calm down. The colors will ensure the continuity of the species. That's our inheritance, proof the circle is perfect, proof of Fermat's last theorem and twenty-two others he couldn't even fathom. It's a legacy of men for men."

Leon skewered Paul with an intense gaze.

"I must tell you the greatest tale ever told, one my people know and pass from generation to generation, but I must be certain that you can listen to it. A deaf man cannot hear stories."

A stronger tinkle of the shells drew Paul's gaze to the

entrance. A tall figure in dark clothes blocked the light from the fire outside.

Leon picked up a clay bowl, drank, and offered it to Paul.

"Drink, Mr. Reece. We will test your worth."

"What will happen if I'm found wanting?"

A new voice, soft as gossamer, issued from the entrance. "Then you will die, Mr. Reece."

Paul gazed at the thick, dark liquid in the bowl and then looked into the old man's sorrowful eyes.

"Are you afraid?" Leon asked.

After a slight hesitation, Paul shook his head and drank the contents. The liquid burned his throat, and for a second Paul remembered the *quitapenas* of Colquizate, but only for an instant. The drink tasted of jungle, of moist primal earth, a texture that stuck to the palate, wafted the smell of rain and fresh semen, the smell of life into his nose. He laid the bowl aside and closed his eyes to a tale of wonder and magic.

When Paul opened his eyes, the embers lit the room with strong radiance. Leon Kibassa had grown. He was powerful, with an air of indescribable majesty. A white halo surrounded his head. Paul glanced toward the door, where the light of the fire flitted on the shells' edges. The tall shadow was no longer there.

Suddenly Paul felt overwhelmed by tenderness, an irresistible urge to hold the old man, to feel his own body against Leon's, to enjoy his warmth. With a deep sigh of need, he opened his arms and embraced the pygmy.

The old man stroked Paul's hair. "Welcome home."

part two

sphere

I must go deeper
and even stronger
into my treasure mine
and stint nothing of
time, toil, or torture.

zane grey

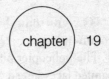

Gordon Turner leaned against the webbing restraints and scanned the tree canopy through powerful binoculars. Nothing moved. He glanced at the other two Sikorsky HX70 choppers holding station over the river and spoke into his headset.

"Okay, guys, we play it by ear. Hold your position. Keep us covered. We're going in."

The helicopter backed off at top speed, skimmed the treetops, and gained height on full power with a deafening commotion. The pilot threw the machine into a hard bank, traced a 180-degree turn to hover over Shawaiti. Clouds of dust billowed in all directions, engulfing the huts, scattering the fire's embers like tracers.

Four ropes snaked through the trees and toward the ground, disappearing into a dust cloud. Like trapeze artists after a performance, armed men clad in combat fatigues rappelled down the lines. Gordon came last and dropped to a crouch, peeled off his leather gloves, and shoved them into his kidney pouch.

"Give us some breathing room!" he yelled into his comm-link.

The helicopter pitched hard and vanished. Men with painted faces spread out to prearranged positions. Gordon stood motionless in the clearing's center, waiting for the dust to settle. *Where's everybody?*

A dead silence hung over the village. Even the jungle, always noisy and lively, was hushed as if an invisible hand had covered every mouth.

The huts wavered through the settling dust. The men readied their weapons, safeties off. They scanned the area for any movement. One by one, they found each other's eyes. The village was deserted.

Gordon spotted the SUV between the largest two huts. The previous day, after bailing out of the chopper by the river and reaching Shawaiti on foot, they had found more than a hundred people; now it was a ghost village. Gordon peered through the SUV's mud-caked window without touching it. He squatted beside the vehicle and ran an expert eye along the underside, taking in the leaves, mud, and grass encrusted on the shock absorbers. Yesterday there had been no trace of the Hummer anywhere.

Still he avoided touching the SUV. He circled it, peering through the front grille and the air-conditioning compressor, then he inspected the winch, fenders, and spare tire. A trembler switch would have triggered already.

One of his men waved toward a hut. Gordon nodded. Stepping on the outside edges of their feet, silent as cats, two soldiers neared the shack with smooth, choreographed movements. They stopped at either side of the door and exchanged glances. One dashed inside at a running crouch while his partner stayed high to cover him in front of the door opening. After a short hesitation, the second soldier followed him into the hut. Gordon marched in after them and stopped dead in his tracks.

Through a round opening in the roof, a feeble ray of morning sun highlighted a tranquil scene. Shermaine, her back propped against the thatched wall, leaned on a cushion, caressing Paul's hair. His head was resting on her lap. Gordon glanced around the hut and gestured for the shocked soldiers to wait outside.

"Paul's asleep," she said. "He drank too much at the party. He'll be fine in a few hours."

"I'll be damned," was all Gordon could say. He removed his cap and scratched his head. He bent, placing two fingers on Paul's neck. His pulse was strong and even.

Gordon swiveled on his heels and abandoned the hut, slapping aside the entrance strings as if poisoned.

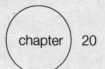

chapter 20

When Paul awoke, Shermaine's was the first face he saw. He lay for a long time, savoring the stillness of the hut, her smell, and the texture of her hand. Paul listened to the rhythm of her breathing, the sound of peace, love, and security—the sounds of life.

Outside, Paul squinted up at the sun, straight overhead. He glanced at three soldiers standing guard under the eaves of another hut, their faces streaked with green, black, and tan lines. He eyed their headsets, cameras, and an array of telltale lumps in their combat fatigues. Paul nodded. He didn't ask what they were doing there; he accepted their presence. Neither did he ask about the villagers. Their absence was natural; they had known *mondele* would soon be arriving in force. Shielding his eyes with one hand, he looked toward the choppers holding station high over the river. Without releasing Shermaine's hand, Paul ambled to the Hummer and turned the ignition. The men dashed to the SUV and piled into the backseat as if it were the last chopper out of Saigon.

The return trip was much faster. Paul drove over the recent tracks. He slowed only when they reached the big mud hole, which he edged around through stands of bamboo. He wished they could stop at the waterfall again, but it wouldn't be the same.

Shermaine lit a cigarette.

Paul saw the puzzled looks of his babysitters through the rearview mirror. He chuckled, maneuvered the SUV back onto the track, and drove in silence toward camp.

He'd accepted the gauntlet Hugh threw at his feet out of curiosity and the challenge to accomplish a record engineering feat, one for the Guinness Book of World Records. But that had been before, when all he knew about was the existence of something "magical," to borrow Milford's word. Later, he dreamed of the impact the wondrous new materials would have for his company, his nation, and mankind. IMC could do much good, and he would have ensured that the products of his exploration propelled his country to global preeminence. Later still, when he found out about the wonders hidden in the third layer, he had realized they might be alternative sources of energy. A miracle to ward off the nightmare of fossil-fuel depletion, and IMC would have no right to keep the source a secret. Shortly after arriving in Ituri, Paul had decided he would never sit at IMC's helm. He would have to give up his life in exchange—a life he wanted to spend with Carmen. But he would have kept control and made damn sure the technology became available to all nations: those who could pay *and* those who couldn't. But these were moot points now.

His mind flew to Leon Kibassa and his tale of

recurring civilizations. In his mind, he replayed the story of a slate periodically erased by cyclic cataclysms, the missing cause in evolution mechanics. Man, almost wiped from the face of the earth, returned to the beginning—a new start, to rise from the ashes like a phoenix. The details, and humanity's only hope of salvation, were buried deep under the surface: in a room holding the colors of the rainbow.

In just a few hours, he had begun his transition from mere mortal to mythological hero. No mundane quests for him, nothing like chasing lost temples full of precious stones. No, that was for Indiana Jones and other adventurers. Tearing the entrails of the earth in search of a patent that would revolutionize the construction industry? No, that was for the scouts of earthly corporations. His quest embodied the crazy essence of myth.

What would you say is humankind's foremost duty?

To help one another? To strive for equality? To respect the environment? Paul had asked in turn.

No, my friend. Leon had joined his hands as if to pray. *Helping one's brothers is a fine endeavor, but teaching would be even finer; men should strive to learn, because the wealth of a society rests in the knowledge and culture of its citizens. Think of China. They lost centuries thinking that they had nothing to learn. Equality, you said, but there will always be inequality among men and, often, discrimination is the seed of eventual destruction. For decades, the superpowers have been scared of Muslims, without realizing that any society excluding the woman— half of the human race—is doomed. Care for the environment is a means, not a goal.* Then Leon had waited until

Paul shook his head. *The human species' foremost task and unshakable duty is survival.*

The sheer surrealism of what he was to attempt left him winded. Ulysses had dragged his men past mermaids, one-eyed giants, and beautiful sorceresses in his quest for the Golden Fleece and fountain of eternal youth. The concept seemed puny compared with his task. A pygmy Wizard of Oz had tasked him to travel not down a yellow brick road but down a metal chute to the bowels of the earth for the colors of the rainbow. He felt a smile tugging at his lips.

Paul kept exchanging looks with Shermaine, but nobody spoke a word the rest of the way back. For a while she rested her hand on his thigh and hummed *"La Golondrina,"* the Mexican rebels' freedom hymn. Paul joined in.

○

They reached the camp at mid-afternoon. Paul noticed the men's puzzled glances, the half-hidden leers, and knowing looks of complicity. By the camp office, he caught sight of Michael Didier and spotted a look of relief in his eyes. Paul had learned many things in Shawaiti. True, Michael was probably glad to witness his safe return. But he'd be even more delighted to learn that Shermaine was softening. Softening toward Michael.

Five minutes later, Paul was in the shower. He squatted, reached into his anus, and forced out a lustrous black sphere no bigger than a walnut. He deposited it on a shelf and stayed in the shower, unconcerned about using up all the hot water.

Fluid life, ever-changing waters, *panta rei*. Everything flows. His life had changed after his time with Leon Kibassa. He had a purpose, a reason. No more improvising; now he had a script to follow.

His heart was heavy with the implications. An evolution was imminent. A tabula rasa for humankind. It was unavoidable; the stars would stop in the heavens. Paul replayed Leon's words.

The colors of the rainbow are a guide for the children of Terra, her heirs, whoever they may be. They must not fall into corrupt hands. The colors are not only here in Ituri. Copies are buried in many places, and some have already been found, their meanings ignored. The outcomes were terrible.

In 1908, in Siberia, an explosion leveled over one thousand square miles of forest. The center of the explosion was easy to determine: The trees fell radially from a single point. There was no crater, just a swamp in the epicenter.

Scientists theorized a comet had exploded in midair. That would justify the lack of a crater but not the circular arrangement of the fallen trees. The disaster was never explained.

Truth is, the Russians clandestinely drilled a shaft to access something they knew nothing about. They also concealed the death of over eight hundred technicians. They could have changed the course of history but for their own greed.

Long before, in 1623 B.C., men also tried to reach for the colors, in Santorini. They weren't ready.

But why the explosions? Paul had asked.

Another safeguard. Whoever removes the colors of the rainbow must know what will happen and work out a way to race the colors to a safe place within a few hours. It can easily be done with a good horse, or better legs.

After toweling off, he picked up the small sphere. Through his mind flashed an image of French convicts on their way to penal servitude on Devil's Island. They, too, carried a *charge*, a metal capsule stuffed with banknotes, inside their rectum. *Take this, my brother, there's life inside,* Leon had said when he gave Paul the container.

Life? Paul had asked.

To a man wasting from a burning fever, a pinch of cinchona bark—the quinine Jesuit fathers kept as their closest-guarded secret to treat malaria—would mean life. In this capsule, there's no cinchona bark, but its contents may be your lifesaver.

He dressed, locked the spherical capsule in his safe, and raced to the administration block, taking the steps two at a time.

Paul greeted Matthew—hands full of documents and face full of anxiety—on his way to the coffee machine and his daily ritual before tackling the pile of papers he'd spotted on his desk.

"You had us worried," Owen said when he showed up at the door of Paul's office.

"I'm sorry."

"Is that it?"

Paul felt a stab of anger but suppressed it. It was natural that Owen expected further details.

"I didn't call at prearranged times. I'm sorry to have given you a headache, but I can't undo anything. I'm sorry," Paul said again. "I'll plow through this right away." He tapped the papers on his desk to ward off any further questions.

"Have you seen the drilling sheets?"

Paul picked up a pile of forms held with paper clips. "I haven't had time to go through the details, but I suppose not much has happened in a single day." *Here we go.*

Owen looked bewildered. "A single day? It's been two full days."

Paul raised his eyebrows without answering. He dropped the papers back on the desk and neared the window, his hands deep in his pockets. Driving back to the drilling site, he had considered possible excuses to justify two days of radio silence. He couldn't tell Owen about his experience with Leon Kibassa or the trip upriver to a pygmy village.

"What day is it today?" Paul asked.

"Sunday. You left on Friday morning. The same night, when we didn't hear from you, we called the radio, but it was disconnected. The Hummer's transmitters showed it moving downriver."

"I was never even *close* to the damn river."

That wasn't true. He had been on the river, with Leon, Shermaine, and Jereh. They all were tipsy and almost crashed the Zodiac pneumatic boat against the reeds twice. At the same time, the SUV's locators flew over the water in an old but fast Vosper river-patrol boat, all the way to Kisangani. No lights. It must have been a hell of a ride and a devil of a skipper.

"There must be something wrong with your gear," Paul added.

"Since we have no helicopters with night-flight competence, we waited until dawn. There was no trace on the river. You're right there. We triangulated the signal to Kisangani. We've been on full alert for two days with the Gécamines people, embassy personnel, and all our spare men following the signal."

"How did you know the signal was moving?"

"Come on, Paul. We used two satellites."

"I'm sorry you went to so much trouble."

"That's not all. Later it moved again, fast. *Real* fast."

"Do you mean airborne?" Paul tried not to smile.

"No, I don't mean *that* fast. That's the weird part. I mean damn fast considering that after bolting down the river, it moved in thick jungle. The signal moved overland the second time we tracked it."

"There ya go. Your equipment is faulty. Nothing can go fast through virgin jungle." Another lie. He thought of the monkeys Jereh and his bunch used as homing pigeons.

"We went to the stinking village twice and didn't find a trace of you or the woman. The villagers said you came and went without stopping. The SUV was nowhere in sight. The rest you know. Before dawn today, the signal reappeared in Shawaiti. Strong. We sent the choppers again, only to find the Hummer nicely parked between two trees and you sleeping in a hut."

"There's nothing mysterious, Owen. We reached Shawaiti. The villagers hid the car because rebel choppers fly over unannounced." Paul gathered speed as he started to deliver his yarn. "I went with a group of young people, somewhere in the jungle, but don't ask me where."

He moved from the window and reached for the coffeepot. He looked at Owen, who nodded.

"We had a hell of a party," Paul continued. "Lots of music and dancing. All I can say is, I'm fine. I haven't suffered any harm."

Owen sipped in silence, obviously miffed.

"Look, Owen, I've been on my own for a long time without having to check in. It slipped my mind. I was on a binge, okay? I can't tell you anything else because I don't remember much."

"And the signal? And the speed?" Owen asked.

"Don't know."

"We thought you were lost or abducted or being held for ransom. We've been pestering the Congo government, the embassy, the state department, even the army, to say nothing of the commotion in Dallas. Your grandfather was beginning to think IMC would have no Reece to be bequeathed to."

"I understand. As for the transmitter"—he lied with aplomb—"perhaps some circuit glitch was at fault. We weren't driving on the river or in Kisangani, at least not that I can remember."

Paul was now certain that Owen had nothing tangible to throw at him.

"How's the drilling?" Paul asked, to change the subject.

"We're at twenty-two thousand, and if it weren't for the time wasted pumping mud, we'd already be at the target."

Paul opened a drawer and drew out a folder, which he placed on the table. It contained calculations he'd finished before leaving for Shawaiti.

"I wanted to talk to you about this the other day, but we didn't have time. If I remember right, the photographs indicate the structure consists of two concentric spheres."

"Well, that's as much as we could make out from the film," said Owen.

"The measurements"—Paul pointed at the diagram on the paper—"are more or less one hundred fifty feet for the outer sphere and thirty for the inner one, with walls about twelve inches thick. It's logical to assume the outer shell is for protection and the support network, with the neoprene to absorb shocks."

"What are you driving at?"

"Bear with me," Paul said as he refilled their mugs. "If the inner sphere is hollow, access could be anywhere—a door or opening of some kind, on one of the sides, or even underneath. The photographs don't show anything on top of the inner sphere. The supports are sixty feet long, and that's the distance between the spheres at any given point."

Owen listened in silence.

"We've had to pull out the mud to remove material dislodged by the drilling bit, but that's no longer necessary. I don't think we need to pump out any more mud, since we're within five hundred feet of the upper sphere. When we drill into the structure, the slurry will run down into the bottom inner surface of the outer shell and settle there. There's enough room for the whole job's mess before reaching the inner sphere. We can drill at twice the rate now."

He riffled through the file for a sheet of calculations, aware that he was treading on thin ice. He now knew that the outer sphere was there only to protect and support the inner one and that the faint image on the film's background was real. There *was* a door into the core. *There's a door into the room, and two keys guard the colors of the rainbow: body and mind,* Leon Kibassa had told him.

"Originally we planned on reaching the outer sphere in a week. Now we can be there in, say four days. If the concrete is not harder than the coring sample, we can pierce the shell in two to three days. That's at least two days early. We can schedule the descent a week from now."

Owen didn't look happy. "You might be right, but I don't know if we should bring the date forward."

Paul's face remained stony, but a shiver ran along his spine. "Any reason in particular?" He collected his papers and returned the file to the drawer.

"Of course not," Owen answered, with too much denial. "But access might be more difficult."

"In what way? If there's access, it can't be on the underside of the outer shell."

"That's obvious, but we're working on a precise schedule; maybe the equipment..." Owen wrung his hands.

"When does the Autonomous Manned Probe arrive?" Paul asked.

"It's already on its way." Owen checked his watch. "It should be in Kisangani already. We should be able to load it on the Skycrane right away."

"Great! Then we have no problem. I'll tell Mark to go ahead with my plan and bring the schedule forward by two days. I imagine the head office will be happy about that."

Owen stood, stoic, with a patently false half smile. "Fine, we'll do as you say. I'll speak with Milford in Dallas to tell him the good news."

With a hand on the doorknob, Owen stopped and

turned around. His eyes roamed the office. Owen sniffed the air and stared at the empty ashtray. "Say, are you not smoking?"

"Nope, I quit," Paul answered without looking at him.

"Just like that? From two packs a day to cold turkey?"

"Yup." Paul moved over some papers and leaned back in his chair. "People quit smoking all the time. Filthy habit, really." He smiled inwardly at Owen's perplexity.

"Well, I'll be damned," Owen mumbled as he left Paul's office.

As soon as Owen left, Paul punched the communications pad. "Gordon, listen carefully. In a minute Owen will make a phone call. I want to know the number, and I don't want anyone to know about it. Can you do it?"

There was hesitation at the other end. "Without telling the company?" Gordon finally responded.

"Without telling *anyone*."

Another pause.

"Of course, Paul. You're the boss."

"When you have it, come to my office."

The only unknown in the equation was who to trust. In Colquizate he would know; he could trust most people there. Here? That was another matter. He couldn't afford a mistake.

○

A rap on the door pulled Paul away from the sunset he was enjoying from his office window. Gordon laid a sheet of paper on Paul's desk and, without a word, sat down.

Paul picked it up and unfolded it, peering at the unfamiliar numbers from an exchange that was not for Dallas.

"Recognize it?" Gordon asked in a guarded tone.

"No. You?"

Gordon shuffled his feet underneath the chair. "It's a number in Virginia. I tracked the exchange to Langley."

"How did you do that?" Paul asked as he took a seat facing Gordon.

"I called in a favor. Nothing to do with SA. First Owen called Milford's cell. It was out of range. Almost at once, he dialed that number."

Paul felt as if a heavy load had been lifted off his shoulders. "Good thinking."

"What the hell's going on, Paul? What's Owen doing talking to the CIA?"

"All I know is it affects this operation. Maybe the government wants to keep tabs on us, but it may go much further."

"How *much* further?"

"We may be doing the dirty work for someone else."

"The government?"

"Perhaps, though I wouldn't discard any other theory."

Gordon frowned. "This is the first time anybody's called this number. I have the list in my computer. I'm positive about that."

"Perhaps because up to now there's been no need. There's been a schedule change. I moved up the descent by forty-eight hours. Looks like it's important enough for Owen to risk making that call."

"If you're right, it means that up to now he hasn't needed to make direct contact. The people he's talking to must have other means of knowing what's happening here."

Gordon was nervous, his security detail clearly in jeopardy.

"When you outlined the security measures to me, you said that all the operational details were being channeled through a single conduit: from Security Associates to IMC. It's logical to presume the source of information is there."

"You think SA could be feeding information about this operation to the government?"

"It's a possibility," Paul conceded. "A possibility you must have considered also. Of course, it may be someone from IMC's top brass."

"What should we do?"

"*Do?* There's nothing to do, because we're not supposed to know what's going on. I imagine Owen doesn't know that his telephone and mine not only go through the switchboard but are monitored. There's no reason he would suspect his call was traced."

"How did you know the telephones were monitored?"

"I didn't, but if I had designed the setup I would have never left that big a hole in it."

"Which brings us to the doctor and her mysterious cell phone."

"No, Gordon, she has nothing to do with this. If there are two sides in this, she's on ours. You can rule her out."

Gordon seemed surprised. "You sure about that?"

"I am," Paul replied at once. "My life rides on it. Don't ask me questions I can't answer yet, but forget about Shermaine. She's out of it."

Gordon nodded. "Fine. Now what?"

"Make sure you always carry a weapon and see to it

that Didier does the same." He thought for a moment. "Don't tell the men about this. Carry on as usual."

"How do you know you can trust Michael and me?"

Paul remembered Shermaine's words. *Gordon is a good man, and Michael — he's beginning to come around in a whole new way.*

"Someone I trust told me you two were with the good guys."

"Oh, really? Who's ratting on us?"

"When you contact SA, limit the report to the day's activities." Paul ignored Gordon's question. "Skip over the call and this conversation."

"You know the Hummer had been tampered with?"

"Yes, and that makes two of us. Let's leave it at that. When the AMP gets here, I want around-the-clock security with everything we have. Tight, Gordon. *Really* tight. And it wouldn't be a bad idea to keep the Hummer tanked up and with a stack of hardware as close as possible to an exit."

Gordon raised an eyebrow but said nothing as he left the office.

○

I envy your wisdom, Paul had said.

Leon shook with laughter. *My brother, wisdom is one of the dubious perks of old age. The more sand has escaped from the hourglass of our life, the clearer we should see through it.*

Paul hadn't replied, but Leon seemed to read his thoughts. *You've repressed the urge to mention, out of respect, that I've pilfered the quote from Machiavelli, the*

Renaissance diplomat, political philosopher, and poet.
Thank you, but don't be disturbed, my friend. To drink the
wisdom of others is the essence of learning. Although, you
must never forget wisdom is not necessarily a good thing if
used badly. Take Machiavelli. He wrote much wisdom,
later used by friend and foe alike. Politicians the world over
adopted one of the master's teachings: "Men are so simple
and so much inclined to obey immediate needs that a de-
ceiver will never lack victims for his deceptions." And so did
the mob: "Men should be either treated generously or de-
stroyed, because they take revenge for slight injuries—for
heavy ones they cannot."

Which is your favorite? Paul had asked.

A difficult choice, but perhaps: "The wise man does at
once what the fool does finally."

○

Paul found Shermaine bent over some papers. She raised
her head as Paul stepped in. "Don't tell me you're already
here begging for my coffee."

Paul shook his head and took Shermaine's hard hat
from a hook on the wall. "Let's go to the drilling rig and
have a look around."

They slipped by the cabin side, passed two laborers
snatching a quick drag on a reefer, and continued toward
the drilling zone.

In a low voice, Paul described the recent events affect-
ing the project. He stopped in the middle of the clearing
and nodded at the mountain of drilling rubble, for the
benefit of anyone watching.

"The AMP is in Kisangani and the Skycrane is already

there. They'll try to ground it or delay the loading. We can't let that happen."

Shermaine traced a line with her boot's toe. "We won't."

○

A gentle crush of gravel underfoot snapped Paul from his reverie. He turned to see Gordon's approaching figure clad in his sempiternal desert-rat regalia, a six-pack of beers dangling from one hand.

"I've been watching you for a while from my office. You were miles away. Thousands, millions?"

"You could say that."

Gordon pressed an icy beer can against Paul's bare arm. "Well, it's time you come back."

They drank in silence, staring at the jungle darkness beyond the electrified fence.

"What about you?"

Gordon rubbed the sole of his boot on a clump of grass, as if trying to dislodge something unpleasant. "Renee and I divorced six months ago."

"I would say I'm sorry, but that's a cliché. What about your daughters?"

"Sondra and Marianne now live with their mother and new father, a car mechanic with a thriving local garage."

Paul didn't say anything. He tossed the empty can into a bin and waited to give his friend room.

"The weirdest thing about it is I don't hate him," Gordon said in a low voice. "He'll give my girls what they need most—a father with a steady, simple job and lots of time for the family. Just what I couldn't manage, or perhaps I never tried hard enough."

Paul relaxed with the drone of the derrick engines. "Déjà vu," he muttered.

"Why?"

"I never had any kids, but my marriage went sour for similar reasons. I was never home. And now...I've left my woman alone, again."

"You know what they say about humans."

"What?"

"We're the only animals capable of stumbling twice on the same stone."

"Have you ever wondered if it's worth it?"

"I can't answer that question. Look at them." Gordon gestured toward the derrick and the yellow-clad roustabouts. "They spend a few days at home between jobs. Good providers, no doubt about that, but most people need love and company more than money."

Paul reached for another beer, pulled the ring, and blew the froth before taking a long pull.

"Are you sure about dropping down that hole after Owen's call?"

"I have to do it."

"Have to? Come on! For your grandfather? For the company? You could walk out and let another crazy bastard pull the stunt."

"No, I can't." Paul reached for Gordon's arm and pressed to still his rejoinder. "I can't explain, because the information is not mine to give, but I'm going down that shaft if it's the last thing I do."

"What the fuck is down that hole?"

"Would you believe me if I said the colors of the rainbow?"

"Shit, man! What did they give you in that village? Acid?"

"No, Gordon, they gave me a reason."

Gordon didn't say anything for a long time. Then he nodded, tugged on Paul's arm, and started walking toward the dormitories. "To live?"

"You got it."

Silence. When they reached the cabins, Gordon ran a hand over the dome of his head and inspected the empty plastic ribbon that once held beer cans.

"I always suspected you were a lucky bastard."

chapter 21

Aaron Greenberg was late. Dario Hindman cast a sidelong glance at CIA Director Foust, who drummed his fingers on the table's polished surface. In the cafeteria an hour before, Greenberg hadn't hinted at any problem. The meeting had been slated for 08:00 on floor seven, in one of the smaller workrooms, a light-wood-paneled enclosure with none of the recording paraphernalia embedded in the main meeting suite. Fawn-colored vertical blinds covered an oversize window, translucent strips hinting at a blazing sun behind. *Another deception.* Hindman knew the walls were lead-lined foot-thick concrete, clad with a platinum mesh to prevent eavesdropping. The window was a prop, the sun an illusion recreated with artificial light sources.

Director Foust checked his watch again. His teeth clenched.

Hindman didn't offer a comment. Could be bad news. He tried to relax by bunching his toes.

A few tense minutes later, the doorknob twisted.

Greenberg rushed into the room, steadying his eyeglasses. "Sorry I'm late," he muttered. He walked over to lay a yellow folder and a tablet on the tabletop before taking a seat.

"Well, now that Mr. Greenberg has privileged us with his presence, we can start," Foust said. "Hindman?"

Hindman glanced at Greenberg before opening his leather portfolio. Perhaps his delay had nothing to do with today's agenda.

"At the close of yesterday's meeting," Hindman began, "Paul Reece was still missing. They were chasing him all over the Congo. According to the latest data, he's shown up alive and well at a village forty miles west of the camp, after a two-day jag with the notorious doctor. No explanations given. This was at 04:30 UTC. It seems the wonder boy needed some fun—"

"Let me see the file."

Hindman pecked at his tablet, transferring a copy of the file to Foust's.

"No explanations?" Director Foust asked, running a finger over the shiny screen.

Hindman shrugged. "The explanation is that he has no explanation. He went to a neighboring village with some new pals, got himself juiced up, and slept it off with Dr. Mosengwo. Claims not to remember much more than that."

Foust finished scrolling the text and then leaned forward, his reading glasses sliding toward the tip of his nose. "He didn't offer any account of the SUV wandering at high speed down the river and through the jungle?"

"Nope. A glitch with tracking equipment is what he

suggested. He swears the Hummer didn't move from Shawaiti."

"Can he be right?"

Hindman glanced at Foust with a sinking feeling. The agency director could be naive at times. He shook his head. "No, sir, he can't be right. We triangulated the locator's signal and tracked it for over twelve straight hours. The signal traveled down the river *and* through thick jungle. The speed peaked at thirty miles an hour, with short bursts even faster. The locator would stop, speed up to thirty or more miles an hour, stop, and start again. Often this was repeated several times in the interval of one minute. Inexplicable. No SUV can do that."

"Thirty miles isn't much speed. There are tracks, clearings…"

"Not there, sir. We checked with reliable large-scale maps, superimposed on satellite takes. We're talking about thick virgin jungle. No tracks. No trails. You couldn't walk six paces without a machete, much less barrel a two-ton Hummer through the environment."

"We've already argued the case," added Greenberg. "It's impossible."

"I believe those were Paul Reece's exact words," said Hindman. "Still, we're calibrating equipment and running over the tapes. I suppose we'll have more data before the day is over."

Greenberg nodded. "It seems as if my hunch wasn't off target. Reece is playing a game of his own invention, and we don't know the rules. So far we know nothing of the mysterious Mr. Kurtz he was supposed to meet."

"Say again?" Hindman requested, staring at Greenberg.

"According to our contact, Paul Reece traveled to Shawaiti to meet a Mr. Kurtz."

"Reece has a wicked sense of humor," Hindman said with a smile.

"Care to elaborate?" Foust asked, peering at him over his specs.

"Sir, Mr. Kurtz is a character from a famous novel set in the Congo. It's hard to believe there's someone with the same name living in the middle of the jungle." Hindman pecked at his pad. "Coppola adapted the novel for the script of *Apocalypse Now*. I'll run a trace through our Congo station, but I'm sure they'll agree."

"I see. Carry on."

No, you don't see at all. "On the other hand," Hindman said, "drilling continues according to schedule. The AMP and the technical personnel from IMC will arrive on-site later today. According to the analysis, the descent is slated for the eighteenth, five days from now."

"Your information's obsolete," Greenberg said, drawing a paper from the file and placing it on top. "Mr. Reece pulled a rabbit out of his hat with a technical maneuver. According to this message, decoded fewer than fifteen minutes ago, the descent has been brought forward two full days."

"Can they do it?" Foust asked.

"Technically, yes. Reece has advanced a procedure the technical team overlooked. He must have had the change in mind before he disappeared; he hasn't had time to weigh the calculations and contingencies since he's been back."

"Where does this leave us?"

Hindman cringed at the overtones in Foust's voice. The operation was becoming more complicated by the minute with small, seemingly unconnected issues. Paul could have known before setting off, in which case he didn't confide in the on-site team or head office, meaning he trusted no one. He could have worked it out during his trip, an unlikely assumption if the binge caper was true. Of course, there was another possibility: Someone else could have suggested it to him. This alternative wasn't worrying; it was downright frightening. It meant another party knew what was cooking in Ituri. Anyway, Paul had chosen the moment with care; he'd fired a broadside when it could do the greatest damage.

"Mr. Hindman?"

The director's voice pulled him from his thoughts.

"We can attempt to delay the AMP and technical personnel at Kisangani airport when they try to clear customs and immigration." Hindman hated it. He was playing his trumps, the cards he always liked to save as backup. *Now I have only an ace left. Well, that's not true. I have another two aces but in side suits I can't play in this trick.* "Our people are in place and we can force a forty-eight-hour delay. I'll send a signal as soon as we finish here. Our man is already in Goma, coordinating air-transport troops and the ground group across the river with General Kalundo." Hindman paused. At least Kalundo was reliable. The fat Ugandan would sell his mother for loose change, but he had his eye on southern Sudan and the vast mineral fields below its surface—a yearning also shared by the CIA. Fortunately, he couldn't hit Sudan without help. Both the Russian and the Chinese had already turned him down, and beggars couldn't be choosers. Kalundo would play along because he couldn't do anything else. "We're not going to hit the camp from the air alone. Too risky. The assault on the installations must be a coordinated effort to include a ground column and the chopper group."

"Why ground troops? Wouldn't an all-airborne attack be more efficient?" the director asked.

Hindman glanced at Greenberg and nodded.

"We discussed the issue," Greenberg said. "Our problem is the security detail. These guys are pros and armed to the teeth." He scrolled down his screen. "I have a list of their weapons. The men pack Heckler and Koch OICW M29s, capable of firing high-explosive twenty-millimeter air-bursting ammunition."

Director Foust raised his eyebrows. "What are these guys doing with state-of-the-art gear? They plan to start a war?"

"No." Hindman said. "They're betting to win if one starts. Funds were no object when they designed this operation. The security bosses made damn sure the men had the best money could buy. I mean, the modular fire-control system of these beauties will determine position and distance before locking onto the target with day or night optics and communicate the data to the ammunition-fuzzing electronics."

"What's the use of that?"

"The target can't hide. The shooter aims. The carbine corrects and sends the projectile overhead, exploding it right over the objective."

"How nice," Foust said.

"Yes, but that's not the real fix. These guys have Spike shoulder-held missile systems, Russian RG-8s six-barrel grenade launchers, and sundry goodies from rocket-backed RPGs to personal ballistic shields."

"Security guards on duty with RPGs?"

"Of course not. All their heavy gear is stored in four purpose-made cabins. Ground troops would neutralize these before the choppers arrived. At least, that was the original plan."

Hindman's ears perked up. *Would neutralize? Was the original plan?* Greenberg must have concocted in the past fifteen minutes whatever new idea he had on his mind. The original plan called for ground troops—perhaps two hundred soldiers, or warriors, or whatever Kalundo could put together—to hit the camp just before the choppers flew in and zero in on the stores where the security company housed their serious gear. *Access denial* was the euphemism Greenberg used when thrashing out the plan, removing the security detail's teeth to render them manageable.

"What happens now?"

"We can't hinge the success of the mission on the ground troops."

A mild and puzzled smile crossed Foust's face. "I've just voiced doubts about ground troops and Hindman insisted they were necessary. Now you say even those won't be enough? We're securing a drilling camp, not toppling the Congolese government."

Greenberg nodded. "I'm sorry, sir. I agree with Hindman. Reducing the fire capacity of IMC's security is essential for an airborne raid to succeed. What I question now is our ability to move ground troops in place after reducing their deployment time almost in half."

Foust leaned back and narrowed his eyes.

"Go on."

"I propose we ask Kalundo to outfit his guerrilla fighters in Congo army uniforms. To fire on government troops would be an act of war, and the security guards are IMC employees. If someone from the corporation's top brass warned them of the arrival of government troops— say for their protection against an impending guerrilla attack—it's reasonable to assume they would obey an order to keep away from the artillery."

"Would Paul Reece give such an order? He's the boss."

"Not if he's already on his way down."

A charged silence fell.

"We could do with additional time, but I'm sure we can repaint the choppers with Congo air force insignia and find uniforms in three days."

Hindman had been following the exchange. *This will be touch and go,* he thought. Precision planning in Africa would be madness. If IMC managed to bring the descent forward two days, there would be no time for accidents; everything would have to run like clockwork. He suppressed an internal shudder. The vehicle and the technicians had to be delayed at all costs.

"What about General Kalundo?"

"He'll play ball, though it's frightening to see the shopping list he's demanding in return." Greenberg slid some sheets across the table toward Foust.

The CIA director swore under his breath as he browsed the lists. "What does that son of a bitch want with all this hardware? To invade China?"

"He knows we need him and he's got us by the balls."

"How many people has IMC got in place?"

"Besides drilling personnel—who are unimportant,

because they'll be repatriated as soon as the sphere is breached—there are about one hundred forty security operatives."

"How many rebels do you need in the choppers?" Foust asked.

"Around two hundred."

"So many?"

This is it, Hindman thought. *I will spell out what this is all about so there is no misunderstanding.* "Once our people secure the field and deal with security personnel, there shouldn't be anyone left to rescue in the camp."

Hindman stared at the director, who remained stiff, as if chiseled from rock. With blinding clarity, he realized Foust didn't give a damn about the problems or a couple of hundred dead. Nothing would make him pull the plug from the exercise.

Director Foust removed his eyeglasses, sighed, and laid them over the papers, massaging his nose. "The schedule is tight enough as it is. Let's get this show on the road."

chapter 22

The forklift backed at a snail's pace down a ramp extending from the cavernous hold of an old Boeing 747 cargo plane. Dylan Hayes, in charge of the AMP engineers, watched the last wooden crate wobble on the prongs of a forklift as the operator stacked it with the others a short distance away. The three other technicians accompanying the AMP waited on the tarmac, surrounded by large blue canvas bags and aluminum chests with white IMC labels.

Dylan flopped on a trunk near his colleagues.

A man with a nose like a mountain at sunset and a jiggling double chin, in a dirty white suit and a straw hat, bellowed and waved his arms at a customs officer. The officer gestured to a clipboard with papers and shook his head. Perched in an olive-drab jeep, two other customs officers smiled in the inane way of those who don't know what the hell is going on as they followed the scene from a distance. After stacking all the crates, the forklift sped out of the blazing sun into a nearby hangar.

"What's the matter with the geezer?" One of the engineers pointed with his chin to the irate man.

"He's the IMC agent in Kisangani; the one arguing with him is the customs inspector. The other two in the jeep are customs officers." Dylan watched the gesturing match. "It looks as if we're having a problem with the AMP. They want to inspect the crates at their leisure. That means delays. For how long . . . Well, your guess is as good as mine."

Another jeep closed on the group at breakneck speed and screeched to a halt, laying burned rubber behind it. Two tall officers, their khaki uniforms impeccably pressed and starched, stepped down as three soldiers spread out, leveling Kalashnikovs at the customs men.

One of the officers—a young man with lieutenant's stripes—stood ramrod-straight by the vehicle. The other approached at a sedate pace, as if taking a stroll. Dylan eyed the officer's epaulets and frowned: three stars over two horizontal bars. A full colonel.

The customs inspector, after running the fingers of one hand through a sparse beard that imparted a cloudy look to his face, stood at attention and raised one hand sharply to his forehead in a crisp military salute. The IMC agent backed up several paces.

The colonel faced the inspector and barked a volley in rapid Lingala. The customs officer wagged his head with a mocking smile and pointed to papers on his clipboard. The colonel backhanded him, the blow reporting like a whip crack, knocking the customs officer off his feet, and echoing with the metallic snaps of weapons' safety catches. Two of the soldiers aimed at the customs officers in the jeep. The third soldier, a boy not older than sixteen, drew back a few steps to cover the inspector who lay on the ground, rubbing his jaw. Suddenly the inspector's face contorted into a mask of rage as he twisted, reaching for a pistol on his hip. Without batting an eye, the soldier-boy fired a short burst, point-blank. The inspector trembled and clutched at his chest in an attempt to stanch the blood pouring from the wounds. He half-propped himself on the ground with his other hand, looking up like a hurt dog.

The lieutenant approached, unclipped his holster, took out a Makarov pistol, and fired twice at the customs inspector's head.

The colonel nodded, as if accepting a glass of water. "Thank you, Pierre."

"Sir?" Pierre arced his weapon toward the jeep with the customs officers, whose hands had hurriedly flown to rest in plain view over their heads.

The colonel looked into the sky as if to forecast the weather.

Pierre nodded and returned the pistol to its holster. "Hot, indeed. We'd better adjourn somewhere cooler."

"That's a sensible idea, Lieutenant." He then pivoted and, in a soft voice, gave instructions to the IMC agent.

Two of the soldiers marched the remaining customs officers to nearby barracks, and the lieutenant followed at a sedate pace, as if reluctant to mar the knife-edge of his trouser creases. When the group disappeared through a door, the other soldier jumped in a jeep, gunned the vehicle, and drove out of sight behind the warehouses. A stream of rapid automatic gunfire issued from the buildings, followed by two sharp pistol cracks. Within two minutes, the jeep reappeared, driven by the lieutenant;

the other three soldiers were crammed in the rear and made a beeline for the colonel and the IMC agent.

"Please, proceed loading your craft," the colonel said. "Now we'll adjourn to the control tower to negotiate your takeoff permit, although I foresee no further delays." The colonel waved a polite farewell, and as soon as he settled beside the lieutenant, the jeep gunned toward the airport's main building.

Heralded by a thundering roar, a Sikorsky landed, its huge rotor scant feet from the crates. The forklift returned from the hangar at full speed.

The IMC agent trudged over to the helicopter, his face haggard. He stopped in front of Dylan and produced a large, stained handkerchief to mop his face and neck. "Welcome to the Congo, gentlemen."

○

Ignoring the muttering behind him, Robert Lukesh wiped some grit from the windowpane to gaze out at the Virunga Mountains hemmed between Mount Nyiragongo and Mount Nyamuragira. Lukesh never tired of the sight. The view seemed like a watercolor, a composition of such awesome beauty it looked false, and a contradiction to the grubby surroundings. He eyed thick smoke plumes rising from active volcanoes. A few years before, Goma had burned to the ground, and large quarters of the city disappeared under a lava onslaught.

He could do with a beer. Instead, Lukesh popped a stick of gum in his mouth.

High on the slopes of Mount Goma, the house had been spared the worst of the volcanic eruption, but time and neglect had taken its toll. Lukesh moved from the window, releasing the decaying curtains he had been holding aside. Grime-encrusted netting dangled from broken poles, adding to the dismal atmosphere. He sat down by the desk, eyeing the room.

Once upon a time, the place must have been elegant. The room felt like a parlor, even a music room, with plaster moldings and walls hung with fabric. Men and women from colonial ages might have gathered there to play bridge and enjoy a sedate afternoon tea. Now a line of bullet holes punctured the wall by the door, shredding the wallpaper. The ceiling fared no better. The plaster had come loose in places, baring the bamboo and rough timber beams.

Lukesh watched with dismay as General Kalundo, sitting behind the table, selected a wad of hundred-dollar bills and counted them one by one. Considering the number of precariously piled bundles, the task could last for hours.

He eyed the sweat on Kalundo's bald black head. Rows of scars lined his cheeks—small lumps, like grains of barley—forming lines to his small eyes and disappearing beneath puffy eyelids. With exaggerated deliberation, Kalundo licked the thumb of a hand with short, thick fingers. He moved sideways, scratching his back against the chair and counting hard, stacking bills in piles of ten.

I'm getting too old for this shit, Lukesh thought. *Just one more week.*

On a ripped horsehair settee by the door, a peasant with colonel's epaulets darted greedy glances at the briefcase bulging with banknotes.

After counting out two bundles at random, Kalundo

seemed satisfied and tallied the packs, noting the partial results on a piece of paper. A drop of sweat traveled down the bridge of his nose and stood poised at its tip, until a sharp exhale converted it to a fine spray dewing the table's mahogany surface.

Lukesh slumped back and shook his head, feeling weary, in need of cleaner air. He glanced toward the mountains and sighed.

"My dear friend, this looks correct, but I do not see the other part of the deal anywhere. Where are my weapons?"

In a gesture of exasperation, Lukesh rolled his eyes. "General, you expect me to bring sixty tons of hardware under my arm? The weapons will be handed over within a week, on the Rwandan border."

The general leaned to one side and farted. "It's the diet," he said, poker-faced. "Too many vegetables. You like okra?"

Lukesh shook his head. "I'll take steak anytime."

"Nah! Okra and mutton stew tops steak. Pity about the gas, though. But back to the weapons. That, my friend, was not the agreement."

"As I've already explained, the plans have changed. We don't need ground troops, only a couple of hundred men outfitted in Congo army uniforms. Good men. Disciplined. It must be a credible army contingent." He was about to add, "Not a band of *shufta*," but thought better of it. "Half the men, but the same goods in exchange; it's a good deal."

"I see no weapons."

"There's been no time to move so much hardware without arousing suspicion. You don't have anything to worry about. You'll get your weapons, the same as you've gotten your money."

"I'm afraid I won't have time to organize special troops and uniforms. I hope you understand."

Unperturbed, Lukesh stood and lay a hand on the briefcase. "In that case, we'll leave negotiations for another day."

The general grimaced. The soldier shifted.

"Reckon you could get out of this room with that briefcase?"

Lukesh had the answer ready before Kalundo finished. "I don't doubt it; you are a trustworthy man who always honors his commitments."

Quietly at first but with increasing violence, the general laughed. His whole body shook like jelly as his laughter echoed around the room. The man on the settee applauded. Lukesh eyed the peasant, in uniform and '50s-style mirrored aviator glasses. *What am I doing here? There must be an easier way to make a living.* Lukesh had repeated the same self-scolding many times over the past twenty years.

"Of course we've got a deal! Come, sit, let us study plans as friends and allies do the world over." Without warning, the general stood, raised a finger to his lips as if remembering something, farted again, and reached for the briefcase. "My best officer will attend to details. Colonel Daulne will handpick the cream of professional soldiers from our regiments and lead the raid with the choppers. Don't worry about uniforms; we have thousands. I'll see you later to work out final details for the weapons delivery."

Our regiments, Kalundo had said. Why not divisions?

Robert pictured Daulne raiding neighboring villages and recruiting every farmer he could lay his hands on.

Kalundo walked around the table with the briefcase in one hand, rubbed the other on his khaki shirt, and offered it palm up.

Lukesh slapped the hand and peered at a wet stain spreading across the general's trousers.

The general followed his gaze and shrugged. "It happens when I laugh."

As he watched Kalundo leave, Lukesh remembered the CIA's failure during the Iranian hostage crisis decades before. Now the agency was about to place the fate of the operation in the hands of a man in sandals with a fruit salad of medals on his chest, most of them religious or commemorative.

The idiot officer laughed when Lukesh almost stepped into a pile of stale vomit, then shut up abruptly when he stared him down.

The media will have a field day if we screw up.

○

Paul and Michael Didier waited a short distance from the landing pad as the Sikorsky settled on the concrete slab, kicking up a dust cloud.

As the AMP technicians descended from the narrow cabin on ladders, Michael radioed the tractor to approach the craft. Paul raced toward the group of men unloading their canvas bags onto the pad. He held a hand out to a pale-white Dylan Hayes, the lead engineer whom he'd worked with in Dallas.

"I'm sorry about the problem at the airport," Paul said,

patting a fax folded into his shirt pocket. "The agent got in touch with us as soon as you lifted off. It must have been terrible."

"Terrible? You shoulda seen that son of a bitch's eyes! He didn't blink, I swear. I mean, the customs guy is bleeding to death on the ground, and that lieutenant bastard moves like he's about to give him a hand, then shoots him like a dog. Damn, Paul, his eyes never moved! Then the colonel saluted and waved, like the President at a photo op."

Paul put his arm on Dylan's shoulders. "I'm sorry, man. Law and order don't exist here, and life is cheap. You're among friends now, Dylan, and we need you."

"Sorry, Paul. You can count on me."

"Never doubted it."

Dylan shook his hand with a forced smile, then froze. "Damn! I almost forgot." He fished an envelope from his backpack. "A love letter from Milford. Dr. Kennedy asked me to give it to you in person."

Paul took it, then gestured for Michael to escort the technicians to their cabins. Meantime, he joined the pilot and ground personnel in releasing the webbing securing the crates in place and got them ready to unload.

"I appreciate the late trip," Paul told the pilot.

"Sure thing, Paul. By the way, you know the colonel and his men, the ones who shot the customs officers?"

"What about them?"

"They have fancy tastes."

"What do you mean?"

"I saw them hopping on a private Learjet."

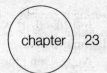

chapter 23

"I have bad news," Greenberg said as he withdrew a folded sheet of paper from his coat pocket.

Hindman leaned back in his chair, as if readying himself to receive a blow. Greenberg sounded as if he'd found out Grandma was turning tricks to support her crack habit.

"Right this minute, the AMP and the technicians are arriving at the camp. They lifted off from Kisangani an hour ago," Greenberg said, settling into a chair.

Hindman drummed his fingers on the table and waited for more.

"According to confusing signals coming in, customs officers went to the runway to check cargo and paperwork. They were under strict orders to delay clearing permission forty-eight hours. Both the IMC agent and our contact—who saw everything from the control tower—say an army colonel and a lieutenant appeared out of the blue with three armed soldiers and ordered the immediate release of the goods."

"Just like that? No documents, orders, or anything?" Hindman asked.

"Nope. Don't forget, the country is at war and all airports are under the Congo army control. When the inspector refused, the lieutenant shot him twice, point-blank in the head. Then they marched the other customs officers behind a shack, shot them, and left them there. That's not all. The colonel removed to the control tower. There, he produced a Congo army ID with the name of 'Colonel Jacques Kleber' and some orders nobody could corroborate and demanded immediate clearance for the helicopter transporting the AMP."

Greenberg leaned closer to the table and lowered his voice. "Now here's the best part. When our controller in the tower stood up to the colonel and demanded the order's confirmation, he was directed to call the ministry in Kinshasa. He did. Kabila's rep confirmed that the colonel acted on the president's orders."

"You're saying Kabila ordered the AMP's release?"

"I'm not. The whole setup was a sham. Sakombi Inongo *is* President Kabila's rep, but he's with the president in Lubumbashi, over six hundred miles away, and inaccessible. We checked. His office denies having had any contact with the Kisangani control tower, although that shouldn't worry us, because Colonel Kleber doesn't exist. He doesn't belong to any Congolese army command structure. Fifteen minutes ago, however, our controller picked him from photographs our embassy worker took to the hospital."

"Hospital?"

"When the controller hung up the phone, he apologized to the colonel and the guy kicked him in the crotch. Hard. He's heavily sedated; looks like he'll lose one of his balls."

Hindman's fist hit the desk. "Christ, Greenberg, cut the crap!" he shouted. "Who's this damn colonel?"

"Well, at least his rank is true. He's Hilari N'dende, forty-nine. Head of President Kabila Senior's secret police from 1998, a ruthless motherfucker from head to toe, and perhaps the most powerful man in the DRC. He's untouchable."

"And the lieutenant?"

"So far we have nothing. A mystery."

Hindman stared straight ahead as he weighed the news, the implications, and the immediate results.

"Maybe we're being shortsighted," Greenberg said. "We're familiar with intrigue and outsmarting the rest of the pack. None of this should surprise us. The operation—I mean the IMC operation—is of enough importance for the corporation to sink billions into a godforsaken hole. We appear on the scene and try to read events our way, without considering that the others are anything but stupid."

"Bullshit. Why would people close to the president, including the head of the secret police, be mixed up in what they've been told is nothing more than a routine mining project?"

"Why?"

Hindman raised his eyebrows without answering.

"Isn't it possible IMC covered its ass?" Greenberg asked. "Hugh Reece has enough money to bribe the whole damn country."

Hindman shook his head. "Our source at the top of IMC would know it. Let's face it; everything concerning this project crosses his desk. Besides, our controllers decode communications from the camp routinely. No, it's something else. A third element."

"A third entity siding with IMC?"

"Perhaps not. It could be playing its own game. We're assuming only we and IMC know about Project Isis and its potentially lucrative profitability. But there could be other actors involved." Hindman raised his hand to keep Greenberg silent. "Imagine for a moment Gécamines didn't swallow the drilling story or uranium prospecting. The permanent posting of Dr. Mosengwo to the site *and* all her phone calls add weight to the theory. What in God's name is a mining inspector doing with a miniature microwave-pulse transmitter–receiver? We don't know where her calls are going. Could be to a station in the jungle or on the river or up a gorilla's ass. I think we should reconsider the operation."

"What? You want to drop everything when it's possible the Congolese government wants to steal the goods? The ground is theirs, but that's it. The hole and whatever comes out of it, even if it's just cow shit, is American property."

Hindman listened, astonished at Greenberg's deranged logic. The premises were wrong, the conclusions stank, and Aristotle would have a fit. The land, or the capsule, or the contents, didn't belong to them. And IMC was in the DRC under false pretenses, illegally.

"The Congolese government doesn't have the resources needed to exploit whatever comes out of that hole," Hindman said.

"No. But the French do. Gécamines is a remnant of

the Belgian empire, staffed by French scientists and technicians. They have muscle, technology, and scores to settle."

"You think these developments give us no cause for concern?"

"I didn't say that," Greenberg replied. "It could well be Gécamines or even the Congolese government behind it, but they're having a rough ride. They have a real revolution going on, and they're spread thin on the ground. We control communications that can deactivate site security. We can also get out of the way and let the situation follow its course. Don't forget, we're not involved directly. We don't need to get in until the last minute, and only if the place is secure. We can control whatever happens when the descent begins."

"You think we should go forward?" Hindman asked.

"Yup."

Hindman stared at Greenberg, regretting his earlier suggestion to shelve the operation. Director Foust wouldn't back off. The agency's boss had been inoculated with adventure's venom; the man wanted his moment of glory and his pound of flesh. Besides, when he got a whiff of the possible French involvement, he would go ballistic.

"You may be right," Greenberg said. "We're missing something important. The single detail that terrifies me the most is the ability of an enemy to react, *any* enemy."

"What do you mean?"

"Five hours ago, Paul Reece decides to move the descent forward and catches us with our pants down. After bringing into play some awesome resources, we manage to slap together a forty-eight-hour delay. Two hours later, up pops the most powerful motherfucker on the continent, in the right place and just in time. He executes half the customs department, sends our man to the hospital, and blows our scheme to hell. All in two goddamn hours. Hindman, we're being played like fools."

chapter 24

Like pagans gathering around a totem, hundreds of people crowded the derrick under a surreal gray light to share a momentous event: the instant when the drill head would reach 22,500 feet, the deepest large-diameter bore in history. The few who couldn't desert their posts—security officers and communications personnel on duty—stood on the camp's perimeter or leaned against guardrails, eyes glued to the yellow steel monster. Even those who had finished their shift hours before waited, ears inured to the din of screaming turbines straining to twist four miles of shaft with a ton of diamond-studded cogs at its end.

Beyond the clearing, a lumbering shadow—followed by another, and another—slowly traveled the length of the fence to stop at a point closest to the derrick.

Overhead, a low-frequency rumble reverberated, echoing in Paul's chest. He darted a glance to the leaden sky. It was midday and already it felt like late afternoon. The deluge had stopped half an hour earlier, almost as suddenly as it started, but the sky looked heavy, the sun a memory. Lightning flashed, bathing the camp for an instant in clear light. Paul speed-counted until thunder boomed again. The storm was moving toward Kisangani and away from the camp.

He squatted by the rapidly rotating shaft and peered at the gauge. Almost there. Next to him, Owen, Mark, and Shermaine stared at the frozen numbers on the laser gauge installed by the shaft.

"It hasn't moved for"—Owen checked his watch—"ten minutes."

"It will," Paul shouted. He looked at Shermaine, but her eyes didn't shift from the gauge.

"Damn—jade. That bitch is harder than we thought," Owen grumbled, obviously for the benefit of everyone but Paul and Mark.

Paul saw the edge of Shermaine's lip twitch. He knew the core sample they had produced to explain their unusual drilling schedule was a fake, and so did Shermaine.

For Gécamines and Shermaine's benefit, their drilling schedule included a strange procedure when they reached the false vein of nephrite jade. They had to raise the bit, exchange it for a special one, and then start its rotation very slowly, for the cutters to adjust. Adjusting the cutters was nonsense, of course, but it had seemed to the Dallas think tank a sufficiently obscure explanation to cover the real reason: going through the rubberlike compound.

Unlike six months ago when they core-drilled the same spot, the roughnecks had been briefed about what to do when the drill stopped its normal progress: raise the bit and exchange it with one of the advanced crowns guarded day and night in a separate container. As soon as the crown was in place, Mark O'Reilly, the tool-pusher, had taken the derrick's controls from the shift machinist. For over fifteen endless minutes, Mark had played torsion and speed like a virtuoso, the momentum of the steel column increasing with each tiny adjustment of speed. During the operation, the shaft dropped eight inches, as the front bit teeth pushed the rubber aside to bare the concrete.

Although the technical team in Dallas had pored over computer simulations, discussed and planned minutely the steps to bypass the cladding rubber, there remained an unsolved riddle. What would happen when the drilling head was brought to the speed required to drill into the concrete? Would the displaced rubber harden? Would it weld together? If it did, the crown head would seize. The simulations suggested that the rubber would break off into small chunks, but even so, to ward off the possibility of seizure, the only plan they could all agree on was to bring the drill to speed in tiny increments, to break down the rubber into ever smaller fragments. But that was 22,500 feet below the surface. For the onlookers, Mark's bringing the machine up to speed at a snail's pace was what the crown head required to "adjust its cutters."

Instrument engineers had affixed a sleeve with minute black-and-white bands, spaced at 1/32 inches apart on the shaft, and had deployed a laser sensor just clear of the rotating table a few feet away. The thin laser beam—reflected off the white bands—excited the sensor and gauged the shaft's progress with uncanny accuracy.

Paul straightened, the muscles of his legs aching from sitting on his haunches, and caught a strange look from

Shermaine. She rotated her eyes a fraction in the direction of the back fence, then stared at him. Paul frowned and glanced past her, did a double take, and froze. Six elephants stood along the fence, like spectators at a ball game.

Pandemonium erupted.

The blast of a siren sent a shock wave through the crowd as the clutch controlling the shaft speed slammed into the steel and the explosive bolts retaining the brakes fired. Numbers raced on the laser gauge, stopping when the sleeve played out. The turbines screamed when the torsion dropped and the automatic shutdown system engaged.

Paul jerked his head to look at the still-rotating shaft. The depth gauge was visible over the table's massive slab—stationary, not sinking any deeper—the twelve-ton string of tubes suspended from the derrick's brake array.

Like a receding tide, sounds dimmed gradually, replaced by the growing clamor of shouts, whistles, and hurrahs.

In a daze, Paul watched the table slow down, only to stiffen when Mark dashed forward and engulfed him in a bear hug.

"Son of a bitch! We did it!"

Shermaine stepped over and slapped both men's shoulders. "Wow! Well done!"

Paul darted a look toward the drill crew. They were dancing a jig around the table, joined by Owen and the other engineers. He slapped Mark's back and squeezed Shermaine's shoulder before glancing toward the fence. The elephants had gone.

From a far corner of the camp, impromptu tenor

voices tried the first stanzas of "The Star Spangled Banner," and soon a chorus of four hundred thundered over the Ituri forest.

Paul couldn't recall exactly what happened when the voices, swallowed in a thundering applause, died down. His eyes had filmed over and he blinked to clear his vision. He caught the looks between Shermaine and Mark, and between Mark and the drilling crew. He also spotted the beginning of a coordinated movement, but his reflexes were dampened by emotion. When he tried to react, it was too late. In seconds he'd been lifted off his feet and dragged by the brawny arms of the drilling crew into the mud pit, where a fierce mock battle ensued, soon joined by scores of others.

○

"Like postcoital *tristesse*?" Shermaine whispered.

Paul eyed the silent derrick as a group of mechanics worked at taking it apart. By morning it would be disassembled, the steel frames stacked aside, ostensibly for erection at another point within the site, but Paul knew it was a ruse. There wouldn't be any more drilling. Breathing in the cooler air, he raised his head and gazed at Shermaine, holding his hand up against the sun as it dipped below the horizon.

"When will you leave?" Paul asked.

Shermaine didn't reply at once. She scooted her butt closer on the crate they had appropriated as a makeshift bench, lit a cigarette, and took a deep drag. "Tomorrow."

Paul nodded, his mind alive with contradictory emotions. Leon hadn't been forthcoming when Paul questioned him about his organization. Need to know. Beyond satisfying Paul's curiosity, the information was useless. But an organization existed behind their superb communications and intelligence, now uncoiling like a sleepy snake to stretch across continents. Men, women, and materials would be moving into place, chess pieces carefully adjusted by a remote hand on the Ituri board. Shermaine had the closest task and the most dangerous: to receive the colors of the rainbow from his hand, and to accomplish that she and her team would have to be close. The paper she filed announcing her intentions to remove to Shawaiti was only a smoke screen. Somewhere in the jungle, other pieces would be gathering. Besides communications and intelligence, her organization would bring muscle to bear for the endgame.

"Chopper?"

"No. The chopper flies to Kisangani. Leon needs me; I'll grab the Hummer."

Paul smiled, remembering the treacherous track. Jereh and his bunch would be tree-hopping, keeping an eye on her. "You're not going alone, I hope?"

"Could you spare Michael? For escort purposes, of course."

You're making your move. "Are you finally going to relieve him of his misery?"

Shermaine unfastened a head scarf and shook her hair loose. "No more undressing me with his eyes. He gave up. Now he avoids me like the plague. I think he's having a hard time."

"Biko-batà bo?"

She jabbed her elbow in his ribs. "I didn't mean *that* hard."

"I suppose poor Michael will feel a great ego boost when he gets the prize," Paul said, teasing her about her tactics. Most women played the game. He wondered if it was part of the double X chromosome. "He'll assume that he's worked for it."

"He has, but he doesn't know it."

A commotion drew Paul's gaze to the rig. The mechanics had removed the bolts securing the upper section of the tower, and the crane maneuvered the forty-ton assembly. A high-speed drill started up somewhere close.

"Can I ask you a personal question?"

Shermaine frowned. "You've never asked permission before. Shoot."

"Why Michael?"

She didn't answer right away, and when she did, her voice had a different color, darker, almost prayerlike. "The simplest of questions usually beg for a complex answer. I've attended the best universities and it would seem I'm a thoroughly Westernized woman, but that's just a facade. I'm a tribal animal, a clan woman." She turned to peer into Paul's eyes. "Have you ever observed how primates choose their mates?"

"Gorillas bang their chests, gesticulate, and make a show of strength," Paul offered, failing to catch her drift.

"That's the paraphernalia, the show, but the subjacent theme is to afford a female and her offspring the best possible chance of survival."

"I can't believe it. You mean Michael is a sounder bet?"

"No, I don't. I'm attracted to Michael, and that's a bonus. But I chose him as my partner because he's a survivor, a fighter. Where I'm—" She bit her lower lip.

"Where we're going, I need a man with the resources to fight and win, to look after me and my pack. Not a desk executive."

Paul nodded. Still dazed by the far-reaching implications of their quest, his mind hadn't adjusted to making decisions based on different rules. "Thank you."

Shermaine ground the butt in the mud and turned toward him, her face serious. "For everybody there's a line." Shermaine peered at the dirt patch at her feet and made the gesture of scoring a line with her boot's toe. "It's invisible but, once you cross it, there are no comebacks. I crossed it a long time before you, but we're both on the other side: different priorities and different horizons." Drilling stopped, and the sudden quiet sounded exaggerated. "How are you feeling about your quest for the colors?"

Paul sighed. "Scared, eager, weary. That tube is frightening, but I'm all right. Determined. After all, I've been groomed for the task."

"You're a brave man, Paul. But, remember, you're not on your own." She stroked the side of his face.

"I know."

There was nothing more to say. He'd felt a strange calm since the day he returned from Shawaiti. Perhaps *calm* wasn't the correct description; rather, he had a feeling of purpose and security. He turned his head toward the jungle's darkness, imagining affable eyes in the gloom.

"Have you thought any more about Milford's letter?" she asked.

"No. The issue is clear." Paul thought about the letter Dylan had given him at the helipad. "A great disappointment and an unexpected gift. In a strange way I've found out I'm much loved by my grandfather. That's priceless."

Shermaine nodded. "What about Owen?"

"He'll be unable to check with Lynne Kennedy in Dallas. She left on vacation yesterday."

"Convenient."

"Necessary."

Shermaine's fingers toyed with her scarf. After a deep breath, she slipped the yellow silk foulard around her neck. "Paul, I know this is easier said than done, but don't worry about the surface. We'll take care of things. Your task is in the sphere. You must rescue the colors for all of us." She leaned her head on his shoulder for an instant, then she stroked the nape of his neck and kissed him full on the lips.

Paul closed his eyes. Not mangoes, like Carmen, but wild forest. Heady. His stomach fluttered. He hated farewells. "Good-bye?"

"No," she said with a wink. "Good night. You must rest. Tomorrow's *the* day, and I won't be able to kiss you when I leave." She grinned. "I've wanted to do it for a long time." She stood, her hand outstretched. "Come, I'll walk you to your cabin."

Paul thought there were worse ways of sending a man to the scaffold.

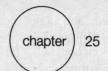

chapter 25

"We've drafted a contingency plan based on the IMC operation's new agenda," Dario Hindman said. "The descent begins tomorrow at twenty-two hundred local time, and the AMP will reach the sphere one hour later. The pilot has three hours to explore and remove portable objects. With three hours for the ascent, the AMP will surface around zero five hundred. Take it from here, Bouchard."

Anthony Bouchard, the Africa controller, poked at his tablet. "We have four Sikorsky HH-53Cs from Namibia now waiting in Rwanda—"

"Just a minute," Luther Cox interrupted. As external operations controller, he would stage the Autonomous Manned Probe's raid. "Are we talking Jolly Greens?"

Bouchard nodded and glanced at Director Foust.

"For heaven's sake!" Cox exploded. "Those contraptions are over forty years old. Where did you dig 'em up? A museum?"

"Those are the only choppers we could find on the

continent with the range and capacity we need," Bouchard said. "They're in perfect condition, similar to a few the Congo air force uses and reasonably painted with the right insignia. We can't use anything else, because it would look suspicious. Besides, they're part of our payment to General Kalundo."

"Mr. Cox," Director Foust said, "limit your comments to relevant issues."

Cox lowered his head at the rebuke. Hindman glanced sideways, noticing a vein pulsing at Foust's temple. *Bad news.* Cox's hostility toward Bouchard was over the limit. Something would have to be done about it, perhaps a desk posting.

"We have an agreement with the Rwandan authorities to hold and refuel the choppers," Bouchard continued, after exchanging quick glances with Hindman. "At the scheduled time, the choppers will lift off and fly north to Goma. There they will pick up Kalundo's troops— dressed in Congo army uniforms—and our man."

"Communications?"

"We have a real-time observer, Robert Lukesh, overseeing the exercise—experienced and reliable. He'll travel with the troops on orders not to intervene, with an American passport and a *Washington Post* press card."

"Press card?" Cox asked.

"Right. We thought it would be a sound cover, given the Congo is swarming with journalists. The world's too tame. There's a shortage of news and gory footage." Bouchard paused and glanced in turn to the other men. Nobody laughed. "Anyway, the troops will reach the campsite at around twenty-three hundred. Once the camp's secure, they'll lift off at zero four hundred."

"Fine." Foust nodded as he ran his stylus over the schedule. "We hit the IMC drilling camp at twenty-three hundred. Go on."

"Cox's team is already in Kisangani," Bouchard said. "They'll take off at zero two-thirty on the eighteenth and reach the site by zero four-thirty. If there's something in the sphere and Paul Reece brings it up with him, they will recover the AMP's contents and send it back to Kisangani, where a jet will be ready for the extraction to Saudi Arabia."

"That sphere itself is priceless. If the container is a miracle of engineering, what might it contain? But anything down there may be too large to carry in the vehicle. What if the AMP returns empty? I mean besides the pilot."

"Nothing changes. They will leave the pilot inside the AMP."

"And then?"

"Either way they'll call in reinforcements from Blackwater Worldwide and get out on the same choppers they'll be using to transport a couple of hundred of their men in to secure the place."

Cox nodded and selected a paper with a chart. "According to my data, first light will be at zero five-thirty, with dawn in full swing by zero six hundred. We'll have under an hour to lift the AMP from the tube, recover whatever, and get the hell out of there."

"You didn't say anything about communications, only that our man would travel with the troops," Foust insisted.

"Lukesh carries a secure set with direct sat-link," Bouchard replied. "We've repositioned a satellite with high-resolution infrared cameras to record the camp's movements. The action will take place at night; no other way to do it, since we might have cloud cover. Once the site's secure, we'll cut heat sources and kill the lights so we can follow heat signatures from here."

"What about here?" the director asked.

"Rhea Paige is preparing a situation room in basement three to follow the operation and control communications in real time during the exercise. I also think it's essential we preserve radio silence from the zone, in particular from the IMC informer. His last signal should announce the AMP is moving. Camp communications are our first target. It must be shut down before we secure the area."

"For argument's sake, if Reece returns empty-handed, what would have been the purpose of the whole operation?" Foust asked. "I've mentioned it before to Bouchard. If there's any artifact in the sphere, it could be too large to remove in one piece."

Hindman smiled. He'd been expecting the obvious question. "Remember, the sphere itself is the prize; anything in the sphere would be a bonus. But I don't think your scenario would alter events. A paramilitary group will have attacked American interests. We stay to ensure the operation continues."

"Yes, I know. It occurred to me we didn't need to wait. We could've taken over before."

"I don't think so, sir."

"Explain."

"We don't know if the AMP works or if the tubes are practicable or aligned. Reece is marching point for us, doing a test run. Once we know the road is clear and feasible, we'll follow through."

Foust nodded.

"I think that covers it all," Hindman said. "Cox, a chopper is waiting to taxi you to the air base and your flight to Kisangani. I'll be in my office in an hour." He glanced at Bouchard. "Let's join Paige and Greenberg to go over the final details. If there are any last-minute doubts or questions, this is the time."

"What happens if our recovery team hasn't arrived when the AMP surfaces at five?" Bouchard asked.

"The damn thing will stay put, suspended like a fish out of water," Hindman responded. "There won't be anybody left to help."

"What about the pilot?" Foust asked.

"The pilot has a small emergency tank with twenty minutes of air clipped onto his suit. He will use it to leave the capsule and reach for the two ninety-minute portable exploration tanks the capsule carries on its nose. On his return, he will use it again until he can hook to the capsule's main air supply—a large reservoir on the topside of the vehicle with a six-hour capacity—for the trip back."

Bouchard frowned. "If the descent takes one hour, that leaves five hours worth of air in the tanks for a three-hour ascent, right?"

"Right, but the overhead tanks have a valve, inaccessible unless the AMP is taken apart. One of the IMC engineers will install a mechanical plunger on the valve. The plunger will trigger when the second set of tanks kicks in during the return trip. The capsule will have no air one hour before it surfaces."

"Greenberg told me you worry about the exercise's integrity," Foust said, looking at Hindman. "You still do?"

The DDO shifted on his seat to unglue his sweaty buttocks. "Yeah. I still think we don't have the whole picture."

"Meaning the massacre at Kisangani airport and Dr. Mosengwo's behavior?"

"That too, but I have a gut feeling. I think we're messing around with something that may blow up in our faces."

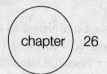

chapter 26

In the final hours, activity around the perforation zone
was frantic. Over the wellhead, technical personnel and
IMC engineers had assembled the containment housing
and raced to ready the AMP.

Twenty-four hours before, when the crown bit drilled
through the sphere's outer shell, the first group of workers
prepared to leave the camp.

Outfitted with a passenger cabin, the Skycrane was
back from the first of four trips to evacuate the drilling
crew and most administrative personnel.

From the office window, with a pang of nostalgia, Paul
eyed the group waiting next to the landing slab. They
were going home for a rest after the weeks of drilling—
some of them a half million dollars richer.

Paul gazed at the three-story-high prefabricated containment housing over the shaft and derrick. He heard
Gordon and Owen chatting in the hallway.

"Owen wants to post no-smoking signs all over the

place now that you've quit," Gordon said as he and Owen entered. "You agree?"

"Nah, I'm not a zealot," Paul said, still looking out the window. "Unless there've been any last-minute changes, we're reducing staff here by two hundred forty people. Right?"

Gordon scanned his tablet. "Eighty-two from security and thirty-eight technical, administrative, and catering personnel. One twenty total left on site. We have twelve security men around the clock in the AMP's area; the rest are off duty or patrolling the perimeter, but we'll limit that after eight tonight."

Paul went to check the lists on his desk. "Dr. Mosengwo will leave this afternoon too. She wants to return to Shawaiti. Something to do with a relative."

Owen's careless drumming on the desk stopped cold.

"Good timing, especially if I bring up samples," Paul added. "It would've been hard to find excuses to keep her away from the shaft. I think we owe her some considera-tion as a government rep, but we also need to keep an eye on her. I suggest someone from security goes with her, for her own safety, of course."

Gordon nodded. "Good riddance."

"Since the schedule we gave Gécamines says we won't start any tests until next week, she has nothing to do here for several days. Can we spare Michael Didier?"

"Didier's too important in the security scheme to send him off on a babysitting errand," Owen said, obviously annoyed with the suggestion.

"We've reduced the operation," Paul argued back. "Security will concentrate on the shaft. It would look better if someone with more weight than a simple guard went with her."

"I've no problem with that," Gordon agreed, stealing a glance at Paul.

"All settled, then. Tell Michael to inform Dr. Mosengwo. She wants to leave around noon. Get the Hummer ready, and make sure the localizers are working."

Paul watched for Owen's reaction. *Now you're wondering if Michael and Shermaine's departure is a coincidence or something darker. Traitor.*

Owen didn't respond, except for a jiggling foot giving away his nervousness.

"I'll be with the technicians for the rest of the morning," Paul continued, "testing the operating systems and the suit again. This afternoon I'll catch a nap. It'll be a long day. I'll see you later if there's any change in plans. Gordon, will you excuse us?"

Gordon raised his eyebrows but left as requested.

"One of the techs brought me a note from Milford the other day," Paul said after Gordon closed the door. "It may be nothing, but it could be important. I thought you might want to read it." Paul was sure Owen knew about Milford's note. He had seen Dylan talking with Owen several times.

Owen reached over the table, unfolded the creased sheet, and flattened it on the desk with the back of his hand.

Miner:
The communications with the camp are not secure. I think they're somehow compromised. CIA personnel, posing as defense department officers, urgently re-

quested copies of tapes from the AX54A satellite, covering the dates when you were absent from the site. We have handled with absolute discretion the real reasons behind the drilling; therefore, I'm very confused by the sudden developments in this project.

The operation security was supposed to be airtight and I'm at a loss about the sudden interest at the agency about you and our work. Because of the imminent resolution of this job, I urge you to be careful and vigilant. Our hopes ride with you.

Use your charm and good luck.

Milford

To fine magical raids.

"I never thought my outing would warrant the CIA's intervention," Paul said. "Milford is right, and there may be a loose end in Dallas in security. I imagine you'll want to look into it when you go back."

Owen left the note on the table. "The CIA clowns want to poke a finger into everybody's pie. Don't worry. When I get to Dallas, I'll look into it. I have good contacts at defense."

"I feel better knowing you'll check the leak." *You're wondering what this is all about. You suspect this letter isn't from Milford, and I'm counting on you believing I fell for it. Now you'll check. Milford will deny it and you'll be left to wonder about the letter's author.* "Get in touch with Milford. If the old miner's worried, put his mind at ease."

Paul picked up the note and held it over the ashtray. He was about to light it when Owen asked for it back.

"What does it mean when he says *use your charm?*" Owen asked.

Paul smiled and burned the note, then ground the fragments to fine ash with a pencil. He drew a thick gold chain with a worn jade disk from around his neck.

"I've had this since I was twenty. It's Neolithic, close to four thousand years old. According to legend, it's the symbol of the sun. My lucky charm. If I wear it, I'll always surface from any mine. I'll see the sun again."

Owen reached over the table and fingered the disk.

"Extraordinary," he whispered. "I've never noticed it before. Paul, thanks for the trust, and I think it was a good idea to keep Gordon out of this. I'll see you later at the AMP," he said as he left.

That was easy, Paul thought as he straightened up his desk. He could have described disks from several dynasties; he had a collection of about two hundred.

He also didn't tell Owen the disks were called *pi* in Mandarin or that Milford didn't know the *pi* around his neck was a present from his grandfather.

When Paul had received the letter, he recognized his grandfather's longhand on the envelope at once, and he hated having to destroy it. A long time had passed since he had received a letter from Hugh.

The Hugh in the single typed sheet sounded confused, perhaps frightened, without his usual humor and vulgarity.

Why should I use my charm? Why should I use my pi? Then it had hit him. *Pi!*

Pi is 3.14. It couldn't be every third word. That wouldn't make sense. The third, first, and fourth wouldn't work, from the beginning or from the end. What do you mean, Grandfather? Let's start again. Pi: 3.14.

On a blank sheet of paper Paul had written 3.14159265. He'd listed the words in positions 3, 1, 4, 1, 5. It made no sense. He wrote 3, 14, 15, 92, 65 and underlined the words. The hidden message had appeared in front of his eyes:

> **Miner:**
>
> The *communications* with the camp are not secure. I think they're somehow *compromised*. CIA personnel, posing as defense department officers, urgently requested copies of tapes from the AX54A satellite, covering the dates when you were absent from the site. We have handled with absolute discretion the real reasons behind the drilling; therefore, I'm very confused by the sudden developments in this project.
>
> The *operation* security was supposed to be airtight, and I'm at a loss about the sudden interest at the agency about you and our work. Because of the *imminent* resolution of this job, I urge you to be careful and vigilant. Our hopes ride with you.
>
> Use your charm and good luck.
>
> **Milford**
>
> **To fine magical raids.**

"Crafty son of a bitch," he'd mumbled, smiling. His grandfather had thought of something simple and effective to signal five words. *Communications compromised. CIA operation imminent.*

His grandfather had known whom to trust. But the letter contained another piece of information. Hugh could have signed it or asked Lynne to do it. Instead, he'd used Milford's name. Why? Paul had reread the letter for the hundredth time. The answer was in the strange postscript. Now Paul eyed the sheet where he had worked out the anagram.

Hugh had a lifelong fascination with anagrams. Whenever Paul received one of his letters at college or the university, Hugh had inserted a line with the clues to collect Paul's allowance at a different bank or agency. Unless Paul deciphered the message, he couldn't get his money. *In deciphering each word, you shouldn't underestimate the contextual assistance provided by the adjacent words or by what you have read before.* Paul remembered Hugh's advice and discarded using a Vigenere matrix, hashing functions, or hash collision techniques to tackle the anagram. *Milford* had to be the key word.

After writing the anagram's eighteen letters, his first step had been to remove the *Milford* characters.

TOFINEMAGICALRAIDS—OFIMLRD—MILFORD

The weeded line then looked thus:

T NE AGICA AI S

Agent stood out, written almost back to front and clearly identifiable.

T NE AGICA AI S

After weeding *agent* only two consonants and four vowels remained:

ICA AI S

Simple transpositions yielded:

IC ASIA
I ISAAC
I AS CIA
A CIA SI
I SIC AA
IS A CIA
MILFORD IS A CIA AGENT.

The anagram's revelation had slotted scores of seemingly unconnected pieces into a picture of appalling treachery and confirmed Paul's suspicions about Owen. Only he liaised daily with Milford; the security protocol had made sure of that. Their ploy became clear, as did the American government's involvement; Owen had reached a CIA number. They couldn't allow Paul Reece to own IMC *and* whatever came out of the sphere. Milford and Owen were playing a ruthless hand to secure the IMC control, backed by the CIA.

How had the discovery of Owen and Milford's double role affected the operation? It hadn't. IMC had a schedule and the CIA another, but, unknown to either of them, the crazy capsule rider—aka the idealist Paul Reece—had

changed sides and was about to stage a different performance for his chosen audience.

After collecting the sheets with the word combina-
tions, he burned them one at a time. When he finished,
the office stank. He opened the window and rubbed the
ashes between his fingers.

He walked to the door. With Shermaine and Michael
off the site, he needed to spirit Gordon away and place
his own life in the hands of a tiny man with pitch-black
skin and large, sad eyes.

chapter 27

Shermaine didn't speak a word during the first couple of miles, as Michael maneuvered the heavy Hummer around the raised roots. *You're really going through the mill, aren't you?* When they reached the turnoff to Shawaiti, she rested a hand on his bare arm. Under her fingers, his muscles rippled. *For a moment, you were tempted to yank your arm away.*

"Please stop the car."

Michael braked and disengaged the transmission without taking his eyes from the road.

"We're not going to Shawaiti." She'd switched to French.

"I gathered as much."

She leaned sideways against the door and studied his profile, glad to discover his professional instincts were unimpaired. Shermaine tried to keep her face inexpressive, to hide her internal turmoil. Thoughts of running her fingers through his wavy hair warmed her loins. Shermaine suspected the answer to her next question but had to ask.

"How did you know?"

"I spoke with Gordon after Paul's binge. You're plotting something. It doesn't make any sense to leave the site now that we're about to send the vehicle down."

"And what are you going to do about it?"

Michael shook his head. "Look after you. Paul trusts you. He told Gordon his life is in your hands, and he's my friend."

Look after me? Darling, we're finally finding common ground. Paul's ability to bond with the unlikeliest of people, often rough or dangerous, was disconcerting. Men would follow him to the end of the world. She shuddered at the thought.

"We must wait here."

Michael didn't comment. He killed the engine and lowered his window a fraction.

"You talk funny. I mean, your French has a strange lilt. Is that your Quebecois accent?" Shermaine asked.

"Been reading my file?"

"Aha. Weeks ago. Born in Quebec 1969, high school, Canadian army, transferred to a special unit of the U.S. marines, American national since 1996, mercenary to IMC, and now part owner of a security outfit with Paul, Rolf Bender, and Gordon. I know it by heart, and I'm also well versed about your private life."

He didn't react.

"Don't you want to know?"

"I suppose you'll tell me anyway." The tone of his voice changed. He was angry.

"You're single, though very much attached to a lucky woman."

Michael turned and stared into her eyes.

Shermaine held his unblinking gaze as her fingers danced to the front of her shirt. When she ran out of buttons, his eyes didn't waver. She sighed and reached for her belt.

"Michael Didier, you're not doing a very good job of looking after me."

He made a strange noise, and for a moment Shermaine feared he'd choked.

○

"You smell and taste like my dreams."

"Mmmm." Shermaine floated in a warm and blurry haze. She wrapped her legs tighter around his waist and nuzzled his neck, oblivious to the discomfort of the cramped rear seat, wanting to prolong her inner glow forever.

Michael drew her even closer, as if he wanted their bodies to melt.

"I've missed you."

"I know," she whispered. "At night I would picture you asleep, just a few cabins away. The thought of your sad eyes and that little scar by the side of your mouth drove me wild."

"You could have knocked on the door for a cup of sugar."

"No, I couldn't, sweetheart. There was too much at stake to think of us."

"Want to tell me about it?"

She straightened and ran the tip of her tongue over his scar. She couldn't tell him that the end was so near, every moment was precious.

"Not yet. You can only have what's mine to give."

Michael grinned.

She reached for him. "Monsieur! You've been deprived—"

"Sorely. It's all your fault."

"You reckon reparations are in order?"

"With accrued interest."

She leaned closer. "And what rate are you thinking of?"

"Usury." His fingers brushed her neck.

"I'd better start repayments, then."

○

The light had shifted. Shermaine finished dressing and checked her timepiece.

"We must get going."

Michael maneuvered his frame through the gap between the front seats, then wiped at the door window to remove the condensation and froze.

"What's wrong?"

Keeping straight, his hand dropped to a weapon fastened under his seat.

"There's a group of soldiers outside," he whispered.

Shermaine leaned over him and peered out the window.

"Hilari!"

Michael frowned.

"Don't worry, they're friends." She opened the passenger door and jumped from the car.

A few yards to the side of the vehicle, Hilari, slumped on a raised root, stared at her, deadpan. Behind him, she eyed eight or ten soldiers in Congo army drab fatigues and felt heat creeping up her neck after checking their leers.

"Why are you staring at me like that? You could have said something." She tried to hide her embarrassment.

Hilari stood, glanced at Michael, and nodded. "You know what they say in America: 'If the van's a'rocking, don't come a'knocking.'"

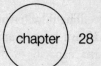

chapter 28

Robert Lukesh walked to the center of the runway, leaving the welcoming shadow of the hangar behind. Out the corner of his eye, he watched four lines of boy soldiers marching toward the choppers and he edged closer to one of the machines, sliding a hand over the fuselage and eyeing the craft with respect. He had not seen one of the venerable Jolly Green Giants since Vietnam: a Sikorsky HH-53C, the beautiful machine that had rescued hundreds of downed pilots and countless soldiers. He checked the telescoping probe for midair refueling and the external extra tanks, with internally operated quick-release latches for ditching in flight to lighten the load and gain maneuverability if things got hairy. The machines were stocky, heavy, painted the dirty khaki of the Congo air force, the undersides white to afford better camouflage in flight. Namibian mechanics had maintained the choppers well, even lovingly, surprising for aged equipment in a country not noted for the care of hardware.

The pilots—young men who flew the choppers from Kenya—eyed him inquisitively from the cabin. Although the capacity of the HH-53C was theoretically twenty-seven men, Lukesh knew that many more could jam inside. During an evacuation less than twelve miles from Da Nang, one of the machines had managed to lift seventy-two soldiers in a single trip, and several more could have squeezed in. In the last, tragic days of the war, a CH-47 Chinook with a capacity of forty-five soldiers in combat gear carried 147 refugees to safety on one flight.

Satisfied, Lukesh had ended his inspection and joined Colonel Daulne, who waited on the chopper's opposite side, when he noticed movement at the edge of the airfield. A jeep burst into the open from a track half hidden by stands of umbrella trees and barreled toward them at breakneck speed.

After the vehicle skidded to a stop, leaving behind twenty yards of burned rubber, General Kalundo extricated himself from the cramped seat and struggled upright. "Here you are!"

Lukesh stiffened. *What on earth...?*

"I'm coming along. This operation deserves the highest authority."

"But..." The thought of having the bumbling peasant interfering added unfathomable new angles to the mission.

"You're worried about my safety? Don't be. My army will protect me."

The idiot had mistaken dismay for concern.

Before reaching the chopper, Kalundo turned. "You *mondele* have a thing about calling blacks 'blacks' or Negro 'Negro,' no? You like beating around the bush with 'African-American,' 'colored citizens,' and the like, no?"

Lukesh remained immobile, waiting for the punch line.

"We'll spare your conscience. For you, we'll be green. You know what I mean? Like in a green woman with a big fat green ass? We are green citizens." Kalundo drew a finger to his lips as if pondering a spiny conundrum. "But to uphold the forms, dark green travel coach and light green like you may ride in front." He reached for the handhold and negotiated the steps, shaking with laughter.

Lukesh attempted a smile, but his clenched jaw prevented it.

"You may travel in this one and I will go in one of the other choppers," Daulne said as he donned mirrored sunglasses. "Now we have free corridor all the way to Kisangani, but that guarantee nothing. Many crazies loose, love to shoot anything that flies." After looking around to assure that all the men were aboard, the colonel dashed toward the farthest machine.

Lukesh negotiated the steps and glanced in dismay at Kalundo, who was sprawled in the farthest reaches of the chopper, already pulling the cork of a whisky bottle with his teeth. The general was surrounded by a sea of smiling faces: boys who had never flown before, children eager for a long roller-coaster ride. Trying to avoid eye contact and holding his breath against the odor of rancid sweat from unwashed bodies, Lukesh pushed his way through the cabin and took a seat next to the gunner.

He pulled his hat forward to avoid witnessing the pilot's performance and tried to sleep.

chapter 29

The entire CIA building was secure, but nowhere in the facility was security taken more seriously than in sublevel four. Once the door was shut, the central computer in another part of the building sent a high-frequency alternate current to the thin mesh embedded in the concrete walls, floor, and ceiling. This sealed the room, barring the entry or exit of any electromagnetic signal.

Dario Hindman entered room three with Director Foust, Rhea Paige, and Aaron Greenberg. They took their usual places, chairs they knew well. Behind Greenberg, a sergeant closed the door.

The situation room was identical to any other meeting room, with an oblong table, plush armchairs, chilled-water dispenser, and a stocked credenza, save for the three large plasma screens that hung side by side on one wall.

Four chairs lined the table, two on the long side facing the wall screens and two at the ends. Hard rubber mats lay on the table in front of each chair. Small fiber-optic lamps with green shades provided the only light. On the right arm of each chair was a telephone pad with a series of buttons to hold, resend, or feed calls to a set of speakers.

Three clocks, showing the local time in Dallas, Congo–Kisangani, and Washington, D.C., flashed on the screens.

Director Foust sat at the long side of the table with Hindman at his side. "It's noon here, eleven in Dallas, and eighteen hundred in the Congo. Ms. Paige, please bring us up to date."

Paige tapped several buttons on a handheld. The central screen lit up, displaying a map of the Democratic Republic of Congo with two flashing colored dots and another motionless in white.

"The white spot is the operation zone in Ituri. The yellow one is the rescue team led by Luther Cox. Right now they're waiting at Kisangani, four hundred yards from the airport, checking in every thirty minutes.

"The red spot marks the four choppers. They're refueling, also at Kisangani airport. They take off in four hours; ETA at the operation zone is twenty-three hundred local time."

"Any news, Hindman?" the director asked.

"The usual glitches. Lukesh had to insist Kalundo's troops wear boots instead of sandals."

Foust peered over his eyeglasses at Aaron Greenberg. "Any problem at the camp or with IMC?"

"Reece has sent Dr. Mosengwo out of the camp with the security team's second-in-command, Michael Didier. According to our sources, the move could be a ploy to deny Gécamines access to the real purpose of the shaft."

"How?" Hindman asked.

"By ensuring that their inspector is elsewhere when the AMP drops."

"You don't think that's an auspicious move?"

"Perhaps, but after the woman's strange behavior, her continuous coded conversations, and her patently false reports to Gécamines, it's hard to believe she'd agree to leave just as the operation reaches its climax. Among other things, it would be an irresponsible move for the government's on-site inspector."

"Maybe not. The AMP shouldn't make the first trip until next week. This has been filed as a test drop. The new schedule has never been filed with Gécamines. There's nothing for her to do until the second phase starts. However, I still think if they bought the uranium-mine story they wouldn't have kept her there all this time. Gécamines may now be a government organization, but it's still run by French scientists and they aren't stupid."

"What other reason would Paul have to get rid of her at the last minute?" Paige asked.

"No idea," Greenberg admitted, "and that worries me."

"Anything else?" Foust asked, looking at Hindman.

"We've landed a signal from the camp. Someone handed Reece a message from Milford Crandall at IMC. Crandall told him we requested their satellite data under cover of the defense department for the days Paul was gallivanting around the jungle. That's true, and it tells us there's a leak we'll have to look into." Hindman knew that he walked on thin ice here, as he was omitting the fact that Milford had never written to Reece. A Dr. Lynne Kennedy had given the letter to one of the AMP's engineers. All efforts to locate the whereabouts of Dr. Kennedy had been fruitless.

"Damn the leaks," Foust complained to no one in particular. "And damn the defense department."

"The signal also confirms the descent is slated for twenty-two hundred local time."

"Fine," Foust replied curtly. "When do we get satellite images?"

"Not before twenty-three hundred local," Paige replied. "Too much cloud cover to get a good optical image."

"What about infrared?"

"Infrared relies on a temperature contrast. We need a minimum difference of fifty degrees Fahrenheit. The temperature seldom drops below eighty-five in the equatorial zone; the human body is ninety-eight point six."

"I see," Foust conceded. "We could have a panzer division at ten paces and never be the wiser—until they started their engines."

"That would be too late, sir."

Foust removed his glasses and proceeded to polish them with a small chamois square. "Amen."

chapter 30

In thick jungle, Hilari N'dende checked the tritium hands of his timepiece and breathed deeply the damp night's air. Moving in almost complete darkness, he retreated to a stand of trees and dense vegetation that hid a windowless box truck and checked that the thermal blankets were firmly fastened over the roof and engine compartment. When he was satisfied, he rapped twice on the side.

After a short delay, the back door opened and a calm face peered at him. Hilari gazed past Tshul into the van's interior, crammed full of electronic consoles with dozens of blinking lights. Mkhas sat at the controls, apparently whittling a stick with a penknife.

"Time," Hilari said.

Tshul nodded and turned to Mkhas, whose deft fingers already flew over a keyboard. The vehicle's roof opened and a large aerial deployed, thin wires spreading like an inverted umbrella frame.

"I hope you know as much medicine as electronics," Hilari said.

Mkhas toggled a switch and nodded to his knife. "I could do with some practice. Shall we?"

"Forget it." Hilari bowed his head and closed the door.

Giving wide berth to a dense clump of thorny acacias, Hilari reached into his pocket for a tiny LED flashlight to guide his way along the hundred-yard trail to the clearing where his men, Michael, and Shermaine waited by the Hummer. The clearing was bathed in a ghostly light from a hurricane lamp dangling from a low branch.

"Well, no more communications after ten minutes."

"And after that?" Shermaine asked.

Hilari shrugged. "Your guess is as good as mine, but things will start happening. Fast."

○

Paul stopped at the door and checked his watch: 21:00. He lifted his gaze to the sky. The night was clear, scattered with a myriad of stars, the air still warm and moist.

Dylan Hayes and Hailey Brown, one of the technicians who remained behind to oversee the launch, waited for him on the other side.

"Ready when you are," Dylan said when Paul entered. "You remember Hailey?"

"Yeah, from Dallas. Another from your geek squad," Paul said with a wink.

"That's *Mr.* Geek to you," Hailey said as he popped open a can of Coke.

Paul knew the drill; he had practiced three times already during the day. *Well, not quite the same drill,* he silently corrected himself. He eyed Dr. Laura Carrillo, the site's medic, with a hint of apprehension. Paul slumped on a stool and bent to remove his sneakers and socks. He smiled. When he was a boy, learning the ropes at a mine during a summer vacation, Milford had coached him on the rules for proper undressing, in particular when women were present. *First shoes, then socks, followed by the shirt,* the sage had insisted. *Flaunt your class, my boy; that'll get the old juices running. Nothing kills passion faster than a buck-naked guy in socks.* Paul never forgot to flaunt his class. His chest constricted under a wave of sadness. *Milford, my friend, my Brutus.* After a deep breath to exorcise the thought, he removed the rest of his clothes and stood naked. Milford's treason wasn't important anymore. Not as important as the rainbow.

Dr. Carrillo tore open a sterile bag. With deft fingers, she lubricated a transparent catheter and inserted it into Paul's penis.

"Ouch!"

"Never had any complaints from horses," she said, securing the tube to a leg bag on Paul's thigh with a Velcro strap. "I doubt you'll produce any urine at all, not with all that sweat." The physician backed up a step and eyed the contraption. "Well, that's my contribution. Good luck, Paul." She turned toward Dylan. "I'll be at the infirmary if you need me, guys."

Dylan passed Paul a flexible one-piece suit. Contorting, he donned the sheath to his waist. From there he needed Dylan's help to push his arms through and raise the garment and its hood, enclosing his head except where an oval cutout showed his face.

Paul started to sweat at once, the sheath becoming transparent. He stepped into a silvered suit made from layers of microfiber and Kevlar with two large connectors on the chest. As soon as Dylan closed the suit and checked joints and gaskets, he attached a tube to a connector. The interior cooled, and Paul breathed easier. "Let me have a sip of that Coke," he said as he sat back on the stool.

Hailey passed the can over to him. Dylan squatted and slid the socks, fashioned from the same material as the inner suit, onto Paul's feet. He secured the tops with fasteners. The boots, with thick white soles and internal magnesium sheets to protect his feet against sharp objects, came next. Hailey snapped them onto rings on the suit.

"During the trip you'll produce considerable liquids, which will collect in the containers at the top of your boots. These valves"—he pointed to a nipple on each side—"are drains. Don't forget to vent them when you reach the sphere and before the return trip. Portable cooling equipment will freshen you up, but you'll still sweat like a hog once you disconnect from it. Now gloves."

Paul stood and offered his hands to Dylan, first for the superfine sheaths and then the silver gloves, sealed at the wrists.

Owen stared as he entered the cabin. "I'll never get

used to seeing you dressed like an astronaut." He swiveled to Dylan. "The AMP's lower section is aligned and inserted."

Hailey brought Paul a bulky helmet with several dangling connectors. Dylan adjusted a small canister of compressed air on Paul's chest, affixed a thin tube to a valve, and opened the spigot. While Hailey fastened the helmet, Dylan connected lines to plugs spaced along the neck's metallic rim. Then they snapped the gasket shut.

At a signal from Owen, four workers stepped into the cabin and took positions around the portable air-conditioning unit.

"Can you hear me?" Hailey's voice echoed inside the helmet.

"Too loud!" Paul complained. "You almost busted my eardrums."

"Better?" Hailey had to be fiddling his dials.

Paul nodded inside the cumbersome helmet.

"We'll do some more tests after you connect to the AMP's system, but nobody knows how long the link will hold. It'll depend on the radiation level."

The workers hefted the cooling system, and the bizarre parade got under way.

The AMP's technical end was already inside the tube. The rest of the cylinder, suspended from the crane, shone under the fierce lighting.

Paul climbed the containment enclosure and ran another check of the AMP's readiness. The AMP was suspended over the sealed shaft inside the enclosure, surrounded by two expanded metal platforms. The upper stage, three feet below the AMP's top, had been used by the technicians to install and adjust motors, batteries, and compressed-air deposits. The lower one was level with the AMP's door. Narrow ladders interconnected the platforms.

Paul slid a thick glove over the AMP's skin, smiling with pride at the faultless construction. The metallic surface looked uniform; only a closer examination betrayed hairline joints. He descended through an opening in the upper platform. The two-story-high AMP was shaped like a double-ended sex toy, a sleek cylinder with both ends rounded. *I hope it doesn't vibrate too,* thought Paul ruefully. Internally, it divided into two superimposed modules. Paul ran his fingers over the door's waterproof seal and squeezed into the top module, negotiating hand and footholds with rehearsed movements. The inner room was so tight, his shoulders touched both sides. He disconnected the portable air-conditioning hoses and hooked himself to the craft's air supply, fumbling at the bushings with his gloves. Dylan raised one hand in a farewell salute. Paul leaned out to close the door, activating the hermetic seal with a large handle. He insisted on carrying out all the operations unaided. Where he was going, he wouldn't have any help.

He sensed movement. The overhead crane would be lowering the AMP inside a three-foot-long sleeve bolted to the shaft, after Hailey checked the diaphragm-valve seal. When the valve triggered open, the AMP would be free to drop.

Paul climbed into the upper section, let down the narrow seat, and fastened a safety belt. He gripped a cable hanging overhead and connected it to the helmet's side. At once, he heard Hailey's voice.

"Are you in position?"

"Affirmative. I'm turning on the systems."

"Fine. We're disconnecting external power supply."

The lights doused. Paul's eyes adjusted gradually until he could see again with relative clarity.

"Starting descent sequence." The tone of Hailey's voice changed. "Battery-bank one on, primary and secondary on standby. Starting insertion."

Paul chuckled. "Should I cough?"

"Diaphragm valve open."

The AMP inner walls transmitted a slight shudder.

"Braking segment in position. Pressure and traction good. We're going all the way now."

Paul eyed the shaft's rim as it inched past the portholes.

"Top wheel train is in. You can release traction."

Paul moved a lever, locking powerful hard metal cylinders with sharp striations into the shaft's steel.

"Good. We have brakes. We'll disconnect the cable. Two minutes."

Paul remained propped on the narrow seat, trying to forget the four-mile drop under his feet and the myriad things, some ridiculously minor, that could go wrong. He checked the instruments once more, trying to keep his mind occupied. Before taking apart the rig, they had several times dropped a cleaning head, a contraption similar to a cutting bit, bristling with steel brushes instead of industrial diamonds. In theory, the tube was aligned, free from anything that might foul the AMP's passage.

So much for theory, Paul thought. If the AMP jammed, recovery would be impossible. He would die locked inside a sleek titanium cylinder shaped like a vibrator. *Way to go.*

"Paul," Owen's voice sounded inside the helmet, "you're free. Start the descent. Good luck, boy."

"Okay, releasing traction wheels," Paul announced, trying to sound cool despite his racing heart. He flexed his hand twice and moved the lever controlling the hydraulic jacks in the tungsten cylinders. He felt a faint vibration and an emptiness in the pit of his stomach as the AMP slipped free and slid downward.

Numbers rotated on an overhead counter. He dropped at six feet per second—cruising speed. Paul remembered the tests in Dallas. If the brakes failed, the AMP couldn't drop any faster. The air pressure inside the tube acted like a natural brake, as a plunger in a syringe, making free fall impossible. The engineers' principal worry was how long the AMP might slide down the shaft. Wheels and cylinders braked and centered it, pressing against the inner walls. Adding mechanical counters to translate each rotation of the wheels into feet had been easy. Any major difference between the counters would warn of slippage; not all the wheels could skid at the same rate.

As added security, in the event of a full-speed entry into the sphere, a mechanical feeler would detect the shaft's end and fire hydraulic jacks overhead, which would bite into the steel lining. With luck, that would prevent a free fall.

He could have sworn the counters rotated faster.

"You look good," Dylan said. "Constant speed at six feet per second."

Paul lay back until the helmet touched the curved metal plate. He closed his eyes and tried to think of Carmen and overflowing tin bathtubs.

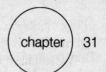

chapter 31

"Are we going to wait here all night or are you going to tell us what's happening?" Director Foust asked Rhea Paige after she finished her phone call.

"There's a wave of static in the area. We can't reach the camp. The recovery team is in Kisangani and the airborne troops still a hundred miles away."

"ETA?"

"Thirty minutes."

"What about the interference?" Foust asked.

Paige checked her notes. "It's from more than one source. The first is a fast-changing frequency across a wide band, and the other resonates with the first."

Hindman frowned. "Similar to what we use?"

"I don't know—"

"It's your job to know," Hindman snapped.

"It's not my fault; the spectrum is unlike anything we've seen before."

Hindman gripped the table's edge and leaned closer

to her. "I know it isn't your fault, but we expect accurate information!"

"We still have airborne communications?" Foust interrupted.

Paige nodded. "The interference covers an area from ten to fifteen miles in diameter. It's stronger in the center; communications are impossible there. Now, and until they reach the disturbance outer circle, the link holds."

"For how long?"

"Ten to fifteen minutes."

"It may be wiser to send a chopper first to check and have the other three wait at a distance," Hindman suggested.

"That's stupid," Greenberg snapped. "Say the first helicopter is in trouble and can't radio back. What do they do if it doesn't return? Send in the next? All four must fly over at the same time. They'll have a better chance to radio back. If there are no problems at the camp, the operative will have to ride one of the choppers out of the dead zone and report."

"Sounds reasonable," Foust agreed. "Send a signal."

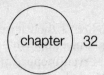

chapter 32

In the control cabin, Owen leaned over a dial registering the depth of the AMP's center wheels. After the first three hundred feet, the speed steadied. He knew radiation would soon kill the radio link with the AMP. "I'll be at security. Call me if there's any news."

Hurrying toward the office block, he dug a radio pad from his pocket and entered Gordon's number. The call failed several times. He grew more nervous with each try. He had spoken with Milford several times during the day and everything was unfolding according to plan, but the radio glitch was an unforeseen development. Now he had to ensure that Gordon would rein his men in and keep them away from the hardware.

When he reached the cabins, he was almost running. The men at the switchboard looked worried. Gordon was there.

"I've been trying to reach you on the radio," Owen whispered, out of breath.

"We have no comms," Gordon replied. "The sat-links

crashed. There's heavy clutter, some interference. It's not us. Our equipment's working fine."

Owen mopped his brow with the back of his hand. "Now what?"

"Nothing *we* can do. Anyway, it doesn't affect the AMP. What's the hurry?"

"We have to get in touch with IMC, tell them the descent is under way. They'll be trying to contact us. We have to do something."

Gordon shook his head and sighed. "There's nothing to do but wait."

"Let's go into my office." Owen pivoted on his heel and headed for the stairs. He gave a curt nod to Matthew and marched to his office, closing the door after Gordon.

"In less than an hour, army forces will take control of these installations," Owen said, falling into a chair.

"What the hell are you talking about? They can't do that. This is a private American operation."

"They can and they will. Milford warned me on his last call." Owen avoided looking at Gordon. "You have to tell the security crew to lay down their weapons."

"I can't do that," Gordon said, surprisingly calm. "The camp's security is my responsibility."

"I don't think you understand. The Banyamulenge rebels are retreating in this direction. You and the rest of the security personnel will have to yield to the military authorities."

Gordon shook his head. "They can't put us under military orders. We're civilians, and foreign."

"To them you're an armed paramilitary group. I'm warning you, if you don't obey the soldiers, this could be a bloodbath. Paul's in that chute and he's our priority. As the highest IMC officer here, I order you to have all security personnel lay down their weapons and wait outside until the army arrives. If the army finds armed paramilitaries when they get here, they'll butcher all of us."

"Okay," Gordon conceded, "but without radios I'll have to do it on foot."

"Whatever, but do it in a hurry."

Owen stood and then sat again, feeling weakness in his legs. It was going to be much easier than he had thought.

○

Gordon ran down the row of cabins and grabbed a jeep. *It's happening, just as Paul predicted. This is madness.* He drove at full speed around the perimeter, barking orders. At the entrance, he stopped and gestured to the sentries.

"We're expecting visitors: soldiers!" he shouted. "Open the gates, then go to the esplanade. You'll get instructions to cooperate with the army. Anyone outside?"

The men hurried to open the gates. "No, everyone's in."

Gordon nodded and drove again like a maniac around the inside perimeter, shouting to the running men. He glanced around and took in the general confusion. For an instant, he doubted. *What are you doing, man? You're betraying these poor bastards.* Then he pulled himself together as he thought about Paul and Shermaine. When he neared the gates, he didn't slow down. He barreled out of the camp and into the jungle.

○

Hilari N'dende lowered his night binoculars, climbed down from a forked branch in a tall iroko tree two hundred yards from the camp's fence, and approached the group by the Hummer. Suddenly he jerked his head toward the camp, listened, and gestured to his men, who melted into the jungle. He rose halfway, a finger on his lips, and doused the hurricane lamp. The sound of an engine neared. Hilari drew a pistol from his holster, pulled off the safety, and screwed on a silencer. He stole away, disappearing between the trees.

The irregular glow of an approaching vehicle's headlights shone over the treetops for a few seconds, then a jeep burst into the clearing. The driver slammed on the brakes. The jeep skidded sideways and stopped scant inches from the Hummer.

Gordon jumped out and spotted Shermaine and Michael. "What the hell are you doing in the dark?" Gordon asked, his teeth clenched.

The sharp metallic snap of a safety catch sounded loud in the jungle's silence, soon followed by a chuckle.

"If I weren't a peaceful man, you'd be dead." Hilari moved into the open and continued laughing as he offered Gordon his hand. "Hilari N'dende is my name, and in this war I'm with the good guys."

chapter 33

The helmet's speakers had been silent for ten minutes. Paul heard only the soft hiss of static. He reached for a plug on the side and pulled. The cable reeled overhead. Careful not to foul his air hoses, Paul lowered himself with measured movements to the base module and peered through narrow portholes at eye level. The shaft's inner wall passed by in a moist red blur, dimly lit by faint light escaping from the AMP. The AMP vibrated, its noise dampened by the helmet.

Paul threw a switch to light the AMP's nose lamp. A rectangular screen came alive with a fantastic view of the shaft disappearing in the distance. Nothing but an inverted periscope—a set of mirrors reflecting the nose's image onto a frosted piece of glass. After a moment he switched off the lamp to save energy and checked the counters once more. Almost 14,000 feet.

The temperature in the suit was comfortable, although the vehicle's thermometer showed 93 degrees Fahrenheit. Eventually, the temperature inside the tube would climb above 176 degrees. Paul moved his head sideways in the helmet and sucked warm, salty liquid— water with added electrolytes—from a tube connected to a reservoir on his waist.

For a moment, he thought about the surface: the plots, betrayals, and deaths that would happen before he returned. If he managed to return. *A room with the colors of the rainbow.* Suddenly a jolt snapped Paul from his reverie. One of the rollers must have ridden over a lump of mud. His hand shot out in reflex, but he couldn't find a handle.

A wave of terror gripped him, and Paul shivered in a cold sweat. Slowly at first, but with increasing violence, his muscles convulsed. He opened his mouth to scream.

"I've got to brake!" he shouted into the metal and plastic bubble around his head.

He tried to climb up, shoving the tubes aside. His foot slipped. A trickle of urine rushed into the leg bag. Paul was perched on the ledge, gasping and staring at the lever to fire the brakes and halt the descent, when Leon Kibassa's counsel echoed in his mind.

Fear is a woman, logical and fanciful. You cannot tame her, just as you cannot tame the wind or the tide. You must live with her; make her your companion. You must learn her; get to know her fancies and whims. Do not try to avoid her embrace. You cannot hide. She will find you. She will become you. You cannot run away. Stop. Woo her, calm her, until she sleeps again.

Paul labored to control his breathing.

As if a spectator, he saw his hand, clad in silver, caress the lever gingerly, only to pull away. A narcotic calm suffused his sweat-drenched body.

His eyes found the counters: almost 22,000 feet.

Paul slid down into the lower module and turned the wheel controlling the speed of the middle and lower wheel trains. He switched on the headlight, but the image was unchanged. Paul reduced speed to one foot per second, his eyes never leaving the frosted-glass window. Time slowed, compressed. He blinked. The dot in the middle of the screen grew. He watched as it enlarged, and he reduced speed still further. When the end of the shaft occupied most of the screen, Paul released the upper rollers, slowing the AMP to a crawl as he switched on the sidelights. He peered through the narrow portholes.

Warning lights blinked. Black and gray bands slipped past the portholes. He released the power brakes. Then the structure's shining braces, supporting a sphere visible farther down, crisscrossed the screen.

Paul giggled like a schoolboy. "I made it!"

Nobody cheered.

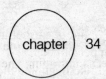

chapter 34

Four helicopters appeared from the east and flew over the camp in formation at flank speed, raking the ground with the powerful beams of their nose projectors. They banked to the right, losing altitude and cutting speed as they lined up for a second pass.

On the third run, the choppers hovered above the concrete slab before landing in unison. Doors opened and soldiers spewed out, sprinting for cover.

Robert Lukesh negotiated the steps and glanced around, assessing the disarmed security guards and IMC personnel. Colonel Daulne, a pistol in his hand, climbed down from one of the other helicopters. Satisfied, Lukesh headed toward the shocked group.

"Where's Owen DeHolt?" he shouted over the din of the rotors.

"Right here," Owen said, lifting an arm.

Lukesh did a mental comparison with the photograph beamed from Langley into his palm-held.

"I'm the vice president of IMC," Owen said once they

were out of earshot from the group of security and civil-ian personnel.

Lukesh ignored the offered hand and glanced around. "Robert Lukesh. What's wrong with communications?"

Owen shrugged. "No idea. Nothing but interference."

Most inconvenient. "Have you had this problem be-fore?"

"Nope. First time since we opened the site."

And too much of a coincidence. Lukesh felt his alarms tripping. "What about the AMP?"

"The descent went as planned. No incidents for hours." Owen paused. "Well, that's not quite true."

"What do you mean?"

"I ordered the security chief to round up the person-nel, and he did, but he hopped into a jeep and bolted."

"Where to?"

"No idea. He drove through the gates and into the jun-gle. There's a track two miles long, down to the river road."

"Is everybody outside?"

"The technicians and two mechanics are in the con-trol cabin. I can vouch for them."

Lukesh didn't hide his contempt. His life's work meant lies, conceit, a continual bartering with traitors, cowards, double agents, and mercenaries who would sell their own mothers for pocket change. However, work was one thing and ethics another. He'd never read a manual on how to enjoy the company of traitors, regardless of the side. His instructions, nevertheless, were clear. He had to protect Owen DeHolt and the technical team at all costs.

"Where is the control cabin?"

Owen nodded toward the metal compartment next to the containment enclosure.

"Mr. DeHolt, these men"—Lukesh gestured over his shoulder—"are not soldiers, at least not in the strictest sense of the word, regardless of the uniforms and weapons. They're warriors, hunters, farmers, and fishers. They see the world from a different perspective. The situation we've planned calls for deception. It will seem as if Banyamulenge rebels have hit this place, men with no sympathy for *mondele*—that's what they call white men around here." Lukesh eyed the pale executive. Perhaps he could tarnish Owen's silver shekels. "You see, Mr. DeHolt, tomorrow this place will look as if the Banyamulenge had fun. These . . . let us say, men, will do a fine job. Once their leader turns them loose, nothing will stop them. They consider white ass a true but rare delicacy, *bocatto di cardinale, capisce?*

"Join the technical crew in the cabin and bolt the doors," Lukesh went on. "Don't come out until you hear the choppers take off in about four hours. Now I will fly out for a few minutes."

"No, you can't mean that." Owen wrung his hands, his eyes open in stark terror. "Nobody told me about people getting hurt."

Lukesh felt a bleak smile steal across his lips. The same age-old play with different actors. In their minds, stupefied by greed, idealism, or whatever happened to drive them, traitors seldom considered thermodynamics—the universal laws dictating that one can't get anything without its corresponding cost to balance the equation. Owen DeHolt had just discovered the cost, a hefty sum that wouldn't affect his bank balance but might play hell with his sleep.

"Hurt? This is the real world, Mr. Honcho." Lukesh paused and mentally counted to five. "You'll be all right while I'm gone—I think." The promise of the fifty thousand dollars he carried in his knapsack would secure Colonel Daulne's collaboration after Kalundo passed out. He glanced toward the obese "green man" leaning against a cabin, the bottle of whisky almost empty in his hand. Daulne would keep his mob from the descent zone, but Owen didn't need to know that.

Owen paled. Without a word, he turned and headed toward the control cabin.

I bet you've pissed your pants, big man. Lukesh climbed the steps and whistled for attention, then, with staccato hand signals worthy of a top NFL coach, gave the order.

○

Colonel Daulne nodded and his soldiers converged on the terrified personnel. With a volley of shouts and blows, they herded the men into two empty cargo containers and bolted the doors. The soldiers then searched the cabins to flush out anyone hiding and to pillage for loot. They set fire to all of the mattresses, and soon a thick cloud of smoke billowed over forty cabins in flames.

At the clinic, a group of soldiers dragged two women out by their feet. Kalundo raised a hand as if to issue an order, then reached to one of his men and grabbed his weapon, mounted a bayonet on it, and impaled the first woman, pinning her to the ground. The soldiers laughed and followed suit, stabbing and hacking away, reducing both medical employees to bloody pulp.

Lukesh, back from the short trip outside the interference zone, slumped by the containment module and watched the scene dispassionately. He'd already seen the glorious Congo fighters in action. The rebels would tire of a warlord after a few months at most and desert in droves. They would take their weapons and regroup as *shufta*—bands of marauding murderers working the roads. They would have a whale of a time in the lull until the next leader emerged. Out of the corner of his eye he spotted Kalundo scurrying into one of the cabins, a fresh bottle in his hand. *Sweet dreams.*

When the site—except the containment module and the area around it—was in flames, the band zeroed in on the remaining site personnel. Soon the screaming began—inhuman howling and ululations. It was impossible to say whether these came from the men's throats, or from their victims.

Lukesh lit a cigarette. He reckoned if the *shufta* rationed the poor devils, they could well last them the night.

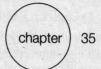

chapter 35

Despite the acoustic isolation of the airtight helmet, the difference in sensations from the AMP's motion was evident. No vibrations, noise, buzzing of machinery, or sound of moving air disturbed the silence.

Paul took a few deep breaths in a bid to slow his racing heart. After a few seconds, he mentally ran through the procedure he'd memorized to put together his equipment for the climb down to the inner sphere. His stomach fluttered. From the control panel, he detached a battery the size of a paperback novel and slipped it into a pouch fastened to his belt. Then Paul connected a plug, lit his helmet lamp, hoisted the door levers, and pushed, breaking a seal around the opening. With the door open, a chasm opened at his feet. Holding on to both sides of the aperture, he leaned forward to gape at an intertwined forest of metallic bars caught in the powerful beam of the AMP's main lamp. The light bounced at odd angles, dappling other bars with reflections and transforming the void into a sea of dancing lights.

Despite his breathing exercises, Paul's heart thumped in his chest, the euphoria of success ebbing before the vastness of the cyclopean sphere. A couple of feet over his head, the inner surface of the outer shell that had been pierced by the drill yielded no reflection. The effect was unsettling, weird. The word *alien* came to mind. Tentatively, he stretched out his hand and ran the tips of gloved fingers over the sphere's inner surface. How long had it been since anyone had touched it? Thousands and thousands of years? Twenty-five hundred generations? He tried to picture the builders of such a wonder and found he couldn't. Paul swore, itching to feel the strange material with his bare hand. Discipline. He played the narrow beam down toward the core, picked one of the shiny bars, and followed it until it disappeared into nothingness. *I'm wasting batteries.* He leaned back into the vehicle, reached by feel to a switch, and doused the head projector. Then he toggled another switch to kill the vehicle's internal lights. *I've made it! I'm here.* He wished he could shout.

Once more, he leaned outward to pan his helmet light through the gloom, following the swiftly moving pattern of lights as the beam caught on the bars. He stopped and tried to keep the light steady on the closest bar. It shone like the ram of a hydraulic jack. *This is a hell of a photograph.* Paul held the helmet with both hands and twisted his neck to reach a curved pipette with a mouthpiece. After gripping the plastic piece between his teeth, he rotated a knob on the helmet's side to release the camera's safety catch and blew into the mouthpiece to trigger the camera shutter.

The construction was much more precise than could

have been gleaned from the grainy photograph Paul had seen in Dallas. The sphere below, about thirty feet across, was anchored in midair by hundreds of metal bars—a giant pincushion.

Enough sightseeing.

From the door's edge, Paul unwound a steel safety cable and fastened its carabiner to a ring on his belt. He then leaned out of the AMP, pulled a handle to deploy a vertical footrest, and climbed downward until he felt the steel cable tighten and tug at his waist.

The lower tip of the technical module had two levers to open the whole section. Paul pulled them, moved the panels aside to reveal a storage compartment, and released the fasteners holding one of the two compressed air tanks inside. He disconnected the suit's cooling line and secured it to a loop on the side for the return trip. At once, the chiller built into his suit vibrated. He patted the oblong protuberance on his midriff, took a deep breath, and released the AMP's air supply, then connected the portable equipment to the suit and, with a series of movements he'd practiced dozens of times, slipped the cylinder over his head.

Hampered by the thick gloves, Paul straightened web straps over his chest. He pressed the button on one of the watches built into the suit's arm to record his air reserve. Ninety minutes. From a side loop, Paul picked up a small auxiliary cylinder with twenty minutes of extra air and snapped it to clips over the cooling unit. He recalled the hours spent before a full-length mirror rehearsing each movement with the suit on. *Here is where I start looking like a pregnant astronaut.* He fastened a portable lamp, a small tool pouch, and two folded canvas bags to the belt.

Then he paused and rotated his helmet slowly, a sensation of strangeness deepening. Something was wrong. In the gloom outside, the flashes of light where his beam played over the bars' darkness had changed. Now he could discern the ghostly contours of the farthest supports. A muscle on his thigh twitched. *I'm secured by a cable. I can't fall.* After directing the beam directly overhead, where it disappeared, absorbed by the strange inner surface, he tilted his head further toward the roof but rotated his eyes downward as far as he could. Over the edge of the spherical core, sections of the bars appeared brighter within a rectangular area. *There's light issuing from the other side of the inner sphere.* Paul drew one hand to an upper quadrant of his helmet and depressed a dimple to douse his light. The rectangular pattern disappeared, swallowed by thick darkness. Perhaps it was never there. One finger still on the rubbery protrusion, Paul was about to turn his helmet lamp back on when he froze. Myriad tiny lights danced before his eyes. He blinked repeatedly, but the lights stayed. The inner surface of the vast cavernous volume became an endless field of diamonds repeated on the shiny bars until the void sparkled like a captured nebula. As Paul's eyes adjusted, the sphere's sheer size became apparent and he felt dwarfed, awed at the feat of engineering and advanced technology enveloping him. Darkness had retreated enough to see the contours of his surroundings but not sufficiently to delineate sharp lines. Everything seemed to have its edges blurred in softness.

He recalled the wording on Donald Watson's report.

Buckyballs: BB#1 displays a strong luminescence without local temperature increase or apparent energy source.

Role of these structures and nature of the phenomena: unknown.

Well, Paul knew the roles of the inner layer—at least, a few. Some buckytubes would help to move the air and probably cool it by accelerating its molecules with their unusual shapes. The others perhaps gathered energy. The fullerene layer would be some sort of housing for the other structures. Finally, the buckyballs had been shown to provide a source of light and a gift to the explorer who dared breach the wondrous structure.

Paul grinned. *Me.*

Drunk with sensations, Paul tore his eyes from the lights and shifted his feet on the precarious hold. *At this rate, I won't go past this point.*

Another flush lever released a trapdoor with a coiled conductor and a small box with two push buttons inside. Paul grabbed the device and pressed the top switch. A weighted safety hook at the end of a steel wire unwound. Once he had enough cable, Paul secured the hook to his belt, switched off the craft's main lamp, and slipped underneath the AMP. He depressed the button once more. The winch unwound to lower him fifty feet onto the sphere's surface. As he descended, the sensation of sinking into a luminous fluid deepened, although Paul realized it was an illusion caused by his continuously changing angle of vision. The stars seemed to fold into lazy tendrils, turning, enveloping him like a luminous veil.

With his feet on a solid surface, Paul unhooked the cable and secured it with the control box to one of the bars. Beneath the AMP were telltale signs of drilling. Slurry, rocks, and debris had poured into the void. Tons of mud had left rivulets, like a reddish-brown spiderweb, over the central sphere. He glanced up to a blinking red light on the AMP's nose. The bars jutting out from the core soared above him at odd angles into the black surface of the spherical cavern and disappeared among the stars. The perspective inside the sphere fooled the eye. The craft looked miles away. Suddenly, he felt terribly alone.

The cooling unit spluttered erratically.

Unconsciously, Paul held his breath and drew a hand to the hard shape below his emergency air tank. After a burst of erratic flutters, the vibration died down. With his feet on the hard inner sphere's shell, Paul drew an arm around the nearest support and tapped harder on the cooling unit. With an ambient temperature of 180 degrees F, his body would overheat in minutes. Paul swore. He could withstand edema, rashes, cramps, and exhaustion—the typical symptoms of high-temperature exposure—for a limited period, but not heat syncope, stroke, and hyperpyrexia. Standard sauna temperature was 180 degrees, but the design of the suit kept his skin continuously bathed in his own sweat. High temperature on wet skin would result in excruciating pain. He tapped the unit again, his mind racing, when a sudden thought intruded. Paul jerked his head to the sea of pinpricks on the inner surface of the sphere: the fullerene structures and weirdly shaped nanotubes. Then his gaze dropped to the mechanical instruments on the right sleeve of his suit. Not enough light. He switched his helmet light on: 70 degrees F. A physical cold wave of relief washed over him, anguish replaced with awe. The sphere was a controlled environment, probably sustained by the complex inner layer. He checked again. No mistake. The hygrometer registered twenty percent humidity—irrelevant since the values inside his suit would be close to one hundred percent, but also remarkable. The cooling unit had not malfunctioned. On the contrary, its inner regulator had switched it off. When heat built inside the suit, it would kick in again. His feeling of wonder deepened.

He followed the bars, constructing the pattern in his mind, attempting to glean their structural disposition but failing. The symmetry of the bars was an optical illusion. From the horizontal equator of the inner sphere, the supports bent at subtle angles, following a helical pattern. He could have descended using the tubes as steps.

Paul moved sideways to rub his hand over a brace, solid and shining, as if made hours before. *Fifty thousand years old and no rust?* The bar he'd inspected should have been caked with slurry and debris after the crown had pierced the shell. But the bar's mirror finish was spotless, obviously so perfectly polished that the cascading drilling slurry couldn't cling to its surface.

Paul descended to a point where the bars were horizontal. Grabbing on to one, he squatted and switched on his helmet lamp, panning the light toward the supports spreading downward.

The bars below curved, forming level steps even a child could use. Paul tried to keep apprehension at bay. He thought about the builders, thousands of years before, patiently designing the internal structure to let a man step down to reach the underside without tools.

There had been the hard shell of the outer sphere to contend with, but the main difficulty was due to the depth. It was obvious now that the sphere had been built much closer to the surface, probably at the bottom of a canyon or fissure, but over the millennia alluvia and shifts had piled miles of deposits over it. When Paul had arrived at IMC's labs, everybody had been baffled at the physical properties of the materials. The concrete resisted grinding but sheared off like flint, the metal armatures of the cradle embedded in the concrete were butt-jointed, and the rubberlike material could be cut with a knife or any other object providing the action was slow, keeping friction to a minimum. One of the technicians back at IMC labs had proved that a man with a chisel and a hammer could breach the outer shell in a few days.

The conclusion was inescapable. The sphere's accessibility was proportional to the technology used to breach it: the humbler the tools, the easier the entrance. The builders of the sphere had included a lesson in humility into the design. If additional material hadn't piled over the sphere, it was reasonable to assume a deep shaft with timber props could have reached it.

Paul took several deep breaths and negotiated the bars, bending his bulky headgear down to avoid the upper braces. When he reached the lower curve of the sphere, the lamp's beam highlighted a platform crafted from the bars. He panned his head left and right over the inner sphere, but the light beam followed an unbroken surface. There must be an opening. It made no sense otherwise. So much effort to visit a ball within a ball? Although the light was sufficient to move around, it wasn't strong enough for a detailed inspection. Somewhere, there had to be an opening device, a lever or button or something. He reached for the flashlight dangling from his belt and switched it on. In the background, the tiny stars faded.

The light-emitting particles, whatever their role and working mechanism, seemed to react to different light levels, but in his mounting anxiety, Paul didn't waste time theorizing. The lack of a visible opening to access the inner sphere spelled disaster. Although smaller than the formidable outer shell, the core sphere was huge, and it would take many hours, if not days, to scour its surface for an opening device. Then he remembered the mirage-like rectangular glow. He backed a few steps to the far edge of the platform and once more switched off his helmet lamp. A tremor, and then his cooling unit vibrated steadily.

After a few endless seconds, a rectangular section of the sphere, perhaps eight feet tall and four feet wide, glowed faintly, as if driven by inner phosphorescence. Paul neared, reached out with his hand, and pushed it into the lighter area. His gloved hand sunk an inch into a soft surface. He pushed harder, but to no avail. The putty-like material gradually hardened until it was like a rock. Paul tried different places within the shape, with similar results. In frustration he switched his lamp on and examined the surface, his helmet a scant distance from the sphere's surface.

Although there was no visual clue, the continuous surface abruptly changed from hard to a weird jelly-like consistency within the contours of the lighter rectangle. It *had* to be the door, the shape suggested one. Opening it was another matter. Tension mounted as Paul ran his hand over the edge. Then he enlarged the area of his inspection a foot to either side. Nothing. He tried a little farther, and his fingers caught on a depression. Paul swiveled his head to aim the lamp and jerked his hand away when he identified the indent. A handprint. He squinted and a tremor ran down his spine. Not a human hand. Paul neared, his eyes running over the contour of the shape. It looked vaguely human, with five fingers, only this hand had three fingers and two thumbs. Two opposing thumbs. Kibassa had been clear. The sphere had been built by ancestors, but he hadn't mentioned humans. Only perhaps they were human, only different.

Paul maneuvered his hand, clad in the bulky glove, over the indent, but nothing happened. He splayed his fingers to conform to the recess, but the sphere remained impervious to his efforts. *It may need a similar hand.* He backed up a step, his helmet light trained on the depression. In sudden anger, he slammed both hands onto the place where he'd guessed the door to be, but there could have been steel under the soft surface. It didn't shift.

Two keys guard the colors of the rainbow: body and mind.

Well, he was using his body. He slammed his palm onto the indent again and pushed harder. Then it hit him. *I'm using fabric, not my hand.* As he reached for the airtight clasp fastening the glove to his suit, Paul brushed aside the craziness of what he was about to do. Would someone build an air-conditioned structure, with lights and steps, only to spike it with germs, nerve gas, or killer viruses? They might, but his gut told him he had to risk it. He looked at his bare hand as if seeing it for the first time. Wet, white, and pruned from stewing in his own sweat. He flexed his fingers, then he waved and felt his skin cooling. *There's air. I could probably remove this damn suit and be no worse for it.* But he wasn't about to try. He

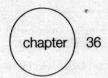

"*You* do not understand, sir. We are experiencing traffic congestion." Pierre Oyono spoke English, pronouncing each word as one would speak to a child. "As soon as possible, we will squeeze you in."

Luther Cox reddened and crowded into the lieutenant's personal space.

"It's *you* who doesn't understand. Our mission is sanctioned by your ministry and communicated to your superiors. Anyway," he jerked his thumb toward the helicopter, "it's a fucking chopper, not a 747. It doesn't need a runway. Vertical takeoff, get it?"

Cox's team of marines watched from their vantage point next to the helicopter.

"I do not know about the law in your country, but here you need a permit to take off. Besides—"

"Take me to your superior!" Cox interrupted.

Oyono stared. After some consideration, he sighed. "Fine. Follow me, please, if you would be so kind." He performed a parade turn and marched with long strides toward a squat building about fifty yards from the chopper. When Oyono reached the door, he opened it and stood aside to let Cox in. He followed him and closed the door.

The building was a cavernous hangar, empty except for a small table and a chair. Bulbs hanging from twisted cords, thick with grime, emitted dim islands of light at intervals. Oyono marched past Cox with the same military gait until he reached the table, where he deposited his clipboard. Without altering his indifferent demeanor, he turned to peer at Cox, still standing by the door.

"*I* am it. I am in charge of this airport, at present under military jurisdiction."

"You're a fucking clown, that's what you are."

"Mr. Cox, I have addressed you with politeness," Oyono said evenly. "People like you are adept at intimidation. But I am afraid your technique has no effect on me."

"Is that a threat?" Cox edged forward with a hint of a smile on his face.

"No, sir. No threats. Just facts. Your party lacks takeoff sanction and will remain grounded at my pleasure. I am also bringing to your attention another reality: You're a big-mouthed motherfucker."

Cox twisted on the ball of his right foot and aimed a savage kick toward Oyono's chest. Oyono shifted his body weight and recoiled out of the kick's trajectory. Then he flexed his knees, squatted, and sprang into the air, kicking Cox in the face. Cox grunted and fell backward, eyes widening. Before he could straighten, Oyono kicked him in the side. A sharp crack echoed from the grimy walls, like splitting bamboo cane.

With labored movements Cox stood, his gaze unfocused.

Oyono drew closer and deflected a chop directed at his larynx, then grasped the hand and brought it sharply down on his knee, snapping the arm at the joint. In the same fluid movement, he smashed his elbow into Cox's nose.

With a thud, Cox flopped down and lay in an impossible position, his arm twisted upward like that of a broken doll.

Without undue haste, Oyono picked up his clipboard and strode outside, stopping for a moment to breathe the moist evening air.

> *Black wing, brown wing, hover over;*
> *Twenty years and the spring is over;*

Thomas Stearns Eliot, the American poet turned Brit. *I wonder why?*

Then, with his characteristic martial bearing, Oyono marched ramrod straight to the chopper as he pondered how such dimwits managed to build the world's most powerful nation.

When the marines saw him return alone, they exchanged glances and moved toward the helicopter.

"Gentlemen, I ask you not to try anything foolish. Please, behave yourselves like civilized people in a foreign country. If you draw a weapon, I beg to point out that, behind me, on the terrace above, there are three M-60s aimed at you. They are old," he conceded, "but in fine working condition. They would reduce you and your craft to shreds. Now I suggest you tend to your superior officer, who has sustained some damage, and wait here for your takeoff warrant."

Oyono stared at the tense-faced marines. "Good night, gentlemen," he said, performing a smart military half turn on his heel and marching toward the airport's main building.

○

At the Langley situation room, the bloodshot eyes of three disheveled men and a woman betrayed the stress of the past hours.

"The camp is ablaze, except for an area around the shaft," Dario Hindman said, approaching the screen sideways. "The first piece of good news so far."

"The camp is under control, but the interference continues," Rhea Paige added. "The AMP's descent started on schedule."

"There's the security chief," Aaron Greenberg said. "It's strange the camp's officers managed to vanish, except for our contact and his men."

"I can't see any great danger here," Director Foust said. "The IMC people wanted Dr. Mosengwo out of the way to avoid embarrassing explanations about the AMP's unexpected trip. The security man who accompanied her is under orders to keep her occupied. As for the other—he's a pro. Maybe something didn't smell right and he got the hell out."

"Agreed," Greenberg said. "The plan's working so far. Even if that guy hides in the jungle and sees the whole thing, what could he testify to? Witnessing a bunch of soldiers on a rampage?"

"Don't forget there's a white observer, and the area around the shaft is intact," Hindman added, returning to the table.

"But the shaft is the only valuable asset in the camp," Director Foust countered. "The man could well be a Gécamines inspector. They employ Europeans."

"Problems will start when the army leaves the camp before the rescue team arrives."

Foust stared at Greenberg. "Why do you say that? How long will it take them to come from Kisangani?"

"About two hours, starting ninety minutes from now. The army, or the rebels—whatever you want to call them—will leave at four, half an hour before our team arrives. We've arranged for a dead zone, a thirty-minute interval to keep them apart at the camp. There can't be any contact between our men and those people."

Hindman shook his head. "You worry about the missing security chief. I doubt he'll cause problems. The AMP will be on its way up, and I can't see what difference thirty minutes will make. Besides, there should be seven men in the control cabin."

"I wasn't thinking about the security chief," Greenberg clarified, "but the interference. You have any more information about it? Anything?"

"We tried to triangulate the disturbance's origin with satellites," Paige said as all eyes swiveled to her. "There are two sources broadcasting. If that was all, we could zero in on the transmitters within a couple of minutes. But what causes the interference is a third frequency originating in the ionosphere, where the primary ones bounce back. It's like an umbrella over the ground."

"Then how do you know there are two transmitters?" Foust asked.

"You need two separate sources to create resonance."

"Who has the technology?" Greenberg asked.

"Nobody we know of. We've been testing frequencies for years, and it's hell to uphold resonance, because of the atmosphere's absorption."

"Your information must be flawed," Director Foust said. "Someone has the technology and is using it with excellent results. We've been deaf for hours. Unless the interference has something to do with the damn hole. I haven't heard that possibility considered."

All faces turned to Foust.

"You mean from the shaft?" Paige asked, eyes wide.

"If the rubber and concrete samples are advanced, why not the interference?" Foust asked. "Maybe the AMP triggered something."

A yellow light blinked on Hindman's armrest. He lifted the phone. Everyone knew the news wasn't good, because the operations director blanched.

Hindman listened in silence and replaced the handset on its cradle. "That was Bouchard. We have problems. There's a hitch in Kisangani. The airport's full of army personnel who won't let them take off. They're trying to raise somebody with enough authority to issue a permit. Luther Cox tried to muscle his way out and is wounded. Bouchard will call back as soon as he knows more."

"Unless there's an act of God, the thirty-minute dead zone may be hours. *Long* hours," Greenberg added. "The interference began minutes before the capsule's departure, right?" He glanced toward Rhea Paige for the answer.

She nodded, and Greenberg sucked in a long breath of air.

"If it's the shaft," Greenberg went on, "that sphere isn't just advanced; it knew what we were going to do. It was ready for us."

chapter 37

After climbing a few steps, Paul stood on the solid flat floor of the inner sphere. The light from his helmet bounced back, and the brightness increased until it was as intense as daylight. Paul's eyes widened as he looked around and etched the scene in his memory. On impulse, he reached for the lamp hooked on his belt, switched it off, and then put out the light on his helmet. His hunch was right. The walls continued to emit extensive bluish light. He blew twice into the mouthpiece to operate the still camera.

A small circular table supported by a thick metal cylinder occupied the center of the room. Paul stepped forward. Centered on top of the table was a gleaming sphere the size of a beach ball. The polished metal reflected the room's blue light. Above it, six curved wedges floated in midair. *Magnetic?* Yet he didn't notice any pull on the metal instruments peppering his arm when he neared the objects. On the tabletop, there were five shallow indents the size of small bowls. All but one contained multiple egg-size metallic marbles. He eyed the wedges. No wires supporting them, no struts; the things just floated in an arch over the table. Otherwise, the room was bare, with no loose elements. No colors. No rainbow. Nothing.

Paul walked gingerly around the table, neared the curved inner surface of the room, and ran his bare hand over its surface. On impulse, he unfastened his other glove and stowed it away with its companion in one of the bags dangling from his belt. When he pressed his fingers on the wall, the surface gave, dimpling an inch or so, only to recover its previous shape as soon as Paul withdrew his hand. He panned his eyes along the line where the platform met the curved walls, looking for any distinguishing features. On the left of the opening and the steps, Paul counted six circles on the floor, like inserts of the same material but slightly lighter in color. He squatted and rubbed his fingers over the circle's edges, without feeling any joint. *Decoration?* So far he hadn't spotted anything that could be remotely construed as decoration. Everything seemed to have a function, only he didn't know what those might be.

He straightened and turned slowly for another look at the featureless walls. Besides the table, the sphere was empty. Paul returned to the table and inspected its contents. A sharp tone echoed in his helmet. Paul checked his watch, and his chest tightened. His ninety minutes were spent. He disconnected the main air cylinder and opened the valve of the reserve canister on his chest. It felt funny handling his equipment with bare hands, but he could be much faster now. Paul removed his portable breathing apparatus and left it on the platform outside the spherical room, lit the helmet lamp, and, now familiar with his surroundings, returned at once to the underside of the AMP.

When Paul reached the point where he had left the cable, he clasped the hook to his belt and maneuvered the winch to reach for the second compressed-air cylinder. He contorted in slow movements, hanging below the AMP like a hooked fish being reeled in. Paul secured the second cylinder on his back and closed the valve of the reserve canister. He'd entered the room and found no colors. *Now what?* After resetting the timer on his wrist, he returned to the core sphere with an increasing sense of urgency.

At the platform before the stairs, he knelt down, obeying a sudden intuition. Paul directed the lamp's beam to the underside, to confirm his suspicions. The metal column supporting the table continued downward through the inner sphere's wall and pierced a pool of slurry at the bottom of the containment sphere. Paul weighed the implications. The sphere could be sitting over a buried structure. According to Kibassa's tales, there had been past instances where people had messed about with other spheres. Every time, the place had blown to smithereens soon after, and the column looked suspiciously like a plunger.

For the second time, he climbed the steps to enter the spherical room and darted a quick glance around, now a little more apprehensive about doing something wrong. But nothing seemed to have changed. He neared the table and peered at the shallow indents and the balls. He reached for one—a little larger than a table-tennis ball and shiny like a ball bearing—and picked it up. As he withdrew his hand, the ball seemed to hit an invisible wall, and it escaped his fingers, dropping down to the edge of the table. After a flurry of tiny bounces, it stayed there. Paul eyed the ball with mistrust. Then he reached again and hefted it onto his palm. It was heavy, perhaps half a pound. Then, with the ball sitting on his outstretched palm, he started to withdraw his hand. When the ball reached a point Paul assumed was perpendicular with the table's edge, it started to slide along the palm of his hand toward his fingertips, as if halted by an invisible barrier. He closed his fingers around the object to prevent it from falling again, rested it on the table's edge, and tried to nudge it over, his other hand lower down to arrest its fall. But the ball didn't progress past the end of the table. Paul was about to return the ball to its original dimple when he thought it over and placed it in a different one.

He nodded as a picture formed in his mind. The sphere builders must have considered different scenarios. If the palm imprint outside could identify a species, no other animal would have been able to deactivate whatever held the door together. Only a man could. Perhaps any man—and that could pose a problem. If a savage managed to breach the inner sphere, the only loose objects would be the balls. He would certainly try to take them with him. Paul was only guessing, but if he found the objects fascinating, a primitive man would have been entranced by their sheer strangeness. Surely the balls were magical talismans; gifts from the gods. So the builders must have considered that scenario and ensured the balls couldn't leave the table.

The five dimples, arranged in a semicircle around the

sphere resting on the table, contained different quantities of balls. He picked the ball he'd used to test his theory and returned it to its original place. From left to right, he counted the spheres in the dimples: two, three, five, nil, eighteen. The first three were prime numbers, the last one wasn't.

Two keys guard the colors of the rainbow: body and mind.

Two, three, five, _____, eighteen.

If he was right and his body had acted on the door's lock, the problem before him was mental, and it couldn't be too hard. Could it? What would the builders seek? Surely not a cryptanalyst. Intelligence? Knowledge? How much? Perhaps only enough to determine that the discoverer could reason and owned a modicum of scientific knowledge. Paul nodded. If Leon Kibassa was right, the colors of the rainbow would be useless to a cave dweller.

Two, three, five... The following prime would be seven, and the one after, eleven. Seven and eleven— eighteen. Without further delay, Paul scooped seven balls from the last dimple and placed them into its neighbor: two, three, five, seven, eleven.

All around him, the inner sphere underwent a transformation. There must have been clicks and hisses, but Paul couldn't hear them over the roar of blood raging in his temples and a faint high-pitched noise, like tinnitus.

The sphere walls rippled and seemed to dissolve like a startled swarm of minute insects to rearrange into a three-dimensional 360-degree image: hundreds of men and women with raised hands, palms forward in the universal gesture of welcome. Hands with two opposing thumbs.

Paul stepped back until the heel of his boot rested on the stair's edge, his heart thumping in his chest.

The bodies were beautiful—skinny and obese, youths with tight-muscled chests and old folks with wrinkled skin, children with innocent stares and women with pregnant bellies, wise-eyed old sages. Babies with huge eyes in the arms of old women with deflated breasts.

It's the faces! Paul realized. He gasped. *They're so proud, it shines in their faces!*

He never imagined such a force—a proclamation of human kinship—could be captured in a single image.

Time slowed. Paul let his gaze wander over the images. He searched the nuances of each face, the sensitivity, the intelligence, the gradations of copper and tans.

No whites! No blacks either, or Asians, or any other division by color.

There were Oriental cheekbones, Mediterranean noses, and thick Negroid lips: beautiful. But no one face fit any racial archetypes.

Then he understood. Individual races had mixed and disappeared. Before him he saw the end result of thousands of years of interbreeding. "You beautiful people!" Paul cried out, and laughed at his impulse.

He neared the wall and reached out to touch the picture. His finger sank into the image as though it was etched into soft foam. The eyes of those pictured followed his gaze, beaming. *It's a visual effect.* Paul forced himself to swallow. *The eyes don't move.* He stepped away from the image and glanced around. From the six circles on the floor had sprouted six columns, each with a height similar to the tabletop and about a foot in diameter. On top of each cylinder was an engraving of the mysterious hand—not a recess this time, but only an outline. Without thinking, Paul laid his bare hand on the shape and the top of the column rose, exposing beneath it a rack stacked with scores of metal rings like thin bracelets. *I'm getting better at this.* He fished one out and watched as colored waves rippled across its narrow surface. Colors. *Is this the rainbow?*

On the wall, the images stared back, smiling, their deformed hands raised. He did a quick calculation and glanced down at the canvas bags clipped to his belt. He could carry all the rings and have room to spare. Suddenly, Paul became calm as his training took over. He collected the rings from all the columns and transferred them to his empty bag; the other held his bulky gloves.

Back at the table, he noticed that the center sphere had split along its equator, separating into two halves. Paul hunched down to examine the hemispheres and the space between, the only place so far left unchecked. Inside, on the flat circular surface of the lower half, sat six disks the size of large casino chips. Six colored disks. Paul paused, then smiled at his own stupidity. He had expected seven colors, not six. Newton had named the colors of the rainbow red, orange, yellow, green, blue, indigo, and violet: ROY G BIV, a mnemonic from his school days. But Newton believed in numerology and thought that seven was a special number. Seven continents, seven days in the week, seven endocrine glands, seven openings in our head, seven double letters in the Hebrew alphabet, seven seas... The list was endless. Of course, any Christian would point out seven virtues and seven sins. But the rainbow colors merged gradually into one another and there were literally millions of hues. He peered at the colored disks: red, orange, yellow, green, blue, and violet. The builders of the sphere didn't concur with Newton and had skipped indigo. With his forefinger, he slid one out. He jumped back when one of the wedges on the band above shone in the same color as the chip. Paul replaced the disk, and the slice dimmed. Somehow, the wedges and the disks were connected. *But how?*

The wedge floated in midair. Paul tried to move it, but it was held solid. He pushed it again with more force and identical results. Then he glanced again at the wall's image. The group seemed warmer, their smiles more animated. Paul checked his air timer. Fifteen minutes left.

The only objects that could be removed from the sphere were the rings he already had in his bag and the disks. He slid the disks from between the hemispheres, stowed them in a sleeve pouch, and stood back. Six curved wedges flashed in violet, blue, green, yellow, orange, and red: the colors of the rainbow.

Then Paul detected movement, and his heart skipped a beat.

Slowly, the image on the wall dissolved. In unison, the wedges of the band drew together, changing color to form a solid ring of blinding white. Underneath it, both hemispheres closed until they formed a single unit.

In quick succession, Paul snapped a stream of photographs, pausing only to advance the film.

Then the ring of light dissolved and the shining ball slowly fell toward the interior of the central column.

Something stirred on the far wall. Paul darted a glance

and saw fish swim from the edges of his vision to arrange into a slowly rotating circumference. Then another image superimposed over the fish. The image of two hands, thumbs outstretched and fingers folded, drew together and touched.

The circle was complete. Perfect.

Paul stood transfixed, watching the upper edge of the sphere sink below the surface of the table. On his left, the columns that held the stacked rings had closed and were retreating noiselessly into the floor. *Wow!* Euphoria welled in his chest. The sphere seemed to be wrapping up its show. That could only mean his task was complete. He looked around. All motion had stopped, except the circumference of fish turning slowly inside the hands.

His air supply almost exhausted, he hastened down the steps and out of the room. Once he was outside, the opening shimmered and disappeared, replaced by the sphere's unbroken surface. He knelt again on the edge of the platform of tubes and panned his flashlight underneath it. The shiny column he had spotted on his way in was slowly sinking. And somewhere, Paul suspected, a clock had started its countdown. He had no more time to explore. Paul retraced his steps to the upper crown of the inner sphere, clipped the winch's cable to his belt, and pressed the button to hoist himself to the AMP. As he dangled in midair, Paul eyed his bare hands. Inside the AMP, the temperature would be stifling and all surfaces too hot to touch. In measured movements to prevent imparting a swing to the cable, he recovered his gloves and slipped them on, swearing when he fumbled with the second one. Once under the AMP, he hooked his suit to the vehicle's air and refrigeration system. A welcome coolness washed over him. Paul opened the valves on his legs and watched his own sweat gush out. His lips felt parched; he was burning with thirst. Paul sucked from the tube inside his helmet, guzzling the salty emergency liquid stored in the suit pads. His body soaked up revitalizing electrolytes as it recovered from dehydration.

After struggling to negotiate the narrow door into the vehicle, Paul turned around and leaned over to gaze into the sea of stars, to imprint in his mind a unique image. An image no man alive had ever seen.

Fullerenes? Disintegrating surfaces? Solids held in midair? Two-thumbed hands? The sphere had yielded objects he hoped would fulfill the purpose of his mission, but it had held on to its secrets and technological wonders. Over the next couple of minutes, Paul considered that the sphere's technology could change his world. The hidden source of power had withstood the passage of millennia unscathed; the very materials of the construction seemed indestructible, crafted to last unimaginable spans of time.

He then climbed back into the AMP, closing the bottom door and awkwardly reversing the steps he had taken when he first arrived. When he was strapped back into his seat in the upper portion of the capsule, he pushed the lever to start the ascent, lit the periscope lights, and watched the bottom of the shaft recede.

Somewhere in the bowels of the sphere, something had primed. Why would the builders bother to destroy it? It seemed as if they had planned that whoever found it

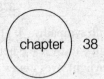
Hidden under dense foliage for several hours, a few yards away from the now-inert fence surrounding the camp, the group had grown inured to the screams and howls of the mutilated men. Hilari N'dende glanced at Gordon, who slouched on the ground with his back propped against a tree, his eyes red-rimmed and vacant. A thin trail of clotting blood from a lump on Gordon's forehead ran down the side of his face, soaking his collar.

When the terrible shrieking and howling began, Gordon had leaped with homicidal fury toward the fence; Hilari's men restrained him to avoid detection. A violent fight ensued. Eventually Hilari dropped the enraged security chief with a blow to the head.

Next to him, Michael shook his head nonstop, perhaps unable to assimilate the butchery inside the IMC concourse despite Shermaine's advice about the futility of trying to stop the carnage. The security on Paul's return was the only consideration now.

Hilari walked toward his men and peered at Gordon

with sympathy. "It's ten minutes past two in the morning. They must leave before four if they don't want to fly in daylight over zones they don't control. Accept fate and stop recriminating yourself. All you would do is die and get us all killed."

"They're our men!" Michael growled in return. "We brought them here!"

Shermaine laid a hand on Michael's arm. "Michael, those men out there are part of a plan. I don't believe anybody wanted this to happen, not even the CIA, which orchestrated this debacle. They crossed paths with destiny and found themselves where they should never have been. It's all part of a cycle."

She put both her hands on Michael's waist and moved in close. Hilari raised an eyebrow and smiled inwardly as he considered that good old Shermaine was definitely hooked on Michael. *For fun or for keeps?*

"When the dry season comes, wildebeest migrate to water and pasture thousands of miles away, from the Serengeti to the savanna."

"What does this—" Michael started.

"Wait. Listen," Shermaine insisted. "When they reach a river, sometimes the first animals sink into the mud and are trapped. The bodies form a bridge over which the rest of the herd crosses. The herd isn't concerned with the dead. Without the ones providing the bridge, none would survive. Mike, this is much more important than any of us. We don't matter. When this is over, you'll agree that any cost is acceptable."

Gordon raised an eyebrow and folded his arms. "Any cost?"

"That's right, my friend," Hilari answered. "Any price.

I have forced this nation's government into backing this operation. Hundreds, thousands of people have their eyes on us."

"We could have spread out along the fence and shot them like rabbits—anything to stop this obscenity," Gordon insisted.

"You're right," Hilari admitted. "We could have done that. Nevertheless, we couldn't kill them all. Someone would run for it. The CIA would put two and two together. Don't misunderstand me. I wouldn't lose any sleep over that, but I don't want Uncle Sam sending better muscle than these clowns to hunt us down.

"Anyway, that would be the least of our worries. If we started shooting these idiots, we would have had a full-fledged battle. You can't control action in a battle. Just one grenade down that shaft would cut off our future—if we have one." Hilari thought of Tshul and Mkhas, the two men he'd left manning the electronics in the van, and how much the operation's success hung on their expertise. "Can't take the risk. So far we've not been detected; the ground is too hot to afford good infrared contrast. Those gold-foil blankets over the vehicles help avoid detection."

"What's in that shaft?" Gordon asked.

Shermaine moved away from Michael and squatted next to Gordon. "With God's help, Paul will be bringing up our future."

"Answer me, Shermaine."

"I can't."

Hilari walked away a few paces and returned with a long leather case. "Shermaine said that perhaps all this is the result of several unfortunate circumstances and that maybe even the CIA didn't want it this way. I disagree. They could have had the same results by other means, but that's academic now. That white man," he pointed with his chin toward the control cabin, "is already dead, though he doesn't know it. I planned to do it myself, but I'm feeling generous. I'll give him to you."

Gordon stood up, baring his teeth in a fierce grin, looking alternately at Hilari's face and the case in his hand.

"In this case is a connoisseur's rifle: a Brno twenty-two caliber. The bullets are tiny and subsonic, with a weak charge. It doesn't need a silencer. It's no louder than a sneeze but has a short range. That's the bad news. The good news is these are hollow point, mercury tipped." He held up a cartridge between his thumb and index finger for Gordon to examine. "From the other side of the fence, about fifty yards from the tent, there is a spot with an unobstructed view. Now, listen to me, Gordon. When the *shufta* are ready to pull out, that man will stand up and walk toward the choppers. That's the moment, and not a second before. They'll have no time to investigate. Give me your word that you'll wait until then."

Gordon lowered his gaze and shuffled his feet. "You have my word," he said as he took the rifle.

"You were in the army?" Hilari asked.

Gordon nodded.

"Marines?"

He nodded again.

"Breathing, it's all in the breathing; my sergeant drilled that into me during my training days. Wait until you are at the bottom of an exhale, when you have no air left in your lungs and you hang between breaths. That's when your body is at rest. That's when you squeeze the trigger. One of my men will show you the ideal spot. And remember, a head shot."

○

The esplanade of the camp could have been a scene out of Dante's Inferno. A low mist, the breath of the earth, fell like a shroud and licked the blackened cabins. As if a crazed hand had shaken the camp, twisted antennas and crooked storage tanks lay entangled with burned-out machinery, empty beer crates, and corpses: the remains of mutilated men. Cadavers without ears or genitals, objects jutting from tortured orifices, littered the ground like empty, nonreturnable containers. The *shufta*, tired of the orgy, sat on crates or slept in groups, impervious to the penetrating smell of excrement and burned matter floating over the installation.

In the center of the tableau, the choppers stood still, their pilots asleep inside, the only ones who could not share in the party. Moisture covered the machines, and a thin film of water, broken into minute dewdrops, glistened over airframes and windshields like tiny diamonds.

Somewhere an unseen hand opened a can of beer, and the hiss blended with the noises of the forest, a call to silence and calm after the savagery.

Robert Lukesh lit another cigarette. He'd been almost motionless for the past few hours, detached from his surroundings, his eyes darting in all directions, registering details, shapes, colors, and sensations. Lukesh mulled over his status as an observer. He was a machine, a drone posted to a faraway place to analyze and reduce the unspeakable to words in a report. Lukesh had obeyed his orders not to intervene but to stay on the sidelines and watch, evaluate the job without questioning.

From the corner of his eye, he noticed movement. General Kalundo exited a cabin, buttoning his shirt and shouting at the same time. Colonel Daulne rushed out the door of a container and darted about, kicking inert forms and yelling at the top of his lungs. From all corners of the site, groups of dirty and disheveled men picked up their weapons and collected obscene souvenirs of their night of debauchery.

Lukesh ground out a cigarette butt with the heel of his boot and stood. He glanced sideways at the locked door of the control cabin, behind which the trapped technicians and Owen DeHolt had experienced their own particular hell. The sounds would torment them for the rest of their lives. Lukesh yawned and stretched, looking up at the clear sky and the moon's faint yellow halo as he began walking toward the choppers. It was his last vision before his head exploded in a fine mist of bone and fluid.

○

Kalundo saw the American fall. In an irrational reaction, he ran toward the headless torso. Then reality clawed its way through his bloated brain and he raised his gaze toward the jungle's impenetrable screen. In an unfamiliar but real hallucination, he felt the gun sight's crosshairs slowly travel his body, over his distended belly, fluttering on his chest and neck, to stop with cool deliberation between his eyebrows.

A cold sweat trickled down the valley of his back.

During the next everlasting seconds, Kalundo stood without blinking, knowing death stared at him with the same intensity. With blinding clarity, he realized his stupidity. If death wanted to reach its hand from the jungle, nothing could stop it.

Without moving a muscle on his face, Kalundo turned around and set off, his eyes glued to the now-blurred image of the choppers reverberating like a mirage over hot asphalt. It was the longest walk of his life. When he finally reached the first machine and could hide from the line of sight, he stopped, feeling a sudden cool breath on his wet face. Without looking back, Kalundo mounted the steps and collapsed onto a webbed seat.

The lead chopper rose into the wind, joined by its mates in an echelon formation that veered to the east, heading for Kisangani.

○

At a few minutes to four in the morning, the jeep bore toward the chopper at full speed and skidded to a stop with a screech. While the driver, a boy no older than eighteen, remained motionless behind the steering wheel, Lieutenant Pierre Oyono got out with studied composure.

The American soldiers, clad in combat fatigues, their faces drawn by the long wait, stood and moved away from the airframe, eyeing the approaching lieutenant with open hostility. Oyono knew his order to leave their weapons in the choppers made them feel unpleasantly vulnerable.

Oyono saluted, but his greeting was not returned.

"Could you *please* advise the pilot to come down?" he asked no one in particular.

A huge sergeant cracked his knuckles and disappeared inside the craft. He reappeared a few seconds later with an officer, a set of earphones around his neck, its spiral cable dangling.

"Here's your flight plan," Oyono said, offering the captain a folded sheet of paper from his shirt pocket. "You may take off at once, although you will have to stay below three hundred feet until you reach the first radio beacon. And please avoid the river. I apologize for the delay and wish you a swift and pleasant journey."

Oyono pivoted smartly on his heel as the driver gunned the jeep's engine.

"Son of a bitch," the sergeant muttered in a low growl.

The lieutenant, despite the engine noise, turned and locked eyes with the sergeant. Finally, Oyono stood to attention and drew a rigid hand to his right brow.

"Good night, brother."

dream, he sank into a deep mental and physical drowsiness and closed his eyes, filling his mind with the extraordinary image of his kin, the people who had handed him a legacy.

Men and women smiled in a sign of recognition. Paul approached the center, and the group came forward as one with open arms. A pleasant sensation overwhelmed him as he mixed with the people now gathered around him.

Eyes smiled and sparkled as if dusted with stars. A woman, her skin textured with the canyons of age, reached for his hand and ran gnarled but pleasantly warm fingers over his own. She turned his hand over and leaned closer before nodding. Then they hummed. A soft drone at first, the sound grew and modulated into a melody without cadence, like the soughing of wind and tame rain. Colored shafts of light coalesced into whorls of thick warm air, a dancing pageantry of swirling hues, swimming, rotating into a lazy vortex, becoming denser, tangible, and alive. Then the color eddy tore into ribbons of pure light, fanning out from its center in an orgy of sparkling colors.

All around, arms pressed and held him with increasing strength. More bodies crowded in closer and squeezed, until Paul found it difficult to breathe. He tried to shake free, but the bodies bore on him relentlessly, smothering him.

Paul opened his eyes and tried to inhale but found no air to take into his lungs. Terrified, gasping for air, he grabbed the helmet with both hands and tried to remove it. From the depths of his mind, a tendril of sentience guided his hand to the tubes connected to his chest and removed them. On the edge of unconsciousness, Paul connected the small, almost-exhausted spare cylinder. A rush of air flooded his lungs with revitalizing force. His vision cleared, and his body started to respond.

The counters read 13,000 feet and 04:00. With increasing awareness, he calculated that it would take another hour to reach the surface. Then he looked at the small spare cylinder. Ten minutes of air left.

Fully conscious, he reached for his tool pouch as he checked dials showing the main air tanks half full. After clipping the pouch to his belt, Paul took a small screwdriver and a roll of tape. With the tip of the tool, he peeled the end of the roll until he had enough tape to grip in his gloved fingers. He grasped the air hose and placed the tape over the valve. With the tip of the screwdriver, he depressed the inner nipple. The compressed air should have caused the tape to flutter, but the ribbon did not move. Paul darted a glance at the dials and understood; regardless of the readings, the tanks were empty.

Paul undid his safety harness and slid into the lower compartment. From the tool pouch, he selected a thin blade to cut a slit in the suit and body stocking to one side of his crotch. Paul flinched as he felt blood trickle down his thigh. He pushed his hand inside the opening as he pressed with his sphincter until he felt the implanted ball's rounded shape. Paul withdrew his hand and, with a movement he had practiced hundreds of times, twisted both halves and opened it.

From inside the hollow ball, he removed a triangular arrow. Reaching inside the slit, Paul plunged the arrow into his thigh.

After a few seconds, he let the small triangle drop and

with the tape attempted to seal the slash in the suit's fabric, working with only one hand.

Feeling weak, he climbed the steps and fastened himself into the harness. Deep convulsions racked his body. After a short agonizing rattle and a violent fluttering of his eyelids, Paul's heart stopped.

part three

circle

This is not the end.
It is not even the
beginning of the end.
But it is, perhaps, the
end of the beginning.

sir winston leonard
spencer churchill

Hailey Brown, Dylan Hayes, Owen DeHolt, and the three other technicians stood in a semicircle around Robert Lukesh's corpse, numb from the sights and sounds of an endless night.

When the screams started and the outcome of his treacherous scheming became apparent, Dylan jumped on Owen and tried to strangle him. Hailey pulled him off and Owen curled up on a chair, trembling. The other men cowered against the far end of the room, as far away from the door and Owen as possible, as if distance could reduce the horror in progress outside. Hailey, perched on a stool facing the door, watched his men. He supposed they no longer considered a fistful of dollars worth the price. No one made eye contact.

The real terror began when the howling stopped. The men fixed their eyes on the door, waiting for the kick of a boot followed by black faces with pitiless eyes. When they finally heard the choppers taking off, Owen rushed out before the others. He'd aged ten years; a spark of madness lurked in his sunken eyes. Hailey panned the camp's smoldering wreck and spotted the headless torso first, realizing the viscous fragments clotting and sliding like slugs down the door and sides of the shelter were all that was left of the CIA man's head.

Dylan was the first to react. He rushed to the control panel. "It's on its way," he yelled. "The AMP's returning."

The other men paid no attention. In unison, they pivoted toward the sound of an approaching vehicle. Hailey backed off several paces and leaned on the cabin. With measured movements, he unbuttoned his lab whites. *About time,* he thought as he produced a pistol from a holster strapped to his chest.

The SUV stopped a short distance from the group. The first to alight were Gordon and Michael, followed by Hilari and Shermaine. Michael and Hilari quickly spread a gold-foiled sheet over the front of the Hummer.

Hailey glanced at stealthy silhouettes clad in black closing in from the edges of the camp, floating like ghosts, jumping from cover to cover as they zeroed in on the shaft area. He caught Gordon's eye and nodded, noticing in his peripheral vision the shadowy men spreading out in their direction.

"Hello, Owen," Gordon said calmly as if all were normal.

Owen glanced around, perhaps fighting to preserve his self-control, and played one last card.

"I'm happy to see you. Things have happened, terrible—"

"Why, Owen?" Gordon interrupted, tears welling in his eyes.

Shermaine stepped forward and stopped between Michael and Gordon. "I can answer that. IMC is a private corporation, and old Hugh can't last forever." She peered into Owen's eyes. "The CIA would be happy to see Owen in the driver's seat, to protect and control the precious product from that hole."

"But there's Paul," Michael interrupted. "He's the last Reece. He would control the corporation."

"The AMP is almost back," shouted Hailey. "Shouldn't we try to raise Paul on the radio?"

"Paul is dead," Shermaine said. "Murdered. Right, Owen?" she said, staring at him coldly.

Michael's eyes and Owen's mouth jerked open simultaneously. Michael wailed in pain. In a movement too fast to follow, Michael snaked an arm around Owen's neck and with the other hand delivered a sharp blow to his temple, snapping his neck like a twig.

The soldiers raised their weapons.

"Are they all involved?" Shermaine asked.

Hailey nodded. "Dylan has been Owen's accomplice throughout. And these three," he raised his chin toward the technicians, "each got half a million in blood money to keep away from the upper life-support module in the capsule. When the butchery started out there," he pointed with his chin toward the esplanade, "they spilled their guts and blamed Owen."

Hilari nodded and raised his arm. The soldiers surrounded the technicians and held them at gunpoint. "Kenjo," Hilari called out. "Take the *mondele* to the esplanade and make them pile up the corpses. We'll burn the bodies before we leave. I'm not going to leave them for hyenas and vultures."

"What will you do to us?" Dylan screamed as two soldiers manhandled him.

"Do?" Hilari asked, feigning puzzlement. "We're not barbarians, Mr. Hayes. We're not going to *do* anything to you. Torture must have justification, and in your case it wouldn't have any. You sold your boss for a handful of coins—and there's nothing wrong with that. The trick is not to get caught, and on that score you're out of luck. When you finish your work, we'll shoot you. That, at least, will have a certain ring of justice."

"You're no better than them!" Dylan screamed. "Murderers!"

"I agree with you," Shermaine said to Dylan. "We're no better, but we're the winners—so far."

Dylan jerked around, and Hailey felt their eyes lock.

"What about him?" Dylan shrieked, pointing a finger at Hailey.

Hailey laughed. "Nice try, chum, but in this war, I'm also with the winners."

"You bastard—you didn't move a finger."

Hailey considered the issue and shrugged. He uncocked his pistol, slid the safety catch, and with slow movements replaced the weapon in the holster.

"No need; you weren't going anywhere, and I had my orders. Pay at IMC is fine, but there's nothing wrong with another job on the side." He glanced at Gordon and winked.

A giant man wearing a corporal's insignia grabbed Dylan by the hair and yanked him backward, backhanding him and splitting his lip. With a shove, he sent Dylan tumbling down among the mutilated corpses.

"Is it true?" Gordon asked Shermaine. His voice was weak, mournful. "I mean, what you said about Paul." He wrung his hands. "If you knew it, how come you didn't say anything before? What's going on here?"

Shermaine gazed at Gordon with red-rimmed, sorrowful eyes. "I didn't lie, Gordon. They murdered Paul." A weak smile tugged at her lips as she pictured Tshul and Mkhas racing through the jungle and toward the river as soon as they completed their task at the van. "But perhaps we can revive him."

Michael looked at Shermaine, who nodded at Hilari.

"I hate doing this, because it will show on the sat, but you know the British saying. 'In for a penny,'" Hilari said, smiling. He produced a signal pistol from his shoulder bag, loaded a cartridge into the chamber, pointed it upward, and fired. A pink flare rose and returned to earth, tracing a wide, curving, smoky trail. After a couple of minutes, Shermaine's radio buzzed. "AMP arriving," she announced, and killed the communication.

"Clear the area and prepare the crane," Shermaine said. She turned to Hilari. "If we can have a few soldiers, the work would go faster."

"The cowboys are on their way," Hilari responded, pocketing his radio. "They'll be here by six, with enough daylight for sats to scour the zone. It's four-thirty. In an hour, dawn will be in full swing. Their infrared doesn't work and so far it's cloudy, but it won't last. Let's make a smoke cover so at least they can't take pictures."

"By six we should be as far away from here as possible," Shermaine replied.

Gordon stared at her, looking unsettled by her words.

Hilari's brow furrowed as if he didn't understand either. "In that case, we need to evacuate at once so we can get to our meeting point with the boat at the river. My men can go on foot; it's less than thirty minutes' march away. We can follow in the Hummer as soon as we recover Paul. Let's meet at the river between five-thirty and five forty-five."

"It'll be tight," Shermaine said, nodding, "but there's nothing else we can do. Get that crane, Mike. We'll move the containment enclosure a few feet to the back."

"Are you sure?" Michael asked.

"Of course I am. There's nothing poisonous coming out of the shaft."

Michael nodded and jogged toward a Liebherr crane.

Hilari marched to the center of the esplanade, where the men carried out their macabre task. He shouted orders to a beefy sergeant, who followed him with a few men.

Hailey and Gordon left to remove the security pins anchoring the enclosure. A soldier opened a wide swath in the fence with bolt cutters and disappeared into the jungle with several others. Michael brought the crane forward.

On the esplanade, single barks from an AK-47 rifle were followed by a long rosary of automatic fire. The soldiers danced two fifty-gallon barrels of kerosene toward the pile of corpses.

Loaded with bulky haversacks, the soldiers reappeared

through the hole in the fence. The sergeant gave a command and the men took up position around the esplanade and drilling zone. They set smoke canisters on the ground and ignited them. In a short time, the whole zone was shrouded in thick fog.

Shermaine and Hilari finished removing the last of the enclosure fasteners. Michael had the crane in position. Gordon directed the operation of lifting the protective structure to uncover the shaft. With the enclosure out of the way, Michael killed the crane's motors, jumped down, sprinted to the control cabin, and returned with a flashlight. He directed the powerful beam down the shaft. Shermaine and Hilari were quickly by his side.

"I reckon about ten minutes," Michael said, standing up.

"It will be best if you go with your men and prepare everything to get us out of here in a hurry," Shermaine said to Hilari. He opened his mouth, ready to complain, but then thought better of it and smiled. Shermaine understood her friend's reticence. "Hilari, we've only one vehicle, and we need as much room as possible to move Paul," she explained.

He nodded. "Don't forget to replace the containment module over the shaft." Hilari touched his lips to Shermaine's before heading after his men.

"He's almost here," Gordon said as he joined them. "Get the crane ready, Michael. Swing the boom over."

Shermaine neared the shaft. Sixty feet further down, the AMP's flashing light on its rounded top was visible.

While Michael fired the engines and maneuvered the

crane's long arm, Shermaine stepped into the cabin and reappeared moments later with two cylinders of compressed air and oxygen, the latter with a short tube and a face mask.

In seconds, the AMP's top emerged from the shaft and continued to rise until its ribbed wheels lost traction and snapped out of the tube, disconnecting the motors. Gordon gestured for more cable and then clamped the hook on to the vehicle's top ring. He stood aside and signaled to tighten the line. Slowly the crane pulled the AMP from the shaft until its door was clear. Gordon prompted Michael to brake the cable drum, leaving the lower part of the AMP in the shaft. Mud and moisture dripped from the AMP's metallic skin as Gordon opened the door. Shermaine brought the compressed-air cylinder and opened its valve, directing the jet into the interior. A powerful stench of sulfur, like rotten eggs, billowed out and sent them back, coughing.

Shermaine took a deep breath and entered the AMP. She hoisted herself a couple of steps, squeezed past Paul's legs, and toggled his harness release. She backed up so Gordon could drag Paul out by his boots. Outside, Gordon laid Paul's lifeless form over a tarpaulin stretched out on the ground and peered into the steamed-up helmet's visor. Shermaine unsnapped the seal, removed the helmet with care, and gasped at the paleness of Paul's face. His skin was gray and sallow, his eyes half closed. He wasn't breathing.

Shermaine fixed an oxygen mask over his face and opened the valve wide.

Gordon and Michael quickly removed Paul's suit, and

Shermaine cut away the body stocking with scissors. She threw aside the garment, making a face at the powerful stink. *What have we done to you?* She ran her hands over his chest, her gaze clouding. Paul's naked body had the pallor of a cadaver, pruned and whitish, like an oversize larva. "Hang in there, baby, we've almost made it." From her bag, she produced a hypodermic with a long needle. After searching for an intercostal space, she injected the full contents of the syringe into Paul's heart, feeling his neck with her fingers.

Gordon brought blankets from the control cabin, and they carefully wrapped Paul into a cocoon. Shermaine peered at the skin of his inner thigh and found a hairline cut and, next to it, a small incision. Cellular poison had slowed his metabolism almost to zero. She breathed with relief.

"Paul's in a coma. Now we have to get the hell out of here."

Taking a deep breath, Shermaine crawled back into the AMP. She climbed to the upper section, grabbed the canvas bags, and came down again, coughing, her eyes watering from the gas. She rummaged in the bag and drew out a metal ring. *Where are the colors?* Her heart racing, Shermaine returned to the AMP, only to come out a minute later empty-handed.

Please, please, let them be here. She knelt by the discarded suit and searched it, running her hands over the sleeve pockets, freezing when she felt hard shapes under her probing fingers. Shermaine pulled the pocket flap open and dug out the disks. Holding the chips gingerly, she stored them with the rings. Back to the AMP's lower

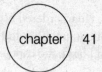

The venerable Vosper speedboat, painted dark gray and hidden by tall reeds, was almost invisible in the Aruwimi River's predawn gloom. With over forty years in service, it was a true relic and proof of the solid engineering of its design. On the open bridge, Hilari checked his watch every five minutes, glancing sideways at the captain, who didn't know what to do with his hands. Hailey checked his watch also. Soon it would be daylight.

Minutes before the Hummer arrived, they knew it was coming, as its headlight beams flashed intermittently over the treetops. Hilari nodded to the captain, who gunned the motors. Their deafening roar brought the jungle to life. Soon the forest's cacophony competed with the engines.

Several soldiers rushed down a plank to meet the SUV as soon as it was in sight. Two men opened the rear door and another took Paul in his arms gingerly, as if holding a child. He strode quickly onto the boat and down a flight of steps to the lower deck.

Hilari ordered his men to push the Hummer down the embankment, into the dark waters. When everyone was on board, the captain opened the throttle.

◯

In the sick bay, Paul's inert body lay on a table. Two slight Asian men leaned over him, searching his body with bare hands. Michael opened his mouth to say something, but Shermaine silenced him with a glance. The older of the two Asian men placed both hands on Paul's neck and concentrated. Without looking at his companion, he offered his hand palm up. The other man unwound a roll of felt, revealing dozens of long needles, one end wrapped in thin, coiled wire.

In quick succession, the older man pushed needles into Paul's face, neck, chest, wrists, and legs, often touching one and adjusting another, like a virtuoso performer on a strange instrument. Subtly at first but gaining in intensity, Paul's color returned. A slight tremor ran through his legs.

"This will save his life?" Gordon whispered to Shermaine, his eye on the needle pusher.

The younger man, head shaved except for a thin ponytail, turned, smiled, and nodded before rolling an IV stand to the table and inserting a needle into Paul's arm.

Paul's cheeks gathered tone and color as his breathing became deep and even. One by one, they removed the needles, until only four remained: one over each eye and two at the sternum, near Paul's heart. The older man felt Paul's neck again and then ran his hands along his sides, groin, and ankles. Nodding, he returned to the head of the table and removed the rest of the needles. Only the IV drip remained. He slapped the soles of Paul's feet, a blow that sounded like a whiplash and made the observers cringe.

Paul's eyes opened and closed. He moved his mouth as if chewing and squinted as Gordon and Michael neared the table. Then he closed his eyes and smiled weakly.

"The world is full of beauty and I have to wake up looking at two bums," he whispered before falling asleep.

Her eyes full of tears, Shermaine brought her palms together and bowed to the two men. Next to her, Michael and Gordon also bowed. The Asians exchanged quick, amused looks and returned the compliment. Then she deposited the canvas bag she'd been carrying into Tshul's hands.

The man's face lit up and changed into an expression of wonder when he accepted the bag. He bowed again, this time much lower.

Shermaine bowed once more before following Michael and Gordon up the steps to the upper deck, leaving Paul in the hands of his caretakers.

The day was already bright, and a strong breeze hit them in the face. Hilari and Hailey neared, holding on to the handrail's taut steel cable.

"I see in your faces the monks were successful," Hilari said, and checked his watch.

"Monks?" Gordon and Michael said in unison.

"Yes, genuine, from Tibet."

"*Medical* monks?" Michael pressed.

"Yes, Tibetan medical monks," Hilari said.

"Experts in acupuncture techniques thousands of

years old," Shermaine added, laughing at Hilari's dead-pan delivery. "Paul was in a self-induced coma. That's the reason he's alive."

"Would you *please*—" Gordon began.

"We knew there would be an attempt on Paul's life, but we didn't know if it would be in the AMP or when he got back. If the idea was to wait for the AMP to surface, we could take care of it, but Paul would have to look after himself on the trip back. The obvious way would have been to tamper with the craft's air supply, which is what they did. They couldn't mess with the AMP, because they needed it to surface intact. Paul carried a powerful cellular poison with him."

"Where?" Hailey asked. "I was there when he suited up. He was buck naked."

Shermaine smiled. "He carried it in him."

"*In* him? He poisoned himself?" Gordon asked.

"It lowers the metabolism down to a comatose level. In such a state, body requirements are minimal. I'm sorry we couldn't let you in on this, Gordon," Shermaine added softly when she realized the security chief was blaming himself for a professional lapse.

"Is it an herbal concoction?" Michael asked.

"It's frog sweat."

"Frog sweat?" Michael said, looking at Gordon.

"The humidity must get to them too," Gordon answered before the group broke out in nervous laughter. "Are you kidding? How on earth do you collect frog sweat?"

"You'll have to ask the experts."

"But what happened to the people in Shawaiti? Where did they go?"

Shermaine worried her lower lip. "Far away, toward the east and the mountains."

Michael frowned. "Before, you said *we* knew. Who knew?"

"I can't tell you," Shermaine said, holding his hand. "Perhaps Paul will someday."

"What happens to us now?" Gordon asked Hilari.

"When we reach Ekilo we'll split up," Hilari said, ignoring their surprised expressions. "A chopper will fly you to Buta. There you'll board another chopper to Bangassou, in the Central African Republic. A private jet will fly you out of Africa. The monks and Paul will go with you."

"Go with us where?"

"To Tibet, of course."

"Of course! I should have guessed. Stupid of me. Tibet; where else?"

So this is the real Gordon. No wonder Paul likes him so much, Shermaine thought as she watched his body language. He was finally beginning to relax.

"I'll stay in Africa," Hailey said. "There may yet be more to learn about frog sweat."

Soon everyone joined in the laughter, even the captain, who had not heard a thing.

When Shermaine stepped away from the group and reached to grab a rail, her eyes on the rapidly moving bank, Michael followed. She closed her eyes, ready for the blow.

"And now?" Michael asked.

"I must stay in Africa. You have a choice."

"I don't think so. Paul already has his minder. Will *we* ever see them again?"

She let out a long held breath. "I guess they'll eventually catch up with us. It's a small world."

For a while, Michael didn't say anything and then his hand slid along the guardrail next to hers. "I'll stay."

chapter 42

"1 degree 3 seconds north, 24 degrees 18 seconds east, on a west approach to the IMC installations, dense smoke, altitude 300, speed one-forty, passing over the site now, visibility poor—"

"Take her down to one-fifty," Sergeant Santiago interrupted Corporal Williams's constant chatter to the boys at Langley. After the American Consulate had hurriedly arranged transport for Luther Cox to a hospital, Santiago had been ordered to take over control of the operation.

The pilot nodded, adjusting torque and cyclic to throw the chopper into a tight turn.

"Maintain speed?"

"Affirmative."

On the second pass, Santiago peered through a maelstrom of dark fog eddying from the machine's powerful downdraft. Visibility was still patchy, but he'd caught sight of rows of charred cabins. Fires still burned on the ground, fed by scores of shapes looking much like human bodies, and to one side, untouched by flames, he spotted

his target: a gleaming construction with the IMC logotype in bright white letters.

"There," Sergeant Santiago gripped the pilot's shoulder and pointed to the helipad's markings. "That's clear.
Turn around and take her down. Keep the power up."

He glanced over his shoulder at his men and was rewarded by a rosary of snaps as they readied their weapons.
Garcia crouched by the door, ready to yank the handle
and roll the sliding panel on Santiago's prompt.

○

In 1908, in Siberia, an explosion leveled over one thousand square miles of forest. The center of the explosion
was easy to determine: The trees fell radially from a single
point. There was no crater, just a swamp in the epicenter.

In the jungle, the ants detected the subtle vibrations
first. They abandoned their stern group discipline and deserted the nest in a mad race, scampering, leaving behind
larvae, stores, and the product of hard work. The tiny insects dashed in blind terror, filling the air with a faint out-
pouring of pheromones, warning others of the imminent
danger. The jungle hushed. Even the leaves of the trees
seemed to pause.

○

As soon as the helicopter's wheels settled on the concrete,
Santiago stepped next to Garcia, his eyes darting to the
pile of burning corpses revealed as powerful blades dis-
pelled the smoke.

Santiago studied the flames; something about the different colors of smoke wasn't right. They had drenched the corpses in fuel, provoking the heavy black smoke, but there was something familiar in the white mist, just like—then he spotted a smoke canister.

"What the . . . ?"

His eyes darted toward the dark jungle.

○

The elephant's trumpeting was the signal for a stampede. Birds took flight in unison, and thousands of creatures bolted toward the east: hyenas, okapis, porcupines, and antelopes, leopards, and mongooses. Predatory instincts forgotten, hunter and hunted gathered and fled in a wild run for salvation as monkeys dashed across treetops, screaming.

○

Through the window, Santiago suddenly saw flocks of birds rising from the jungle. Then, under the roar of the chopper's turbines, a low-frequency rumble shook his gut. "Abort!" Santiago yelled, slamming a hand on the metal bulkhead. "Get the fuck outta here!"

○

A deep vibration filled the air and made it unbreathable. The earth moved. Torn and cracked, the surface swallowed huge trees and terrified creatures. The ground trembled with a muted tearing at its entrails, and the helipad's thick concrete slab danced like a fallen leaf on a stream.

A vast explosion expanded, spewing steam and gases at five hundred miles an hour, leveling everything in its way.

○

"Holy—" The sat-link drowned in a flurry of static.

○

When conditions stabilized twenty-four hours later, the most violent eruption in modern history had produced a cone half a mile high. Magma and pumice covered large surfaces of jungle, and over two million people died all over the continent.

Tsunamis punished the world's coasts, and dense clouds of cinder spreading over whole continents rewarded humankind with breathtaking sunsets.

Many miles away from the majestic new volcano, other ants gathered. A sense of purpose suffused the minute insects as their limited nervous systems detected the arrival of a new day. Slowly at first but with increasing enthusiasm, the tiny African ants concentrated with frantic resolve on the task of building a new nest.

chapter 43

"You must have needed the sleep," Paul said, his voice thick. "You look like hell."

Gordon leaned over to Paul. "*I* look like hell?"

"Where are we?" Paul asked.

"At Asmara, Eritrea, on a jet with the monks, on our way to Tibet." Gordon searched Paul's face. He didn't look well, despite the smile. Dark rings framed his eyes; his skin was pale and pasty. "You look like a guy who's been in a fight with a steamroller, pal. How do you feel?"

"What monks? Where's Michael? Where are the others?"

"The monks are doctors; at least I think so. Anyway, they saved your life. Everybody else stayed back in Africa. Michael too."

"Ah, Shermaine bagged him."

"I'm a lousy security man. Why am I the last to find things out? You should fire me, you know?"

"I had inside information about the ambush."

"So Michael didn't stand a chance?"

"Let's just say the dice were loaded and he wasn't shooting. I'm happy for them. Somebody had to put a stop to Michael's carrying on." Paul blinked repeatedly, as if returning to reality. "What happened to *you?*"

"Ah, this?" Gordon ran careful fingers over the lump on his forehead. "A branch got me."

"I bet."

"There was an explosion when we took off. It was like an atomic blast, with a mushroom cloud and everything. Something like an earthquake and a volcano happened at the same time. Congo was ground zero. The pilots heard on the radio that there have been hundreds of thousands of casualties. Looks like we got out in the nick of time."

Paul remained silent, his eyes glazing over.

"Why don't you look surprised?" Gordon asked when Paul's expression didn't change.

Tshul, the younger of the two monks, entered from the forward cabin before Paul could answer. He smiled wide. "Good. No more coma," the monk said, reaching out to shake the hands of both men. Tshul sat next to Paul and peered into his eyes. Then he took his hand and checked his pulse. "You look well."

"I feel like an old rag. How much worse would I have to feel to be bad?"

Tshul chuckled but didn't let go of Paul's hand. "I mean you are recovering fast from the poison. I will bring you a tea you will need to drink several times a day to clean your system."

"Coma. Poison. Sounds serious," Paul joked after the monk left.

"No shit," Gordon replied, yawning. "Man, you're a toxic dump."

○

When they landed at Lhasa airport, an ambulance was already waiting on the tarmac. Gordon stood aside as the monks transferred Paul from the plane to the old rickety vehicle. Soon a small gray car with an elaborate insignia approached the aircraft. Two uniformed men stepped out and climbed onto the plane, reappearing a few minutes later. They shook hands with the pilot and then glanced toward the ambulance. Gordon cringed and forced a smile. He had no money, no passport, and no identification other than the IMC tag on his wrist, but the officers climbed back into their vehicle without a second look and drove off.

Tshul gestured toward the open rear doors of the ambulance. Gordon waved to the pilot, climbed in, and settled on a side seat. He realized with some surprise that the floor was covered with an inch of sawdust; a faint whiff of manure tinted the air. Gordon sighed. Tshul climbed into the front; the other monk sat across from Gordon, then tightened the straps securing Paul to the stretcher.

The driver latched one of the twin doors and craned his neck inside before closing the other. "We go to Tashilhumpo Monastery, Hou-Tsang Province, Nepalese border, thirteen thousand feet." He sounded like an airline flight attendant. Gordon smiled, inclining his head. The driver must have found the gesture pleasing, because his face lit up and he bowed back.

Gordon shifted on the hard wooden seat. The monks seemed to have everything under control, but he hadn't survived this long by placing his life in the hands of others. He glanced at Paul and softened. Well, maybe once or twice. He wondered if he should at least ask the monks about travel documents but thought better of it. They drove through the airport checkpoint without stopping and headed for the mountains.

Paul opened his eyes a few times but didn't speak. At his side, the monk laid a hand on Paul's neck, muttering under his breath. When he appeared satisfied, he glanced over, then handed Gordon a quilted coat. Gordon's nose wrinkled at the smell. Brief imaginings of what would cause the odor crossed his mind, but he dismissed them as he shrugged on the garment. At least it was warm.

Gordon turned his attention back to Paul. He slept. Gordon suspected the herbal infusion the monks had given his friend must have contained something to help him rest. He envied him. After the horror of the past hours, he would never again sleep as peacefully as Paul seemed to now.

After a while Gordon turned his back to the rear door, leaning against the vibrating ambulance wall. He sighed, resolving to endure the jolting trip as best he could. The landscape was breathtaking: green, dotted with woods and cultivated fields against the imposing background of the Himalaya cordillera. He'd always imagined Tibet would look something akin to the North Pole. He was surprised to find a country so fertile, exuberant, where the cold seemed to come only from the altitude.

They saw Tashilhumpo from a distance just before dusk. "Is that the monastery?" Gordon asked. "It looks like a fortress."

Mkhas smiled, nodding. "In other times the monks

were warriors. Most of the monasteries are fortified; Tashilhumpo is the largest of them. The lama lives there."

"The Dalai Lama?"

"No, Mr. Turner. Not that lama." There was a hint of displeasure in his voice. "This is the home of the Panchen Lama, the Amitabha Buddha's reincarnation. Do you know anything about the history of Buddhism in Tibet?"

"No . . ." Gordon made a gesture, his eyes roaming the fortification rising toward the clouds. He knew that constructions on hilltops loomed larger from below, but this was one mother of a castle.

Tshul laughed from the front of the ambulance. "You have just displayed an unforgivable void in your education, Mr. Turner. Mkhas will make sure your culture is furthered in the days ahead."

"I'd like that. It'll be interesting."

Tshul laughed louder. "That makes matters even worse. Now he will not let you get away until you know our entire history."

The ambulance crept up the steep road and finally entered a tunnel that zigzagged into a vast courtyard surrounded by buildings. Gordon smiled. Someone had to be thinking. The tunnel was a first-class defense against anyone or anything ramming through the walls. After driving through narrow cobbled streets, they reached large steel gates. Dim lights appeared everywhere, dispelling the shadows and revealing files of monks. Feet whispered against ancient stone as saffron-robed fireflies danced the dusk away. Monks stepped forward to crank a horizontal wooden drum. The ropes creaked.

They stopped in a square surrounded by tall stone

ramparts and crowned with pitched roofs. Scores of narrow, barred windows opened in the stonework. Another
group of monks neared the vehicle. They opened the
back door of the ambulance, then wheeled the stretcher
through long corridors, up to a large chamber equipped
with stout wooden furniture.

Gordon followed but kept out of the way and admired
the procedure. A monk warmed the tall bed with a copper
brazier bright with incandescent coals at the end of a long
pole. They lifted Paul from the stretcher and laid him in
bed. Not a movement was wasted; all activity was well rehearsed, as if the event were commonplace. Once Paul was
settled, Tshul turned around. "Come with us, Mr. Turner.
Your room is next door. Your bath is ready. Later they will
bring you food and clean clothes. Mr. Reece must rest now.
You can see him tomorrow morning if he is feeling better."

They walked along the corridor until they reached another door to a room similar to the one they left. Mkhas
stood aside to let Gordon in, then retired with a slight bow.

"The bathroom is through that door at the rear. Good
night, Mr. Turner."

The monks closed the door. Seemingly he didn't merit
the bed-warming routine. *Most discriminatory*, he thought.
Gordon waited until his eyes grew used to the dim light. In
one corner, oil candles floated in a large dish on the floor;
embers glowed in an open hearth. With apprehension, he
crossed the room, peering into the long shadows. He
opened a heavy door, stepping back in surprise as a cloud of
water vapor escaped. He walked a few cautious steps and
stopped, taken aback by an enormous bath opening in the
floor, the surface rippling as faint tendrils of steam escaped.

"Well, I'll be—this is large enough for an army."

Gordon undressed quickly and stepped into the bath with careful movements. The water was hot.

When he returned to the room, he found quilted pajamas and slippers placed neatly on the bed. On a round table, two squat tallow candles illuminated a tray with food, fruit, and a large steaming mug, probably tea.

Gordon looked toward the bed and smiled. He padded to it and slid his hand under the covers. It was warm.

○

The next day started well before dawn, when Tshul woke Paul up with a cup of tea. Then he accompanied him to the bath, where a brute with the looks of a sumo wrestler gave him a brisk, energetic rub with a handful of hemp. The creature followed with a massage, which at times seemed more like a thrashing. Afterward, Paul returned to bed for a couple of hours to sweat and recover from the beating.

"Any chance of getting some sun today?" Paul asked Tshul when the monk presented him with a breakfast of brown bread, yak butter, yogurt, prunes, and figs.

"You are always free to do so."

"I'm a visitor; I didn't want to commit a transgression."

"Transgression? This isn't the Vatican."

○

When Paul finally risked a stroll, the sun was high, the air crisp and cool.

"Hey!" Gordon yelled from behind him. "What've you been up to?" he asked when he reached Paul.

"I don't know what I can tell you and what's a state

secret," Paul said, smiling. He could sense eyes watching him from several windows.

"You look good for someone who died."

"Yeah, the resurrection took a bit out of me, but I'm ready to be worshipped."

Gordon laughed, then sobered as he told Paul about the butchery that had taken place at the camp.

"So that's what Tshul wouldn't tell me. He keeps saying, 'When you've recovered.'" Paul's eyes watered. "So many good men dead. Damn."

In seconds, Tshul appeared and clasped Paul under the arm. "Too much too soon," the monk said before guiding Paul back to bed.

"See you later."

They watch us like hawks. Jesus! Or is it Buddha in this part of the world? Gordon wondered as the monk and his patient disappeared behind a door.

○

Paul and Gordon met up again in the afternoon and walked a walled garden so large it disappeared into the distance of a huge space crisscrossed with narrow red brick paths, laid geometrically in small squares. In each frame grew a different kind of aromatic or medicinal herb, resulting in a breathtaking kaleidoscope of colors and shades of green. Gordon relayed the information supplied by Tshul. The narrow paths ensured that when the monks walked in meditation, their robes brushed over the herbs and released the plants' fragrance. Afterward, Gordon drew Paul to a squat building jutting out by the side of a ravine. They wandered down three floors on a long set of stairs. Once on the third level, they followed faint sounds and found a room with an expansive bay of windows and scores of monks sitting on floor mats.

"Translating manuscripts from Sanskrit into Hindi or Chinese," Gordon told Paul, and pulled him away from the door.

"What did you do?" Paul whispered. "Ask what they do for a living?"

"Basically. They also produce a vegetable dye to color their robes."

"You asked them about their wardrobe?"

"I sure did."

"Did you also ask if there's a mess hall? I'm hungry."

"This way."

○

"I suppose you've already thought about what we're going to do when we leave here?" Gordon asked after the monks had served them a vegetarian dinner. There were no more jokes; he looked worried.

"As far as the outside world knows, we're all dead," Paul said. "At least, I hope so. IMC and the CIA will be able to relax."

"Who was their man in Dallas?"

"Milford Crandall."

Out of the whole episode, Milford's treachery had hurt Paul more deeply than he would have thought possible. Gordon didn't seem surprised. Paul could have sworn the ex-security chief was relieved. In an instant, Paul understood.

"I see. You thought it might have been retribution, vengeance, a settling of old scores."

"Your grandfather's been on my mind for some time," Gordon replied after finishing off his tea. "I'm glad it wasn't him."

"You remember the letter Dylan brought from Dallas?"

Gordon nodded.

"It was from my granddad. Hugh didn't trust site communications. In retrospect, it must have been easy for him to flush the mole.

"Think about it," Paul continued when Gordon didn't reply. "If you had access to the site's communication log, so would Hugh. When I changed the descent schedule, Owen phoned the CIA. By doing so, he risked blowing their secret scheme."

Paul could tell Gordon wasn't convinced.

"I still don't understand why Owen would place a direct phone call from the site. It was the first time, and he knew we kept a log."

"I suppose if their plan had succeeded, the call would have been justified if anybody asked. When you mentioned it was the first time, I knew the mole had to be at IMC headquarters. Someone at the head office, someone high up who ran Owen. He reported daily to Milford Crandall. You see, Owen never used that number before because he could pass on the information each day during his chats with Milford."

"That still doesn't explain the call."

"Yes, it does. Milford was at his daily meeting with my grandfather."

"So what? He could have taken a call on his cell."

"No, he couldn't, and he *wouldn't*. Hugh is paranoid about interruptions. Besides, Hugh's offices are built like bunkers and include a powerful cell-phone jammer.

When I returned from my escapade, Owen had to call Milford and knew he was unavailable. Owen panicked."

"So you say, but I checked the transcripts of previous conversations. No mention of you, nothing. The exchanges were clean."

"No, they weren't."

Gordon opened his mouth to protest, but not a sound came out. He was responsible for security and it looked like he had let many people down. "How do you know?" he finally asked. "You didn't read the transcripts. Those were locked in my safe—unless you had access I don't know about."

"I don't need transcripts. I'm only guessing how I would have done it, had I been in their shoes. The scheme could be ridiculously easy." Paul smiled, knowing Gordon was struggling and in pain, trying to put the pieces together. "I'll give you an example. You remember me mentioning Carmen?"

Gordon nodded.

"The first time we made love, she laughed."

"Appalling technique?"

"You could learn something from my technique, bud. She was happy, so she laughed."

"I don't follow you."

"Later, she'd say things like 'I could do with a good laugh,' or 'I could laugh all night.' Things like that."

"I see." Gordon turned serious. "You mean they had a plain English code and could exchange information—providing they didn't need precision."

"Even precise information could be exchanged. Don't forget, drilling involves much data, numbers, ratios. I could devise a simple code with a dozen words, and so could you."

Gordon nodded. "And your grandfather found out..." Gordon trailed off.

"Grandfather must have used Milford, the same way I used Owen."

"You used Owen? How?"

"Proper care and feeding of the mole, once you know who it is. A good mole is like a courier. I doctored the information I gave Owen about Shermaine."

"So, what about your grandfather? He doesn't know you're alive?"

Paul shook his head. "Nobody knows. When I disappeared in Shawaiti, I spent most of the time at a pygmy village. The people there knew of the sphere *and* of the CIA operation. They also guessed someone might try to kill me on the return trip from the sphere. Their instructions were clear. If I had to use the poisoned arrow, I would have to disappear afterward and forget about returning to the U.S. or getting in touch with anybody even remotely connected with IMC or this operation."

Gordon frowned. "Where did you—"

Paul didn't let him finish. "—hide the arrow? In my ass."

"It figures; there weren't many places left. I wondered if you had it taped to your skin someplace."

"Damn painful at first, but you get used to it."

"I bet," Gordon said dubiously. "Say, I've been meaning to ask you for a long time. How did your friends make the Hummer travel fast through virgin jungle?"

Paul met his eyes. "Monkeys carried the locators."

"Monkeys?"

"They use them like carrier pigeons. Monkeys raised in one village are taken to another. When freed they hurry back home."

Gordon stared at him stonily. "Don't they escape into the jungle?"

"Nah! The pygmies keep females in the original village. Males race back to their honeypots."

Gordon laughed and slammed his palm on the table. "I love it!"

"You see, that's a fallacy of so-called civilized nations."

"I don't follow."

"We assume primitive men are stupid, when they're as intelligent as we are. Maybe they lack technology, but they're as sharp as a tack."

"More tea?"

Paul nodded. "We'll be pissing all night at the rate we're going."

As Gordon poured, Paul checked his watch. It was almost 20:00.

Gordon rotated his mug around absently, staring straight ahead. Something worried him.

"We can't ever go back to the States or show our faces anywhere?" The realization must have hit him.

"We'll need to keep a low profile, cut communications with anyone from our past lives for a while. That's the price we pay for being alive. If any of us showed up, the shit would hit the fan."

"What are you going to do?"

"First, we need to get some answers here, at the monastery. Later we'll go to Colquizate in Honduras. I have friends there, and we'll be able to stay with them."

"We?"

Paul nodded. "Our destinies are bonded, like those of Michael, Shermaine, Hilari, and hundreds of other people—though you may not have noticed. Right now nobody's looking, but if any of us showed up, the lid of Pandora's box would be off. This is all too important to risk with rash foolishness. I'll have to vouch for you; we'll have to be together. There are many people involved. You told me about Shermaine's tale of the wildebeest. The same issues may apply here." If the people around them felt threatened, their lives would be worthless. Paul knew it and hoped Gordon had caught the drift.

"Does it mean we'll have to hide for the rest of our lives?"

"Of course not. First, Colquizate is not a place to hide. I'd like to spend the rest of my life there if I could. You don't have to like it, although I think you will. There's another issue, though. The world's days are numbered, in its present form anyway. The change may come in many years or a few, or it may be next week."

"Come on, Paul, you can't be serious. You can't believe that crap. You're a scientist, for God's sake."

"Yeah, I made science my religion. This is different. Don't ask me for details, because I don't have any. One reason we're here is to find out. In the jungle I listened to a wise man, one of the keepers of ancient knowledge about a cyclic phenomenon, something that will affect the whole earth. The shaft, the capsule, the earthquake, and the volcano are all related."

"What do you mean? Like a climate change? They've been warning about it for decades, but so far nothing has happened."

"I don't think so. More like a cataclysm—something more sudden and unpredictable."

"What was down there? You've never explained."

"A message, data, a warning, or something like that,

and a hologram of people. I can't explain my feelings...
my emotions. It was amazing."

"What was in the message?"

"I don't know. I brought back colored disks and rings a
little larger than bracelets. I spotted rainbows in their surface, like a DVD. I think they're recordings of some sort.
But I think the important objects were the disks and their
colors." Paul explained, joining thumb and index finger
for emphasis. "The whole place seemed built around the
disks. Everything I found is here. Tshul said the monks
were studying the items I recovered."

"You have no idea what's in those disks?"

"No. But we will before our stay here is over. I think
the bad news is just ahead."

"Have you noticed any effects of altitude?" Gordon
asked, changing the subject.

Paul took a long breath. "Just the first day; I had trouble breathing. But it could have been the poison and
plain exhaustion. What about you?"

"Nope, but I haven't done anything demanding. Hard
physical work must be rougher here than down below."
Gordon paused and glanced around. "It's amazing how
well they keep the monastery. Built in the fifteenth century
and all the materials original. Dry climate helps, I guess."

"Great place to get away from it all, if you like translation or gardening."

Gordon shook his head. "Two months of this would
drive me crazy, but I wouldn't mind buying a time-share
here. You know, for a Christmas vacation."

Paul laughed and shivered.

Gordon must have noticed. "Yeah, bud, I know. *If*
we're still here next Christmas."

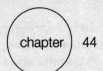

The atmosphere around the table was tense. Although the facts had never leaked outside the agency, it was obvious the exercise was never under their control.

Director Foust didn't look happy after returning from the White House. He folded his arms and peered over his tiny eyeglasses. "On this occasion, we've had the luck of the Irish. Everything is under wraps and will remain so. I informed President Locke about the agency's efforts to secure a discovery of national importance. She knows a natural disaster thwarted our hard work. From the IMC side, their undertaking has been a total failure. Their losses will end in God-knows-which account and the taxpayer will foot the bill, as usual. Hindman, any news?"

Dario Hindman glanced at Rhea Paige and Aaron Greenberg before pulling a few sheets from a folder and fanning them before him. He placed his elbows on the table and leaned his face into his hands to scan the papers.

"It's all unreal. Never before have I faced such a multitude of unexplainable—and disconnected—details. A late report from Anthony Bouchard says our embassy has received a long document from the Kabila government. The communiqué denies N'dende could have taken part in the events we're complaining about. In particular, observers in Angola and Zambia confirm he was at President Kabila's side during the time we thought he was at the Kisangani airport. If we still believe that man to be Hilari N'dende, then why is President Kabila lying?"

Hindman roamed the documents.

"As for the source or sources of interference, we haven't found anything; searching the zone is impossible. About the installations, you know as much as I do. The place is beneath a volcano, with millions of tons of lava on top. We've gone over the tapes a hundred times. The recovery team arrived just when the area exploded. We must presume all the men are dead.

"We have a few extra snippets and signals related to strange happenings," he continued. "According to a reliable observer, Cox's unfortunate fight in Kisangani was with Pierre Oyono." He selected a single sheet with a small photograph stapled to it. "Mr. Oyono, besides being an ex-instructor of the British SAS, is an expert in commando training, karate fifth dan, and an expert of kendo—among other lesser-known arts. Mr. Oyono is Mr. N'dende's right-hand and, of course, never left the president's entourage. Questions are: What was a bone-breaking machine doing at Kisangani airport? Are we wrong? Was the man in Kisangani mistaken for Mr. Oyono?" Hindman nodded to Paige. "We have only a few photographs, and they aren't very clear." Rhea Paige produced several black-and-white prints and spread them on the table so they faced the director.

"Difficult to see without magnification, but it's the best we have." She pointed to a print. "This one, a few seconds before the first explosion, covers the drilling zone. The containment module is intact and there's no trace of the AMP, only what appears to be a body. But we're not sure; it's the wrong shape. Nothing suggests the AMP ever surfaced. It could be inside the containment module. We must assume when the photo was taken the AMP was in the tube. There isn't a trace of the security people or Mosengwo either. This print here shows our chopper landing. They were down an instant before the place blew up."

"About Mosengwo," Aaron Greenberg cut in, "we have a report from one of Bouchard's agents confirming that her family, including her father, Étienne, celebrated a Kasai funeral ritual. They believe she's dead.

"As for the AMP, I've analyzed the photos and I agree with Paige. Perhaps the AMP surfaced, was emptied, and was sent back, but it's unlikely. The smoke over the installation was thick. No chopper could take off after the rebel forces left without scattering it. River traffic shows a few barges and a river police speedboat well before the eruption. I think the cataclysm caught them close to the camp. IMC's private security manager confirms he's not heard from his men."

"What about the interference?" Director Foust's rhetorical question elicited no immediate answer.

"We'll never know. Everything in the area is underneath a volcano," Hindman said.

"That's what I can't swallow," Paige muttered. "Too many *coincidences*."

Director Foust peered over his reading glasses. "Are you suggesting the eruption was intentional?"

"Of course not. Perhaps the shaft had something to do with it. It could have weakened a formation, or maybe the sphere was a bomb after all."

"If you're right," Hindman said, "Paul Reece found the unexpected."

"What about IMC? Any developments there?" Foust asked.

"Hugh Reece is finished," Paige said. "Owen DeHolt is presumed dead. Milford Crandall waits on the sidelines. Chances are he'll take over. The corporation will go public."

Foust stood up and stretched, stifling a yawn. "Project Isis is officially closed. Regardless of how much we argue, we'll never know what happened in that goddamn shaft."

Paige sighed. "Amen."

chapter 45

After his morning program—a bath and a thorough roughing up at the hands of Bidi, his jumbo masseur—the routine changed. Instead of returning to his room, the monks guided Paul up three flights of stairs to a library with stone walls and a floor of dark-wood planks smoothed by age. Gordon was already there.

A monk knelt, leaning over rolls of parchment before a low desk, little more than a plinth. Without raising his head, the monk gestured to an area by the desk. Paul knelt on the floor. Gordon followed Paul's lead.

After a while, the monk removed his glasses to lay them with care on the table. The monk's dark pupils sparkled before his gaze moved to the ceiling, as if in search of inspiration.

"You have recovered, Mr. Reece. You, Mr. Turner, have also a good aspect. If we consider your recent experiences, it's a small miracle—"

"Excuse me," Paul interrupted. "I need to know. Did I bring up the colors?"

The monk folded his arms, hands disappearing inside the saffron tunic's wide sleeves.

"Indeed you did, Mr. Reece. Your mission was a success."

Paul relaxed a notch. The possibility he'd overlooked something in the sphere had been playing on his mind.

"My first thought was to speak in private with Mr. Reece, but there are bonds between you. It may be that Mr. Turner can share the enlightenment. In a way, your destinies are intertwined."

"We sorta figured that out," Gordon said as his knee popped.

"I'm sorry, but are you the Panchen Lama?" Paul asked as he rearranged his long legs into a different position. His kneecaps ached.

The monk chuckled. "My name is Kunchen, which, in Tibetan, means *all-knowing*. Nothing could be further from the truth, I assure you. My parents were optimists."

Paul eyed the small man. Kunchen had a round face with pronounced dimples when he smiled. No hair on head, face, chest, or arms. *They shave? Hell of a daily chore, unless they're hairless*. Paul made a mental note to ask Tshul.

"I am a kind of curator, you see?"

They didn't. Paul caught Gordon's expression from the corner of his eye.

"Besides our more publicized philosophical endeavors, we translate books and manuscripts from ancient languages. Later we archive and cross-reference texts. We have been doing it for centuries." Kunchen shrugged. "It's a labor of great patience, most acceptable for monks."

Either the monk was abstruse by design or Paul missed the point. He cast another glance in Gordon's direction.

What was Kunchen driving at? Unless old texts were connected to the sphere. "I...We thought you would explain, er—things."

"Where should we start?" Kunchen adjusted his robe and ran a hand over the dome of his head.

"It doesn't matter. Everything is...bizarre, to say the least. I suppose the beginning would be best," Paul answered. "Somebody orchestrated all of this: logistics, intelligence, people—"

"Monks," Gordon added.

"Yes, and from a religion that concerns itself little with earthly matters," Paul said. "Then there's the shaman of a pygmy tribe teamed up with you and a corrupt African government. You are the *strangest* bedfellows. None of it makes any sense." Paul bit his lip, thinking perhaps he'd gone too far, but Kunchen broadened his grin.

"Your confusion is understandable, but it's a question of perspective. Strange bedfellows," Kunchen repeated with a gentle laugh. "I could not describe it better. Pygmies are the oldest race on earth. They are the original people of Africa, India, Australia, Malaysia, the Philippines, and even North America."

An eyebrow raised, Paul darted a quick glance at Gordon's face.

"Pygmies are the original native Americans?" Gordon asked.

"That is not what I said. You are thinking about the modern Indian nations. I meant the original dwellers, hundreds of thousands of years ago."

Paul could have sworn the monk's eyes flashed with a mischievous glint and considered with a sinking feeling that the unexpected was still to come.

"Say..." Gordon leaned forward with sudden interest. "You mean pygmies—you know, people with beautiful colored skin like me—were the earth's first?"

"You could say something like that, yes."

Gordon's booming laughter echoed off the study walls as he slapped his knees with glee. "I knew it, man, I swear I knew it!"

"But shouldn't there be remains?" Paul asked. "Something paleontologists would have found?"

"They have. Take your country. In Cochocton, Ohio, archaeologists discovered a burial ground with two hundred thousand pygmies. Near Hillsboro, Tennessee, another burial site contains over a hundred thousand pygmy skeletons. In Wyoming, the oral history of the Shoshone Nation tells of wars with the Nimerigar, a small race who used tiny bows and poisoned arrows. All pygmy people share a common ancestry and language. For example, the word for jungle is the same on all five continents—*jengi*—regardless of the language later inhabitants adopted from their neighbors."

Paul's mind kicked into overdrive. "Why didn't they evolve into a technologically oriented society?"

"That they have not developed technology means nothing. Their wisdom of earth is unparalleled. Their oral traditions are five hundred thousand years old."

"Are you Buddhist?" Gordon asked.

The monk paused, shifting on his mat.

"Yes, I am, but Buddha was not a god or a prophet and never said he was. He was a man who taught others out of his own experience. Buddhism is a philosophy." Kunchen leaned toward Paul. "Do you know the meaning of philosophy?"

434 carlos j. cortes

"The love of wisdom," Paul answered, calling on his memory of a college class. "But I've heard many definitions."

Kunchen nodded. "Indeed, we strive for wisdom, to preserve wisdom regardless of man's folly. But we must move on. There is little time."

Kunchen's smile widened.

"We are fortunate, my friends. A pilgrim is with us, a visitor most eager to meet you. He has the answers to your questions."

As Kunchen spoke the last words, the door opened. The synchronization was remarkable, perhaps too much so. Paul started to rise, but Kunchen stopped him with a gesture. No one spoke. It was as if they were in a cinema with the sound switched off.

Framed in the doorway was a tall figure dressed in a black two-piece suit and a turtleneck sweater, his feet encased in thick tabi. The dim light and the monochromatic effect of his ebony skin and dark outfit made it difficult to see details.

"Nestor," Kunchen said. "A pilgrim from far-removed lands and your host for the balance of your stay with us. I am sure you have much to discuss." Kunchen stood with a fluid movement. He hesitated, glanced at Nestor, pointed toward his side of the table, and strode from the room.

He obviously knows who we are, Paul realized when Kunchen didn't introduce him and Gordon. *He's taller than me,* Paul realized. *Watusi?*

Nestor smiled with both his mouth and eyes. When he looked at Paul, it almost felt like the physical touch of fingertips.

"This is indeed a fine day," Nestor said, folding his legs as he sat down across from them.

Paul tensed. He'd heard Nestor's voice in Shawaiti, issuing from the shadows in Leon's hut. The voice was rich, deep, textured. Nestor shifted his gaze between Paul and Gordon, his smile broadening.

"I have followed your progress these last months."

Paul studied Nestor's chiseled face, the long nose and the lips—proportioned the same as Caucasian lips. "You've been tugging at the strings?" Paul asked. All of them—Shermaine, Leon Kibassa, and Kunchen—had avoided his questions or plainly refused to answer.

Nestor lowered his head; the taut skin of his skull became alive with the candles' reflection. For an instant, it looked as if a band of errant fireflies had landed on Nestor's head. He shuddered with soft baritone laughter. "Rather than tugging, I have been watching." Nestor sighed. "Both of you have been very brave."

"Isn't it time somebody filled us in about the sphere, the items I brought back, the reason I risked my life?"

"Of course, Paul."

Paul waited and stared, but Nestor offered nothing more, returning his gaze evenly.

"Well?"

"It's always wise to start at the beginning."

Those were Kunchen's words, but so far beginnings had only posed more questions.

"In this case, *my* beginning. I'm not from the earth."

Paul winced at Gordon's loud snort. *This is too much.* He shifted his legs, feeling light-headed, the surrealism of the scene unbearable. Nestor's eyes seemed to gather the scant light and brighten.

"Are you . . . an alien?" Paul tried to hide his discomfiture.

"That depends on your definition of an alien. My origins are elsewhere. On the other hand, I'm as human as you are."

"Another planet?" Gordon asked.

"Something like that."

"As in flying saucers?" Gordon asked.

"Just a signal from another planet."

"Scottie beamed you down?"

"Scottie?"

"Never mind."

"Go on," Paul prodded Nestor.

"In the Upper Congo, in the Sudan, there's a meteorite crater called Tamaa. A few thousand years ago, after an earthquake, a cleft formed a small volcano in the center of the crater. Imagine an upside-down umbrella with a cone in the middle, where the stick is supposed to be. The cone is Mount Mzimu."

"Never heard of them," Paul said. "What do the names mean?"

"Mzimu is a Swahili word for *soul*, not attached to religion but to mythology." Nestor paused. "Tamaa means *hope*."

Gordon darted a glance in his direction but didn't comment.

"For centuries, during the summer solstice, pygmy brides met their men on the summit. A story that has passed from generation to generation says a woman will conceive a guardian from the stars in times of danger. Thus I was conceived, although more as a pilgrim than a guardian."

Paul mulled over the tale and lifted aching buttocks from his sore feet. "What do you mean by *conceived*?"

"A manner of speech. As you know, some craters have

interesting shapes, like an inverted dish. Tamaa is such a natural formation, although the people of the last civilization refined its profile before the cataclysm. A signal from space, captured by the crater's shape and concentrated onto the apex of Mount Mzimu, reprogrammed the DNA in a woman's ovum. My mother."

"But you said you were human. You look human to me," Gordon said.

"Thank you."

"Are you?" Gordon insisted.

"Am I what?"

"Human."

"I suppose so."

"You told us who your parents were," Paul said. "It infers you're human also, no?"

"I spoke about my origins. My father and mother are pygmies. My mother gestated me for nine months and my father supplied his seed."

"But I saw people in a hologram at the sphere. They were ... mixed, no—"

"No blacks?" Nestor shrugged. "Yes, I've often pondered that point. I suppose there were no instructions to alter my skin color, so I inherited that of my parents."

"What about knowledge? Memories?"

"Those waited for me here, in the monastery. The monks were the keepers of such things."

"The monks had the knowledge?"

"No, but they kept a language, the means to communicate with those who did have the knowledge. They taught me the language, and then I gathered the facts."

"Who controls the knowledge? Who are they?" Paul pressed.

A tap at the door—an announcement, not a request. Two monks entered the room, deposited a legged tea tray, bowed, and left.

"Ah, tea." Nestor uncrossed his arms and rubbed his hands together.

The temperature seemed to drop several degrees. A shiver darted along Paul's spine as he caught sight of Nestor's hands. "I'll be damned! I've seen hands like yours—in the sphere."

"Yes, my relatives," Nestor said, chuckling.

"Why two thumbs?" Gordon asked, staring.

"Two thumbs?" Nestor held out a hand to inspect it. "Oh, I see what you mean." He rested his mug on the table and fluttered both hands. "My hands are more evolved than yours, that's all."

"What's more evolved?"

"Human hands have a wondrous design. What makes the human hand unique is the ability of your small and ring fingers to rotate across the palm to meet the thumb. The only weakness in this structure is your little finger, weaker and with shorter reach."

Gordon clenched and unclenched his fist.

"In the previous civilization, the weakness of the little finger was understood, and genetic engineering did the rest. Mine is an improved hand, balanced, symmetrical, stronger, and much more dexterous."

"You know a lot about hands," Gordon said.

"Only because I've studied evolution. Consider that about a quarter of the motor cortex in the human brain is devoted to the muscles of the hands. Evolution of the hand allowed primitive men to handle and count objects, an activity that stimulated logic paths in the brain to create abstract mental models. This led to manipulating first physical counters and then symbolic counters, the forerunners of mathematics. Yes," Nestor fluttered his hands, "a wondrous design."

Paul had listened to Nestor's words with growing unease.

"I gather there's something troubling you," Nestor said.

"Your people tinkered with the human genome?"

"Some did, but I wouldn't call it tinkering. Rather, it was an accelerated process. The human genome has certain built-in evolutionary paths, such as the gradual recession or change of unnecessary or weak appendages. Take your small toe: It's been shrinking for a long time and will eventually disappear. I have only four toes, broader. The little one went the same way as your tail."

"My what?" It was obvious Gordon also was having a hard time digesting Nestor's words.

"Over the millennia it shrunk into a coccyx." Nestor reached behind and patted his lower back. "You know, the bone at the end of your vertebral column."

A puzzling detail still gnawed at the edge of Paul's consciousness.

"My friend," Nestor turned to Paul, "you're still troubled. You wonder why your hands are not like mine. If humanity evolved along certain lines, why are we different?"

Paul nodded. "Before you said, 'Some did.' That implies that some didn't. Were there different factions?"

"Yes." Nestor's face clouded. "One part of the human race achieved unprecedented technological advances. The other, mainly on the African continent, didn't, and chose to stay here at the time of the great exodus. All of you are descendants of those who stayed behind. But that's a very long story. Perhaps one day, when we meet again, I will tell you the tale of two civilizations and what drove them apart."

Paul extended his hand over the table, palm up. "May I?"

"Of course," Nestor replied quickly, as if expecting the request.

The silky softness of Nestor's hands warmed his own. Paul brought up his other hand and rested it on top of Nestor's. For a moment he remained motionless, hunched over the table, fingers sensing the energy they found there.

"*In the absence of any other proof, the thumb alone would convince me of God's existence,*" Paul quoted.

Nestor's smile broadened. "Isaac Newton, a great man, but I prefer, *You can't shake hands with a clenched fist.*"

"Yours?"

"Alas not. Indira Gandhi coined it."

"What a strange sensation." Paul tried a smile and failed. "Is the rest of your body the same as ours?"

Nestor laughed and drew back his hands. "No. I have no reproductive system. Those who sent the signal made sure I could not reproduce."

"Say, if you have no—" Gordon started, fidgeting. "You know, how you do . . ."

"I use a toilet like anyone else."

"Nowadays they can clone from a single cell," Paul said, afraid to ask overtly whether Nestor could have sex.

"My DNA can't be cloned. I'm one of a kind and have no desire for little Nestors. But my life has a purpose."

There was a slight tremor in Nestor's voice that spoke of more-complicated emotions. Paul liked him.

"Whatever I say will sound fantastic to your ears," Nestor continued. "Please, allow me the benefit of the doubt while I tell you the entire story, the story that Leon Kibassa started in that magical hut on a magical night."

Paul narrowed his eyes, his mind suddenly flooded with images, smells, and sensations. "It was magical. You were there, yet you didn't introduce yourself."

"It would have only confused you further."

"You've known Leon for a long time?"

"Indeed. He's been my mentor and dearest friend since childhood. Master Kibassa is also the last of a kind, in that we share a destiny. The world is orphaned of wisdom, as people strive for the knowledge that can be bartered for cash or services, not to enrich the soul."

Paul thought of the hands in the sphere's hologram, hands the same as Nestor's.

"Stellar bodies, like ants or bees, are parts of an organism with its own entity, like the anthill or the hive. Motions of an individual bee are nothing but the beat of the hive."

Gordon nodded, although Paul suspected it was a polite gesture rather than agreement.

"Each frequency has amplitude in time, however, which we can measure. This way we could predict, with our limited means and intellect, a timetable of periods and the extent of the beats."

Nestor glanced at the teapot and the cups on a tray to one side of the table. Gordon hurried to refill their mugs, as if he had been issued a direct order. His hands trembled.

"Forgive me," Paul said, "but I still don't know how you managed to outsmart the best brains of a powerful nation."

"Best brains?" Nestor repeated, smiling. "We knew what was under Ituri. They didn't. That gave us an advantage. We have scores, hundreds of young men and women working in the most advanced research facilities around the world. And we have access to the beings on this planet who hold this information and the collective memories. We've acted on their instructions, become their tools."

Nestor uses the same words as Kunchen. Is he hinting at more aliens?

"Humor me," Nestor added, acknowledging the incredulous expressions of his listeners.

"No problem," Gordon said. "It's like having the Sci-Fi Channel in three-D."

Nestor laughed heartily, and Paul wondered if he ever took a break from his mission to watch television.

"Let me save some things for the end."

"To be continued next week," Gordon said, smiling.

Nestor laughed again.

"I promise, when you leave the monastery you'll carry answers with you. I don't think you'll *like* them, but you'll share my burden."

Paul was tempted to insist about the "beings" but thought better of it. Nestor wanted to save the punch line for last; that much was obvious.

"Paul, you're a geologist, so you understand magnetism, of course."

"Of course," Paul repeated.

"One of earth's cycles is a switch in the planet's magnetism. That causes the lithosphere to lose cohesion and slip over the core. So the earth's crust decelerates a fraction, only to speed up later. Think of it as a pronounced wobble. It happens every fifty thousand years, give or take a century or two."

Paul's mouth opened but words failed.

"Pole shift?" Gordon blurted out.

"The man knows his science fiction," Paul explained with a smile. "I've heard many theories about pole shift, about the weight of the ice caps or certain planetary alignments messing with the earth's crust. Scientists can't find evidence, though." Paul felt the uncomfortable weight of Nestor's smile. "The laws of physics say pole inversion or displacement of the earth's rotational axis can't happen."

Nestor rose to his feet and offered a hand each to Paul and Gordon. Gordon's knees popped again as he stood up.

"Let's go," Nestor said, holding the door open.

○

He led them down a long corridor to a small room with masonry walls but no windows. A single electrical bulb, suspended from the ceiling, cast a bright yellowish radiance. An old wood table held a modern laboratory stirrer, in stark contrast with the room's ancient atmosphere. A large glass beaker held an opaque metallic liquid. Copper wires coiled around the beaker.

"This beaker contains over two hundred pounds of mercury. It has a hole and has been fitted with a shaft and a propeller connected to a motor in the base," Nestor explained. "A normal stirrer, working by magnetic induction into an element on the bottom of the beaker, would float."

444 carlos j. cortes

From one side of the table Nestor picked up a square mirror and floated it on top of the mercury. He then pointed a finger to the ceiling, where the mirror reflected the lamplight as a bright square.

Nestor pressed a button on the stirrer. The propeller's edge rotated as the counter read five revolutions a minute. He fingered a dial until the counter read one hundred revolutions a minute. Stepping away from the table, Nestor pointed again at the ceiling, where the mirror's reflection remained stationary.

"The metal molecules slide one over the other because of inertia. The movement doesn't transfer. The mirror doesn't move. Now watch."

Nestor connected the loose ends of the copper wire to a battery. The mirror rotated. Paul watched the mirror's reflection on the ceiling in fascination and tensed when his mind leaped to reach the conclusion Nestor was demonstrating. Unconsciously he shrank away, a line of fear scraping like a claw down his spine.

"I created a weak magnetic field, enough for molecules to mesh with one another. Now the column moves as a solid.

"The earth's core is spherical, as you well know," Nestor said. "A fluid layer rotates with the nucleus and, because of its lesser density, expands to create its equatorial bulge—but only on the outside, in the solid layers. Its inner surface, the liquid one, has no bulge. There are two concentric spheres rotating in unison because molecule meshing is magnetic. If the polarity value changed, there would be slippage because of the differences in density between core and lithosphere. Coupled with other forces and the different weights of the mantle, it would trigger a tiny repositioning of the earth's crust."

"But…Wh-what about angular momentum?" Paul couldn't accept the theory; the premise was absurd. "Earth would break into pieces."

Nestor laid a hand on his shoulder and squeezed gently. Paul felt the symmetrical thumbs. *The hand.*

"You are picturing a sudden, significant deceleration, Paul. It takes only a *tiny* deceleration, since the earth's surface travels at over one thousand miles an hour at the equator. The deceleration effect will pile the oceans into a mountain of water.

"Before long, water will raze this civilization," Nestor finished, his voice now hushed.

Gordon's mouth opened and closed like a carp in a fishbowl.

"A slight deceleration of the crust will shake the lithosphere," Paul told Gordon. "Tectonic plates will rip; magma will pour to the surface, earthquakes off the Richter scale. Billions of tons of ash, steam, and smoke will shroud earth."

"A new Stone Age," Gordon whispered.

"Yes."

Nestor disconnected the wire, and the mirror slowed. When he restored the circuit, it picked up speed again.

Legs shaking, Paul stared at the mercury beaker and the reflection on the ceiling, absorbing the terrible implications of the simple experiment. He felt his breath catch, certain now that Nestor's tale was true.

"Is that what happened to the last civilization?"

Nestor's shoulders slumped. He seemed to have suddenly aged. "Yes."

So it's true after all. Nestor's origins were in the stars.
"Where are you from?"

"Ardhi, a planet of the star Dunia, the one you know as Alpha Centauri B."

"Ardhi," Paul repeated. "What does it mean?"

"*Earth* in Swahili. *La ardhi na la mbingu, neno lake husadifu: Concerning the earth and the sky, His word is true.* An African poem Leon taught me."

"What's it like there?" Gordon asked.

"I wish I knew. I've never been there and never will be." That part came out dry as a wasteland.

"Of course, you were beamed down," Gordon said. "So the old earth inhabitants emigrated to Ardhi?"

"Yes."

"They left? Everyone?"

"*Almost* everyone."

"How?" Paul asked.

"Large ships."

"Just like that?" Paul asked, snapping his fingers.

"Yes. It took close to ten years."

"Four light-years in only ten years?"

"We had help. There's a permanent passage open between earth and Ardhi, but only in one direction. Are you familiar with Krasnikov tubes?"

A vein throbbed on Nestor's temple. The man was human, just like him. Paul considered his question, trying to remember an obscure article he'd once read in *Scientific American*, then shook his head. "No."

"When a ship travels at high speeds, there's a space warp created behind it, a distortion of space that can be used to travel almost without delay. It works only in the same direction, though. We can send messages from earth and they are received almost at once, but not in reverse. Causality laws forbid it."

Paul was frustrated. He wanted to grasp it all at once, but Nestor spoke methodically, as if itemizing his points in a seminar.

"Messages from earth have reached Ardhi for millennia. Crater footprints make excellent focusing devices to concentrate signals into tight beams. Those in the know only have to wait until a tube is overhead and beam a signal. When Shermaine met you, Chodak, a young man working with you at IMC, sent such a signal. We even received it here when it bounced off the moon."

"Are there several tubes?" Paul asked.

"Yes."

"How do you know signals have ever reached Ardhi? You've never been there."

"Genetic memories. I know some things about Ardhi."

"Ardhi must be technologically advanced," Gordon said.

"Yes, but they use technology to further the species, not to destroy it. Universal cycles can be gleaned through millennia of computing and observation. You haven't had enough time, but others before you could evaluate the pulse frequencies. We only need to know the date, direction, and amplitude of the slippage to gather where on the planet there's a chance of survival. That's what is in these disks."

Nestor pulled the disks from his jacket pocket and rotated them between his thumbs. They looked like plastic chips.

"The colors of the rainbow."

Paul and Gordon peered at the objects without understanding.

"Perhaps a recording?" Gordon tried.

Nestor nodded and placed the disks on the table. "Have you considered the possible reason behind the different colors?"

When Paul had seen them in the sphere, they had a slight shine, like silk, but he hadn't noticed that each had a dent on its outer edge. He took a disk and raised it toward the light. The chip had three tiny holes. He looked at Nestor.

"The colors may be a key," Paul thought aloud, "or perhaps a sequence."

Nestor nodded. "The colors are a sequence, but of what?"

"The rainbow?" Paul studied the disks again and arranged them on the table: the violet disk on the left, followed by blue, green, yellow, orange, and red on the right.

Nestor clapped his hands once and laughed like a child. "Right! The sequence of light, from fast to slow, from high to low energy. I knew you would get it. Now, what about the holes?"

Paul altered the positions and tried to superimpose two. After a while he shook his head and laid them back on the table. "No idea," Paul conceded.

From his trousers pocket, Nestor produced a small flashlight. He selected a disk, placed it over the flashlight pointed at the ceiling, and switched it on. Three brilliant points of light appeared, each with a different diameter.

"Sirius, Arcturus, and Procyon, the first, second, and sixth brightest stars in the sky as viewed from earth's northern hemisphere. The groove in the disks shows their relative position to the sphere's magnetic axis. The red circle shows star positions before the previous calamity, the orange their horizontal deviation, and the yellow the vertical. The green disk shows the star locations when the new slippage will occur—the blue toward their horizontal plane and the violet toward the vertical. That's the message and the legacy from our forebears: the date of the next cataclysm."

Paul glanced at Gordon. His head was slumped forward. He looked like a captured prisoner. Nestor collected the disks and put them away in his pocket.

"The monks are working at the observatory. We'll have the coordinates by tomorrow. We can talk more after dinner. Okay?"

"But what about the rings I collected, the wire rings?" Paul asked in response.

"They contain the artistic and scientific knowledge of the last civilization, but you shouldn't be concerned. They're worthless right now. It would take years, perhaps centuries, to transcribe their contents. Besides, if a country or corporation got the rings and managed to translate their contents, they'd be disappointed. There's only philosophy, natural sciences, art, literature, and music, what they considered valuable, their treasures."

Nestor's voice dropped to a whisper. "Besides, there may be no time left."

chapter 46

Dinner, served by silent monks, was the usual: yogurt, rice, lentils, curried vegetables, and fruit. Paul wondered how they could tolerate such monotony.

What wasn't usual was the room: a semicircular dome chiseled out of solid rock and walls covered with tiny, tight Sanskrit writing. Paul studied the script, wondering how many years and monks were required to put it there.

Nestor picked at his food but drank several glasses of water and the strong tea that followed the meal.

"They should have offered you *chhang* with your meal," Nestor said. "It's a beer brewed with fermented cereals. But they left us some *raksi*." Nestor held up the dark bottle. "It's wheat liquor popular in Tibet. The locals mix it with their tea."

Gordon took the bottle from Nestor. The stopper was clay, sealed with wax. After a struggle, he removed the bung and sniffed the contents. "Smells good," he announced as he poured a generous dose into the tea. Nestor declined, a hand over his mug. A strong, pleasant aroma spread through the room.

"Is this a meditation room?" Paul asked, eyes fixed on a wall.

"Any room is good for that," Nestor said. "No. The writing is a tale of humankind, a story about heroism and altruism."

"It must have taken many years."

"Centuries. There are over sixteen million signs here, and I'm told a good scribe could manage twenty a day."

"That's more than two thousand years," Paul said after a mental calculation.

"For a single scribe perhaps, but this isn't the feat of a single man. The room is a ball, or a sphere if you like. There's another room below, a mirror image of this one. The walls are thick and independent of the building. The room could roll down a mountain slope and remain intact."

"Or remain buried throughout millennia," Paul added.

"Precisely." Nestor's voice echoed softly off the ancient stone. He paused to drink from his mug, holding it with both hands. Paul remembered with a pang of longing that Carmen, Lupe, and Shermaine drank the same way.

"What number are we?" Gordon asked.

"The fifth human civilization."

"And all managed to leave their tale?" Paul asked.

"It's now obvious the people from the first civilization didn't understand the problems involved," Nestor replied. "There were logistical difficulties in leaving something in a way that would last thousands of years. That's part of the problem, because the term *first* civilization is confusing; it covers at least two hundred catastrophes."

"But *some* things must survive," Paul insisted.

Nestor sighed and intertwined his fingers. Paul peered at Nestor's twin thumbs. Moses had offered engraved stones as proof. Nestor had his hands.

"Many cycles elapsed before man understood the sequence of cataclysm and reemergence. It wasn't an easy phenomenon to detect. You can only write about what you know, and man remained ignorant for millions of years."

"There must be *something*," Paul insisted again. "Structures can last a long time, and somebody would have found remains, however small."

"Are you thinking about pyramids, perhaps?" Nestor asked with a smile.

"For instance, yes."

"Pyramids are young constructions, built in stable times. In a primal earth with hurricane winds lasting for decades, the pyramids would revert to sand in a short span. Have you seen the Sphinx?"

"There's not much left of the face, I know," Paul said. "I played tourist around Cairo a few years ago."

"Precisely."

"But what about men? What about evolution?"

"The cycles are the most important mechanism of evolution. Only by wiping the slate clean can you further the species. Ever hear of saltational versus progressive evolution?"

"I've read some papers on *punctuated* evolution," Paul responded.

"Yes, punctuated equilibrium is such a theory, but

cyclical disasters are the mechanism. The process can spread over millions of years. Intermediate cataclysms are of little importance, because survivors, regardless of the number, are developed and don't have to start from zero. After a catastrophe, the species continues its development."

"And the written records?" Paul asked, mind reeling.

"A huge volume of data has survived, spread all over the world and in various media. In places, comprehensive libraries exist, deposits of knowledge belonging to the survivors. Individuals and groups have tried to look after them."

Nestor leaned forward, and his dark eyes seemed to gather the scant light of the candles.

Like Leon's, Paul realized.

"If I wanted to leave a piece of writing to my kin," Nestor continued, "I would need to write it and give it to someone. The problem is what may happen between writing and reading. The catastrophe that follows a crust shift is unimaginable."

Nestor's voice trembled.

"Cities and populated areas disappear in an instant, but earth may be unstable for centuries. Survivors have a single advantage: their genetic development. This may be the only thing to remain intact. Metals aren't available from a cold earth. A technological mind is useful, but only with the resources of a primal and convulsing environment.

"The new man will have to be always on the move in search of food, with few animals left, all the time trying to escape earth's convulsions. The question remains: how to conserve data that will be useful thousands of years later?"

Paul glanced at Gordon, who stared immobile at Nestor, as if mesmerized. This was the mother of all tales.

"Engraving on stone is slow. You need large surfaces, and will the next group of survivors know the written language? How long will it take to figure out? Oral tradition corrupts with relative speed and after a few generations can become incomprehensible. I don't know how survivors manage to catch up."

That answered Paul's unspoken question about whether Nestor was speaking from experience.

"Libraries have been managed or mismanaged by all kinds of people, all in the name of religion, power, or ignorance. Scientists venture inaccurate suppositions based on observations of a few cosmic laws, mathematics, and the properties of matter. Theories are mistaken for fact. Polarity reversals, the dinosaurs' disappearance, the presence of marine fossils on high mountains, and many other of science's inexplicable facts are the keys, but dogma gets in the way. People are more concerned with their reputations than getting the facts right. Paul, you in particular have had plenty of proof."

Gordon glanced at Paul, who only shrugged.

"I'll give you an example of how blind a whole species can be," Nestor went on, ignoring their puzzlement. "In the Muslim year 919—1513 in the Christian calendar— an admiral of the Turkish navy painted a map on parchment. His sources were twenty other maps, some dating from the time of Alexander. The parchment has America and Africa at the correct longitudes, surprising because sailors had no way to fix longitude. Even more astonishing is the detailed contour of Antarctica."

Paul jerked his head.

"Antarctica wasn't discovered until 1818," Nestor continued, "and dry land isn't visible at the South Pole. The soil is under miles of ice. The first modern map was made in 1920; explosives and seismic tools were used to locate the land. Not long ago, scientists produced a better map with sonar technology. The last chart is identical with the one drawn in 1513. By the way, the map I'm talking about uses spherical trigonometry with a fiendish projection. A powerful computer needed sixteen days to calculate the details. Science cannot explain such a map. It's a puzzle inside an enigma. Isn't that the term used?" Nestor asked, smiling, apparently amused at the colloquialism. "Where did the data come from to map Antarctica in the sixteenth century?"

"From members of a previous civilization, who wisely emigrated to another planet and left information in a way they hoped would reach the right hands."

"Why me?" Paul finally asked. "I'm a scientist, not a shepherd of men."

"You're a rare man, Paul." Nestor turned toward Gordon and smiled. "With rarer friends, if I may say so."

"You may," Gordon said, smiling in return. "I was wondering if anyone knew I was here."

"It's been a small miracle you were chosen to lead the Congo operation for your company," Nestor told him. "Shermaine couldn't believe our luck, even though it meant redesigning our previous strategy."

"I *still* don't understand," Paul said. "What's so rare about me?"

"Your character," Nestor said bluntly. "Your morality."

"Morality?" Gordon asked, laughing. "Are you sure you have the right guy?"

Nestor laughed back and then turned to Paul. "It's more complicated than religious norms. You're a wealthy man in earth terms, the heir to a huge corporation, yet you chose to work with your hands. In more than one way, you have remained close to the earth. That singles you out as a rare man."

"That's it? I play in dirt?"

Nestor laughed again and nodded. "Perhaps you're not a leader, but that should not be a cause of concern. The new age does not need leaders."

Paul bowed his head, awed by the horror soon to be unleashed on the human race. He had seen the sphere. That had been no dream. It had been built by men, buried at an unimaginable depth, and made from advanced composites. *Proof? Did he need extra proof?*

Nestor leaned and placed a hand on Paul's arm, the warmth soothing and comforting. For a moment Nestor looked at Gordon and extended his hand toward him. Gordon held the proffered hand, his face an image of wonder. Paul felt the magic of the moment as he stared at the men's communion.

"I'm not suggesting you play God and decide who should live or die," he explained. "There will be small groups, scattered, facing the same dilemma. Who do you think will survive? You, me, anyone you gather within your group? You would be wrong. The survivors will be those who can deal with the hand they're dealt without egos and opinions getting in the way. The single thing you'll be able to secure is transport for a group of people.

You can take them to a place where the effect of the catastrophe will be less, but you cannot guarantee their survival. Not many will survive a year."

After a long silence, Gordon shifted on his cushion. "There's something I don't understand," he said. "Where are the remains? You know, the knowledge left by past survivors?"

"Huge quantities of data survived in the knotted *quipos* the Jesuits burned by the thousands in the New World. There was a great deal of information in the pyramid engravings and in codices and clay tablets in the Alexandrian libraries. *And* in the Vatican Library, in the vaults and crypts of governments, to name just a few. The monks have been collecting and hiding data for over two thousand years."

"You mentioned there were *beings* with the knowledge," Paul prompted.

"We knew about the spheres in two ways. Any dowser could point to the exact location of the capsules. You don't need satellites. On the other hand, some survivors are trying to give us the necessary information. We need only to communicate and listen."

Paul glanced at Gordon, confused. Gordon shrugged. Apparently he didn't hear the answer about the beings either.

"Come," Nestor said. He stood quickly, with surprising agility after sitting such a long time.

He led them to a door, but it didn't open. Instead, the floor below it moved forward, uncovering a flight of wide stairs. Gordon jumped back, not expecting the unexpected.

The bottom of the stairs opened onto a circular

library, its stone shelves crammed with thousands of ancient books.

"The monks use these books for their studies," Nestor explained as they descended. "If unwanted visitors ever reached this point, they would see only books. They'd probably stop here since there's no other visible entrance or exit. But..." Nestor paused and smiled to heighten the drama.

"But?" Gordon repeated.

Nestor touched a wall candle and the entire wall rotated 180 degrees.

"Ah, but," Gordon said, nodding. "Concrete?" he asked, eyeing the room that appeared.

"With a steel door," Nestor answered. "And..."

"Dare I ask?" Gordon said, laughing.

Nestor smiled and pressed the button on the door.

"Voilà, an elevator."

Nestor gestured for them to enter the tiny box ahead of him. Seconds later, the distinctive void in the stomach confirmed that they were descending at notable speed.

"Eighteen hundred feet?" Paul asked. "As tall as the Sears Tower?"

"A bit more," Nestor replied. "About two thousand, and built by the monks."

The door opened and the three men entered a vast natural cavern with rows of metallic shelving. Floor rails spanned each battery of shelves. The entire area was brightly lit.

"Electricity," Gordon noted.

"Other than the monks and me, you're the only ones who've entered the library this century," Nestor told them. "There are more than eighteen million items written in Sanskrit, the language of the third civilization."

"They had only one language?" Paul asked.

"That's right. As I said, they were advanced. They made this cavern. Twelve hundred years ago, the monks built the monastery on top. Then they worked on the shaft and other access for centuries. The rings you found will enlarge this library. Perhaps a new civilization will be able to enjoy their contents."

"Okay to touch?" Gordon asked, eyeing a flat black object that looked like shale.

"Sure," Nestor answered. "The fourth civilization ensured that the details to find any of the eleven spheres spread around the planet would reach us without a hitch. The beings you're understandably curious about are in charge of the data. They've been telling us about it daily, from all over the planet. All men need to do is listen and they'll understand. It's a simple language. The monks have spoken it for over five hundred years, and *they* taught *me*." Nestor flipped a switch on a desk, and a wall rose, disappearing into the ceiling and revealing a thick pane of glass.

"An aquarium . . ." Gordon muttered.

Inside, a dolphin somersaulted in silence. It stopped to peer at them with intelligent, expectant eyes and made several quick clicking sounds.

"He's asking about the image you saw inside the sphere," Nestor said. "Could you describe it?"

"He's speaking and you're interpreting?" Paul asked after grasping that the sounds were speech. He glanced at Nestor, who seemed also to be waiting for an answer.

"Well, I didn't understand the mural in the sphere," he said.

Nestor whistled, clicked, and wheezed in succession. The dolphin's head bounced up and down.

"It's nodding," Gordon said.

It then uttered a string of sharp clicks.

"It's what I heard in the Congo!" Gordon shouted. "Shermaine," he added in almost a whisper. "She was talking to a dolphin?"

Nestor chuckled. "No, Gordon, she spoke with me."

Paul shook his head, incapable of processing the sudden avalanche of slotting pieces. "But... why dolphins?"

Nestor drew closer. "You remember a conversation— a briefing, really—when you first arrived at the IMC labs? Milford Crandall said: *Imagine we want to leave something for our posterity far into the future or we're faced with a catastrophe, something that threatens the survival of the species. We would be in deep shit. How could we leave our message? How could we design a structure sufficiently robust to withstand millennia and to ensure discovery at the right time?*

"Then he added: *Imagine the following scenario. According to history as we know it, ten thousand years ago we lived in caves. One of our ancestors finds a container, a book, or a chip. First, he would check to see if he could eat it. Then he would throw it away or burn it. Anyway, it would be lost.*"

Paul's mind raced. "How do you know that? Were you listening? The place was secure, scanned for bugs twice a day."

"That's true, but your security people checked in the

evening and first thing in the morning, before and after workers used the premises."

"And?"

"Our friend Chodak placed the bug after the morning sweep and removed it ahead of the evening check."

"But how?"

Nestor smiled. "He attached it to the base of your coffeepot."

The sharp clicks continued.

Paul glanced at Gordon, who leaned on a wall, his mouth once again wide open. They had heard the same noises many times in the Congo, as they pored over the tapes of Shermaine's phone conversations.

"He wants to know if there were animals in the hologram," Nestor translated.

"Yes, some fish," Paul said, his voice trembling. "But I don't remember—" He stopped and snapped his fingers. "Yes, they were dolphins, and they formed a circle."

After listening, the dolphin nodded and clicked again.

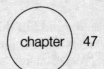

chapter 47

Two monks he didn't recognize shook Paul awake before dawn. "Come," one of them said, grasping his upper arm. His cotton tunic was green rather than saffron, seemingly the regulation dress. Paul guessed from his high-pitched voice he couldn't be more than twelve years old.

Paul dressed quickly and stepped into the corridor, adjusting his stride to the monks'. Instead of following the passageway to the outside, they went in the opposite direction and turned at the end of the corridor to a narrow staircase, which they mounted for several floors. When they finally reached a semicircular landing, one of the monks opened a heavy oak door and bowed before turning on his heel, his silent companion in tow. Paul walked onto a dark terrace housing a large garden with clumps of plants, a small lake, a bridge, and sinuous gravel paths.

Nestor stood from his seat on a wooden bench and smiled in the near darkness. "This is the lama's garden, one of rank's privileges, an ideal place for meditation. Care to hear its history?"

Paul breathed deeply, nodded, and walked beside Nestor along a narrow path.

"An extraordinary monk planted it in the year 1465. Cheng-t'ung: the sixth emperor of the Ming Dynasty. A weak man ruled by the court eunuchs and especially by Wang-Chen. His reign was a sorry one. The Mongols held him prisoner. He lived as a recluse and continued as emperor when his successor fell ill. China's history tells us that he died in 1464 at thirty-five, but that's not true."

Nestor's voice was barely above a murmur but audible over the slight soughing of the wind.

"Through a ruse, he managed to fake his own death and came to this monastery as a simple monk. Besides being the first emperor to abolish the law calling for his concubines to die with him, he planted and tended this garden for more than thirty years. Therefore, this is truly an emperor's garden. The monks look after it and replace the old or sick plants with others of the same type. What you see here is the garden that Cheng-t'ung planted."

They walked along gravel paths, both men silent for a long time, lulled by the crunch of gravel underfoot and the rustling of leaves. They crossed a wooden bridge over a tiny lake as the shadows melted into timid dawn twilight on the horizon. The play of light from the new day's sun enlivened the plants, highlighting the soft contours of lavender stalks, wild sorrel, and the inimitable green of rosemary and thickets of thyme sprouting between the rockeries.

The reddish tints of dawn melted slowly away. Stronger light bathed the garden, revealing the flowers' true colors. Paul reveled in the rare sensual experience.

Nestor sat on a flat stone and motioned for Paul to sit

at his side. On the horizon, the awesome Himalayas' perpetual snow basked in the early sun, outlined sharply against the blue sky. The wind shifted, bringing with it the tang of evergreen alpines.

Paul looked at the greenish water. "I'm afraid," he admitted. "Nestor, what am I supposed to do?"

"Kunchen will give you new identities, travel documents, and access to funds. You'll need much money if you're to put together a large group of people."

"I have money."

Nestor stopped and ran his hand over a lavender bush. Then he sniffed and turned toward Paul. "I know you do. But you're supposed to be dead. You can't touch your assets."

"I have safe funds scattered everywhere—South America, Asia, Europe. Over twenty million."

"Including the proceeds of your opal adventure?"

Paul smiled. "I won't ask how you got that information."

"Irrelevant. But let me congratulate you on your friends. You have many. That singles you out as fortunate."

"I know."

Nestor stared at the sky. It was a cloudless day.

"I'm no Moses," Paul said. "I can't be a leader of men."

"But you can be a Noah. You'll deliver some of earth's creatures to the safety of a mountaintop. Don't be hard on yourself. In the coming voyage to the unknown, you'll be one of the drivers. The ultimate explorer."

To Paul, it all seemed unreal, as if they had discussed the plot for a theater play. Yet his gut churned with foreboding.

His face to the sun, Nestor stood up.

"It's time for you to journey to a new era. I can't give you any expensive luggage, though."

Paul tried to laugh, but it came out like a cough. He shivered.

Nestor turned back toward the monastery.

"You'll meet others, you'll combine your collective intelligence, and you will survive," Nestor said as they walked. "Civilizations will form again. There will be religions, economies, peace, and conflicts."

Nestor took an envelope from his breast pocket and handed it to Paul. "I think you might like to have this. It's fair you enjoy it," he said, before nodding solemnly and heading toward the door.

Paul pulled out a thick piece of navy-blue plastic the size of a playing card. When the sun hit its surface, Paul could see Terra's children, hands raised, welcoming him.

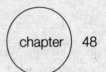

chapter 48

In an atypical gesture, Hugh Reece didn't walk straight to his seat at the head of the table. With short steps and a grimace of weariness, he detoured to stop in turn beneath each of the four oil paintings presiding over the board-room.

The patriarch knew he'd aged beyond recognition over the last few weeks. From the date of the Congo ca-tastrophe, he had not set foot in his office. Now he was a weak old man, propped up by little more than his steel re-solve.

Hugh raised rheumy eyes to the portrait of Amos: a strong face with large sideburns. John Reece came next, with the coppery skin of the Kutchin, an ancestry as old as the mountains. A few steps farther, Hugh stopped be-low the portrait of Tobias Reece, his father, a huge man dressed in buckskin, a smile on his thick lips. This was the man who'd chased a legend and unearthed a fortune. At last he gazed upon his own canvas, as if it were a stranger's.

The rest of the empty wall blurred as Hugh closed his eyes on welling tears. As in a dream, he imagined the portraits of his son, Walter, followed by his grandson, Paul. His progeny; what should have been the future. He opened his eyes and absorbed the empty spot after his own picture. The chain had snapped beyond repair. There would never be another Reece.

He turned to peer at the expectant faces. Hugh trudged around the table and stopped by Milford, his own Judas. He ran his hand along the back of Owen DeHolt's empty chair, the man perhaps buried under tons of lava. At last his eyes reached the vacant seat of Walter, his son, ripped to pieces in a dissecting room. His board room was peopled by ghosts.

When he reached her seat, Eula Kauffmann offered her arm as support—a crutch for the failing walk of the elderly and infirm.

After he settled, Hugh remained motionless, staring straight ahead. When he spoke, his voice shook, a mere shadow of the deep growl that had once made strong men tremble.

"There isn't an agenda for this meeting. What I'm about to tell you I could have done by internal mail or in writing." Hugh stopped, weary from the effort of speaking. He met their eyes in turn. "This is the last board meeting of the International Mining Corporation."

Stewart, Justin, and Eula jerked in unison and exchanged glances. Milford remained deadpan.

"The board of directors is dissolved until the new president takes over. He will assume control of the corporation until its public offering." Hugh paused to catch his breath. "Milford will take over tomorrow; that's the agreement reached between his lawyers and mine."

Eula, the vice president in charge of the corporation's formidable legal apparatus, paled but remained silent. Hugh fixed her with his stare.

"Most shares will be available, including those of my grandson, Paul. Until he's declared dead by law, the proceeds will have to be set aside. As you know, there's no body yet, and chances are there never will be. You have options as part of your respective contracts. In addition, I have arranged for transferring packets of shares to bring each of your equities to two percent of the corporation. This is true of you and Owen DeHolt's widow." *It's not the poor woman's fault her husband was a bastard.* Hugh turned to stare at Milford. "When my grandson is declared legally dead, the sums from the public offering will bankroll a foundation to assist the people of Africa."

The three directors exchanged glances again. Hugh could almost hear the whir of greedy mental cogs, weighing, calculating the value of two percent. *Greed's a mightier passion than sorrow.*

"Milford will also run the Paul Reece Foundation." He locked eyes with him. *For what you are about to receive may the Lord make you truly thankful,* Hugh thought, silently reciting the Catholic litany. He hoped there'd be no eternal punishment for misusing it with scorn over someone he hated.

The old man straightened and glanced at his directors.

"What I have just told you is my decision, registered and legalized, with my will. I have already sent copies of the original legal document to your offices with fuller details.

"Don't even think about contesting my decision or bringing legal action because you think I've not treated you well or that I'm not in full possession of my faculties. If you interfere in any way with the smooth changeover, my guess is your life span will be decreased. That's all." He made a dismissive gesture, as if swatting a fly. "Now I want to be alone."

When the directors left, Hugh reached under the desk to a hidden switch and disarmed the signal-blocking system embedded in the walls. Then he pulled a cell phone from his trousers pocket and opened its back cover. With difficulty, Hugh removed the sim-card and inserted a new one, stolen and hand-delivered to his house the previous evening.

Hugh keyed in the number he had memorized months ago on a magical night, the last time he saw his grandson.

I have a friend, Paul had said, raising a tumbler in an unsteady hand. *And my friends are yours. If ever you need anything, call him and he'll be there.*

There are no friends left.

Perhaps, but there are soul brothers, and he's mine.

After a short delay, when he heard the voice of a man he'd never met, thousands of miles away, Hugh demanded justice, the kind courts of law would never grant him. The voice just asked for a name and address. When Hugh finished, he exchanged sim-cards again, fed the minuscule piece of plastic into a shredder next to the credenza, and collapsed into the nearest chair.

Breathing in ragged gasps, he looked once more at the faces of his forebears and at his own. He searched the eyes and found them strange, cold, and unloving.

Hugh leaned over and reached to one of his tall moccasins. His hand closed around the caribou-horn handle of a knife. As he drew it, the blade caught the light and glinted.

Hugh changed hands, taking the knife with the left and drawing a deep slash across his right arm. Without blinking, he repeated the procedure on his left. He dropped the blade with a sigh of relief and eased his arms to the side as blood streamed down his fingers and fell onto the carpet.

When he lifted his head, Amos, John, and Tobias looked down with affection. Hugh, the patriarch of the Reeces, felt his spirit rise, expansive and free over the northern lands, as he died with a smile on his lips.

Eldorado Brougham—and slid a hand over the polished ·
sage-green trunk.

Milford rested the coffee mug on a shelf and filled a
bucket with warm water, a squirt of detergent, and a dose
of liquid wax. From a drawer he selected a couple of
chamois leather squares. He carted everything toward the
rear of the car and opened the garage door with the remote.

A reddish dawn outlined tile roofs on the opposite side
of the wide residential road. A boy darted by on a mountain bike and tossed a folded newspaper. It arced through
the air and landed with a soft thud three feet from the entrance door. *Good throw*, Milford thought as he sipped
with one hand and washed the car with the other.

Ten percent of the shares would not be on offer; those
would remain with him, Stewart, Eula, Justin, and
Owen's wife. He should have no problem controlling
them; after all, they were rich now, beyond their wildest
dreams. Riches bred cautious, conservative behavior. Yes,
they would side with him. Through them, he would control IMC. The pieces fit admirably. In the evening, he
would join Hindman at his club for further flushing of
the bilges. Hindman would press once more about Paul's
whereabouts during his two-year absence. Milford would
never reveal that Paul had been hiding in Honduras.

There was a good reason for his discretion. Milford
smiled. In fact, there were twenty-five million good reasons. He never considered involving IMC in the opal
deal. Yuji Murakami had bought the lot. Milford's cut on
the twelve tons of first-quality black opals had fattened his
Swiss account by almost twenty-five million dollars—
twice what he had paid to the Honduran hillbillies.

Milford squeezed the chamois between his fingers. *Paul, my boy, an idealist to the end. You never grew up, did you?*

As Milford crouched to rub the fender, he caught sight of a cleric heading toward the open garage door. In one hand was a large brown bag with grease marks, in the other, a doughnut. *I thought they packed doughnuts in boxes,* Milford thought, dreading the visit. *Alms for the poor? A contribution to missionaries in some godforsaken place? A rest home for wayward hookers and other worthy causes? What will it be this time?*

"I'm sorry, Father; I don't have any money with me," Milford said before the priest could ask.

The priest stopped, the hand with the half-eaten doughnut frozen in midair. Up close, the man seemed odd, more like a linebacker. The collar, a little on the tight side, dug into a beefy neck. The loose-fitting jacket barely disguised powerful shoulders. Milford eyed the wraparound sunglasses blending with the black skin, the square jaw with the cleft chin. *How does one shave that? A distant memory fought to surface in his mind. Where have I seen that chin before?*

In one movement, Milford rose and the priest let the doughnut drop to the ground. Milford followed the chunk of dough as it hit the concrete slab and rested there, cosseted in a sprinkle of crumbs. A strange calm suffused his body. He suddenly realized that Charon, the imperturbable ferryman, could call to offer his services cloaked in the unlikeliest of disguises: in this instance, as a doughnut-eating parson. Milford remembered the cleft chin—Honduras! *Where Paul had discovered the opal seam.*

Lazily, with unbearable weariness, the arm reached

toward him, growing. It was much longer than before or, at least, that's what it seemed at first glance. Milford's eyes inched down the arm, stopping at the impenetrable darkness of a silencer. The weapon was being held steady, as if nailed in midair, held by a man without fear. T. S. Eliot's words echoed through his mind.

I've seen the moment of my greatness flicker, and I have seen the eternal Footman hold my coat, and snicker, and in short, I was afraid.

Milford waited.

After an eternity, he felt a mighty kick on his chest, followed by another, softer, more like a tap, as he jerked backward. He didn't feel his back slam against the concrete.

epilogue

Muhammad Ibrahim Ega, president of Somalia, looked with ill-concealed skepticism at the two Americans sitting in his office. The ruler was a pragmatic man who detested Yankees. He'd always considered them vulgar, pretentious, and patronizing. The pair facing him across the desk were no exception. Their affected mannerisms and the way they ogled each other made him nervous, although the letter of introduction from President Kabila meant he had to grant them an audience.

"My people need the altitude, Mr. President. They must be at the right spot to receive the telluric current bath and be in tune with the New Year. Don't you understand?"

Muhammad stared at the thin white American with his cord necktie and thick silver slide. *Of course I don't understand. What the fuck is a telluric current?* Muhammad shook his head.

The black American leaned forward, pouting at his companion. "If Your Eminence allows it, I'll explain.

Our congregation needs to take a year-end cruise, visiting points where the cosmic forces are at a peak. According to our calculations, the summit of Mount Surud Cad is the essence of... how shall I say it, my general? The ideal place to tap into the currents, to receive a new era and bathe in the cosmic forces."

The president stared for an instant at the black American's cleft chin and shook his head with determination, already weary of the two idiots. *First he calls me Eminence, like I'm a fucking cardinal; then general. The bastard will crown me emperor before this is over.*

"I cannot agree to your request," Muhammad said. "I can't issue five hundred visas for as many tourists to spend a few days camping on a mountaintop. These are difficult times. We have, shall we say, internal dissent."

The white man, who had introduced himself as Charlie Martin, shook his head and raised a hand to his mouth as if he were going to be sick. Muhammad stared at the thick gold coin ring on the man's hand.

"Oh, Lord, what will we do now?" Charlie whined. "It's all organized. Our poor flock awaits. Oh, my God."

The black man embraced him, uttered cooing sounds as he patted Charlie's head, then turned a sorrowful face to the president. "This is a catastrophe, Eminence. The faithful have already paid for the cruise, including a donation for your magnificent country. But now... Please, Charlie, stop crying."

The president felt his ears tremble like the antennae of a moth capturing a female's scent. He adjusted his ample anatomy on the seat and cleared his throat.

"A donation, you said?"

"Peanuts, my general," the black man continued,

pouting now straight at the president, who flinched. He glanced sideways at Charlie, who had covered his mouth again, racked with convulsive sobs. "Now that I know you, I'm ashamed of our boldness. Two thousand dollars."

The president straightened, a hand on the security-alarm button.

"Two thousand dollars?"

"Per person, Your Eminence."

"In cash?" he asked, his expression softening.

The black man leaned to one side and picked up the briefcase he'd deposited on the floor. Without a word, he placed it on the desk and undid the clasps. The president raised the lid a fraction and gazed for an instant at the stacked bundles of hundred-dollar bills. Then he closed the case and set it on the floor at his side.

"Did you say telluric currents?"

The black man nodded.

Muhammad tried to uphold a severe expression. Then he allowed the hint of a smile.

"I must say the feelings of your colleague—parson, perhaps? No matter—have touched me. If you want to bring your . . . flock to celebrate . . . whatever, I will issue a block visa for your pilgrimage to our country. A week from now acceptable?"

Charlie sprang up, grabbed Muhammad's hands, and kissed first the left one and then the right. Then he turned around and left the room in a hurry, still sobbing. The black man shook his head and produced a long list on several sheets of paper.

"He's so emotional. . . . Anyway, these are the names of the faithful, if Your Eminence could order the visas."

The president took the papers and hurried to offer a handshake to thwart further effusions of warmth.

"My secretary will have the papers at your disposal tomorrow morning, and I assure you that your people will have a special safe conduct."

"Thank you, Eminence. If things work out, we could repeat this every month," he said joyously before running out of the office.

The twenty-ninth president of one-third of Somalia sat back down, his mind in turmoil. *Every month?* After a quick calculation, he lifted his phone and issued several urgent orders.

○

"If you ever pull another stunt like that I'll tear you in half," Paul warned Manuel after giving instructions to the taxi driver. "Damn! I couldn't stop laughing! How could you blow kisses to that slob? Your *Eminence*?" Paul dried his tears with the back of his hand.

"Go ahead, laugh," Manuel said as he stared out the window and pretended to look offended. "But we have the visas. I told you the congregational bath in telluric currents couldn't fail."

○

The *Norse Witch* raised anchor at Marseilles to start a voyage of thirty thousand miles, from Marseilles to the Canary Islands, the Antilles, and Honduras, and through the Panama Canal to the Marshall Islands. Skirting the Philippines and Borneo toward the Straits of Malacca, the ship entered the Gulf of Bengal, then continued past Sri Lanka and the Maldives to the Somalian peninsula and the Gulf of Aden. At last, on January 3, she dropped anchor at the port of Maydh, fewer than seventy miles from the peak of Mount Surud Cad, 7,900 feet high.

The operation, a jewel of logistics, was designed and directed by Paul. He had gathered 464 people of different races and extractions and equipped them with haversacks containing pemmican, nuts, and vitamins capable of nourishing a person without any supplement other than water. In a parallel operation, Paul shipped over twenty-five thousand blue plastic boxes, each weighing forty pounds, to points in Kenya, Ethiopia, the south of Sudan, and the Upper Congo. Michael, Shermaine, Hilari, and dozens of helpers waited on the receiving ends to store the boxes in natural caves, the safest storage places they could think of. In Oceania and Asia, others made similar preparations, moving huge quantities of supplies and transferring groups of people. The cache contained antibiotics and drugs in sturdy plastic bags of two pounds each, with basic tools and other simple necessaries.

The travelers from the *Norse Witch* crossed the Tabah Pass and spread out over the peak of Surud Cad a scant eight hours before the deadline spelled by the colors of the rainbow. There they waited, huddled beside open fires. A strange quietness descended over the men and women, making the children drowsy and dulling the senses.

At 04:24 on January 5, 2025, the stars stood still in the sky.

In California, the earthquake started with a low-frequency rumble. It wasn't a sound but a sensation that caused an incomprehensible weakness in the legs, a constriction of the bowels, and panic. The sound waves grew, pulsated, and broke free into an earsplitting roar. This time, however, it was not a landslide or a tremor. It was an earthquake like none in recorded history, at least in the present era.

The effect of the crust's minute deceleration caused tectonic plates to crash and separate like floes on a swell.

Along the California inland, mountains moved like reeds before the wind and jiggled like Jell-O as the Pacific and North American Plates collided and the Cocos Plate retreated. A vast chasm opened along the San Andreas Fault. The Pacific Ocean left its bed and retreated on itself in slow motion, forming a colossal wall three miles high before gravity brought it down.

The wind attacked with passion, smashing everything in its way with a mighty curtain of supersonic air. The Pacific wall followed the wind eastward, burying Los Angeles and San Francisco like grains of sand. Inland, ocean filled the gash along the San Andreas line, suddenly cooling cubic miles of incandescent magma. The explosion ripped off a huge slab of North America and set it adrift.

Across the continent, thousand-mile-per-hour winds flattened the landscape like a gargantuan bulldozer and ripped apart everything living. Along faults, soft masses of lava broke through the crust and gushed forth as a sea of liquid fire. In less than three hours, the wall of water had crossed the continent and buried wind-torn land under miles of water from coast to coast.

Central America suffered the same doom by fire and water. The Nazca, Cocos, and Caribbean Plates collided, rebounding and breaching the Atlantic and Pacific Oceans through a narrow slit a few feet across. Within days, the grinding effect of enraged waters would create a gap several miles wide.

In the subduction zone between the Nazca and South American Plates, the ocean rose even higher, blown by cubic miles of superheated steam. The monumental backbone of the Andes was not high enough to stop the water. Ecuador, Peru, and all of western Brazil were seared by liquid fire from the bowels of the earth. São Paolo, Mexico City, and Rio de Janeiro were reduced to shapeless masses of concrete and twisted steel, entombing millions before they could grasp what was happening to them.

Europe was assaulted by the Atlantic Ocean, propelled by the wind. The Alps, Pyrenees, Urals, and the Scandinavian Mountains rose higher, pushed upward by titanic underground forces, before the wall of water smashed them into grit. Paris, Genoa, Barcelona, Berlin, and Amsterdam lay under miles of water, mud, and stone.

West Africa and the Sahara yielded to the savage

onslaught of wind and oceans. Only the zone framed by South Africa, Kenya, and the Congo escaped flooding.

Russia and Asia were overtaken by the Arctic Ocean as the polar placement moved south. Nothing survived in Beijing, Seoul, or Sydney. Jungles and beasts were torn to pieces by the wind and piled into huge mountains of wood, foliage, meat, and bone, to be buried under avalanches of water and mud. In a fraction of a day, all vestiges of civilization had disappeared.

On the sixth day, the oceans retreated, leaving behind the highlands now drenched in salt, making the soil sterile for generations. The mountains of water poured into the atmosphere, discharging thick cloud belts with awesome violence. On the seventh day, a new Stone Age arrived.

○

In the Cal Madow Mountains, on the upper slopes of the Surud Cad, men, women, and children huddled together on the ground, their eyes empty of tears, the horrors of an endless week etched on every face.

Paul stood first, holding Carmen tight to his chest. The deafening silence was broken by a timid chirp and a rustle of leaves. Paul's eyes widened.

"I hear it too," Carmen said. "Look!"

Paul saw the finch land on a small branch of a bush.

It broke into song and, after a short staccato overture, stretched its wings and soared into the sky.

Close to five hundred men, women, and children slowly emerged from hiding and looked west, toward a timid new sun. The cleansing by destruction was over; a metamorphosis would begin. The circle had closed. Perfect.

about the author

CARLOS J. CORTES was born in Madrid. An engineer by trade, he has published a score of technical books in Spanish, and to date has lived in thirty-two countries. He splits his time between Spain and California, where he lives with his family.